I0662203

Girlie: Undeniable Attraction Enemies to Lovers Steamy Standalone

Lori Laidlaw

Published by Lynda French, 2024.

GIRLIE: UNDENIABLE ATTRACTION ENEMIES TO LOVERS STEAMY STANDALONE

First edition. January 26, 2024.

Copyright © 2024 Lori Laidlaw.

ISBN: 978-1998074099

Written by Lori Laidlaw.

Table of Contents

To everyone who understands how hateful lusty undeniable attraction can be... *until their heart thaws.*

About "Girlie"

Escaping a deadly situation the DEA Officer is driven into the arms of her enemies: three tough, morally-gray men who don't need the complication of a hostage or a virgin.

The O'Shea Brothers, Bram, Joel, and Danny, are smart, sexy, and super-hot but also cold, cruel, and calculating. With a target on her back Girlie has no choice, her willingness to give them what they want is all that's keeping her alive. A passion is ignited, but it's got a short fuse.

After a brutal attack, a killing, and a fire, the menage splits up. Girlie is both terrified and thrilled to be alone with Joel in an isolated cabin. Imprisoned by their lustful love Girlie and Joel negotiate their way through buried secrets, emotional turmoil, and sexual exploration.

Warning: These characters are grown-ups living in adult situations that include: acts of violence including fatalities, coerced/dub-con, MFMM menage... See the book's front matter for a full list of warnings.

If your favorite type of MMC is a dominant and domineering dark-haired and dark-hearted touch-her-and-die Alpha then meet Joel O'Shea, your newest Book Boyfriend.

If you prefer the Papa Bear type of older man who rules over everyone with quiet authority - and the iron fist to back it - then Bram O'Shea is the Big Daddy for you.

Warnings:

These characters are grown-ups in adult situations that include:

acts of violence including fatalities

coerced/dub-con

MFMM menage

reminiscing about BDSM activities and impact play

references to Domestic Discipline

voyeurism

misogynistic erotic fantasies

but mostly lots and lots of playful happy sex with plenty of steam!

If your favorite type of MMC is a dominant and domineering dark-haired and dark-hearted touch-her-and-die Alpha then meet *Joel O'Shea,* your newest Book Boyfriend.

If you prefer the Papa Bear type of older man who rules over everyone with quiet authority - and the iron fist to back it - then *Bram O'Shea* is the Big Daddy for you.

This book has been such a fun journey! and I hope you really enjoy it.

Playlist

Here are a dozen of the songs I listened to repeatedly while writing:

"18 With A Bullet" by Pete Wingfield

"A Girl Like You" by Edwin Collins

"Extreme Ways" by Moby

"Here Comes The Hotstepper" by Ini Kamoze

"Human" by Rag 'n Bone Man

"I Wanna Dance Wit'choo" by Disco Tex and his Sex-O-Lettes

"Lay, Lady Lay" by Bob Dylan

"Let's Do It Again" by The Staple Singers

"Play With Fire" by Sam Tinnesz

"Try Me" by James Brown

"Way Down We Go" by Kaleo

"Woman" by Barrabas

PART ONE

"Captivity"

Chapter 1

Joanne

It's all fun and games until the first shot is fired.

Being singled out by your hardass DEA boss for a special assignment reconnoitring a grow operation is a good thing, right? until you get caught... by a really big guy.

Intel reports this is an unmanned field, which means no guards patrolling, but intel is wrong. Actually it isn't a guard so yeah, they got that much right... instead it's Danny O'Shea, the youngest of the owners, who corners me.

Danny is call-the-fire-department hot. In his late twenties he's got an athlete's body, a male model's face, and a panty-melting smile.

The O'Shea family business, run by three brothers, is a marijuana grow op. Now that pot is legal these growers are like moonshiners. They operate in isolated areas off the grid – except for what they can steal - in order to escape government taxes and regulations. And to produce a more potent product. They're a law unto themselves.

When Danny found me I pretended to be a jogger who got lost which worked because, well, when you've got a pretty face and a killer body virile young men tend to go along with whatever you tell them. It stops working when my so-called partners in the agency start shooting at us.

Danny tosses me over his broad shoulders in a fireman's carry and runs like hell. His brothers appear ahead of us, also running. We all head into a hidden underground tunnel not stopping until at least a half-a-mile later when we arrive at their compound, having successfully escaped.

Abraham, known as Bram, and the middle brother Joel, take one look at me and say *law enforcement*. Since Danny is still holding me they neatly pluck my service weapon from its ankle holster. They find my ID badge next:

Agent A. Joanne Dwyer

Special Ops

Drug Enforcement Administration (DEA)

I can't talk my way out of this one so I don't even try.

Before the gunfire Danny had been chatting me up and thought he was getting somewhere. Now that I've made a fool out of him he is mad - really mad.

He moves me from across his shoulders to across his knees and of all the ridiculous things starts spanking me - hard. It hurts!

One of the brothers, it sounds like Joel, points out that the jogging pants I'm wearing can easily be pulled down. Danny doesn't hesitate and yanks everything down and off.

I'm naked from my waist to my running shoes and trying hard to keep my legs tight together so I don't give them even more of a show.

If you've never had a proper spanking then please listen when I advise you to do everything in your power to keep it that way. When a heavy-handed angry man is smacking you it stings, burns, and really hurts.

Even worse is when you're being punished in front of an audience. No matter how appreciative they are! It's really embarrassing. The two brothers have leaned in to get a closer look commenting:

"Plump, round ass... sweet."

"Very inviting, but finish up baby bro because she's getting red so you've made your point."

Danny pauses to glare at them and I enjoy a moment's respite though I quiver in anticipation of the next blow. He doesn't disappoint.

I can hear his heavy breathing between the slap-slap sounds of his hand striking my bare skin. My gasps and squeals of pain spur him on.

Being the entertainment is humiliating, but despite my predicament I still notice that the brothers sure look handsome when they smile. How sick is that? But you can't deny the appeal of straight, white teeth showing through the dark curly hair of moustaches and beards. Damn! These men are hot.

I'm putting on quite a show with all the wiggling, wriggling, and writhing of my hips. My squirming on top of Danny's groin makes him grow hard. He finally pushes me off and when I land on my sore bum I shoot up to my knees, reaching behind to rub my tender flesh. It's burning hot!

Still not satisfied that I'd been punished enough Danny growls:

"I should shove my dick down your throat."

I don't know which one of us is more surprised when I open my mouth wide. He doesn't hesitate even though a brother cautions:

"Be careful!!"

Danny hooks his fingers around my jaw to keep me from biting down. Not being suicidal I wasn't planning to. He jams into me and my mind blanks out everything except his hard cock in its velvety skin filling my mouth and pushing down my throat.

I'm struggling to breathe without gagging. I suck really hard and he ejaculates quickly. He pulls out spraying all over my face and down my front. I take off my jacket and use it to clean myself.

When I told Danny I was a jogger he should have clued in to the fact that female joggers don't go braless, especially when they're well-endowed. Oh, hell there's no point being modest: my breasts are magnificent. Creamy-white, round and full, with small nipples that are normally pink but now are as red as my ass.

So my shapely bod is completely naked and I'm pretty sure all three of the brothers aren't thinking much of anything else beyond that fact. I'm also shamefully aroused – God knows why - but I doubt if they even care.

Bram lifts me up and onto his lap. When Joel protests asking why Bram gets to go first his brother replies *'cause I'm the oldest.*

Joel grumbles: "You've been saying that all our lives."

and Bram laughs saying: "No, only all of your life, bro."

By now he's inside of me and I'm utterly and completely filled and gasping at this new sensation that hurts, but in a good way. I blink in surprise and my mouth rounds to an O shape.

Like his brothers, Bram is a handsome man of intimidating size. When our eyes meet I swear I see a twinkle in his.

I shift a bit and feel him grow even harder. Of course, he's quite a bit older so I guess a full erection takes more time to achieve. I hope this is as big as he gets because I can't handle any more. Luckily I was well-lubricated by my spanking. Who knew?

The moment Bram grunts out a cry Joel hooks both arms under by breasts and pulls me up and off. Tossing me over the arm of an overstuffed chair he takes me from behind. Standing, he lifts my hips up and holding me with one arm across my stomach he uses his free hand to play with my clit.

He's rock-hard and goes in deep. So deep it hurts, but I'm soon matching the rhythm of his steady strokes. I feel my pussy clutching round him and when he explodes so do I.

His big hands are surprisingly gentle as he massages my sore cheeks saying:

"Damn, baby bro, I told you to stop. This girlie's ass is on fire."

"He's right," agrees Bram advising Danny that I deserve a good licking on the other side to make up for it. The two older brothers exchange a knowing look and chuckle.

Danny says he'll take me to the stream to clean their messes off of me first. And he does just that. The water is cold, but so soothing. I glance over my shoulder and cry out at the redness I can see.

I think Danny regrets getting carried away because when he goes down on me he sure takes his time. He's skilled, but in a clinically detached way, I don't sense that he's getting any enjoyment. Still, I orgasm twice before he enters me for a leisurely servicing. My tender pussy is inflamed and aching but the earlier pain has morphed into nothing more than discomfort from the swelling.

Danny carries me back to their home and Joel says I'll be sore tomorrow so they'll try to go easy but they'll still be expecting sex and lots of it. He's such a jerk.

I've had endurance, survival, and weapons training. I've been taught how to fight and I'm physically fit but I'm puny in size compared to the brothers. They are so much bigger and stronger than me that sure, they'll be having sex whenever they want.

I can tell I've got a sour look on my face by the way Joel smirks at me.

Bram gets up saying he's turning in but stops to fondle my breasts. My traitorous nipples perk up in greeting. He thumbs them, giving me his charming smile, then tells me to kiss him good night. I make it quick but he holds the back of my head in his hand and soul-kisses me deeply. His other hand is still squeezing my breasts, but gently. I lean in to his kiss and he hums happily. I can see that he's thinking *I've still got it* and dammit yes, he sure does!

I guesstimate his age in the mid-forties range which makes him about twenty years older than me. His facial and head hair is heavily streaked with gray but his muscular body shows very little thickening and no sag. Definitely not a *Dad bod*.

For a full minute he studies me with a wry twist to his mouth before saying:

"You aren't Joanne Dwyer, DEA Agent anymore, girlie. That person has a target on her back. You're going to have to stay with us for awhile and at some point you'll become our hostage or our accomplice. I'll guess we'll just have to wait and see how that plays out."

Joel follows him out of the room then turns back warning Danny to keep me in his room tonight and make sure I'm tied up or chained. I meet his cold gaze with defiance in mine.

"We'll all be sleeping soundly after the sweet fucking Girlie gave us but she can't be trusted."

He laughs when I stick my tongue out at him. Fucking figures he's got a killer smile, must be an O'Shea Brothers thing.

Chapter 2

Danny

When I was little my Papa told me: "Never, ever hit a woman." That was one of his hard-and-fast rules but then he gave Mama a sidelong look and added: "Unless she's driven you beyond all reason so you have to put her across your knee for a well-deserved spanking."

Mama didn't reply but when Bram sniggered she gave him a sharp look. Both Bram and Joel were old enough to understand something I didn't know about yet. There's seven years between each of us, and yeah we've all heard the joke about the seven-year itch.

Hmm, I thought I'd forgotten, but the lesson from Papa surfaced this afternoon when I was in a rage with Joanne but didn't use my fists on her. Papa often had to beat Mama but I never saw her with a black-eye or a busted lip.

Still, I did go too far with Joanne. I didn't mean to hurt her, but she made me so angry. Anyhow, she got the message and has been very co-operative since. With all of us.

All of us... that's going to take some thinking about. I kinda thought she'd be mine to play with but my brothers took her out of my hands fast enough.

Having Joanne - I guess I should call her Girlie like they do - here is going to change things. They'll probably leave her with me most of the time, but they expect me to share.

I'm not really bothered about it, but I'm way closer to her age so mostly she'll want to be with me.

Earlier, using my belt, I started tying Girlie's wrists to the bedpost but she pleaded with me not to restrain her like that. The sight of her beautiful body naked, bound, and thrashing about was a real turn-on but I could see that she was really upset. It must have triggered some traumatizing memory for her. But damn, seeing her helpless and begging, made her look sexy as hell.

No way am I going against Joel's command though, so I suggest tying her left wrist to my left wrist and the two of us can sleep spooned together. She tries to convince me not to bind her at all and I enjoy the wiles she uses to make her case but afterwards I tie us together anyways. At least she doesn't panic this time.

Once she's secure and we settle down for the night I start to chuckle, explaining I was totally blown away earlier when I suggested a blow-job and she immediately opened up her mouth. She giggles as well saying she surprised herself. I tell her I bet the brothers were shocked too but all she says is:

"The brothers, yeah. Hmmm."

"What? Do you have a problem with them?"

"It's just that, well... they're very different from you, Danny."

"Not all that different, we're all alpha types or type A personalities or however you want to classify it."

I deepen my voice to tease her asking: "So, do you think there's something in the idea of women responding best to men who know how to tame them?"

She sits up as much as she can and turns herself around so she's looking directly in my eyes to say:

"Danny, I stand five foot eight inches and am very fit but compared to me you and your brothers are like mighty oak trees and I'm a sapling.

I am well aware that I have no choice except to behave any way you want me to. I have no control, I have no wants, feelings, or thoughts on the matter because I don't matter. This is what I've been reduced to."

I can see she's fighting angry tears and I don't know what to say to fix it because she's right. I'm crazy in lust with her body, but she really isn't anything to us except a potential problem. I don't tell her that.

Instead, I push her back down on her belly and using my one free hand I give her a soothing back massage, encompassing her neck and shoulders right down to her thighs, with gentle kisses on her rosy-pink ass.

I like the look of my marks on her ass so I stay awake a bit longer admiring my handiwork while she relaxes enough to fall asleep.

We sleep snuggled so closely she can't hide the tears she sheds in the wee hours of the morning. I feel her body shaking with stifled sobs and almost say *what's wrong?* but luckily that stupid question never reaches my lips. Obviously every single thing in her life is wrong.

In less than twenty-four hours she's been betrayed by her fellow agents, shot at, driven into the arms – and beds – of her enemies. She's lost her identity and has no idea what the future holds beyond whatever three horny men have in store for her.

She must be terrified. No wonder she's such a cocky smart-ass, she's using a tough persona to hide her fear. Well, if I learned anything from my psychology course then the least I can do is go along with her pretense, and not acknowledge this moment of weakness. I won't let on that I woke up, I'll just act like I'm reaching out in my sleep.

Despite the unsettling thoughts in my head sleep wins out.

Chapter 3

Girlie

Sunlight wakens me but I'm still half-dozing. It's so cozy in bed with Danny's body pressed up against mine and I don't have anywhere to go so... might as well enjoy this quiet time.

My eyelashes feel sticky from last night's crying jag – I was sure I wok0e Danny up, but if so he didn't stay awake for long. Or maybe he simply didn't care that I was sobbing my heart out. Well, why would he? He just rolled closer to me and fondled my breasts.

In fact, his hand is still spread across both of them. I can feel his morning wood against my hip, and his breathing has changed to signal he's waking up.

He swivels a bit to poke his hard-on between my cheeks and I think *Oh please God no!* I can't do anal with any of them, they're so big they'll tear me apart. Luckily he keeps pushing through, homing in on my vagina.

I am so sore. Yesterday was my first time. My first three... no, four times, actually. Not that I'll ever admit that to them.

I was used well and repeatedly and even though Danny's only entered a short way it really hurts and I can't help giving a little cry. That's no good, I've got to be tough. I'm tense and breathing as shallowly as I can when I shift slightly to see if I can somehow accommodate him more easily but he murmurs hoarsely:

"Don't move."

I hear the urgency in his voice and I realize he's struggling to hold back. Since I'm not on the verge of being rammed mercilessly I feel my body lose some of its tenseness. He's able to slip in a bit farther. His right hand lazily caresses my breasts, toying with my nipples which tingle and respond to him.

I spent the night sleeping on top of his left arm but he isn't suffering from pins-and-needles because the fingers of that hand are busily stroking me. I start to move rhythmically and he pushes in deeper and we both hear the sucking sound of my wetness. It's embarrassing, but the lubrication is definitely welcome!

We both come fully awake making love. It's a wonderful start to a day of God-knows-what they've got in mind for me.

Chapter 4

Joel

I interrupt the lovebirds to tell baby bro that Bram needs to see him right away. I'm surprised when he doesn't seem especially reluctant to leave Girlie alone with me. Doesn't matter anyhow because no one argues with whatever Bram wants. Danny unties his belt from their wrists and leaves.

Girlie sits up in their bed and I get hard looking at her glorious rack. Without making a big deal out of it she manages to cover up – mostly – by bending to pick up a t-shirt of baby bro's from the floor.

"Don't bother with that, you don't need it right now."

She gives me a wary look but doesn't say anything.

"I'm going to introduce you to our shower – it's not fancy but it does the job. Only catch is we just have cold water. Although I suppose a person could heat up a couple of buckets and carry them out back if they really wanted to. Hmm, maybe that would be a good job for you, eh Girlie?"

Again, she doesn't reply, but she stands up so I lead the way. She's a strong girl, holding her head high despite her nudity. She's right to be proud of her beautiful body and I like the way she struts, but I'll like breaking her even more.

Our shower is literally just a few buckets of water in a cistern that opens up when you yank down on a rope.

I knew baby bro had taken her to wash up at the stream yesterday, but obviously they'd been at it again last night and probably this morning, too. She looks like the type who wants a shower every day.

I demonstrate how the contraption works, explaining that you can pull a little for some water, get soaped up, then pull a lot for a big dump of water.

I check to make sure the cistern is full because she can't reach the top herself. Then I tell her to go ahead and start. She gives me a look that makes me laugh as I tell her:

"Oh, I'm staying to keep an eye on you, Girlie. I bet you can put on a real sexy show soaping yourself all over and I want to see it."

"Are you telling me I have to put on a show for you? Or can I just have a shower?" she snaps.

I'm not smiling when I answer: "Let's go with the show."

She just gives me a tight nod and steps in the cubicle. I sense people coming up behind me and turning see Bram holding baby bro back with a gesture. They stop to watch. They won't interfere.

Girlie pulls the rope and gasps as cold water splashes down. Her flesh puckers and she grabs the soap to start rubbing up some suds. She does an all-over soaping first, turning around at my command so we can see her every move, then I order her to start the show.

We use a harsh soap that's strong enough to clean off the farm soil, but I can see it's stinging her pussy when she slips it inside.

"Cunt's sore, eh Girlie? Well then, you don't need to use any more soap, just rub yourself all over. If you put on a good enough performance you'll be able to finish me off quickly."

"Isn't it always that way with you?" She mutters the words, but loud enough for me to hear. I grin at her, adding to the tally that's running through my head.

She's motivated though, because she puts on a great show. Licking her lips while squeezing her tits and pinching her nipples rock hard. She locks eyes with me and her look is dark and sensual.

Girlie really does get into it as she starts stroking inside her cunt and then falls to her knees when she orgasms. Her head is thrown back and what a gift her perfect body is: curvy, sensuous, responsive, and oh-so feminine. I'm sorely tempted to have her blow me, but I don't trust her enough yet.

Instead, I unzip my jeans and tell her to use both her hands, the soapy and the cum-slimed, to jerk me off. I haven't had a woman give me a hand job since my teens and damn if it doesn't feel fantastic.

The size of my cock makes her hands look little and I smile to see her look of concentrated effort. I groan with pleasure watching her tits jiggle and sway as she strokes me to completion as fast as she can.

When it's over I pull hard on the rope and enjoy her screech almost as much as the sight of the icy water cascading over her curves. She figures out what the trough is for and splashes handfuls up to finish rinsing off.

By now she's shivering and goose-bumped. The water droplets on her tits catch the sunlight and her skin sparkles. Not her eyes, though. They're lasering hate at me.

She reaches for the towel I'm holding, but I hang on and spread it for her to step into. I wrap it tightly around her and enjoy doing a thorough job of rubbing her body vigorously.

When I'm done I pull her close and kiss her deeply. A warm and tender kiss, gently exploring and sucking on her lower lip. She clings to me and when I open my eyes I see that hers are still closed. If I'm not careful this little chickie might actually get to me and that's not fucking happening.

Heavy on the sarcasm I thank her for the entertainment and say I might want to make a regular thing out of it, then laugh at her scowl.

Turning away I see baby bro trying to stare me down, but Bram tells him to be thankful I'd seen she was hurting and didn't insist on a fuck.

Chapter 5

Girlie

I'm starting to crack. I can't believe I let myself melt into Joel's arms after his cruel behaviour. I was staring at his muscled torso while I masturbated. God, I can't believe I did that in daylight and in public. Normally I only do that when the lights are out and my eyes are closed!

I could see the black hair on his chest that trails over his 8-pack abs right down past his navel and his Adonis belt. He's so virile and manly. And such a mean, nasty man.

It's seems the more they shame me the more compliant I become. That's bullshit, I need to get my sass back.

I admit that I'm afraid of them because of what they're capable of doing to me, but I think I'm more afraid of losing my bravado. I'm terrified what will happen to me if I ever cave in completely. I've got to keep lipping off so they don't think they've got the upper hand. It's bloody obvious that they do, but I'm not beaten down yet.

Sure, I've been giving in to them because that's better than being roughly manhandled and raped, but I'm acting like a slutty ball-freak. I'm doing such a good job convincing them that I'm even convincing myself!

They've used me for fucking without a hint of lovemaking so what's with them all kissing me like they mean it? Damned if some silly romantic side of me isn't falling into their trap.

I say I don't want to become a victim but really, who am I kidding? I already am, and trying to get them to like me won't make a difference. They're criminals, gangsters, and probably even killers since they're thriving in the violent world of drug trafficking.

Being female in law enforcement is a constant challenge. I've been denying my femininity and hiding my sexuality my whole working life. Now I need to use my body strategically, but it's betraying me by responding so easily to these men.

Back at the agency, especially once I was trained for field-work, I really thought I had blended in well with my mostly male team members and was treated equally. What was I thinking? Acting like one of the guys meant I stopped acting, feeling, and thinking like a woman.

I let my guard down, and that was a big mistake.

When Kendricks, my superior officer, came on to me I should have used feminine wiles to extricate myself but instead I just blew him off. I didn't realize he'd try to have me blown away because of that. Talk about ego!

Now I see that this was supposed to be a suicide mission. I was set up and my fellow agents looked the other way. No, worse than that, they shot at me. Our CO figured if the O'Sheas didn't kill me *friendly fire* would. Charming. That realization makes me go hot and cold with shame and anger.

The O'Sheas might kill me anyhow. The Special Ops team will figure that I'm dead already. I'm supposed to be dead. If I'd been a man I would be dead.

I'm not safe here but there's no where else for me to go. Not yet, anyhow. The only thing keeping me alive is my body and my willingness to use it. And I'll keep using it until I can get free and get my revenge on all the bastard men who hurt me.

I'm definitely putting Joel O'Shea on that list.

Chapter 6

Danny

I realize that Girlie is only here for as long as we have a use for her, but that doesn't mean I have to like what's going on. 'Course that's like saying Joel doesn't have to be a mean asshole bastard but he still is.

Girlie washed her track-suit and spread it out on the picnic table to dry in the sun but she can't walk around naked all the time. For now I find her a clean t-shirt of mine to wear. It hangs on her like a dress. Damn I gotta admit she looks sexy wearing my clothes and baring her long shapely legs.

She asks if she should cook us a meal and I laugh at that. It's doubtful she'd even know how to make enough food for us, and we're all capable cooks anyhow. We've been out here at the grow for weeks now and we're used to fending for ourselves.

Besides, Girlie should know by now that she's just here for sex. Luckily for her she's a fantastic fuck who's free with her great body. Funny, but it's like she keeps surprising herself with her healthy sexuality. She's really got an appetite for it.

At school we touched on sexual pathologies. Now I'm wondering exactly what her motivation is. I mean, sure it's survival, but is it more than that? Does she think we can provide something more? It's way too soon for Stockholm Syndrome to have kicked in.

Maybe she's yearning for the fellowship and acceptance she obviously never had with her team? What about her family? I wonder if I should get her to talk and open up to me? No, that's a mistake because face it, Girlie has no future with me or with us.

Chapter 7

Girlie

The men prepared the meal but decided that I can take care of kitchen clean-up. They have a dishwasher, but it's an older model so everything has to be rinsed before being loaded, table and counters wiped down, and the floor swept. Good, I can do that without any of them bothering me.

Or so I think, but I'm wrong.

Nasty Joel sits back in his chair and announces that he'll supervise while I clean the kitchen naked. When Danny protests on my behalf Joel asks *do you want to wake up with a knife in your chest?*

"And there he is, Nasty Joel, can't even make it through a couple of hours without showing his true colors." "You can't steal a weapon if you can't hide it," he states. Joel will never trust me.

Something inside me snaps. I mean, I'd just sat down to a meal with these men which was friendly enough and now this degradation? I call bullshit on that! I fold my arms over my chest and stare Joel down.

"I won't say it again," he warns.

I don't budge.

He narrows his eyes saying: "Oh, you don't want to make me get out of this chair, Girlie."

I give him a sassy smirk and shrug my shoulders. What is it about this man that makes me want to push his buttons?

If someone had told me a man his size could move that fast I wouldn't believe it but I sure found out different. One moment we're eyeballing each other and the next I'm being held firmly in his lap while he rips the t-shirt off, leaving me completely naked.

I'm squirming in trepidation of what comes next when Danny says in a sing-song voice:

"Uh-oh, Girlie's gonna get it."

"She sure is," answers Joel.

That makes me fight him even more, but of course my struggles have no effect whatsoever. I'm like a kitten in the jaws of a tiger.

"Poor Girlie is really going to get her ass spanked hard!" continues Danny, sounding quite excited at the thought.

"Don't be so fucking stupid," answers Joel in a sneering tone and I'm surprised and relieved! "Spanking, or any kind of beating, is just an angry person expressing their rage physically. I might have to kill her, but I'll never, ever beat her.

Besides, I'm not angry by her antics - I'm amused! She really is entertaining. And I'm really going to have fun teaching her a lesson. I mean, compared to me she's so little – what's she gonna do?

No baby bro, the proper way to dominate a woman is to let her enslave herself to you willingly. Make her ache for you, make her beg for it."

"AS IF, motherfucker!" I cry waving my arms and kicking my legs. All three brothers laugh at my pitiful show of defiance.

I don't know if Danny resents missing out on a spectacle, or if he just feels argumentative, but he goes on to say:

"She got really wet after I spanked her."

Joel replies coldly, "That wasn't arousal, that was fear. Sheer terror."

I give a little cry because I thought I'd hidden my panic so well, how could he possibly know that? I don't think my gasp was heard over Danny's comment:

"What are you talking about? She was so up for it—"

"Joel's right, Danny. Think over the situation. Three really big men, running a grow op, and one girl who's DEA, our enemy. We're all pumped up with adrenaline after running from gun-fire, and she's naked. She's used to carrying a gun and relies on it so without one she's powerless. Unless she can use her body as a weapon and that's exactly what she did."

"She loved it," Danny insists.

"So did I, so did Joel, so did you. I think we all surprised ourselves. Now, you can learn something here, along with Girlie, if you just shut up and pay attention. Joel's going to give us a master-class on making a lady melt."

I still don't know what's in store for me and am fiercely determined not to cry no matter what. I never expect what actually happens. Joel tenderly rubs his hands all over my body murmuring compliments about the soft smoothness of my skin, my lovely coloring, my spectacular body... he proceeds to seduce me with the most attentive and amazing foreplay.

His fingers tease and tickle and torment my clit until I'm gasping for breath and mewling for release. I am stroked, caressed, fondled, kissed... I'm horny and dripping wet but still he keeps on and on taking me to the very edge.

It's embarrassing – humiliating, actually – to make such a fool of myself. My legs fall open and my nipples are red and hard as I squirm and moan under Joel's magic touch. It's bad enough that Joel sees me like this but for Bram and Danny to witness my shameless, wanton, flaunting as well? I'm mortified.

I struggle to escape but he simply lays me down on the table and holds me in place by pulling my legs wide and pushing them up against my chest. With his hands wrapped around the back of my thighs my helpless pussy is at his mercy and he takes full advantage. His hot mouth captures my exposed clit and he sucks and nibbles and flicks it with his tongue until I'm thrashing about and begging for release.

Throughout all of this he maintains a steady stream of compliments about how responsive I am, how my pussy is so warm and welcoming, how much he enjoys making me his sweet, slutty, good girl.

I cave in, assuring him he's right and I'm pleading for him to make love to me. I desperately need him to take me, to fill and soothe my aching vagina. He just laughs saying he'll fuck my cunt when he's ready.

Apparently he isn't ready to let up on me yet. My suffering is exquisite. He's slid two fingers inside me and hooked onto the spongy nerves of my g-spot. The way he's rubbing back and forth makes me scream. I hear Bram clap and call *Bravo!*

Joel tells me he's pretty sure I'll need a number of nasty lessons before I learn my place but once I'm properly tamed and trained he'll be able to put me on my knees with just a look. He's so insulting, so demeaning, so horrible to me... I pray that he's wrong.

As he scoops me up and heads to his bedroom all I can think is how much I hate Joel, and how I hate myself for loving what his hands and mouth can do to me. I'm so hot for him it's sickening. I can't believe I'm begging that bastard prick.

He tosses me on his bed and climbs on top, trapping my naked body. As I lay beneath him, our faces just inches apart, I'm mesmerized by his penetrating stare. I feel like I'm being swallowed up, like he's drawing out everything inside me. We're definitely sharing a moment. I'm motionless waiting for whatever he wants next. I've forgotten how to breathe.... but I haven't forgotten what he said about maybe killing me.

Much later, I'm in the kitchen, naked, cleaning under Joel's watchful eye. I might even be humming... I have no shame.

Chapter 8

Bram

I thought Girlie would turn Danny's head - as expected when you've got two young people close together in a highly charged situation – but this is different. He seems possessive in a *she's mine* kind of way rather than *she's lovely don't hurt her.*

She really is lovely, in fact she's a gorgeous female who gives herself with generosity. I can see problems brewing between Danny and Joel over her.

If I didn't know Joel better I'd think this little girl was getting to him. Except that this is Joel...

I hope having her around will help Danny. He's been sullen and discontented since we forced him to come here. I realize it was hard for him to leave his psychology studies at the university but we needed him here so he had to come back. Duty to the family comes first. That's how the bills get paid. It was unfortunate, though.

I'm tempted to tell Joel that we should leave the fucking to Danny. Let him and Girlie have this time together because it won't last. Soon enough Danny will have to face some tough decisions. But something warns me that Joel will object and I'm not ready to deal with that battle right now.

In fact, I'm not ready to be hands-off with Girlie myself, either.

I call her to come in from the kitchen and she arrives pulling the t-shirt over her head to wear like a dress.

"My turn," I simply say, and she scurries over to climb onto my lap.

My thing is kissing and petting. It's a memory that goes back more than twenty-five years to blue balls in the back-seat of a car. The height of horniness is when you're a teenager trying to get the girl to give in.

The differences now are that I can last much longer, Girlie is far more willing than the girls of my youth ever were, and nobody's worried about someone knocking on the car window!

She curls up against me and I'm deep-kissing her while caressing her arms, her hips, her back back. I must buy her a bra so I have the pleasure of undoing it. I fondle her all over except for second and third base. I chuckle to myself as my mind automatically brings up that terminology.

Girlie squirms and tries to move my hand to her breast but I gently push her hands away. Same when she tries to lift up the t-shirt. The girl is so impatient. I'll teach her to let the passion build till she's bursting out of control.

"Behave yourself, Girlie! Just because Joel won't put you across his knee doesn't mean I won't."

She gasps, but settles for unbuttoning my shirt and massaging my chest through the tangle of curly black hair. I sigh when I notice how gray I'm getting, and not just on my chest!

She finds my nipples and flicks them with her finger. I do the same to her and she giggles. In fact I suck on her nipples right through the thin cotton fabric. Her whimpers tell me she wants much more.

When I reach down to squeeze her some more she tries to remove her t-shirt but I rub her through the cloth. Obviously this girl never made out in a back-seat before. She doesn't know about fumbling over and under clothing but I'm happy to show her the ropes.

She trembles as I trail soft kisses from her collarbone to her ear, which I first lick then blow gently. Girlie shivers with pleasure and arches her back thrusting her chest out.

Finally I lift the hem of the t-shirt and she helps me pull it off. When she tries to press her lovely breasts against me I sigh and hold her firmly. Now she's going to discover that every caress has to be repeated on her bare skin.

By time I've had my fill of soft warm flesh and pull her tight against my naked chest she's whining for more. We both enjoy the electricity of skin-on-skin contact as she rubs back and forth, frantically kissing my throat.

I lift her onto my cock and she's certainly ready to receive me. Our Girlie is always willing and wet. We make love and I re-live the best experience of my life enhanced a thousand-fold by this beautiful, loving woman.

Chapter 9

Joel

At first they don't realize I'm in the doorway watching but then Girlie looks up and meets my gaze boldly. Bram is so deeply into her – in every sense of the word! - that he doesn't know I'm there.

I marvel at how small she is in comparison to his body and, I guess, to mine as well. She's sitting on thighs the size of tree-trunks and she has to stretch to get her arms to reach around his neck. He clutches her ass and each cheek is fully covered by one of his hands. He lets out a deep groan and she joins in with a higher-pitched cry.

Then they share a tender moment when he says he loves his baby girl and she answers that she loves her Big Daddy. I know they don't *really* love each other but part of me wants to pull her out of his arms and claim her as mine.

I'm so absorbed in watching them I don't realize baby bro is in the other doorway watching us all. His face isn't handsome when it's screwed up in a sneer, and his bad mood shows.

He tells me I should take Girlie now, just like I did on the first night when she was already wet with Bram's cum.

"Bend her over that chair again and just fuck her. No foreplay needed, you've got sloppy seconds to slide you right in to that hungry cunt."

I can see rage light up Bram's eyes and I sure don't blame him. He's just winding down from the great fuck he and Girlie enjoyed and along comes smart-mouthed Danny putting us all down.

Girlie feels the tension because she jumps off Bram's lap and positions herself over the chair-arm. She waggles her butt at me but the look in her eyes is scared. I'm tempted to walk away and let Bram deal with baby bro but I know that isn't a good move and, as usual, Girlie is so inviting...

I immediately plug in to her and rub her clit which, already sensitive from Bram's lengthy foreplay, sets her hips rolling. Pushing inside her is fantastic, she's hot and tight and the walls of her cunt vibrate around me. Her slick wetness makes it easy to drive in deep.

I hold her firmly as she wiggles and the sight of my cock sliding smoothly all the way inside makes it difficult to hold back, but I'm hitting her g-spot so I force myself to ride out two of her orgasms before I join in. I don't know if I'm showing off for Danny or her or myself.

Girlie has such a tight grip that I'm going to be damn sore later, and with only myself to blame. When I pull out she collapses on the floor with her limbs splayed every which way. I tuck her under my arm like a football and carry her outside to the shower.

Pulling the rope I drench us both. The icy cold water has us shivering in the dark.

"What the fuck, Joel!" she yells at me and I immediately reply:

"What was with that look on your face?"

"You mean when I saw you with your usual frowny face glaring at me? Can't you ever wink or something?"

"Wink? Huh! We're not friends, Girlie. Damn you almost cut off my dick just now you clenched so hard."

"I needed to plug the hole you were trying to poke through to my stomach," she retorts.

I kiss her then, long and hard and deep. We're lip-locked for so long we'd have drowned if the cistern hadn't run dry. Our flesh was goose-pimpled from the cold water and the chill air but we don't even notice until Bram comes outside with a few towels. Luckily for all of us his rage has subsided.

Caught in the moonlight with her wet hair plastered to her scalp and not a scrap of make-up on her face Girlie is astonishingly beautiful. She glows.

"Stunning," I declare and Bram agrees, rumbling:

"Breathtaking."

Her lower lip trembles like she's going to cry but her eyes sparkle with happiness and she smiles in delight.

Chapter 10

Girlie

What a night. I'm utterly drained but happily so. Too bad Danny's got such a sour look on his face but I really can't be bothered with him. If he wants sex obviously he'll take it but I can't work up much of a response.

What's his problem anyhow? We all know that it's a free-for-all when it comes to having sex with me. That's what I'm here for. Hell, that's why I'm still alive.

So why was he so snarky and mean about it? He knows I'm here on sufferance, I don't need him pushing anyone's buttons or forcing either of the brothers to act out in a violent way. Joel spoke so matter-of-factly when he talked about maybe having to kill me. What the fuck?

Danny ties our wrists together like last night and we collapse on the bed. He grabs at my breasts roughly but without passion. When I don't react he loses interest.

The shower didn't wake me up from my sex-sated stupor and I'm asleep in thirty seconds.

At some point during the wee hours of the night I feel Danny pushing his dick between my butt cheeks, not hard enough to force himself inside my anus, but he does cum. I pretend to sleep through it.

Chapter 11

Bram

Thank God Joel and Girlie took the heat off Danny. I was so fucking angry I think I might have killed him. One moment I'm feeling 110% and the next thing I know this man, because he's not a kid anymore, is mouthing off and I just want to smash his face in to shut him up.

Danny didn't mind sharing Girlie so long as he was first in her affections but obviously he's not. She might say and even act like she hates Joel, but her behavior tells a different story and Danny is jealous. I just hope he's not stupid enough to challenge Joel, I do not want to get in the middle of that, but of course I'll have to if that's how things turn out.

Oh, Girlie. She's nothing but trouble but no, that's not right. It's not her fault, she's an absolute delight. That's the problem: we all want her too much. Joel and I have no problem sharing her, why can't Danny do the same? He's possessive but I don't think he's fallen for her. I sure hope he hasn't, for his sake.

I think things might come to a head sooner than I originally thought. However, I have to put that thought aside for now because tomorrow all three of us have to leave to take care of some business.

I haven't decided what to do about Girlie while we're gone.

Chapter 12

Girlie

I get a real surprise this morning. Sitting at the breakfast table I ask who was playing music last night because I've never heard that singer before and he was great.

Danny starts to laugh saying it was just Joel, not a record or anything. Then Bram says:

"I heard you too, bro. Girlie's right, you sounded great. It was really good to hear you playing and singing again, it's been a long time."

"Too long," says Joel. "I'm pretty rusty."

"I can't believe that was you," I say in amazement. . I can't imagine Nasty Joel having a creative side.

"I didn't know you played the guitar or sang. That's why I asked who it was because I didn't recognize your voice or any of those songs. I thought I was listening to an album."

Joel doesn't stop eating, but he looks up and smiles.

"Joel writes his own songs. He's been making music since we were kids. I was happy to hear him strumming his guitar again." explains Bram, then he laughs and holding up his huge hands adds: "Believe it or not I used to play the piano."

"Well I think Joel should be playing his songs on YouTube or TikTok or something. You do write the music down, right?"

"Well yeah, it's not Flamenco, but I just do it for me, for fun. It's a hobby."

"It's a skill and a talent and you're lucky to have it. Those ballads are wonderful. I'd love to hear you sing them all again." I still can't get over the fact that Joel, of all people, makes such hauntingly beautiful music.

Then Danny breaks into the conversation with a snide remark saying:

"Girlie, I had no idea you were such a groupie. We'll have to make you president of the Joel O'Shea Fan Club." Then turning to Bram he adds: "We've got to get going so what do we do with her?"

Chapter 13

Joel

I tell them in no way can we just leave her behind, she has to be restrained. I get what they're saying about how she can't go back where she came from and there's no way for her to go forward without help, but I don't care. Women can't be trusted.

So it was up to me to tie Girlie onto a kitchen chair and she made it an ordeal. Too bad because we'd gotten a bit friendly over my music. I liked hearing her say she enjoyed listening.

She's fighting me with everything she has which isn't enough to stop me, but that doesn't slow her down. She's strong when she's that frantic, but still no match for my strength.

She squirms and claws and kicks and even tries to bite me. Then, when I have her in the chair and am tying the rope she starts begging, pleading, offering her body in any way I want, promising to do anything I desire.

"Look, I can tell something once happened to Girlie and now she's got a phobia about being restrained," baby bro says, stating the obvious as he tries to stop me.

"She's so scared she's gonna hyperventilate."

"I don't give a flying fuck about that. If she's got a problem then it's her problem to deal with. She needs to get over it."

He tries to block me but I can easily take him so Bram steps in saying we don't have time for this shit. Bram turns to Girlie and tells her to hush.

"I can see you're upset at being tied up Girlie, and I've got to say I'm surprised by how much. I'm sorry for that, but this is the way it's gotta be. We've got to go and you've got to stay."

She's sobbing like her heart will break and tossing her head from side to side. It's hard to watch and hard to hear. I stuff a cloth – a clean one - in her mouth to stifle the noise.

"What the fuck, Joel? What if she chokes and suffocates herself?" Danny asks angrily.

Even through the cloth I can hear her moaning and carrying on. By now I'm fed up with both of them and snap:

"Well then the problem's taken care of itself, hasn't it?"

I push him away and finish the knots saying:

"Listen Girlie, we all know how well you can work that tongue of yours so you'll be able to push away this gag after we're out of earshot."

We leave soon after but baby bro and I kept sniping and snarling at each other until Bram yells:

"Jesus Fucking Christ just STOP!"

We keep our mouths shut after that. As a younger man I once challenged Bram but he laid a beating on me that I've never forgotten. We don't hurry our business in town but neither do we waste time hanging about afterwards.

Chapter 14

Girlie

I am trying to keep it together but it's so hard. I'm so fucking scared my body is just vibrating, and I'm sweating and shaking at the same time. There's no point trying to reason with my head when my flesh is fighting primal urges. I need to get free, I have to get free, need to, have to, need to, have to... I can't bear this.

I don't know why I can't stand being tied up, tied down, restrained, confined in any way. I don't remember whatever it was that happened that caused me to feel this way... and I don't want to know. I don't care why I'm like this, I just care about getting free.

Joel is such an asshole prick. He could have locked me in a room or something instead of tying me to this chair. Securing my arms behind my back is ample, he didn't have to tie my ankles to the chair legs. I find that getting angry is helping. Being pissed off at him is distracting me, and I need that or I'll panic.

Just like the gag forces me to slow my breathing. I bet I could push it out of my mouth but for now it's keeping me from hyperventilating. My nose started running with all my crying but deep sniffs are fixing that. I sound like a cokehead.

I just have to breathe slowly and evenly and wait this out. I know, I'll think about how I'm going to get revenge against that bastard officer at the DEA. That'll give me something to concentrate on so I don't have to think about this predicament I'm in.

At least that's what's on my mind until the intruder sidles through the door.

It's a man, maybe mid-thirties? about my height but much thinner. Wiry, but he doesn't look very strong. He looks like a junkie, a junkie who needs a fix and is mean with his wanting.

I must look like a Christmas present all gift-wrapped just for him.

I can smell him before he gets close and his odor is foul. Unfortunately he gets very, very close. In fact, he puts his hands all over me, jabbing at my crotch and grabbing my boobs, giggling the whole time. He tells me he's the O'Shea's cousin but from the side of the family that doesn't have any money.

He needs money ASAP, he says. He planned to come here and ask. When he sees the brothers heading into town he knows they'll be gone for awhile and figures he'll do better by robbing them then trying for a handout.

I'm pretty sure he realizes that I truly have no idea where they keep their money or their drug stash. I mean, why would they confide in their hostage? Or kidnap victim, or whatever the hell he thinks I am?

Hell, maybe he just thinks a tied-up girl in the kitchen is the O'Shea's idea of some kinky fun.

No, he knows I don't have answers so he's just hitting me for the pleasure it gives him. Slapping my face one way and backhanding it the other. He keeps delivering blow after blow and doesn't even stop when my nose is running with blood that drips down off my chin. He enjoys hurting me.

When my tormentor pulls out a knife my heart almost stops. I think for sure this is it, this is how I die, my death comes at the hands of this smelly junkie. But no, he only wants to slice open my top to get at my breasts. He could have cut the ropes and screwed me but I guess he's already figured out that I'm strong enough to overpower him.

Instead he – ugh, it's sickening – decides to fuck my tits. I've heard of this, but sure as shit never experienced it. He straddles the chair and sits on top of me then shoves his stinky dick between my naked breasts and squeezes them together as tightly as he can. His bony fingers are strong and really hurt digging into my flesh.

Then he starts pumping back and forth all the while singing in a high-pitched falsetto:

"Tittie-fucking, tittie-fucking, tittie-fucking," while he drools his rancid spit over me, and his cock leaks pre-cum on my chest.

I figure for sure he's going kill me once he's done and I only hope he doesn't slice up my body first. My mind drifts into some sort of hazy, fugue state to escape the reality of my situation.

Next thing I know I hear a roar as somebody yanks the junkie off me followed by the unmistakable sound of his neck snapping.

Joel stands over me in a rage with his body tense and his fists clenching and unclenching. If he wasn't a killer before today he sure is now. And I guess that makes me an accessory.

Danny, standing in the doorway, comes out of his shocked state and races over to grab the knife that has fallen to the floor. Before he can cut me free of my bonds Bram scoops me up, still in the chair, murmuring:

"You're okay, we're here, Girlie you're okay, he's gone. You're okay, it's over."

Danny saws through the ropes at my ankles, then my wrists, and Bram holds me tight while the kitchen chair clatters to the floor. The brothers crowd round me.

I see the naked pain in Joel's eyes and a huge shudder convulses me. Cradling me in his arms Bram gently wipes away the blood and tenderly touches my nose to see if it's broken. When I flinch he knows it is.

They keep telling me I'm okay and that's good because so long as they're telling me what's what it means I don't have to think or speak.

I've been weakly crying since my beating and I can't stop. Partly from the pain, partly from my fear, and now from relief, too. I must look so weak to them.

It's easiest just to close my eyes and drift away into my dream state listening to them arguing the merits of witch hazel or arnica for bruises, and should they do something about my nose?

Chapter 15

Danny

When I hear cousin Kenny singing his stupid tittie-fucking ditty I race into the house but my brain can't take in what my eyes are seeing. I freeze while trying to make sense of things.

Joel just powers on past me and plucks Kenny off of Girlie, breaking his neck in one smooth motion. He tosses the body aside like the garbage it is.

Without Kenny blocking my view I can see Girlie's face is a swath of blood from her nose to her chin, She looks like the vampire from a second-rate horror flick. An x-rated film because she's tied to a chair with her bare tits sticking out.

Turns out she's bleeding because her nose is broken, her lip is busted, and she's bitten through her tongue.

Joel growls that he wishes our cousin was still alive so he could kill him again but slowly and painfully this time.

That's when I see red. None of this would have happened to Girlie if Joel hadn't insisted on tying her to that damn chair. Sure, Kenny would still have broken in, but she'd have been able to fight him off. I start to yell at him but Bram tells me to shut the fuck up.

That's when he gets to Girlie and picks her up, chair and all.

It's a good thing Bram's come between me and Joel while I'm holding a knife and fucking pissed.

Chapter 16

Joel

Knowing I couldn't have done things any differently doesn't help when I look down on this badly beaten girl. After holding her for quite a while Bram passes her to me and I've been sitting here cuddling her against my chest for the last couple of hours.

Girlie isn't comatose or catatonic but she's definitely somewhere deep in her own head. It's a good thing because when she starts to waken out of this she'll be in a lot of pain. I gently smooth the blonde strands back from her face to get a good look at the damage.

The torn t-shirt is bloody and wet with spit and cum, based on the smell, so I pull it off her. I warm her naked body by holding her close, sharing my body heat, keeping her safe in my arms.

Both of her eyes are black and I can see that bastard Kenny's red fingermarks all over her breasts which have bruises blossoming already. Her tongue is swollen and her poor nose is twice its size and crooked.

She'll hate me even more then she already does once she gets a look in the mirror.

I feel along her teeth to check that none of them got chipped or broken and none are loose. Yes, I'm a selfish bastard for worrying about getting his dick sucked, but I'm also glad for her sake that she'll be beautiful again.

When I secured her to the chair she tried making all kinds of sexy promises and I was thinking then that I'd take her up on a few of those offers later but now... now I just want to protect her and keep her safe from harm. From me, even.

I just want to hold her gently and try not to notice how soft she is, how she weighs nothing in my arms, or how her round ass is resting like a cushion on my cock.

Finally Danny reaches out to take her to their bed but she comes out of her dozing state long enough to shriek:

"No, no! I want Joel, only Joel."

For a moment Danny's face shows hurt feelings, but then he looks at me with angry resentment. Too bad, Girlie's made her choice and it's me.

Oh Girlie, despite my best – and worst – intentions I somehow got to you. And dammit, you've gotten under my skin, too. But I need you to hate me. I can make fucking me an addiction but even as we're losing our minds I want you to hate me.

None of that hearts and flowers shit - just raging hormones, a wet pussy and a hard dick.

Chapter 17

Bram

Next morning I take one look at Girlie and think *oh sweetheart, you poor thing* but I know pity isn't what she needs.

"Bram, I'm so ugly," she whispers tearfully.

I lift her up to lie down on the kitchen table and explain she will never, ever be ugly. Not possible. But yeah, she is showing the damage of her beating so I am going to do my best to make her feel better.

"I can't bear to put on a t-shirt, my breasts are too sore, and while everything below my waist is fine I don't own any underpants. So, sorry but..." It's hard to understand the words coming from her damaged mouth but she gestures to her nakedness and I understand.

"Oh Girlie, you nude is like my favorite thing in the whole world! Nothing to apologise for." I gently press her shoulders until she's flat on her back saying, "Let's take inventory, then I'll get back to worshipping this gorgeous body."

Starting with the her face I note that both eyes are black, her nose is crooked, her bottom lip has a scabbed-over split, and her tongue is swollen.

"Your eye sockets and your cheekbones are bruised and scratched, but not broken. Do you want a slightly crooked nose or should I try to straighten it."

"No, that will hurt! I can live with crooked."

"Good. You've already got beauty, now your face has character."

My eyes travel downwards and I notice that Bastard Cousin Kenny had spent some time choking her before grabbing and clutching her tits in his bony hands. The bruising is shocking and mixed in with plenty of red weals and more scratches from his nails.

"Antibiotic for the scratches and astringent for the bruising." I announce. Dabbing as gently as I can I treat the cuts. Then, I soak a tea towel in a bowl of witch hazel and lay it softly over her chest. She gasps at the cold but immediately feels the soothing effect and sighs with relief.

"You're young and healthy, very fit in fact, so you'll heal quickly."

I tuck the towel down along the sides of her body where Bastard Cousin Kenny had dug his knees into her. Soon her torso is fully covered in wet cloths, the lovely shape of her breasts and erect nipples showing through.

"Joel and Danny will be back soon and there's something I want to say to you before they get here. It's only advice so you don't have to take it, but I think you should. Anyhow, at some future date – obviously not now, not 'til you get better – you need to climb on top of a man and fuck him with your tits."

"Ugh, no, the memory of that... "

"Is the whole point. You need to wipe out the memory of you being helpless and replace it with a new memory of you having all the power. And I recommend you do it to Joel because he's the meanest, toughest prick you'll ever get naked with. At least I hope so, for your sake."

It's hard to read any kind of expression on her battered face but she answers thoughtfully saying: "I see what you mean... maybe you're right..."

"I think they call it *changing the narrative*. That's what you need to do and put creepy Cousin Kenny the Bastard out of your mind once and for all."

My younger brothers arrive back home then and I can tell Joel is spoiling for a fight.

Chapter 18

Girlie

Joel is vibrating with some emotion and it's probably unspent anger. I know they were going to their cousins' compound but I don't know – or care – what happened there. Bram's right. I absolutely must put that whole incident behind me. I can't forget it, but I can overcome it. I have to.

Danny is complaining that Bram should cover up my nakedness and Joel snaps at him asking *why?* He then goes into a tirade of how there's nothing shameful about me, and my body is beautiful, that I'm beautiful and always will be, that I don't need anybody's pity, that I should be admired for my courage and not hidden away like some unsightly thing.

"But Joel her face *is* ugly. and then to have her lying like this on the table with her cunt showing is cruel."

Bram intervenes then saying:

"Girlie, I can drape another towel over you if you're uncomfortable? It's no problem."

"NO!" thunders Joel. He then hitches himself half onto the table and proceeds to caress my belly, hips, and thighs. He lets his fingers comb through the blonde curls of my pubic hair. He lays his face down on my groin and the warmth of his skin is pleasant.

He places my feet sole-to-sole so my legs fall into a triangular shape, making my pussy more prominent. He starts to stroke me lightly.

"This is fucking sick!" exclaims Danny in disgust. "Look at her! She's hurting and you're getting off on it?"

Joel growls and Bram pushes Danny out of the kitchen, but not before I notice how Danny licks his lips and tents his jeans with a hard-on while ogling my bruised body.

Bram then comes back and pulls up a chair for a better view of what Joel is doing.

"See how pink she is? Well watch what happens," Joel says before giving me a couple of strong licks. "Look there, already the blood is rushing to engorge her clit."

"I've never known of such a responsive girl. Ever."

"I know. We really lucked out with her. Girlie," Joel meets my blackened eyes without flinching and says: "We know you feel badly from here up," he motions from my waist upwards, "so we're going to make you feel good from here down."

I admit I'm a bit apprehensive. I'm sure I can't manage intercourse without causing myself more pain, and my head is pounding. But, true to their word, they do indeed make me feel good.

Joel shows me that there is such a thing as a gentle orgasm. It's simply wetness and a delicious shiver – not a hip-bucking, butt-clenching, shaking explosion. And gentle orgasms, as the men happily demonstrate, can be repeated and repeated and repeated without shattering me into a wet, wrung-out mess.

The two of them discuss how well Mother Nature manages to propagate the species. How the female anatomy turns on the man and if he doesn't produce seed in a couple of pumps her body will start to squeeze him because it wants his seed. If he still doesn't produce, and if he can last that long, she'll begin a rhythmic swaying and squeezing that will bring them both to orgasm.

Even the most inexperienced, unskilled or even uncaring male is capable of impregnating his female.

"Even now, I've got my middle finger inside her hole and while I'm stroking her clit with my forefinger I can feel the walls of her cunt pulsating. She's absolutely marvellous."

"What do you think happens after menopause... have you been with an older woman lately?"

Ridiculously, I feel a twinge of jealousy.

"No, I haven't. I guess we'll find out when the time comes."

"Girlie, do you mind if I jerk off on you?"

That makes me laugh as I croak out a reply: "Please do, Bram." But he's only kidding. He's been gently massaging my feet, ankles and calves until I am utterly relaxed.

Both men bestow kisses and compliments: *love the way she tastes*, and *she's got the softest skin I have ever touched*, until after almost twenty-four hours in a state of trauma, shock, and pain I drift into a calm and comfortable sleep.

I stay awake long enough to realize Joel is softly singing a lullaby as he carries me to his bed. I know he will stay by me, watching over me, while I sleep.

My penultimate thought is relief that I am Girlie again, and not some pitiable victim. My last thought is that Joel O'Shea is an amazing man.

Chapter 19

Joel

Bram and I do our best to keep up Girlie's spirits over the next few days. Danny's no help, he looks at her like she should be ashamed for being victimized. What the fuck?

Being healthy and strong helps her body heal quickly, and it seems like her mind is keeping pace. She isn't showing any evidence of PTSD and hasn't fallen into a depression or fits of anger. Every now and then she'll drift off in her thoughts but they don't seem to eat at her.

One day she completely lost her temper and it was good, it means she's getting back to normal. It really was an oversight on my part because I honestly did forget that we have an indoor shower.

It's narrow and way too small for us so we never use it and I never thought about it. Until Girlie makes the discovery and starts cussing me out.

"Well it's not like I hid it, it's right there! What did you think it was?"

"I thought it didn't work! Why else would you go outside, and make me go outside in the cold for a dumping of icy cold water?"

"So you finally got the nerve to turn it on to see if it works?" I can't contain my laughter any longer.

"Well, yeah. I figured if there's running water in the kitchen and the toilets then maybe that unused shower would work and it did – it does!"

She has both fists clenched and her chest is heaving with deep breaths. She's gorgeous and hot and, as usual, I'm instantly turned on by her. I pull her into my arms saying:

"The outside shower is the only one you and I can both fit into at the same time. Don't you like taking a shower with me, Girlie?"

"That's not the point," she grumps. "Especially in the mornings when it's so cold. I get all goosebumps."

"Oh I've noticed," I say smiling. "Come on. Hop in this shower now."

"I'm not putting on a show for you, Joel."

"Oh honey, it's showtime whenever I look at you. No, I promise I'll behave. You have a nice warm shower and I'll soap your back, deal?"

"Only if you wash my feet, too." she demands.

"I would love to wash your feet!" I exclaim with a grin.

Needless to say the back-washing doesn't last long before I have her wet soapy body out of the shower and bent over the vanity. Then perched on the edge of the vanity. Then up against the wall. Poor Girlie, I don't think she ever got to have a single shower in peace the whole time we were at the compound.

She said she figures she's horny all the time because of all the touching and naked skin.

"I really love being naked. If my boobs were any bigger it'd be uncomfortable not to wear a bra but, they're firm and I like the free feeling.

In fact, I don't even know why I bother with the t-shirt since one of you guys is always pulling it off of me. And then hugging, caressing, touching...

I grew up with people who weren't affectionate, who didn't kiss or touch me or anyone else, either. Everyone was hands-off and kept their distance. It didn't feel bad or wrong, it's just the way things were. I never realized it could be different... and wonderful."

I love how honest she is about her feelings but other than rare glimpses like that one she refuses open up about her past.

I find I've reached the point where just being in the same room as baby bro is a problem. I wonder if I'm jealous of him for being younger and closer to her age. He certainly is a handsome young man and he doesn't hide his face behind a beard.

Bram's worn a beard for as long as I can remember, and I'm too lazy to shave every day so a beard is a good low-maintenance solution for me.

We shut down the O'Shea family grow-op not long after that day of violence.

Somebody – maybe the government, maybe rival growers, maybe Kenny's family – set fire to the fields and the crop was lost. The flames didn't reach the compound so the house and outbuildings weren't burned, but I think we all knew something had to change and soon.

In that regard the fire has been for the best. It's split the family up, but has brought me and Girlie closer together.

Bram has gone on to our childhood home to take charge of the other aspects of the family business, while Danny has happily returned to his university course.

I'm moving Girlie to a remote cabin that the O'Shea family owns. Set deep in a wooded landscape it's rustic and secluded. Our grandfather built it for hunting season, and it's the perfect place for her and me to hide out while she heals and we get to know each other.

We three O'Shea brothers have been living as outlaws but we've never been caught so there are no charges against us, and no police records.

That, plus what we know about the DEA and a certain Agent Joanne Dwyer, probably makes us untouchable. But I worry that Girlie is still in danger from Kendricks and his men. Kendricks sounds like a psycho so there won't be an expiry date on his hatred and lust for revenge.

After the armed assault, and then Cousin Kenny's brutal attack, I'm not letting her out of my sight. She's mine. I've killed for her once, and I'll do so as many times as I need to. Nobody hurts what's mine.

The man I was, who once wrote ballads of heartbreak and redemption, is long gone. After experiencing what I have, and seeing what I've seen, well... Something about Girlie made me think just maybe she could call out my music but no. Trust, faith, love, and hope are lies paving a path too dangerous to follow.

Girlie is mine. I rescued her and now I own her. During our time alone at the cabin I'll teach her how to show her gratitude.

Chapter 20

Girlie

I'm really anxious about us all leaving the compound. I realize we can't stay forever but I feel safe here with the O'Sheas.

Although things with Danny got uncomfortable having the four of us together feels right. The idea of me leaving with just Joel is really scary.

Partly because coming out in the open while we travel puts me at risk, but also because Joel terrifies me just as much as he thrills me. I feel so threatened when he's in one of his dark moods and eyes me like he could kiss or kill.

I get so nervous I start biting my lip and his gaze zooms in on my mouth. Then I feel my legs tremble with the need to drop to my knees all from one look, just like he crudely promised. I'm terrorized and turned on by the control he exerts over me.

Happily he showed me that he has a playful side, too. It happened on what turned out to be the day we left.

I'm outside and spot Joel in the shower. He has his back to me and I'm startled by the sight of his male beauty, muscles dripping with water running in trails down his smooth, unmarked skin. I must have gasped because he turns and gives me an odd look – a half-smile with one eyebrow raised. Like he's asking me a question, asking *do you like what you see?*

I enjoy looking at his wide shoulders, broad back (no hair), tapered waist, firm buttocks (a bit of hair), strong thighs, and long legs but when he turns and I can see his handsome face as well... without even thinking I say:

"You're perfect!"

He grins and replies:

"That's my line."

I quickly apologize for staring explaining:

"I'm sorry but I've just... it's because I've... I've never... I didn't get to have a good look before now... God, I sound so lame. Sorry!"

He lets his arms fall open and invites me to *look all I want* so I do. I admire his chest and his muscular torso, letting my gaze follow the line of chest hair down past his navel to his groin and then I look away.

He is beside me in a moment and, taking my hand, announces:

"You need an anatomy lesson and I'm gonna be your teacher. Follow me," and he leads me back to our room.

He sits me on the edge of the bed while he lies down on his back saying:

"Okay, starting at the top, my senses and my brain are all erogenous zones but physically I'm sensitive at my ears, throat, nipples – although not so much as you are," he pauses to pull off my t-shirt dress and fondles my nipples erect.

"My hands really enjoy how incredibly soft your skin feels. It's smooth and warm and I love touching your naked body.

Any time your touch moves downwards from my chest it's a turn-on because I'm anticipating where your hands are going to end up. Obviously my cock is my most erotically charged body part and... can you tell whether or not I'm circumcised?"

I reach for his penis and gently touched the tip. I immediately feel him harden in response and that turns me on and makes me feel powerful. I study him for a moment but have to admit that I don't know.

"I am. See here? The head, tip, glans as it's officially called, is always exposed. The foreskin has been cut away. Michelangelo's statue of "David" – have you seen pictures of that? it's different, he's uncircumcised.

Next is the shaft and although it's not as sensitive as the head it still feels really good when you wrap your hands around it."

I follow his instructions saying:

"It feels good to me, too." and he chuckles but when I lick my lips – purposely testing my power – he stifles a groan. His voice roughens as he continues saying:

"Now down here we have—"

"Testicles!" I interrupt since I know that answer.

"No, ball-sack. Testicles is for text-books. These are my balls and they love being fondled by you."

"Oh do they? You mean like this? Hmmm?"

He rumbles deep in his throat and it's a happy sound.

"Somebody, at some point in time, named this bit of skin between my balls and my butthole the 'taint'. I think it was originally applied to females meaning the area between her two holes that *t'aint a hole*. Whatever, it caught on. Probably spread through a story in Hustler Mag or something.

It's still in the whole cock erogenous zone area so it likes being kissed."

I comply.

"Some guys like to have a finger shoved up their ass during sex but I'm not one of them. You're probably relieved to hear that."

"I don't know, maybe it would be okay. I trust you to do what you want to do for both of us. Does that even make sense?"

"No, not really," he laughs.

I giggle in response. Suddenly the whole lesson seems incredibly funny and fun. Joel is actually being fun! And I realize that I'm happy and that makes me feel playful as well.

Since he's already lying on his back I bend his arms at the elbow and try to hold him down but my fingers don't stretch wide enough to wrap around his wrists. I shift position so that my knees are pinning his upper arms although that means my legs are spread wide.

I ignore the fact that we can both smell my arousal, in addition to him getting a good look at my gaping pussy, but the sparkle in his eye shows I'm not fooling him.

"How about you just do what I say and stay put, okay?"

"Sure," he answers, smiling at my predicament.

I reach up to place my breasts on his face and rub them back and forth. He tries to catch a nipple in his mouth but I pull back saying:

"Uh-uh. I'm the boss, you don't move a muscle unless I say you can. Got it?"

He nods and I go back to letting the hair of his beard tickle my skin. At one point I squash my breasts down over his nose and mouth and he mumbles:

"I'm smothering, what a way to go!"

We continue to play like this with Joel allowing me to imagine I'm actually dominating him. Next I massage his chest with my breasts, I lick his ear and then blow a gentle breath until I feel him shiver. Exactly the way he did it to me.

I kiss all down his throat and stroke his biceps. By time I direct my attention to his dick he's erect and ready.

I begin the tease by lowering my hips until my vagina barely touches his tip. I know I'm wet when I feel him immediately strain upwards but I lift up and hold that position, quivering, just an inch or so out of reach.

Suddenly he grabs my hips and thrusts me down while pushing up until he fills me. I cry out:

"No fair, I'm not done!" but he just growls at me saying:

"Oh yes, you are." Then he rolls us over so he's on top and proceeds to drive into me with his usual long strokes. He gives me his full length every time, it's something he always does.

Holding my ass and forcing my hips to swivel he hits my g-spot. It makes me cum quickly, and then moments later we orgasm together.

Afterwards he rolls back onto his back with me still attached. He tickles his fingers down my spine and then caresses my bottom saying:

"So you want to be in charge, do you?"

"Oh I am in charge, mister." I reply.

He gives my bum a gentle swat and comments that I seemed to have learned the anatomy lesson well.

"Good teacher, I guess."

"Do you want to be *Teacher's Pet*?"

"Does that involve fetching you an apple? Or should I be getting more hands-on – possibly even mouth-on – with teacher's anatomy?"

"Yeah, that sounds about right."

I slide off the bed and onto my knees. He obliges by scooting to the edge and spreading his legs to give me easy access. Using my fingers to stroke, the palm of my hand to rub, and my tongue and lips to tease, I play for awhile before stating:

"Isn't it amazing that even from this very submissive position I'm obviously still dominating you?"

He holds my head between his hands and just stares into my eyes. I look right back at him, batting my eyelashes flirtatiously, but he keeps staring without saying a word. I try to move my mouth back down but he firmly hold me in place, still staring, still silent.

I try to avoid his gaze but I can't, my eyes are drawn to his. I begin to feel like he's looking right inside my head. After what feels like an eternity he quietly says:

"I will always be your man and I own you, body and soul."

Part of me wants to laugh "Ha!" in his face, while another part wants to cry with all the emotion welling up from my chest, but the overriding part simply holds his gaze and answers:

"Yes Joel, I belong to you."

"And I am yours," he answers then releases my chin with a little nudge indicating I should pick up where I left off. So I do although a giggle does escape me. When I glance up I see him smiling at me with affection.

I'm giving my task my undivided attention so I don't hear Bram hurrying down the hallway until the bedroom door bursts open and there he stands whispering urgently:

"Who the fuck is Matthew Landisman?"

Chapter 21

Joel

I was having a brilliant session in bed with Girlie. It feels weird to think of her as an innocent considering how well she fucks but she truly is. I enjoy watching her face as she explores my body with her little hands.

I laugh to myself when she tries to hold me down but I play along pretending she's in charge. The way she plays with me really turns me on and the sex is really good, in fact mind-blowing. I'm just enjoying my blow-job when Bram interrupts us.

Girlie, looking shocked, repeats:

"Matthew Landisman? Is he here? Now?" and tries to get up but I hold her down while turning to Bram for information.

"Yeah, he's here. He's standing outside in the yard just asking to be shot yelling his name and saying he's looking for you. For Joanne Dwyer. So who the fuck is he?"

I can see that Bram is anxious and angry. This is no time for Girlie to mouth off but luckily she realizes that and her reply is to the point:

"Matthew Landisman is a fellow agent, he's my friend, my very good friend. He's come here looking for me?"

"He's your boyfriend?"

"Eww, no. That would feel like incest. Matthew is definitely just a friend, but I do love him just like I would a brother. I can't believe he's here!"

"Your good friend, *your brother*, was one of the guys who took a shot at you?"

"No, he wasn't part of that patrol. I guess he heard what happened, that I went missing, and now he's come looking. God knows what he thought when he saw you Bram. He's a brave man, but so crazy! " She shakes her head. "What a terrible risk he's taking."

"Yeah, he sure is."

"You can't do anything to him!" she cries, struggling against me to stand up. "He's only trying to help me, he thinks he owes me."

I can't disguise the sarcasm in my voice when I say: "Why? Did you save his life?"

"No, not his, his wife's. But I couldn't save her foot."

Bram and I just look at each other. He says he wants to hear the whole story but first he has to get rid of Matthew.

"Keep her quiet," he orders. I pull Girlie onto my lap and cover her mouth with my hand warning that if she bites me I will torment her cunt until she cries for sex and then I'll withhold it. Repeatedly. She murmurs against my hand but doesn't try to bite. We both strain to listen to the conversation outside.

"Who are you Matthew Landisman, and what do you want here?"

"I'm a friend of Joanne Dwyer and I'm looking for her."

"I can't help you."

"She was seen on your property last Friday and no one has seen her since."

"I can't help you," repeats Bram.

"Look, I don't care what you're doing here. I'm not here in any kind of official capacity in fact I'd probably be in deep shit if they found out, but I don't care, I'm really worried about Joanne. I need to find her."

"As I said, I can't help you."

"Oh man, seriously? Look I'm unarmed, I'm begging for your help, I'm just desperate for news about her. I need to know she's okay."

"I can't help you and I have nothing more to say." We hear the door close and we hear Landisman call out a few more times but eventually he leaves.

Girlie is sobbing by then, saying she feels badly for Matthew and sorry for letting down such a good friend, someone who obviously cares about her.

Once Bram comes back in the room, indicating he's seen Matthew leave, we both turn to Girlie for an explanation. At first she acts angry and stubborn, refusing to talk. Finally Bram tells her:

"Girlie, behave yourself. Now. You gotta realize that no matter how good a friend this Landisman guy is to you unless he can protect you 24/7 your life is in danger. Do you really think your boss is going to let you live knowing what you can say about him?"

"I heard Matthew say he wasn't here officially."

"And what difference does that make? If he goes back and suddenly stops asking questions about you, stops looking for you, goes back to living his best life – what message is that going to send? Look, we're sorry you're hurting but the best thing you can do for yourself and for Landisman is forget he was ever here."

"You mean the best thing for you O'Sheas!"

"I told you before, at some point you're going to have to decide if you're our hostage or our accomplice, and we don't need a hostage. We don't need to barter, we don't even have a crop to protect anymore.

At this point you're either with Team O'Shea or you're against us."

I remain silent throughout this conversation. I can't believe my bad timing in showing Girlie that I care for her and then this happens. Serves me right for letting a woman get under my guard, but I'll make damn sure there's no more of that nonsense.

"Oh Bram, Joel, I'm not against you guys. I just feel badly that Matthew and Anita are worrying about me. I'm sure that not knowing what happened is really upsetting to them. I know how I'd feel if the situation was reversed.

Matthew took a real chance coming here. Once he got a look at you Bram he must have felt like he was David going up against Goliath!

Look, I do appreciate what you're saying and I guess so long as Kendricks thinks I might be a threat then I am in danger. And I am a threat to him because I'll kill him if I can!"

"You better tell us the whole story. Get dressed and we'll go in the kitchen and have a coffee."

"Oh Joel," says Girlie looking at me with a frown making her face sad. "I'm so sorry."

"Why are you telling me you're sorry?" I know my tone is harsh but I can't help it. In fact, I need to stay in this mind-set.

"Because we were having such a wonderful time together. At least, I thought..." she lets the sentence trail off and I don't respond. I just get into my jeans and head for the kitchen pulling on a shirt as I go and leaving her to follow. I hear her sniff and sigh.

Chapter 22

Bram

The three of us sit at the kitchen table with our coffees while Girlie tells her story. At some point Danny comes in, he's been out surveying the damage from the fire and looking for anything salvageable.

"There'd been a raid on a drug house – a cabin, actually – deep in some woods where they were cooking meth. There was only one road leading in and the raid was a success. Anita and I weren't part of the raid, we were sent in next day."

"Anita?"

"Anita Firth. She's married to Matthew Landisman. They met when they were in college, decided to apply to the agency together, got hired and got married. I met both of them on my first day of training and the three of us bonded right away.

Anyhow, Kendricks sent her and me out to check for any paperwork, digital files, anything like that. It was basically clean-up work. Everyone had cleared out after the raid so it was just the two of us."

"No escort, no back-up?"

"It was supposed to be a quick in-and-out job. No perps to deal with, nobody at all at the property.

Anita was on the phone with Matthew when it happened. Thank God because otherwise we'd never have gotten word out, fortunately Matthew could hear what was going on through the open line. We were pretty deep in the woods so we were lucky to have cell coverage.

What happened is we were just walking towards the front of the cabin when Anita stepped in a bear-trap that was concealed in long grass. It shouldn't have been there, the area was supposedly cleared by the previous day's crew. Yes, we still should have been looking and on our guard, but it never occurred to us.

Turns out, someone had come back in the night or early in the morning and laid the traps. If I hadn't stopped when she screamed I'd have stepped in the next one. As soon as Anita screamed they opened fire. I managed to get her lying down, after one glimpse at her leg I couldn't look again, it was so horrible. She was moaning and going into shock.

I could hear Matthew screaming what's going on? over the phone but I was concentrating on returning fire and couldn't answer. He heard the gunshots and immediately mobilized the team to come get us.

I managed to hold the shooters at bay until they figured out it was smarter to take off and make their escape before help arrived. It took quite a while for the rescue party to reach us... too long to save Anita's leg which had to be amputated just below the knee."

"But she survived, you did save her life."

"And my own. That's why it's so wrong for her and Matthew to act all grateful. Anything I managed to do for Anita I was also doing for myself.

The injury ended her career as a field agent but she wears a prosthetic and now works in the agency office."

"I don't understand why your CO sent the two of you out alone."

"Well, it was supposed to be an easy job."

"You mean like sending you to surveil our compound was supposed to be an easy job? Who's to say you were ambushed by the drug dealers? Why would anyone who had gotten away come back? Just on the off-chance that someone would show up? That doesn't make sense."

That has her pausing to think. But then she shakes her head saying:

"Kendricks is a prick but he's not that bad. He had it in for me, but not Anita."

"Why did he have it in for you?" I ask. I have to ask the questions, since Joel is stony-faced and Danny is silent.

"He tried it on with me, got real pushy and obnoxious about it, and I blew him off. Badly, I should have handled it better."

"You shouldn't have had to handle anything at all. You were one of his agents, his team, where did he get off trying to coerce you into sex?"

Danny speaks up then saying:

"Maybe he'd also made a pass at Anita? Would she have told you if he had? Did you tell her about your run-in with him?"

"No, I didn't. And you're right, she probably wouldn't have said anything either. That kind of thing, it makes you feel dirty or somehow to blame. You don't want to dwell on it. Plus, she wouldn't want Matthew to hear about it."

"Sounds to me like Kendricks doesn't like women."

"Oh no, he loves women. He's always telling us what they're good for and what he likes doing to them. He's a real pig but he's the CO so it's a case of laugh at the jokes and go along to get along.

What he probably doesn't like is having women on his team but he has no choice."

"A dangerous man." Joel finally says something. We all just look at him, each of us thinking *well, you should know.*

"You were right," Girlie says, looking at me. "I'm sorry I gave you a hard time." She turns to Joel adding: "You too."

The two of them exchange a long look but he doesn't answer her. I start feeling uncomfortable at the extended silence so I motion that she should come sit on my lap. Girlie is happy to do so and curls up comfortably against my chest.

"We're all heading out tonight," I announce. My brothers immediately go to their rooms to pack up their gear and within the hour we're on our way.

Part Two

"Consciousness"

Chapter 1

Girlie

Joel and I have settled into our routine at the cabin but he isn't an easy man to live with. Everything's great when we're in bed, the sex just keeps getting better and better, but we can't fuck 24/7 and the rest of the time is, well, tricky.

Joel takes care of the cooking and I clean but that takes no time at all since we've only got two rooms and a toilet. Not even a bathtub or a shower stall, we have to make do using the sink. The cabin was built as a place to sleep during a week's hunting and there are no amenities.

We're roughing it well enough because the weather hasn't turned cold yet although we do light a fire each evening because it gets chilly overnight in the woods.

Joel's phone has coverage so we're able to stay in touch but I have no one to call. He talks to Bram regularly.

At first I surfed the news channels but after a couple of days this cabin became my world and what's happening outside these four walls doesn't seem to matter much. There's enough drama happening in here.

I laid claim to a Kindle one of the guys had at the compound and filled it with a bunch of books so I'm content to curl up on the battered love-seat reading thrillers.

Joel sits in one of the armchairs thinking his thoughts. Occasionally he strums his guitar, but he doesn't sing and he doesn't chat. When I ask about his music he just frowns so I guess that's not working out right now.

Unnerved, I look up to see he's staring at me without the slightest bit of animation or any expression at all on his face. I'm not even sure if he's looking at me or if his eyes are just pointing in my direction while his mind's drifted off.

"What?" I ask.

His eyelids flicker and he slowly blinks a couple of times but doesn't answer.

"Why are you staring at me? What's wrong?"

"Nothing, and don't flatter yourself, I'm not staring at you."

"Oh right, it's not me it's the air around my head that you're looking at so intently. Are you psychic, Joel? Are you reading my *aura*?"

"Fuck off, Girlie."

"Well alrighty then."

Now I'm staring right back at him. If he can disrespect me I don't need to show him any courtesy. He holds my gaze and probably thinks he's going to win this contest but Joel doesn't realize that despite my best intentions and his worst behavior I've fallen in love with him. I can look at his handsome face for hours. I'll even end up smiling. I can hate him and love him at the same time.

I study his manly good looks, my eyes lingering over his firm jaw, straight nose, full upper lip, and naturally I start thinking about sex. I guess I signal that through my expression because his gaze becomes more focused, sharper and interested.

"Come here," he rumbles in his seductive baritone.

I put my Kindle aside, get up slowly, then turn away and walk into the bedroom. I hear his annoyed huff when he growls my name in exasperation.

"I'm fucking off, Joel, just like you told me to," I reply without looking back, knowing full well I'm being a brat.

He stalks into the room after me – a small room that's filled by a big bed – and pushing me down tells me I'm going to pay for my sass before capturing my mouth in a punishing, passionate kiss.

We spend a lot of our time this way, but something's got to give soon.

Chapter 2

Joel

I'm fighting a losing battle with my feelings. Girlie frustrates the hell out of me. I want to know what she's thinking, I want to know what she wants. What's going to happen next? How does she define this relationship?

Of course I don't ask her any of these questions because I don't actually want to talk to her. I want to keep her at arms-length, compartmentalized, only touching physically, just fucking, but I can't help being drawn to her.

She's young, she has – or had – a career she trained for, she's smart, she's single and independent. She should be making all kinds of demands and plans but Girlie just accepts everything as it comes. It's not normal, she's too compliant.

But maybe that's down to me? I do have a strong will and domineering ways so maybe she's playing it safe while we're living here in isolation. Is she afraid of me?

Does she play nicely in bed just to appease me? No, there's no way she's faking those orgasms. Her pussy gushes on my fingers and clenches around my cock. My tongue makes her scream.

But there's more to life than fantastic sex. I realize our time here is just an interlude while we wait for things to settle. It's just a little time out for a couple of weeks like, oh fuck, like a honeymoon. Is that it? Has Girlie fallen in love?

She always catches me when I'm staring at her. This time she's lying in front of the fireplace, watching the flames, when she spots me looking. She smiles and without thinking I blurt out what's on my mind:

"Are you in love with me?"

Her cheeks turn pink but she answers in a calm, steady voice saying:

"Yes, I am. What about you?"

"I've never been in love in my life."

She rolls on her side facing me. Propped up on one elbow her figure makes a lovely wavy line of curves from her head to her feet. She's a beautiful and alluring woman.

"Not yet," she taunts.

I slip down to the floor beside her saying:

"I'm definitely in love with your body and how good it feels and how good it makes me feel."

She stretches, arching her back in a way that my dick notices and approves, while commenting:

"Well, that's a start, isn't it?"

I get up and turn off the overhead light telling her:

"Strip. Take everything off. I want to see you naked in the light of the fire."

She gets up into a kneeling position and I hunker down beside her. Girlie pulls off her sweater and pushes down her sweatpants. We never did get around to buying her any underwear. She shifts from one knee to the other until she's slipped the sweats off and now she's nude.

Sitting back on her haunches she stays still while my eyes rove over her, lingering on her perfect breasts, the curve of her hips, the fullness of her bottom, her long legs. My gaze travels back up to her pretty face. Her lips are parted and reflecting a sheen of moisture.

What I feel for her isn't just lust. I'm kidding myself if I think that's all it is. No, I realize that I do love her.

I am so fucked.

Chapter 3

Girlie

I've been thinking back to the day we left the compound.

We'd been having such a good day and then the whole Matthew thing happens and Joel turns really cold towards me, closed off and unresponsive. It really feels like coming away with him is a big mistake.

We drive here in an old pick-up truck so noisy it makes conversation impossible. Once we arrive both of us get busy setting things to rights. En route we shopped for provisions so Joel fires up the generator and plugs in the fridge while I unpack our food onto the wooden shelving. The kitchen is just a corner of the one big dining and living-room so there isn't a lot of space.

I find the blanket-box of linens and make up the bed in the small room at the back. All of the beds in the O'Shea homes are king-size or even larger custom-builds. It's always a production to put the fitted sheets on. Joel comes in and helps when he sees me struggling.

Once we're done he lays me down on my stomach and climbs on top. He pulls down my sweats but leaves the rest of my clothes on. His too. We have sex and afterwards he hugs me really tight. I guess it's a non-verbal apology or something. I reach for his hand and he squeezes back saying:

"Once the place warms up we'll get naked and do this properly."

I half turn so he can see my face when I answer:

"Sounds really good."

Chapter 4

Joel

When she first came into my life I think I had a premonition that this little chickie was going to get to me. She has, she most definitely has.

That disastrous day when Bastard Cousin Kenny attacked her... that was when I realized I was hooked.

She clung to me that night and chose to sleep with me every night after. Baby bro was pissed off but he just didn't get it. He thought Girlie should hate me for tying her up and leaving her at Bastard Cousin Kenny's mercy - and she does – but she also knows that I'm the only one vicious enough to kill to keep her safe.

There are times, not so many as in the beginning, when her fear of me is like a presence. She never admits to being frightened but it's there in her shallow breathing, darting eyes, and timid gestures to pleasure me, even while she tries to toss her head and act like she'd done it all before.

So yes, she fears me but she knows as long as I'm around she doesn't have to fear anything from anyone else. Girlie knew that even before I snapped Bastard Cousin Kenny's scrawny neck.

Danny and I drive out the following day and deliver the body to the cousins' place. That branch of the family lives in a compound as well. If I'm honest with myself I have to admit that taking over the Delgado compound was really just to piss off my relatives.

I toss Bastard Cousin Kenny like the rubbish he is outside the gate. I can hear his sister, my cousin Ella, wailing and yelling but once she gets a look at my face she shuts up real quick.

"Nobody takes from us, Ella. What's ours is ours," I tell her before getting back in the truck and driving home.

Chapter 5

Girlie

Joel does love me, even though he won't admit it. He proves it every day by looking out for my safety and taking care of my physical well-being. It's just... I really need to hear him say the words. That's what I need and want.

The mood swings, the silent and scary simmering, and the staring would be a lot easier to take if I knew, deep down, that he loves me. And deep down I do know that so why is it so important for me to hear him say it? And why is it so hard for him?

I know I'm nagging but I can't help myself.

So now we've reached an impasse. We had this argument a couple of hours ago and ever since he's been sitting staring at the fire, grumpy, and refusing to open his mouth. I'm not backing down. I can keep up the silent treatment for as long as he can.

He's ignoring me but I keep walking in front of him on one pretext or another: to pick up an empty glass, to dump the waste-basket into a garbage bag, to put a box of tissues on the coffee table... finally he grabs my wrist and pulls me onto his lap growling:

"What the fuck is wrong with you?"

"Me? Nothing!" I snap back.

"Nothing? You're being really bitchy. Complaining and nit-picking, sighing and sulking. If something is bugging you just spit it out."

"Why can't you just say *I love you*?" I cry in exasperation. He stares into my eyes for a long moment then says:

"I love you," in a completely monotone voice.

"Huh, could you say it like you mean it?"

"I'm not an actor."

"Oh, I see. You'd have to be an *actor* in order to say the words like you actually *mean* them. Right. Great." I start to stand up but he holds me firm and again, stares into my eyes for a long moment.

I know that sometimes I act childish but only when Joel thinks he can boss me around just because he's a dozen years older. My only weapons against him are sex and my smart mouth. Trouble is I never know which one I'm going to use until it happens.

I'm pouting, waiting for him to reply to my comment when he totally surprises me by taking the conversation in a different direction entirely.

"Why are you trying to pick a fight?"

"I'm not. You're the one who is grumpy."

"Do you want to fuck?"

"Wow, what a romantic offer!"

"Girlie, I'd like to think you and me are beyond playing word games. Right from the start with us you've always wanted to fuck. At first it was because you were scared but boy, you sure were aroused! Bram talked to me about it after and we couldn't get over how a virgin got so horny without being touched up first."

"Wait... what? That's wrong. Why would you guys think I was a virgin?" I give a laugh but know I don't sound too convincing.

"Girlie, I'm not telling you what I think, I'm telling you what I know. You were a virgin when Bram had you. He said to me: *I've got a big dick but I've never seen such a look of astonishment*, and when I took you after him you were still incredibly tight. You didn't bleed, though."

When you're caught, you're caught. No point lying.

"The bleeding happened when I got fitted with an IUD."

"What's that?"

"An intrauterine device. For birth control."

"Oh, I wondered what was happening about that."

"Really? You never said anything—"

He interrupts to say: "Why would I? Pregnancy is your problem."

"Seriously? You're a Neanderthal, a fucking prick! Most men would wear a condom but you've never even offered to put one on."

"Well of course not, they don't fit."

"Bullshit!"

"Sure, I suppose if I wanted to strangle my dick I could squeeze it in to one but that's never gonna happen. So this device thing is always in you?"

"Yeah, it was difficult to get in but I'm not even aware of it now."

"So why does a virgin need birth control?"

"Because she's over twenty-one and going to work in field operations with a bunch of men. Men who..." I can't finish that sentence.

The betrayal of my team still makes me choke up. He gives me a moment to compose myself then says:

"OK, I know Danny always took credit for your horniness by saying you loved being spanked but I'm really not into that. You said you didn't like it but I want to be clear: you're not playing some game where you say one thing but mean another, right?"

"Listen Joel, because this is important to me. The only time I would ever want you to spank me is if I ever make you so mad that you lash out. In that case I would definitely prefer your hand on my ass to your fist in my face."

He holds my upper arms tightly, much too tightly actually, but he wants me to feel how serious he is as he says:

"That will never happen, Girlie. I will walk away and probably drive my fist through a wall, but I will NEVER - and I can promise this 100% - I will never punch you or slap you or shake you." He waits until I nod that I understand, and that I believe him, before adding:

"You know, I hate when you say things like that." Then, before I can respond, he flips me across his knee and pulls down my fleece pants.

"JOEL, NO!" I shriek.

Chapter 6

Joel

She's really worried and no wonder considering how vulnerable she is in this position. She struggles but I hold on tight.

"You really do have a gorgeous ass, you know, and I can't help myself, I want to give it a good smack."

And before she can utter a word I swoop down to plant a loud wet kiss on each cheek accompanied by me saying:

"Smack! One. Smack! Two."

She giggles but I can see her shoulders slump in relief until she tries to get up and can't. Her body tenses again as I keep her pinned down

"Now that I've got you helpless, I'm going to enjoy ogling and playing for awhile."

Stroking my hand along the length of her thigh and along her calf I admire the long muscles I feel under her smooth skin.

"Joel let me up, I don't like being held down like this."

"Oh! being across my knee is a problem for you? Does it make you horny, Girlie?"

"No, of course not!" she huffs in annoyance.

I chuckle and murmur *liar* under my breath, but loud enough for her to hear. Gently caressing her full curves I comment:

"You are as luscious as a ripe, juicy peach. I just want to take a big bite. I should give you a hickey except I wouldn't stop at just one and I hate the thought of marking this soft, smooth flesh. So sexy and so beautiful."

She responds with a wiggle as I continue light trailing my fingers up and down until I see a dimpling where tiny blonde hairs stand on end. I tickle her thighs until she parts them, and she retaliates by rubbing against my cock. She knows exactly what she's doing. Girlie's not the only one getting turned on, I've grown hard in response to her wriggling.

Time to tame this little brat.

Using my thumbs I part the two globes exposing her little butt-hole. She scrambles to get away but I hold her down saying *take it easy, I'm just looking.*

"I don't want you looking at me there," she complains, but when I press my forefinger against the tight entrance she stills as if frightened to distract me.

I tap my finger gently and with my thumbs massage the flesh around her hole.

"Joel," she speaks quietly. "You don't want to screw my ass, do you? I mean, you're too big and that hole's too small so—"

I interrupt to explain that the anal passage is full of muscles and she can certainly accommodate me.

"But if, no make that when, we do try anal it will be because you want to. I hope that when we explore best practices et cetera, it will pique your interest too."

"Don't count on it," she warns.

"It's only fair since Bram took your virgin cunt that I get your virgin asshole," I explain reasonably.

"I was pretty much still a virgin when you had me, it was only minutes later—" she claims indignantly.

"I just know you'll love every inch of me pushing in deeper and deeper and—"

"Oh fuck off, Joel," mutters Girlie.

"Great idea!" I laugh and lift her up and onto my cock. After all my tender touching she's well-primed to receive me.

"I'm tight enough here for you, aren't I?"

"You're perfect here and everywhere, Girlie. Stop worrying about it and just enjoy fucking me now."

As usual I lose myself in that wonderful experience. Every inch of her skin is incredibly soft and her cunt is so warm and wet and welcoming. Her whole body is responsive and taking her to the heights of pleasure is the very best feeling.

Afterwards I'm holding her tight when she whispers: *I love you, I love you, I love you* and after a pause she adds *and maybe we can try it...*

Chapter 7

Joel

I thought we'd got things worked out yesterday but no, something is still bugging Girlie. Since she won't come right out and tell me what it is now I'm getting bugged too.

She pretends it's just about me saying *I love you,* but I know it's something else. She's trying to distract and misdirect me with talk about love.

Girlie just hasn't been herself. She's even having bad dreams at night. Mostly just saying *no, no* and *don't,* flailing her arms about and babbling in what sounds like baby talk.

She's turned awfully moody lately, too. One moment she's cranky and sullen; next minute she's crawling all over me but in a kind of desperate way; or pushing me to talk when I don't want to so I tell her to fuck off and then I've hurt her feelings.

Neither of us has ever been in a 24/7 relationship and maybe we just need a break from each other. Not going to happen though, I'm not taking my eyes off her. We'll just have to adjust and make it work some how.

"Girlie! Come in here."

She stomps in with her mouth turned down and frowning so deeply her eyebrows nearly meet. For some reason her bad mood really pisses me off. I think about getting the upper-hand by demanding a blow job but she'll probably bite me!

Instead I rein in my temper saying:

"Listen Girlie, I know something's up and I could wait for you to tell me in your own time - probably that's what I should do – but I'm not a patient man. I don't want to wait. What's wrong and what can I do?"

I see a variety of emotions chasing across her face. She's annoyed, scared, hopeful, but dismissive as she says:

"It's nothing. I'm fine. Don't worry about it."

We both know she's lying and so blatantly that again I have to fight down my anger. But I do so and decide to play along:

"Okay great. I thought something was up but if you say *don't worry* then I won't. Let's go to bed," I add, which surprises her into saying:

"It's like two in the afternoon."

"And?"

I can tell she doesn't want to and I don't care. I have a plan in mind so I insist:

"Get your ass in the bedroom now and you better be naked by time I get there."

The look on her face says she wants to challenge me but she enjoys it when I'm being the macho man so she walks, slowly and with quite a swivel to her hips, out of the room.

When I join her she's in bed but under the covers. I pull all the bed-clothes back and toss them on the floor. She is naked. She's decided to be a good girl.

I stand there letting my eyes rove all over her body, she is delectable. It's hard to remember how badly damaged she'd been by Bastard Cousin Kenny.

Except for a slightly crooked nose there's no trace of his brutality on her beautiful face, magnificent tits, or smooth skin. She curves in all the right places. She has a peach of an ass, legs that just won't quit, and she's only twenty-five.

Girlie will be getting a bit anxious, wondering why I'm just staring at her, but she'll also be getting hot with anticipation. Girlie loves to fuck and never says *no*. However, I have something else in mind.

I take off my shirt and now I'm the one who's being hungrily studied. I kneel at the end of our huge bed and pull her towards me lifting her thighs on to my shoulders. Having all her weight on her upper back effectively pins her into position. She's spread and helpless, her hands can't reach me and she can't close her legs.

Once she realizes I've trapped her, and why, her eyelids droop and her mouth goes slack with lust.

Having her arms free, even though she can't do anything with them, makes a big difference.

I make darting motions with my tongue, alternating with licks and swirls, and soon she's gyrating at my touch. My eyes are moving from her clit to her face and I see that she's flushed with excitement. Her nipples are hard and she's started playing with them. I watch her squeeze her tits.

"Does this feel good?"

"Oh yes, yes!"

"Am I your man?"

"Yes Joel, you are. You know it. I love you."

"Should I keep doing this?"

"Yes, of course! Please, more, more!"

I stop what I'm doing and say:

"Then tell me what's wrong with you. What's got you all antsy and pissing me off."

She struggles, trying to sit up, and glares at me shouting:

"Never mind! It's nothing. Just go back to doing what you were doing."

"You mean this?" and I tease her some more.

She flops back down on the bed and gives a little cry. I stop immediately.

"Please Joel, pleeeeease, please, please, please."

"Tell me."

"I can't."

"Why not?"

"Because I DON'T KNOW what's wrong!"

"But it's something, right?"

She doesn't answer so I tongue her some more.

"It's Christmas. Christmas is the problem, and it's coming up soon, and I hate it which is stupid because I don't know why!"

Now she's crying, something she rarely does, so I slip her legs down and quickly enter her. I'm not being selfish, she needs to be fucked just as much as I need to fuck her.

Girlie pulls herself so tight against me it's like she's trying to disappear into my body.

She's still crying as she orgasms. I turn her over and we continue fucking while I toy with her clit until she cums again. Tears still stream down her cheeks until the pillow is wet. I don't know what to say so I say nothing.

Afterwards she punches me in the chest and tells me I'm a mean prick bastard. And she's right. I let her go stomping off to the bathroom while I pull myself to the top of the bed and decide to nap until she returns.

Chapter 8

Girlie

Sometimes I just hate him so much. I've let him get way too much power over me but, omigod I just melt at his touch. His big strong hands that always seem to know when it's time to be rough and when it's time to be gentle. And the look on his face when he's smiling down at me knowing how turned on I am... he's so hot. And I'm so weak.

Now he's going to demand an explanation about Christmas and I don't know what to tell him. I'm not hiding anything, or if I am then I'm hiding it from myself, too.

Actually, that's not quite true. I did hide and deny the truth for a long time but during the Bastard Cousin Kenny ordeal the memories surfaced.

Problem is, they're memories from when I'm two or three years old and I don't have the words to describe my thoughts or feelings. I'm getting flashbacks in my dreams which makes me realize something is trying to break through. I'm just not sure if I'm ready to let that happen yet.

I do know that I'm not looking forward to this conversation, but I guess I better get it over with.

I come out of the bathroom and just stand in the doorway looking at him. His hands are behind his head and that position shows off his physique to full advantage. He's still naked and seeing the size of him stretched out on the bed is arousing and intimidating at the same time. He's over six-and-a-half feet tall and all muscle.

I climb on the bed and lay my head on his chest, wanting comfort, but he pushes me down ordering me to clean him off with my mouth. I obey his orders wishing I was sassy enough to challenge him but, to be honest, his demands are always – and only - for things it turns out I enjoy doing. Joel is a clever man.

So I start to move downwards but he stops me and swings me around so that my feet are up by the pillows. I shrug and turn on my side and start licking his flaccid penis.

He starts playing with my clitoris again but I pull back because I can't bear to have it touched right now. Needless to say I'm not allowed to refuse. Joel lifts himself up to pry my thighs open enough to get at me with his tongue again. He pauses long enough to tell me not to stop what I'm doing and then he turns his attention back to my tingling overly sensitive flesh.

I've heard of the sixty-nine position but have never done it. Well, until recently I hadn't done anything so that's no big surprise. Unfortunately what he's doing to me is distracting me from what I'm doing to him.

Of course I melt into a puddle of helpless pleasure as he thrusts his cock into my mouth. It's growing harder by the second and yeah, I get off on knowing how good I can make him feel.

I'm clenching tight with my lips and stroking his balls when he pushes deep and my gag reflex makes me flinch, but I want to take all of him. I concentrate on opening and relaxing my throat and he drives forward, filling me. It feels like he's about to explode but instead he pulls out and rolls on his back so I can scramble on top to ride him.

He's clutching my ass with one hand and squeezing first my left breast then the right one with his other hand. He twiddles each nipple until it's swollen and slightly sore.

I feel the sexy power of my body. My mouth is open, my eyes are closed, and I let me head fall back.

I really am riding him and I move my hips in a circular motion going way up and then way down squeezing with the walls of my pussy. He shouts out when he ejaculates:

"Girlie! Fuck, Oh Chickie."

I collapse on top of him and he hugs me so tight. He's so strong, and I feel so safe and loved when I'm lying in his arms. It's just the sex, right? Sure, I say *I love you,* but it's all part of the deal.

I've never been in love. I don't know how to love because no one has ever loved me so I never learned. I've seen love, my friends Anita and Matthew are very much in love, and when I saw her bloody mangled foot in that bear trap the pain I felt for her was because I love her.

But I can't really be in love with Joel. I mean, he's such a prick I can't be falling for him. I hardly know him. I'd never had sex before meeting the O'Sheas and that only happened a few weeks ago. It was... September? no, I was sent to scout out the grow-op in October and it's sometime in December now, not even two months.

I can't have fallen in love in less then two months with a man who is so uncaring and cold and dismissive of my feelings. That would be like I have Stockholm Syndrome or something.

Chapter 9

Joel

We sleep for a few hours and I wake up first. I love seeing her curled against me, so relaxed and content, her body soft and warm and pliant.

Loving me with her body is such a blessing. How can anyone ever hurt such tender flesh?

I really did give her a scare when I put her across my knee and pulled down her pants. All the muscles in her glutes tightened with tension and she was trembling. When I gave her ass a kiss instead of a spank her laugh of relief was delightful to hear.

When I look down at her perfect round globes all I want to do is squeeze and fondle fistfuls of soft skin. Same as when I bare her gorgeous tits. I just want to fill my hands and caress. When I'm buried deep inside her cunt I love roaming my fingers and mouth over every inch of her beautiful body and I especially love how she responds.

Girlie loves being manhandled by me.

When I finally dragged my attention away from her sexy bum I could see that she's trim and fit all over with visible muscles in her shoulders, thighs, and calves. I feel a pang of anguish thinking how close she came to losing part of her leg to a bear trap, and I feel sorry for the friend and colleague who did.

How did Kendricks get away with running such a sloppy operation? But I don't want to think about him right now, not when I've got this lovely girl in my arms and in my bed.

I kiss her face along her hairline but with gentle, butterfly kisses so she doesn't waken. She stirs a bit and smiles but doesn't wake up so I let her sleep. I feel so lucky to have her.

I mentally give my head a shake knowing I've totally fallen for Girlie, but I'm determined to keep that fact to myself. I'm not sure which one of us I don't trust.

Girlie thinks she's distracted me from the Christmas discussion but we'll get back to it. I won't pester her about the issue anymore tonight, though.

In fact, while she's sleeping I'll go make a call to get her surprise organized.

Chapter 10

Girlie

I'm excited about Joel's surprise but a bit apprehensive too. I mean, it will be wonderful to see Bram and Danny again and to spend few days with them, but I'm anxious about leaving here. I feel safe here. But, I'm sure a change of scene will do us both good. And a reunion will be such fun!

Too bad it has to happen over Christmas, that's a holiday I've never enjoyed celebrating and now I've got to figure out how to manage it under Joel's watchful eye.

Maybe it will be different this time. How can it not be with three big, strapping men? Oh! The dynamic has changed now and I wonder if Joel will still be willing to share me?

Actually, it's up to me whether or not I bed anyone else but despite knowing that I don't want to cross him. If Joel agrees that it's my choice what will I choose to do? Do I want him to object?

Thinking about having a change of scene I asked if we could go for a walk to get some fresh air and stretch our legs. He likes the idea but warns it's really cold outside.

My face falls when I explain I don't have any winter wear. Joel knows his clothes are just too big, but he sees my disappointment and says:

"It's a long-shot, but I'll check the closet in case there's any of my, or Bram's, outdoor gear from when we teenagers."

The closet has the musty odor of long-forgotten clothing that was sweaty when put away but I don't care about that. Joel digs through the old remnants until he's able to outfit me in a flannel shirt under a camoflage jacket, topped with a padded vest.

Next come snowmobile mitts that go way past my fingertips but have a velcro strap to snug them around my wrist. A tartan scarf and a clashing plaid hat with ear-flaps complete my mishmash of an outfit.

Joel insists on taking a picture with his phone. Shaking with laughter he has a hard time holding the camera steady and has to take a few shots. I stick out my tongue and he comments *that's a keeper.*

All the hassle is worth it once we step outside. The snow has stopped falling and it muffles all sound. Bright blue sky pierces through the gaps between the pine trees, and the snow-covered branches dazzle where they're struck by the sun. Nothing is melting, it's far too cold for that, and the view from every direction is Christmas-card perfect.

Joel holds onto my upper arm as we forge a path through the trees.

"It's all new growth by the cabin, so not too tall and not too thick." he explains.

As we move deeper into the woods the density of the trees makes it impossible to walk side-by-side, and it's much darker there as well. Instead of penetrating further we turn to circle the cabin in the more sparsely populated area.

The crisp air has reddened Joel's cheeks and I'm struck again at how handsome my dark-haired man is. The way his eyes sparkle when he looks at me makes me hope he's thinking similar thoughts.

Without warning he quickly grabs a handful of snow and forms a snowball that he hits me with square on the chest. I don't even bother packing the snow, I just start flailing armfuls of it in his direction, scooping up lots and showering it over his head.

Next thing I know I'm tackled to the ground with the threat of having my face washed with the icy stuff.

"Let's make snow angels!" I happily suggest.

"No, let's make sex silhouettes," he replies, rolling on top of me in a tight embrace. His nose is cold, but his lips press warmly as his tongue teases its way into my mouth.

He's told me I'm a great kisser but I think he gets all the credit. His kisses are never too wet, his teeth never clash against mine, his tongue is never invasive, and his lips exert exactly the right amount of pressure to suit our mood of passion or tenderness.

Enjoying the outdoors has brought back Joel's playful side and it's wonderful.

Chapter 11

Joel

For the next couple of days we make the most of the continued good weather. It's cold but invigorating. Just like the outdoor showers I put poor Girlie through at the compound which I enjoyed but her? not so much.

We can't stay outside for too long but it's enough to enjoy some fresh air and a bit of exercise. Coming back to a warming cup of coffee while stretching out in front of the fire is pure bliss.

I'm wishing I thought to pick up hot chocolate when we shopped on the way here. Hot fucking chocolate – who am I these days? That little Chickie has me by the short hairs.

The chance to get out helped make it seem less like we're stuck here in the cabin. I mean, we are, for safety's sake, but getting out for awhile each day allows some freedom. Girlie and I are no longer irritable and snapping at each other.

She's tidying up in the kitchen and when she reaches to put some plates on a high shelf her sweater pulls up, flashing some bare skin around her midriff.

Immediately I have to touch her. I wrap my arms around that warm skin and kissing her neck slide my hands up from her waist to her naked breasts. She is so soft and squishy except for the hard nubs of her nipples. I drag the sweater over her head and now I can see as well as feel her.

"I love that your body is always accessible, tits and ass bare and available."

I hook my fingers at the waistband of her sweatpants and easily tug them down. Now she's nude from the knees up. Her smooth unblemished skin is so inviting.

"As a matter of fact I have, or at least I had, two dresser-drawers full of pretty lingerie in my apartment. If it's still mine and if my stuff's still there, that is."

"But you don't need that, Girlie. Nothing is more beautiful than your naked body, and nothing is better than straight sex. Not sexy clothes or toys or games, just deep hard fucking."

"Oh you don't understand, Joel. Lingerie shopping used to be one of my favorite things. I'd go to the boutiques plus I'd buy online, and I had a beautiful collection of satin, silk, and lace. Wearing it made me feel so sexy and feminine."

I turn around to face me. Her sweatpants have slipped down to her feet so she kicks them away. Now my Girlie is standing naked in my arms in the kitchen while I'm fully dressed and getting hard.

"I love thinking about you putting on fancy bras and panties – they match, right?" she nods. "Okay, let me enjoy this, thinking about you wearing a matched set of sexy lingerie on your virgin body."

"Well, yeah but I wasn't planning on being a virgin forever."

"No that's right, you got on hooked up with a birth control device."

"Yes, I told you I have an IUD."

"How long did you have it in before you had sex?"

"Oh, a bit. I mean you have to wait like two or three weeks before it becomes effective."

"So less than a month."

"Uh, no. No, actually I had it in for longer than that—"

"Three months?"

"Probably....?"

"Six months?"

"Maybe? Oh what does it matter?" she says with a scowl and I can't help but laugh.

"Oh Girlie, the poor little virgin all primed and ready to go with her birth control and her sexy panties—"

She smacks my arm and says: "It's good to be prepared."

"Prepped and ready and just waiting to be discovered by a bad boy, a tough guy, a macho man—"

That makes her smile as she corrects me saying: "Manly male, otherwise it sounds like that old song they always dance to at weddings."

"A Daddy—"

She interrupts again to say: "No, that's Bram."

I think about that a moment before conceding she's right.

"And instead you stumbled into the path of your Master."

"Ha!" she hoots. "NOT a Master, not ever."

I pull her close and nibble on her ear. She lets her head fall, exposing her neck to my kisses. When she arches her back her breasts squash against my chest and I quickly unzip and shuck my jeans. I'm always commando so I'm all set. I slip a finger inside her to check for readiness and my sweetie never disappoints.

I turn her against the counter and she spreads her thighs enough to let me plunge in. She's wet and hot and sensational. I look down to see my cock moving in and out while I rub her ass with one hand and finger her clit with the other.

She starts to squirm as I press hard on that little bundle of nerves and I whisper that I must be her master because I'm the one who can make her howl. She loses her sassy reply in a stutter of oh-oh-oh as she orgasms but I don't let up, I shift my angle so my cock hits her g-spot while my finger keeps teasing her swollen clit.

"Joel, Joel, oh Joel!"

"Call me Master."

"Nooooo," she keens.

"Then howl for me, Chickie."

And she shatters with a drawn-out high-pitched cry, and I share the ecstasy with a growl. Her legs give out and I scoop her up in my arms, then balance her on the counter so I can devote my attention to kissing her slack mouth.

"You did howl. That means I am your Master, right?"

"Maybe my... Fuck-Master."

"I LOVE being a Fuck-Master! All this time I was waiting for you to say you were looking for Mr Right and I'm Mr Wrong but now... Fuck-Master it is!"

Chapter 12

Girlie

Things are really good with Joel now. We're both relaxed and content. I almost never catch him staring at me and if I do he smiles instead of giving me his brooding scowl.

The weather quickly turned much colder which has shortened our walks, but the sky is a hard bright blue with plenty of sunshine for the few hours of daylight. We stay late in bed in the morning and go early to bed at night.

I'm getting excited about seeing Joel's family home after hearing so much about it. It sounds like his childhood was a happy one, adolescence not so much. He was sent away to boarding school, same as Bram before him, and I think those years apart caused a rift between him and his parents.

It's not a long drive but we'll need to get through these snowy lanes until we reach the highway. Joel says there's a secondary road they use as a shortcut but it will be impassable now.

"You know I'm looking forward to meeting up with Bram and Danny again, but part of me doesn't want to leave here," I begin but stop, suddenly feeling shy.

Joel comes to sit beside me on the love-seat. He puts one arm around my shoulders but doesn't pull me close, instead he keeps enough space between us so he can see my face.

"I've enjoyed our time here, too." He adds: "That's why I'm in no rush to leave. I think we can have a couple more days before we have to head out."

I feel my mouth forming a huge grin. I'm so glad he understands. The real world will intrude soon enough, right now I would like more time hidden away.

"You've been really good about roughing it here. You're not a very girly-girl, are you?"

"I won't lie, I've been dreaming of a hot bubble-bath, fluffy towels, and a change of clothes afterwards. Is that girly enough for you? But really, this has been okay."

"Well, I know there weren't many amenities at the compound, but this cabin really is back to basics and you've been great. Thank Christ you're not a whining complainer, that would drive me up the wall."

"Yeah even if I wanted to bitch the thought of being trapped in here with a pissed off you would have reined me in. Hey, don't laugh, that's nothing to be proud of."

"I didn't say I was proud. I'm a prick and I know it. And everyone who knows me knows it too.

Anyhow, we have to figure out what still needs doing. I'd like to eat up the food 'cause I don't know when anyone will be here again."

"We're not coming back after the Christmas holiday?"

"No, there's no insulation and only the fireplace for heat. Plus we'd get snowed in and could mean being trapped for weeks. No, we'll go home for a couple of weeks and maybe stay all winter, I'll see how it goes."

I notice he's saying *I* instead of *we* but I'm still uncertain about where exactly I fit in so I don't say anything.

"Who all lives at your house?"

"My parents are gone so it's just the three sons and we have a few staff members who come in on a daily basis. Maggie Clarke is the housekeeper and cook and she's got everyone under her thumb. And not just the cleaners and groundskeepers but us brothers too.

She finishes each day late in the afternoon and then goes home to terrorize her own family. No one sleeps in."

"I'm scared of her already."

"She's a pussycat underneath the grumpy exterior. She basically raised us so we're used to her ways. You'll be okay so long as you treat me right because I'm her favorite."

"You're my favorite, too," I reply, moistening my lips with the tip of my tongue. That's got his attention.

"Hmmph, easy to say... how about you come over here and prove it."

This sexual episode is lovemaking. Slow and sweet and I climax twice before he cums hard. Afterwards he keeps stroking my body then kisses and nibbles his way down to my pussy.

Thinking back to our earlier conversation I put out my hand to cover up, stopping him, saying:

"Joel don't, I must smell bad."

"What?"

"Well, it's been weeks since I had a shower. Cleaning up in the sink is fine for my armpits but not for down there, not after all the sex we've been having—"

He chuckles answering: "Girlie, I'm not complaining. I must reek too but—"

"Oh, so you admit that I stink!"

Of course that just makes him laugh but I stop him with an evil smirk.

"What? What are you thinking about?"

"Blue balls," I reply.

"What?"

"Well I know there's this thing called a Polar Bear Dip where people swim in icy water on Christmas Day, or maybe it's New Year's Day? anyhow, when it's fucking cold so we should go outside and have a snow bath. And you can get blue balls."

"First of all that's not what blue balls means, and secondly a snow bath? seriously? You think that's a thing?"

"Sure, why not? The Swedes or Norwegians are always having saunas and then rolling around in the snow or something."

"You want to roll around in the snow, Girlie? You couldn't even stand taking a cold shower at the compound."

Now he's really laughing at me but I explain that we don't have to wash all over, just get our genitals cleaned up.

"You want me to wash my cock in snow?"

"No, I'll wash it for you. And then when we come in I'll warm it up in my mouth. We can lie in front of the fire and warm each other up again."

"Doesn't it kinda defeat the whole purpose if we just get all messy again?"

"Ooh, messy, I like the sound of that."

"You're fucking crazy, you know?"

"We're already naked O'Shea so hurry up and meet me outside."

I race outdoors and he's right behind me, pushing me flat out on the snow so that my front is soaked from face to toes. Then he turns me onto my back and pulls my legs apart so he can pack snow between them.

I'm FREEZING! In two minutes Joel's skin has already turned red and I'm turning blue!

While he's making me into a snow-cone I fill my hands with the cold white flakes and reach for his dick.

"No you don't," Joel shouts trying to scoot away but by now I'm too numb to feel the cold so I jump him and roll both of us around until I've got him facedown.

Straddling his hips I scoop snow between his legs while he tries to yell *stop* but can't because he's laughing too hard.

"Where are your balls, Joel? I think they've disappeared!"

"You better run, Girlie, because a hard smack on an icy cold ass is going to hurt like hell."

I squeal and run inside with him on my heels. He captures me in his arms as we stumble inside saying:

"You are the most beautiful girl I have ever seen!" and his words carry such conviction I believe him.

Although my teeth are chattering and every inch of my skin has goosebumps I know my eyes are sparkling, my cheeks are rosy, and my smile is supernova bright because I feel full to bursting with joy.

We collapse in front of the fire and the heat is both wonderful and painful on our chilled, puckered flesh.

This time the sex is hard and fast as we rub tight against each other to get warm.

Chapter 13

Joel

The sound of a car's engine seems harshly alien since it's so still and quiet here. We both wait, surprised, until it pulls up, stops, a door slams, and we hear one person stomping through the snow to the cabin door.

I'm already up and waiting for the new arrival. The door opens bringing Danny in, along with a swirl of freezing air.

He smiles and greets us both while taking off his big jacket and hanging it on one of the hooks behind the door.

"Danny! What a surprise," says Girlie. "It feels like we're in the middle of nowhere but you found us."

"Oh, I've spent a fair bit of time in this cabin. I know how to get here easily enough," he replies.

"How about some coffee?" she asks, then offers food if he's hungry.

"Coffee sounds good but whiskey sounds better," he says turning towards me.

"Sorry baby bro, the cabin is dry. As usual."

"Oh hell, I forgot about that. Dammit I could have brought some."

"No, that's against the rules. You know that," I answer.

It seems like he's up to something but I can't figure out what he's playing at. It was drilled into us from our very first - and every subsequent hunting trip out here - that guns and booze don't mix. No alcohol of any kind has ever been allowed at the cabin.

"Aww, that was when we were kids."

"No, and you're still a kid."

"Oh Joel, you act like such an old man. Hey Girlie, you're looking mighty fine. All healed up and as beautiful as ever."

Girlie smiles to acknowledge the compliment but something seems a bit off with her. Whatever hinky feeling she has I guess I feel it too. It must be Danny who seems a bit dodgy to both of us.

"Well fuckit, it'll have to be a cup of coffee after all. How about giving it to me naked?" he asks with a sidelong leer at her.

"Hey if you want to strip down go ahead and get naked, Danny," Girlie replies. I hide a smile.

"Ha-ha," he answers, then adds: "I've missed you, missed being with you Girlie, and I'm looking forward to making up for lost time."

Out of the corner of my eye I can see Girlie turning towards me but I'm careful not to meet her gaze. I keep my eyes on Danny. The slight smirk I detect in his expression is enough to make my hands start curling into fists but I force myself to relax and be casual.

"If that's okay with you, Joel?"

"Girlie makes her own choices."

"Well that's something new!"

"No, I don't think so. She's always done what she enjoyed doing."

"So it's okay with you if *she enjoys doing me*, eh?"

Without hesitation I reply: "Sure. baby bro. If it wasn't for you she'd be dead."

"I hope you mean by those rogue DEA agents and not you," says Girlie then hastily adds: "Please don't answer that."

She hands Danny his coffee and has brought one for me as well. As I reach for it our eyes meet briefly, but I'm careful to keep my thoughts shuttered.

Danny pats the couch motioning Girlie to join him. She pauses only a moment before sitting down. He cups her chin in his hand while he studies her face.

"Not a mark. You're a fantastic healer, Girlie. That means you're really healthy with a healthy body. But then, I knew that part already."

He puts his coffee on the end-table and lets his hand drop down from her face directing his attention to the buttons of her flannel shirt. It's cowboy-style with snaps and using both hands he pulls those snaps apart and we all listen to the sound each one makes as it pops open.

We never did buy Girlie any bras or panties so when he pulls the shirt wide her naked breasts are revealed, looking magnificent as always.

"Oh! Hello. Wow, I have missed these two something fierce." He fills both hands with her flesh and squeezes hard. I see a fleeting expression of pain chase across her face before she smooths her features back into a mask.

"I heard about you two coming to the house for Christmas so I figured that must mean the honeymoon is over and we're back to normal. And that means I get to enjoy my girl's tits." Danny bends his head down and nuzzles his unshaven face against her tender skin.

"Oh yes, oh yes, oh num num num." Just as I'm wondering whether or not he's drunk he lets out a loud belch that makes Girlie flinch from the stink of his breath.

"What? Somethin' the matter with you?" he calls out belligerently. I started moving over to the couch but he suddenly stands up and launches into a tirade:

"She's mine. I found her, I saw her first, I'm the one who saved her when the bullets were flying. She's my property, not yours, not even ours but MINE, only mine!"

I fold my arms over my chest to keep from taking a swing at him. Now that I've gotten closer I can see the red in his eyes and smell the booze on his breath. I can't believe he was behind the wheel of a car.

I only need to give him a light push to send him sprawling down on the couch. Unfortunately he lands right on top of Girlie.

His hands and his mouth are roaming over her tits and for the first time ever I see real distaste in her look. She turns her head aside and Danny keeps pawing at her, unzipping her jeans and pulling them down and off. She doesn't resist.

Except for the open shirt, now pushed back off her shoulders, she's naked. Danny pauses to gloat over her body. I watch to see if she'll give some sign that I should intervene. Nothing. She doesn't look at him and she doesn't look at me. She does nothing but lie there.

Danny hasn't noticed, he's too busy roughly running his hands all over her flesh. He jams his fingers inside her and I see her flinch from discomfort. After a few moments of sawing back and forth over her clitoris he finally notices her lack of response. He gets angry.

"What the fuck? What's wrong with you, Girlie? You know you like this, you always liked it when I did this. Maybe I need to beat your ass again, hmm? You'd like that. I know you like it when you're manhandled by me. Yeah, first I'm gonna fuck that ass and then take my Papa's advice and teach you your place."

He struggles, sagging into the couch, and is trying to turn her over when she cold-cocks him. One punch and he's laid out.

I feel like applauding but instead I just look at him, sprawled over the arm of the couch tipping towards the floor, and then at her pulling her shirt closed and panting with the exertion of extricating herself out from under his weight.

Without a word or a glance at me she goes into the bedroom and slams the door.

I stay up all night keeping an eye on baby bro in case he starts puking or something. I suppose I'll rescue him if he does.

When he leaves early next morning I think he might still be a little drunk. Girlie must have heard us talking but she doesn't make an appearance until the last sound from his car is gone.

Chapter 14

Girlie

When I get up Joel says he's decided we should head out today. I agree. This idyll in the cabin has been ruined by Danny. I hope I'll feel differently about it when – if - we come back again, but for now I just want to get away.

We're going to *talk about my Christmas issue* before leaving because Joel says it's making me vulnerable. I guess I've been having noisy dreams – nightmares – these last few days.

But for now, I just want to get out of here.

We've spent the morning tidying and shutting everything down so I suggest we just head out and talk on the way. Joel laughs, he knows I remember how that noisy old truck makes conversation impossible.

"I know you think I'm just avoiding having this conversation but now is simply not the time. Right now I'm not even happy being in the same room as you, never mind talking to you."

He just looks at me without any expression at all. I continue my complaint:

"I don't know what the fuck happened last night but I feel so used and dirty and worthless that I don't even want to know you O'Sheas, so let's just go."

Of course he won't let me get away without a full explanation.

"I didn't like what happened last night, and also what didn't happen. At first I thought it was all a joke until I realized it wasn't.

141

Danny really offended me, you know? I mean, what does he think I am? and who does he think he is? So first I was offended and then I got angry."

"I didn't think you were enjoying what was happening but I didn't know for sure. I was waiting for you to say the word and I would have stopped him."

"Hmm, and there I was thinking I couldn't say anything, that part of my *survival package* was always being willing to spread my legs on command."

"It was, but it hasn't been for a long time now and you know that. C'mon Girlie, you know I feel differently about you now. I was waiting – hoping - you'd call out to me."

"I shouldn't have had to say anything, you should have known."

"Listen Chickie, I'm not a mind-reader. You always have to be direct with me because I'm not going to pick up on subtle clues. That's just not me. I feel, I react, but I don't analyze why." That's actually a lie but I'm sure as shit not admitting that to her.

She's getting riled up again, standing there sticking her chin out and with her hands fisted on her hips.

"Well, I'm a big girl and I can take care of myself when it comes to boys..." she gives me a wicked grin adding: "but men are a different story altogether."

"That was a great punch!"

"Consider yourself warned, I'm SuperGirlie."

"Oh you are, huh? You're looking pretty hot right now, Wonder Woman."

Chapter 15

Joel

Girlie steps close for a kiss but I hold her at arms-length saying:

"Good try baby, but you aren't going to distract me that way. You and I are going to have the talk you keep postponing and then I'll make it up to you for falling short of your expectation last night."

I kept feeding the fire during this morning's chores so we'll be cozy sitting in front of it. Girlie doesn't want to talk which means that I have to make her.

Even after all this time she still tries to assert herself with me. Sometimes it's cute, sometimes it's annoying, sometimes – like now – it just means I have to be patient and coax the conversation out of her.

So I'm sitting on the floor in front of the fire, leaning back against the couch, and I've pulled her down so she's sitting between my legs and resting on my chest. Her hair smells pretty and when I sniff down the side of her neck she gives a shiver and tells me to fuck off. That makes me chuckle.

Reaching forward I take hold of her wrists and bring her arms behind her back, holding her firmly. She immediately starts to squirm and complains that I have to release her, she doesn't like that.

"Why not?"

"I don't know exactly, I just don't like it."

"Has anyone ever restrained you and physically hurt you?"

"No, let me go."

"Has anyone ever restrained you and mentally hurt you?"

"Maybe. Sort of..."

"Tell me."

"There's really nothing to say."

"Then it won't take long."

"Ha-ha. Let go of me first."

"No, I think this helps focus your attention so you can concentrate on your memories."

The entire time we've been talking she's been struggling to get free. Her breathing has quickened and I'm sure if I could see her face I'd notice a rosy flush. Girlie is agitated. I'm holding her wrists, not too tightly, while rubbing her shoulders and stroking her arms but she still won't relax.

"Okay but listen and pay attention because I want to get this over quickly and I don't want to repeat myself. Especially since I don't even want to be talking to you right now. I'm still really, really mad at you.

Anyhow, while Bastard Cousin Kenny was assaulting me my mind drifted away to a memory buried deep inside. I'm tied up and I'm terrified. I don't know why I'm bound, I don't know for how long, I mean I do know all of these things now but I didn't know it then.

Lately the memories have been pushing through in my dreams and even day-dreams because Christmas is coming and that's when it happened.

What I was told afterwards – and I mean years afterwards – is that my mother, who suffered life-long mental illness, went extra crazy at Christmas time – probably all the happy families romantic shit. With no one to stop her she would just abandon me while she went searching for my father.

Just to show you how crazy that is my mother never even knew who my father was. She was always a bit backwards and well... I got my great figure from her so you can imagine what easy prey she was. By time anyone knew she was pregnant it was too late to abort.

Why they let her keep me is a complete mystery. I mean, it wouldn't happen now but back then, if family were willing to step up then I guess Social Services was happy to let sleeping dogs lie, so to speak.

Trouble is the same people who let my mother get banged by anyone and everyone were the ones watching over us. So at Christmas time something would slip out of alignment in my mother's brain and she'd go wandering.

Someone must have taken care of me the first year or so because well, I'm here, but the Christmas I was two or three my mother tied me to a chair, to a bed, to the kitchen table, wherever, while she went out on the prowl night after night.

At least that's what the authorities figured when they pieced it all together afterwards. Mum died of alcohol poisoning or technically that thing called vagal inhibition where a comatose drinker drowns or chokes inhaling their own vomit. Her blood alcohol level was something like five times over the legal limit.

Well, when drunks die outside in cold weather no one really pays a lot of attention but eventually somebody notices the huddled mass of rags is actually dead. So they get picked up and carted off to the morgue which is often busy at that time of year so a day or two or six go by before anyone gets around to figuring out who they are and what their story is.

My mother didn't even get that much attention. It was my auntie calling us from across the country and getting no answer day after day who finally involved the cops.

They tried to slough off Auntie Jill's concerns citing the holidays... busy people... grown woman... no cause for concern... if still no word after a few more days file a missing persons report... yadda yadda. Until she said "Sure, my sister is an adult but what about her baby daughter?"

She lit a fire under their ass, thank God, and they came looking and found me on a welfare check. They can't even guess exactly how long I was left alone. How long can a toddler survive without water? I was severely dehydrated, malnourished, and in a coma at death's door.

I could feel the horror of those days and nights but I couldn't articulate my feelings because I had no words to describe them. I was simply too young. Now, when I'm restrained I feel a smothering panic that terrorizes me, it drives me into a mindless frenzy.

Auntie Jill moved me to live with her on her in-law's farm where she worked in their market garden business. They weren't unfriendly people but they had no reason to love me and vice-versa.

Auntie Jill had kept her distance from her own family for a number of years for the sake of her own mental health but she was there when I needed her. The day after my eighteenth birthday she committed suicide.

In her note she explained that she'd been fighting her depression for years and had just been waiting for me to become an adult. She thanked me for bringing her times of real joy but said she was very tired of the whole business of life so good bye and good luck.

There was no reason for the Dwyers to keep me on. They were quite elderly by then, but they were kind enough not to throw me out. I worked for them the summer between high school and college and then I left for good.

There you have it. While tied up I wasn't abused or molested or anything, I was just forgotten, abandoned, discarded... pick a word. And now you know there's a history of mental illness in the family on one side and God only knows what's on the other. So, I'm damaged goods and I guess my story explains a lot about me."

Then she bursts into gut-wrenching sobs and I hold her and rock her and kiss the top of her head until she quiets.

"I knew some of this but not facts, just suppositions, based on things you've said in your sleep and your behavior in general."

"You know what's really crazy? I'm crying my eyes out but I actually feel lighthearted right now. Despite being so pissed off at you. I mean my life's a complete disaster, I'm just drifting along with what everybody else wants but... I feel, I don't know but.. I guess I kinda feel free."

"You are free, you've freed yourself. You just didn't realize you were carrying the burden of a secret from your past. Now you've escaped it. The trauma isn't cured, but identifying and acknowledging it is a great start."

"That's right. I was probably quite young – at whatever age a child starts to question its origins - when I learned what happened. I probably didn't understand it then or not fully. I just went through life never knowing exactly what was wrong, just that something wasn't right.

Is this one of those so-called *silver linings* to Cousin Kenny's assault on me? It doesn't matter, anyhow. Now that I know l feel like I've gained confidence."

"Instead of bravado."

"I guess. I always did try to act tough—-"

Joel interrupts me saying:

"Tough? Chickie you've always shown a crippling need to please."

"Except last night. Danny was a boor and you behaved like a cold-hearted prick."

"I am a cold-hearted prick."

"But you should have defended me."

I'm ready to argue but the words don't come because she's right. I should have set Danny straight. If I'd been wrong and pissed Girlie off well who gives a fuck? at least I'd have been acting like me.

"You're right. I should have stepped up for you. It's not like me to take my cues from anybody else but fuck things are different with you. I'm different because of you."

"Joel that's so sweet!"

"Sweet? fuck me! Oh Chickie you really are special. Your character, your strength, the fact that you absorb love like it's water and you're a sponge..."

Girlie turns in my arms and looks up at me. Even with her eyes red from crying she's incredibly beautiful. Her face is so open and trusting and always looking for approval.

I don't understand why I felt it was so important for her to ask me to stop Danny. She didn't ask and I didn't stop him. Yet I knew she didn't want him, and it turned my stomach to see him pawing her. I just felt it was her decision to make and I couldn't intervene. I guess I wanted her to ask. Everything has gotten mixed up in my head.

She has no idea how easily she can break me.

"The fire is only embers now but we can't leave until it dies down. So, the question is: can you fuck me and hate me at the same time?"

"The way I feel right now? Make-up sex has nothing on hate-fucking."

"That's my girl."

A couple of hours later the journey home is slow but uneventful because of the precautions we've taken. Girlie's life probably isn't still at risk, I'm sure they figure she's already dead, but when the Government's involved it's impossible to know for certain. There's no one to ask because there's no one to trust.

Once I get Girlie settled in with Bram I'll know it's safe to leave her while I deal with that unfinished business.

My father built our family home out in the countryside and although that was decades ago no neighbors have encroached near the property. It's still secluded, peaceful, and lush. A small wood, a stream, a hill for hiking, fruit trees, and a comfortable house.

There's just us now, with no relationship among the remaining cousins. Bram is settled in here and I expect he's found a woman or two for entertainment. He never wanted to get married and having lived this long without getting caught in matrimony I'm sure it won't happen now.

He looks after the businesses, there are only a few companies left now, and they're all legitimate. He tells me that *we pay taxes and everything.*

Danny is supposed to be home for most of the week before going off on a skiing trip with friends from school. I'll need Bram's guidance on how to deal with him.

Chapter 16

Bram

I'm blown away by how beautiful Girlie is, she has thrived in Joel's care. Other than a very slight crook to her nose there's not a trace of the beating she suffered, and she's grown her hair a bit longer so that it curls around her face.

She is glowing with health and well-being. Joel is like a different man too. When dealing with Girlie he's way more mellow than I've ever seen him, and the two of them are doing very well together. And now this mess with Danny. Obviously we're going to have to have a long talk.

Danny came home late last night and left early this morning so I didn't see him and had no idea he'd even gone out to the cabin.

I hope he's smart enough to stay out of the way for awhile. It's a tricky situation though, because much as I love Girlie Danny is family and she's not.

She made me laugh when she first got here and exclaimed: "I always forget how big you are, Bram! Like a friendly grizzly bear."

"Maggie's served up a feast to welcome you home so let's have dinner," I say, leading them into the dining-room.

The table is richly laid out with crystal and silver and linen napkins.

"Maggie sure went all out!" exclaims Joel. "

Well, you always were a favorite of hers."

"*The* favorite," he insists.

"Your family home is beautiful and huge. Instead of just visiting we could live here, Joel. If that's okay with you, Bram?" asks Girlie.

"Of course! If you want your space you can build your own place even. God knows there's plenty of room on the grounds," I add.

"We're definitely staying for the winter. The cabin is cozy but it won't be habitable for these next few months. Maybe we should build something here. Or just share the house with you."

He turns to me adding quietly: "Now that we're safely here I need a day or two to take care of some business and finish up once and for all."

"What business?" asks Girlie, but no one answers her. We all eat in silence for a bit before she speaks again.

"Why a grow-op? I mean, look at this place, you've obviously got money and you didn't get all this from selling weed."

I laugh at that and explain that our grandfather and father had built up a number of businesses.

"To get rich that fast they had to get their hands dirty but the majority of their concerns were legitimate. That whole grow-op was a bit of a joke that got out of hand, frankly, and it was all Joel's fault, too."

"Fuck you!"

"Well... it's true! Have you not told Girlie any of this story?" I ask him.

He just shakes his head and tries to look pissed off but that doesn't work with me.

"Oh wow. Girlie, Joel here is a decorated hero from the Middle East conflict. He was in Special Forces and he's responsible for saving a lot of lives."

"Then how on earth..."

"I got screwed over. Because of a woman, as a matter of fact," he snaps with a scowl.

Girlie tilts her head, inviting him to continue the story. He gives a big sigh and, acting all put-upon, explains:

"You know how in the war movies *no man gets left behind*? Well, that's only in the movies. In real life, spite and ambition and jealousy all get mixed in to people's actions and motivations and next thing you know..."

"Were you captured? Tortured?"

"Of course not. Girlie, I'm good at what I do or rather did. But getting out of there was... difficult."

"And someone set you up because of a woman you had a relationship with?"

"Huh, no. That was the problem. It was because I *didn't* want the woman that she set me up. Women can't be trusted," he concludes, glaring at her. She simply reaches out and squeezes his hand.

"So, completely disillusioned, Joel decides to end his military career and become a drug dealer," I finish.

"So you built that compound..."

"No, in fact we didn't even rent it. We were squatters. That was part of a stupid feud or bet or some damn thing with the cousins. The original owner of that property died in jail and Joel just moved in.

Seriously though Joel, I'm surprised you didn't confide in Girlie because if anyone in this room could understand what happened to you it's her. She was betrayed by her so-called comrades-in-arms, too."

"And that's a bad memory for her, just as my experience soured me, so time to move on. My only reminder is this fantastic body I developed from all my training..." he breaks off fishing for a compliment.

"Really? My body was a gift from God," answers Girlie smugly.

"A gift for Joel, you mean!" I say laughing.

"Hey, you'll be able to get back to running now that we're here. You'll be safe on our paths through the woods," Joel tells Girlie.

I add: "Plus we have a fully equipped weight-room and gym."

"Girlie doesn't like working out indoors. She likes running and hates the treadmill."

"It gets pretty cold here for outdoor exercise plus we get plenty of snow," I caution.

"Then I'll switch to cross-country skiing and work up a good sweat that way."

Her words hang in the air as Joel and I imagine Girlie's body shining with sweat. Luckily at that point Maggie Clarke comes in to clear away the dishes. She looks at the empty place she'd set for Danny and just shakes her head.

We introduce her to Girlie and the two women seem to hit if off right away. Maggie says she's leaving soon and will clean up the kitchen when she comes back in the morning. When Girlie offers her help Maggie stops her to insist that everything be left just as it is.

The three of us then move into the drawing room where a fire blazes in the huge hearth. Coffee and liqueurs, along with other assorted bottles of spirits, are laid out. Girlie takes charge of fetching each of us a coffee but then stops, nonplussed, at the bottles saying:

"I've never seen either of you take a drink before."

I chuckle and say that we do indulge but sparingly because we always had to be alert out at the compound. We both name the drink we want and she serves us before joining Joel on the love-seat.

"So are you two all lovey-dovey now or is there any chance of an old man getting his bed warmed up?" I ask, half-teasing, half-hopeful, and wholly curious.

"Of course, Bram! After all, you busted my cherry." She seems surprised when she blurts that out and I realize she and Joel haven't discussed this before arriving.

"I knew it!!!" I shout. "I was sure you were a virgin. And to think I was your first!" I proudly add.

Chapter 17

Joel

"You know in retrospect Danny giving you that spanking that first night was a stroke of genius – no pun intended!" I say to Girlie.

She narrows her eyes but I've caught Bram's interest because he asks:

"How so?"

"Well, we know that Girlie was terrified but we were wound pretty tight ourselves. I mean, all I could see of her was a female cop in a track suit wearing an ankle-holster and being carried over Danny's shoulders. You and I knew since she was the Law she was a threat, possibly even a danger."

"Yeah, I sure as shit didn't want to go to jail just because I helped you in your rebellion against the Government. The whole grow-op thing was only a break while you got your shit together. That DEA raid was an eyeopener."

"Except that it was never really a raid, was it?" put in Girlie. "It was just a suicide mission for me. Maybe if you had killed me then they'd have raided. Except that I'm pretty sure they've decided you must have killed me by now and they never did raid. They didn't even care about the grow op."

"Unless that's who set the fire."

"Well, it was a volatile situation, touch-and-go, but seeing Danny put you across his knee like a naughty child well, that just made you..."

"Ridiculous?"

"I was going to say harmless but yeah, it certainly defused things. But he went too far. Four or five swats, sure, but he really beat you."

"I heard one of you tell him he should stop."

"Yeah, but I didn't *make* him stop and I should have. Of course I didn't even know if you'd make it through the night with us. You might have had some crazy kung fu moves or a knife or something that would have resulted in, well, you being put down."

"Jesus, Joel no need to be so blunt! Instead, you were just so luscious and sexy. When you offered to blow Danny? That blew me away. I definitely wanted a piece of you, too."

"We all did and we all well... we all did have her. But initially, I think we kind of treated Girlie like Danny brought home a stray and wanted to keep it as a pet."

Girlie stands up, her color high and her eyes flashing, but l yank her back down on the love-seat again. Bram comes over and half-sits on the sofa arm so we can cuddle her between us.

"That was how it seemed before we knew you but even so, you'd already gotten under my skin. Remember? The very next day I was picking on you, trying to get your attention away from baby bro and on to me."

"And when you bossed her into masturbating Girlie's eyes were just drilling a hole through you."

"I know! I felt it." I give her a nudge and a half-smile escapes her lips. Turning to Bram I add: "Girlie told me she used to masturbate at least once a day."

"So much for privacy!" she exclaims, but Bram just chuckles.

"Baby, you don't need any privacy with us. Everything about you fascinates us and we wholeheartedly approve of you exactly the way you are."

"Joel, you can't tell the story out of context. Bram will get the wrong idea."

"Oh honey, I've already got the picture in my head and there's nothing wrong with it at all." He laughs.

I can't help joining in before saying: "I asked Girlie how such a horny girl could still have been a virgin at age 25. She then explained how her experiences with men had only gone from bad to worse. She then blames – or maybe credits? - us for turning her on to her true nature."

"Up until age sixteen I was a beanpole. Tall, skinny, flat. Then puberty hit, better late than never, right? I got periods and boobs and even a few zits. I also got noticed by boys and men. Classmates, teachers, school-bus drivers... They all acted SO gross, and it just keeps getting worse.

If I were to walk into a bar right now wearing this dress I'd be grabbed at, drooled over, and offended by lewd and crude comments – men are such pigs! And the ones who don't say anything, but just look around them like something smells rotten and they're pretty sure it's me, they're just as bad."

That makes me laugh!

"You are lovely in that dress, you're like a pin-up model."

"Yeah and strangers figure they just need to get me out of the dress and they've got themselves a centerfold!"

"Well they do. Owww—" I say as she punches me in the arm. "I'm serious, Girlie. You're a real beauty and you look just as good if not better than any of those girls."

"Women."

"They're girls, honey."

"Whatever," interrupts Bram, "All this talk about ogling you makes me want to ogle."

Girlie sits back passively as Bram slowly pulls the straps of her dress down over her arms. She knows he loves the act of undressing her. The whole scenario is so different from what happened just twenty-four hours ago.

I look at her naked breasts, full and inviting, and enjoy the sight of Bram's fingers gently teasing her reddening nipples. The usual rosy flush has spread across her chest and she smiles up at him and then at me. It all feels so right.

I lift her arms up and hold them behind her head with one hand while I join Bram in exploring the perfection of her tits with the other. Bram looks at her restrained wrists with a question on his face that I answer by saying:

"Another discovery was made during our *honeymoon* at the cabin but it's still a work in progress. We have lots of stories to tell but we'll save that one for tomorrow. For tonight let's just try to answer the question of *why is Girlie such a fantastic fuck?*"

"That's easy: because I love it. Anyhow, I did hear you two talking about the imperative nature of reproduction or some damn thing awhile back, you know.

I wasn't paying attention but I heard, and it made sense because in my head I hate men and the things they say and think, but my body is always getting aroused. Especially when I'm on my period... oh, would you think it disgusting to have sex when I'm on my period?"

"Of course not. There's nothing about you that could disgust me. I mean I wouldn't bother you for sex if you had the runs but..."

"I see. Blood okay, explosive diarrhea uh-uh."

"I didn't say explosive but.. yeah that would do it."

I'm getting so distracted by her obvious arousal that I can't even concentrate on the silliness of our conversation. It's crazy how she affects me.

"The whole point is I was primed and ready when I met you guys. I was acting like a tough girl who has been around the block a few times because geez, you guys have to turn sideways just to go through a doorway! See you're looking at each other like *do we do that? oh yeah, I guess we do.*

All I saw were three huge, manly, and virile men who were also cold and stern and scary. I knew that tears, or pleading for my life, wouldn't work.

Circumstances dictated that you were going to take what you wanted anyhow so I figured it was easiest to spread my legs willingly and find out what was what. Turns out you brought me to orgasm every single time and usually more than once so... it's your fault that I love to fuck. You fuck me so well."

Girlie effectively ends the conversation by arching her back and closing her eyes. I give her a deep kiss then leave the two of them to get reacquainted.

Tomorrow the three of us will play together, but for now I have no qualms about leaving her along with Bram and his big, capable hands.

I know she'll be back in my bed – our bed – to sleep dreamlessly with me for the rest of the night.

Part Three

"Consequences"

Chapter 1

Joel

Danny does show up next day. He's acting like his visit to the cabin never happened. I decide to go along with that because I think it's easiest on all of us. We all know what happened, but it's best to just move on.

With a good education and no military career Danny will live a different life than Bram and I have and that's good. He's lived in our shadows long enough, it's time for him to grow up in his own way.

"You have a wonderful home here, Danny," says Girlie, making conversation over dinner.

"Actually, I'm never here," he replies. "I'm in residence now and planning to stay in the city."

"How is school going? Were you able to pick up again easily enough?"

"Yeah, Joel, it's been good. I really enjoy it."

"That's half the battle," I answer. It all sounds and feels like a poorly scripted play but we're working through it.

"So you have a college education, right?" Girlie asks me. I nod and she turns to Danny saying: "I sure hope you're attending a different school." And we all laugh.

Just then Danny's cell rings and from what we can hear of the conversation it sounds like he'll be leaving much sooner than planned. When he finishes the call he's excited to say:

"There's been a cancellation, and it's already paid for, so we can start the ski trip now meaning an extra week at no extra cost!"

"That sounded like a girl's voice," I say teasingly and he grins in reply as he hurries from the room to put his things together.

When he returns he's already wearing his outdoor gear and telling us that he has to run to catch his ride. We wave him on his way, wishing him a *Merry Christmas*, and he leaves.

No one says anything about it but everyone in the room has relaxed now that he's gone.

"He'd definitely got a girl of his own – or soon to be his," pronounces Bram.

Maggie carries in a tray with a huge bowl of trifle. She remarks that she's passed Danny on his way out, so eager to be gone he didn't even stick around for dessert. I thank her for making one of my favorites.

Girlie states she's never eaten trifle although she has heard of it. She and Maggie converse about what goes in the dish and how it's prepared and... what is it with women? because next thing I know Maggie's telling Girlie that I should shave off my beard!

All of a sudden the two of them are planning and plotting over the framed photos Maggie keeps producing from one end of the room to the other. Photos showing all three of us brothers at different stages in our life, and mostly without facial hair.

Bram's laughing at me but shit - Girlie's getting ideas!

Chapter 2

Girlie

I have to confess that part of me always suspects that a beard hides a weak chin or some such thing, but according to these photos Maggie has just shown me Joel has an extremely handsome face. His beard wasn't grown to disguise anything!

I'm looking at pictures of him as a boy, alongside Bram and a baby Danny. Then everything from a school uniform through rebellious teenage years of long hair to shaved head to grad photos and then a military uniform.

Maggie keeps pointing out what a handsome man Joel is when he's not hiding behind *that great bushy beard just because he's too lazy to shave*. I just love her! She really makes me laugh.

I have to admit that I prefer Bram's neatly trimmed moustache and beard to Joel's wavy mass.

When I turn a speculative eye on Joel he counters with a frown and I laugh when I hear Maggie snort in contempt. Bram starts laughing too, so I'm thinking the days of Joel's wild man beard are numbered.

I thank Maggie for showing me the pictures, I agree that Joel should shave, and she leaves us once I promise to see what I can do about it. She replies:

"Well, see that you do!"

"Joel you better eat your trifle, you need something to sweeten up the sour look on your face!" I remark, knowing that later tonight

I'm going to feel the curly hairs of his beard rubbing all over my body.

He'll hold me down and tickle me with it until I admit I love his hairyness.

Chapter 3

Bram

I'm glad Joel let things slide with Danny. It's true that the boy is almost never here so we should all be able to patch over what happened and move on.

It's obvious to anyone that Girlie belongs to Joel now, and me? I'm just grateful that he's willing to share!

I ask what her plans were before everything went tits up for her at the agency.

"I figured I had about four or five more years in the field, maybe another year or two of training recruits, and then I'd have to take an office position. Probably chasing money trails because I'm trained in the agency's accounting practices. I know it sounds boring – and compared to field work it sure is – but I would have made a good living."

"Well, now you can use your accounting knowledge to work for our family or not. As you've discovered we're wealthy so you don't have to work at all."

"Maybe I should have a baby?"

"Really? Really you'd like to have a baby?"

I'm surprised to see that Joel is delighted by the idea but... why not?

"Yeah, I think it's certainly something for us to think about." She gives him the sweetest smile and his eyes are positively dancing with a light from within.

"What about you, Joel? Do you plan to become one of the idle rich?"

"Oh Bram, I'm sure you can find me some work to do. I definitely plan to loaf around all winter though, playing at songwriting. You can be my muse, Girlie. Of course you'll have to be still as a statue!" and he laughs while she blushes at some private joke they share.

Chapter 4

Girlie

One day in the cabin I'm feeling bored and restless. Joel is strumming on his guitar and I'm pestering him to focus on me. Finally he's had enough and tells me to strip off. I'm delighted, I love being naked and I love claiming his attention.

He positions me so my bum is leaning against the table then he pulls my arms back so my hands are flat on the surface and my breasts are shown off to full advantage. He then nudges my thighs apart until I'm completely exposed. I can feel the excitement rising in me.

Then he goes back to his chair, picks up his guitar, and tells me I'm his Muse and must remain motionless, which also means keeping absolutely silent, for ten minutes.

"But—-" I begin before he interrupts me saying:

"Each infraction will cost you another five minutes of posing."

"Joel, I don't want to—-"

"Now it's fifteen minutes."

"No, wait! That's—-"

"That's twenty." He turns his head to the clock on the wall and we both note the time. Twenty minutes of playing statues? I feel like a little kid being made to stand in the corner!

I know I'm pouting, especially when I notice his amused look. I smooth my own expression into a resting bitch face. I feel his eyes roving over me, enjoying my discomfort.

I'm tempted to move, tempted to say *fuck this* because he's told me repeatedly that he will never raise a hand to hurt me so... but he's also warned me that he'll torment my body until I'm crying for sex and then he'll jerk off on me, leaving me unfulfilled and dissatisfied.

Do I really believe he can resist me when I'm weak with lust and desire? I'm not sure I want to put it to the test.

God knows what my face looks like while these thoughts chase through my head. Glancing down I see that my nipples are erect and my clitoris is probably red, and shiny with moisture.

I don't want to meet his gaze but my eyes are drawn to his. Yes, he still looks amused at my predicament. But his stare is intense and interested, as if he's divined my thoughts and is ready to take up the challenge.

My eyes slide back to the clock. Time is almost up. Good, because I'm trembling and shivering in anticipation. My head hates how he dominates me but my body sure responds whenever he commands my obedience.

Chapter 5

Joel

I'm watching Girlie and see that she's reliving the memory of her punishment in the cabin. We had really hot sex after that and we should do it again soon.

I think putting her in position similar to the old days of being locked in the stocks will do wonders for her.

I can bend her over a table with her forearms flat out but no other part of her touching. Of course her legs will be spread. I'll walk around observing her from every angle.

Then I'll text Bram to come into the room. I'll have to explain that Girlie is being taught a lesson, but doesn't he think she looks awfully sexy when she's finally learning how to behave? I know he'll play along with a few remarks of his own.

Feeling our hungry eyes crawling over every inch of her body assessing, and evaluating how she looks, and commenting on what we're going to do to her will have Girlie trembling with lust.

By time her ten or fifteen minutes are up she'll be so horny and so will we... I think I better plan to do this posing in my room so the two of us can immediately take her on the bed. She'll be a wildcat.

It's a good thing the beds in this house are massive because the three of us will take up a lot of room when we're playing together. Bram can stretch out while Girlie blows him and I fuck her cunt from behind. I like the idea of Bram licking her clit while I'm screwing her in the ass. I doubt if he and I will ever be able to each take a hole at the same time but who knows?

We're going to be stuck indoors for most of the winter so that means months and months to play games of torment and desire. I think we'll have to instigate a rule that once Maggie leaves for the day Girlie has to strip off. She'll love it... and so will Bram and I.

I can picture us sitting in the lounge while a naked Girlie serves after-dinner drinks then sprawls on the couch teasing us with sexy poses.

Chapter 6

Bram

I'm enjoying the last of the wine while watching my two table-mates chase erotic thoughts in their heads. I feel like a voyeur because it's obvious they're both recollecting a sexual experience. When they meet each other's eyes it's like an electric current flashes.

Even though it's still early they look ready to disappear for the night but I want a bit of playtime first.

"Did you know," I inform them, "that the Empress Josephine used to dine topless? Apparently she was famous for a particular style of dress, Empire style, which meant the top part was easily pulled down to bare her breasts.

Supposedly Napoleon loved to have other people admire her tits and he bought her jewellery to wear on her nipples."

They both turn to look at me with polite gazes, obviously still wrapped up in their own thoughts, then my words penetrate. Girlie looks down at the outfit she's wearing which is a sheer white blouse heavily trimmed in lace and tucked into a long green velvet skirt. Very festive for the holiday season.

Her eyes meet Joel's and he gives her the hint of a smile, then she turns to me and I waggle my eyebrows and grin in anticipation which makes her laugh.

She very slowly, very deliberately, unbuttons her blouse and when she pulls it open reveals that the blouse comes with a matching camisole.

She gently tugs at the skinny straps pulling them down over her shoulders and starts to drag the undergarment down then changes her mind and lifts it up over her head.

Her breasts, now fully bared, lightly sway. It's such a sensual movement. Of course her nipples are hard little cherries.

Joel raises his glass in a toast to her beauty and I join in. Girlie turns her attention back to her untouched dessert of trifle. Both Joel and my eyes follow the path of whipped-cream-filled spoon from dish to mouth, hoping to see some spillage.

Finally Joel pushes back his chair, scoops up a handful of cream from his plate and coming round the table smears it over her tits. He then lifts her out of her chair, still in a sitting position, and places her on my lap.

"Go ahead," he instructs me, "I know you've got a sweet tooth."

I'm not going to argue. I push Girlie back in my arms and bend my head to lick the sweet cream from her. With loud smacking sound effects, of course!

Her tits are shiny from my tongue chasing streaks of cream and leaving a sticky residue. Her nipples are pebbled and so inviting. I can't resist sucking hard and scraping with my teeth, making her squirm.

When I'm done I say:

"Okay, I've had my fun so you two can go now and have a whole night's worth of fun yourselves."

Girlie moves back to her chair picking up her camisole and blouse saying:

"I don't want Maggie washing and ironing these and then putting them in my room to let me know that she knows what's been going on."

"You have nothing to worry about, Girlie. Joel is Maggie's favorite and he can do no wrong in her eyes."

"Oh God that's right! Joel, you have to eat your dessert or Maggie's feeling will be hurt." says Girlie.

"I'll tell you what," he answers: "you play with your tits while we're watching and I'll eat every last bit."

Girlie rolls her eyes but is soon smiling at him as she cups her breasts and bounces them in her hands then pulls at her nipples while nibbling on her bottom lip. So, so sexy!

Joel attacks his serving with gusto, he doesn't have to pretend because he really does love Maggie's trifle. When he's done he rushes her with a growl and lifts her over his shoulder. She's thrown her head back, laughing, and I get a good view of her pretty face and her lovely breasts thrust forward. He calls a *good night* to me then turns at the door to confirm he'll be heading out early in the morning and entrusting Girlie to my care.

"You'll be fine going into town but plan to be home once it gets dark. It's safer that way."

"I will guard her with my life, you know that. You go do what you have to get done, and don't worry about your sweetie."

"Make sure she minds you now."

I hear him in the hallway telling her, "I'm giving Bram permission to discipline you if necessary."

Her voice comes back saying: "Promises, promises."

"No worries, Joel, she's always a good girl with me."

Chapter 7

Joel

I slide Girlie off my shoulder but keep her within the circle of my arms.

"You know I heard that *promises, promises* wisecrack you made. So tell me, Girlie: do you fantasize about Bram teaching you a lesson? Punishing you? Hmmm? Are you going to be naughty just to provoke him?"

"God Joel, you're getting me hot just by having this conversation! I heard him tell you I always behave but now I'm starting to have second thoughts..."

"Well, don't!" I rub her naked tits and tweak a nipple. She groans saying:

"I think there's an invisible wire attaching my nipples to my clit."

I love the stuff she says!

I lift her up and suck on first one nipple and then the other, gently nibbling with my teeth. She groans again in response.

"So you don't like my beard?" I ask as I rub the hair across her tits. She trembles with pleasure but says:

"I'd love less of it and more of your handsome face."

"Oh, you think I'm handsome, do you?"

"Of course, because you are and you know it! Even Maggie thinks so."

"It only matters that you think so."

She tilts my head back to kiss me deeply.

It doesn't matter how much sex we have we're both always quickly ready for more. I can't get enough of her. I love pinning her down with my body and feeling her wiggle beneath me when I'm deep inside. I want to envelope her in a tight embrace and never let her go. I'd love it if time stood still.

And the best part is the way she responds to me. Always ready to accommodate my wishes; shifting to match my moves; permanently warm, wet, and welcoming. She must get sore but she never complains and never says no.

I understand and know her not from her words but from her actions. It's not just Girlie's body that's a gift from God, it's Girlie herself.

I suppose I could give the beard a trim.

Chapter 8

Girlie

Joel must have left very early this morning because I didn't hear him go. After a leisurely breakfast Bram drives me into town to do some Christmas shopping.

He drives a big town car and it suits him perfectly although there's no room to spare. He'd never fit in a sports car. He's very relaxed behind the wheel and he's a comfortable person to drive with.

We spend most of our time at a lingerie store. I need a sports bra for running and some underwear. While I shop he's browsing through the glamour racks and presents me with three fancy negligees to try on.

When I go into the change-room he tells me I have to come out and show him each outfit. God only knows what the sales assistant thinks. Especially after he explained to her that these will be his Christmas gift to his brother!

His taste is impeccable. The costumes are all very different but each is beautiful in its own way. A white lacy concoction, a slinky black satin number that's floor-length but slit hip-high, and a piece of silly fun in pink and red chiffon.

Each outfit is duly admired, and then he presents me with a present just for me saying he wants me to wear it on Christmas Day.

It's a completely sheer beige mini-dress. At first glance it seemed like I'm naked but then as my body moves the fabric emphasizes my nudity. An amazingly erotic garment that seems to bare my body more than wearing nothing at all.

"It's just going to be you and me and Joel on Christmas Day. I know that what's been happening between the three of us isn't going to last past the holidays so I want to enjoy every moment.

You can wear the pink and red thing that wraps you up like a present on Christmas morning but I would love it if you wore this for dinner," he said.

"I will, but knowing you two will be watching my every move with your hungry eyes will make me feel like I *am* dinner!"

"No Girlie, you'll always be dessert."

Chapter 9

Bram

"Bram, if you don't mind can I sleep in your bed tonight?" Girlie asks shyly.

"Honey I'd be delighted! Honored and thrilled to have you with me. I should have thought about it myself, since Joel's away you'll be lonely on your own."

"Yeah well, your family home is beautiful, really, but it's still a strange place to me and I haven't slept alone in quite awhile so..."

"Hey, just be warned that I supposedly snore."

"Oh, that won't bother me. I'll be so comfy cuddled up in your arms that it won't even matter if I actually sleep."

"Hmm, you're right. Having you soft and warm and naked in my bed might mean that neither of us gets much sleep!"

"And if everything goes okay with the doctor tomorrow, tonight will be our last chance to make love."

I pull her into a tight embrace and murmur in her hair:

"You're right, we do make love, don't we?"

"We do. Joel fucks me, sometimes I fuck him, and sometimes we even make love, but with you it's always love-making. It's always sweet seductive foreplay then loving sex followed by intimate cuddling afterwards. It's lovely."

"I'll be sorry when that's over, but I do understand."

"Yeah, I need to be exclusive with Joel while trying to get pregnant. If I remember correctly the first doctor told me it might take awhile after the IUD is removed before I'm fertile again, but..."

"Oh Girlie, I understand completely."

"We can still fool around."

"And we have tonight so let's get started!"

"I'm going to change my clothes first, I'll meet you on the couch. You can put the hockey on and pretend you're visiting your girlfriend at her babysitting job."

"Oh yeah, I like that scenario... mmm-hmm."

As I watch her hurry from the room I can't help but envy Joel for the future he will have with this darling girl.

Chapter 10

Girlie

I'd had a quiet word with the bra-fitter at the lingerie store and though she was doubtful because of my size - apparently this style is usually sold to young girls - she did manage to find me a matching bra-and-panties set in white, with tiny blue flowers and a tiny blue bow in the middle of each garment.

I'm sure Bram thinks I'll come back wearing one of my new negligees so he'll get a surprise when he sees I've bought myself a yellow mini-dress that buttons down the back. Exactly the sort of garment he will love to remove from me.

Tonight is my Christmas present to him.

I realize I've never been sassy or lippy to Bram. I always obey him and respect his wishes without question. He's undeniably the leader of the brothers although I think Joel is probably tougher and definitely meaner.

But I have no illusions about Bram. I realize that the incident with Danny could have caused a serious rift between all of us. I believe it was Danny being disrespectful by showing up drunk that swayed Bram's judgment in our favor. I guess the *no alcohol at the cabin* rule has always been taken very seriously, at least by the older family members.

Still, I suppose it could have gone either way. Bram does have a soft spot for his baby brother.

I finish primping and preening then come into the family-room twirling to show off my outfit. Bram whistles and pats the seat of the couch for me to join him. As I draw close he stands up and taking both of my hands in his looks me up and down saying:

"You are my ideal date."

If Joel is a sleek and deadly panther then Bram is a huge grizzly who can sometimes be a teddy bear. He's very big and strong and makes me feel so pretty, petite, and feminine.

He lies back on the couch and tucks me in alongside him. Then we begin a marathon kissing session interspersed with his comments of *such a gorgeous girl* and *you're my little sweetheart*.

I feel nostalgic for a past I never had. At my Junior Prom, which all the students had to attend, I was just a gawky wallflower. I didn't go to my Senior Prom because the only fellow who invited me was a loud-mouthed, braggy, grabby guy who, I learned, only asked me on a bet.

But tonight I feel like *the Belle of the Ball* in Bram's adoring eyes.

He sits me up to unbutton my dress and he performs that job super slowly because he plants a kiss on each portion of skin as it gets bared. When I hear his quick intake of breath I know he's discovered I'm wearing a bra.

"Oh Girlie, you sweetie-pie."

He quickly finishes removing my dress and then stands me up to twirl around slowly so he can enjoy the sight of me in my matching underwear. You can't call it lingerie, it's so utilitarian, although the blue flowers do add a bit of girlishness.

The bikini panties fit but the bra is way too small. My breasts bulge over the top and flow out the sides. Bram loves it. He fondles and caresses skin and fabric and he can't take his eyes off me.

"Oh you darling child. Come here beside me."

He gently pulls me back into his arms on the couch and we neck and pet until both of us are squirming with anticipation. Finally he unhooks my bra – one-handed! and plays with me like I'm a first-place prize.

On the TV the game announcer suddenly shouts *he shoots, he scores!* and we both chuckle.

Feeling unaccustomedly timid I ask: "Is it bedtime yet?"

Looking down with a smile on his lips and in his eyes Bram answers:

"Almost. First, I need to take off your pretty panties so I can enjoy the view while walking up the stairs behind you."

Then he slowly peels them over my hips, down my legs, and tosses them aside.

Bram sits up and spends a few moments looking down at my naked body laid out on the couch. He lets one hand trail down me from shoulder to vagina and when he slips a finger inside we're both aware that I'm sopping wet.

He bends his head to kiss my lips and slides his hands underneath to lift me off the couch, carrying me to the stairs. Then he sets me on my feet and giving my bottom a light smack instructs me to *walk slowly but with a wiggle*. I happily oblige. His wolf-whistle makes me giggle.

I stop at the top of the staircase, unsure which room is Bram's. He lifts he up in his arms again and entering his bedroom tosses me onto his bed. He jumps on after me and we cuddle and whisper like kids.

Bram isn't as tall as Joel but he is stockier and more barrel-chested. Because of that he looks bigger. He climbs on top but has to hold himself up by his forearms to keep from crushing me. I lift my hips to meet him and wrap my legs around his thighs - I can't manage around his waist.

As usual I give a little gasp when he enters me. The girth of his cock is incredible. After a few minutes of gentle pumping he rolls onto his back pulling me on top. This is a more comfortable position for both of us.

He reaches up and plays with my breasts while I run my fingers through the hair on his chest. Stretching one hand behind my bum I'm able to reach down and stroke his balls. That move surprises him into some rapid thrusting that carries us both along the same wave of pleasure to climax.

I collapse on top of him and he holds me tight, panting for breath.

"That was fantastic, Girlie! Now I know what people mean when they say they feel like they've died and gone to heaven. You're my angel."

A laugh escapes me at that but when he quizzes me I hide the real reason and instead explain that I'm feeling very devilish at the moment. Then I slide down to lick him clean. We've never done this before.

Bram cries out: "Jeez, Girlie. Joel must have taught you how to do that!"

I answer *mmm-hmm* but don't stop with my licking and sucking. I figure Bram will enjoy it just as much as Joel and he does... he really does... and gets hard again, too.

Bram's second go is leisurely and so enjoyable for both of us.

"Bram, my Christmas present is just as much of a gift to me as it is to you!"

"Oh Girlie, sweetheart. I've never had an experience like this."

"I'm a good accomplice?"

He laughs and answers: "The best!"

Once we've settled down to sleep I discover that Bram does indeed snore, but instead of a loud nasal sound it's a rumbling in his chest, like a happy house-cat's purr times 100. I feel myself rocked into a deep sleep by the vibrations.

Chapter 11

Bram

I wake up early this morning enjoying the delightful sight and feel of Girlie's naked body warming my bed.

She's a lovely creature in every way.

Today, I'm escorting her to the doctor's appointment Maggie set up. I don't want to have to sit around a waiting room with a bunch of women with women's problems, but I promised Joel I'd guard Girlie closely.

Maybe we should just tell the doctor that I'm the boyfriend – no, fiance sounds better - so I can go in the examining room with her.

Oh, but what if that's not allowed? Yeah right, no man is going to say no to me, doctor or not!

Girlie is stirring and that means she's squirming her soft ass into my gut. Oh Girlie, Girlie, I need to have you just one more time.

I fondle her breasts with one hand and start teasing her clit with the other and she cums before she's even fully awake. Turning around she faces me with an inviting smile and a wet, welcoming pussy. As generous with her loving as ever, and giving me a wonderful start to the day!

I've never met anyone I wanted to be with exclusively for the rest of my life. In fact, my preference is to get two women in my bed to enjoy a threesome. But the time I've been spending with this gorgeous creature is making me think maybe I should be looking for a serious relationship of my own.

I'm definitely too old to be out on the dating scene, though. I never have any trouble finding female companionship in resort towns since a lot of ladies like to get away and let loose. But I've never gone on the make close to home.

How do you go about meeting someone at my age? If it was just for a night or a dirty weekend then sure, I'm certain I could get lucky in a bar, but for something more?

Instead of a bar maybe I should hang out at a coffee shop? but whenever I'm in one of those places everybody's glued to their phone. I suppose if push comes to shove I could ask Maggie if she knows of any likely females but I really don't want to go that route.

Girlie has taken care of me for awhile, at least, so no rush.

Chapter 12

Girlie

Bram is so proud of himself having brought me to orgasm twice last night and twice again this morning. It was so nice waking up all warm and cozy in his bed.

He woke me up properly with his fingers stroking me to ecstasy and then entered me when I was primed and ready. He fills me completely. He was my first – even if it was only by a few minutes! - and I will always remember that.

Our appointment is early in the morning with the doctor, a Doctor Moro, fitting us in before his regular hours as a favor to Maggie. I shower alone to save time.

The doctor's surgery is part of his home, a good-sized property about fifteen minutes' drive away. We follow the sign round to the side door and Bram insists on coming in with me for the treatment.

The doctor is a bit surprised by this but doesn't argue. We are paying him cash for this visit and not giving our surnames, only because I don't have usable ID. I'm sure he knows who Bram is.

Dr. Moro gives me a basic overall check-up taking my blood-pressure, listening to my lungs, palpating my breasts and armpits, then he indicates I should scoot into the stirrups. The expression on Bram's face is one of avid interest mixed with queasiness when he sees the speculum.

Dr. Moro is explaining the procedure as he works, telling me that after the IUD is removed I can expect to wait about four to six months before I'm ready to conceive.

Once the instrument is in place he looks inside and pauses for a moment that feels too long:

"Is everything okay, Doctor?" I ask nervously.

"Yes, fine, fine! It's just... you show evidence of a very, um very active sex life with frequent.. very frequent intercourse..." he pauses again and glances over at Bram with admiration and respect.

"It's entirely possible that, if you continue at this rate, I might have to revise that estimate because you'll probably conceive much sooner."

I manage to hold back my laugh but it's touch-and-go when I see the proud smile on Bram's face.

I can't wait to share this incident with Joel when I give him his Christmas present!

Chapter 13

Joel

It's a relief to be back home with the unpleasant business behind me. Even though now we're free to stay here or go anywhere we please returning home feels so right. And Girlie is safe.

Bram meets me at the door when I come in. He tells me everything has been quiet here and that the two of them have been out twice during the daytime getting Christmas presents.

"Were you successful?" he asks.

Just then Girlie comes flying down the stairs and jumps straight into my arms so I have to hold onto her by her bum and thighs while she plants kisses all over my face.

"What a welcome!" I exclaim with a smile.

"I really, really missed you and I have so much to tell you and it's almost Christmas and it's going to be wonderful, really it is. First time ever. Joel, I just love you!"

Her words make my smile stretch so wide it hurts my cheeks. I lean in to kiss her lips and whisper "I love you, too."

"I didn't hear that, what did you say? Say it louder!"

Bram is bugging me. I try to glare but that's not an easy thing to do when you're feeling happy. Girlie has no qualms about giggling and encouraging him.

Just then Maggie comes into the hall tsk-tsking that I would be easier to hear if I didn't have that ugly beard, and that Girlie can at least let me get my coat off first.

"The two of you, acting like teenagers. Joel, what do you want: coffee and a sandwich? or maybe a whiskey to warm you up?

"Oh Maggie, I'll take care of warming him up," Girlie is incorrigible and Maggie, though she pretends, can't hide her delighted smile. Everyone is happy for us.

"First off, I want to tell the story of my trip and then we can put all of that behind us so Maggie, coffee would be great."

"You three go in the family room and I'll bring it right out," she answers, heading back to the kitchen.

I put Girlie down and we walk, awkwardly since she has herself entwined around me, to the room warmed up by a roaring fire. I toss my coat on a chair and settle down with a contented sigh to relate my adventure to my engrossed audience.

"It took me a while to track down Kendricks. He had leave for the holidays and was supposedly going home to spend it with his wife and kids.

Of course being Kendricks he wasn't taking a direct route. No, he was going to enjoy himself with a few buddies in a red light district for a couple of nights first. That made him easy pickings.

I waited until he came out of a whorehouse and left his pals going to his car on his own. As soon as I closed in on him he knew he was done for.

He struggled a bit but I silenced him with one hand over his mouth and showed him the knife saying *Joanne Dwyer is alive and well, you motherfucker* and one quick thrust took care of him."

Bram is nodding in approval. We both know the job had to be done and, tempting as it was to prolong Kendricks' suffering, it's always safer to just take care of business quickly.

He's saying: "Good job." Just as Girlie jumps up from the couch and shrieks:

"What the fuck did you do? Joel, seriously? I... I can't even, even..." she breaks off, breathing heavily, eyes flashing, color high, and now I'm wondering what the fuck is going on? I get up to face her but she whirls around and runs out of the room.

Maggie is standing outside the door with a tray of food and drink and her mouth a perfect O of surprise as Girlie races past her and back up the stairs.

Bram has reached out, trying to stop her, but she slaps at his hand and dodges around his grip.

He turns an equally shocked face to me and we both shrug our shoulders trying to figure out what the fuck just happened.

And then I see red. I want to march up the stairs and drag the truth out of her but I know I'm too dangerous when in this state. Without a word I grab up my jacket again and leave the house slamming the front door hard.

Chapter 14

Bram

How the hell could things go so wrong so fast? One minute I'm ragging on the lovebirds and the next they look ready to kill each other.

Joel's face went white and he's deep into a rage. Well, I don't blame him. He just went to some risk to ensure Girlie is safe and this is how she treats him? Why would she side with Kendricks? What was Joel supposed to do - turn the other cheek? As if!

I go after him but stop at the door because seeing the set of his shoulders I know he doesn't want company. How the hell did it all fall apart? And so quickly, too?

Maggie's questioning me but I don't have answers. All I can tell her is that there's something from Girlie's past and it's caused this rift. Rift – huh! More like the Grand Canyon.

Maggie gets a determined look on her face and hurries up the stairs. I don't know if I should stop her but I'm not even going to try. I can hear her knocking but the sound is faint, this old building is well-made, so I don't know if Girlie's let her in.

I don't know what to do with myself. Here I am, standing at the front door letting all the cold air in because I can't make up my mind to what, if anything, I should do. Go after Joel? Try to talk to Girlie?

No, I think I have to leave the two of them to figure this out on their own. They seem, or at least seemed, really great together but... it's their life. I can't interfere.

Just as I resolve to stay out of it Maggie comes running down the stairs with a worried look on her face.

"She won't let me in, Bram, and I can hear that poor girl sobbing her heart out. She's going to make herself sick at this rate. She's just broken-hearted. What on earth happened? I was only gone five minutes—-"

I interrupt Maggie to say that I really don't know what is wrong. Joel said something that upset Girlie terribly, but damned if I know what it was and I heard every word he said.

"I can't figure it out at all. I don't know why she flew off the handle like she did but now you say she's crying, not yelling or angry anymore?"

"Not crying, sobbing! She could barely catch her breath through all her tears. Poor, poor girl. What should we do?"

"I think we need to keep out of it. It's their business." I reply, as gently as I can but Maggie is having none of that.

"You were right to let Joel go, let him walk it off or something, but that girl needs help right now."

She folds her arms and gives me a look I recognize from over the years. A stubborn look that says she isn't budging until I do whatever it is she wants me to do.

"You think I should go talk to her?"

"Well I tried and got no where, so yeah, I do."

"I don't know anything about crying girls, Maggie—"

But she cuts me off saying:

"No, but you do know your brother. Better than anyone. You know this girl is so good for him, you can't let him throw that away."

I sigh but have to acknowledge the truth of what Maggie is saying. I sigh again and agree to try.

Chapter 15

Girlie

I've got to stop crying, I can't even breathe anymore. But every time I stop I think about what Joel did and the tears just well up again. How could he? How COULD he???

I heard Maggie at the door but I didn't want to let her in. I don't want anyone to see me like this. I don't want to be like this! I love Maggie but...

Now Bram's at the door. Oh God, Oh God, Oh God. I can't refuse him. It's funny but with Joel I always feel the need to challenge every order but with Bram? I never defy him, I just skip about like a puppy eager to please. And yet, I'm way more afraid of Joel than I ever have been of Bram.

Maybe it's some sort of father-figure thing? Because he's the oldest, because he's the big grizzly bear? I'm stalling but he's not going away.

"Girlie, mind me now. Open up."

Reluctantly I force myself to drag my feet over to the door. I open it but just stand there with my head hanging down, not looking at him. I sense Maggie is further down the stairs but she doesn't say anything and I don't look her way.

"Oh, Girlie. In the last ten minutes I've wanted to shake you, paddle you, yell at you, and demand answers but now... look at you, you're such a sorry sight! Now, I just want to make it all better."

His kind words do me in. I fling myself against his chest and feel his strong arms wrap me in a tight hug while I sob myself into a bout of hiccups. I feel like I'll drown in my tears.

I think Bram feels the bedroom is the wrong place for us to be so he scoops me up and carries me back down to the family room.

We sit on the couch in front of the fire while Maggie silently fusses with an afghan and a hot drink for me. I look up to thank her but my lips simply tremble. She looks like she's going to cry, too!

Bram continues to cradle me in his arms, not speaking, just letting me feel the warmth of his protective embrace. Finally he asks:

"Why were you so angry at Joel?"

"Because I was so scared!"

"Scared? Scared of what?"

"Of what could have happened to him! I was angry that he took such a risk for a piece of shit like Kendricks, and I was scared because he could have been caught or gotten himself killed. Why would he waste even a moment's thought on that asshole?"

Bram pulls back to look at my face. When he sees I mean what I'm saying he just shakes his head.

"Oh, shit. I totally got the wrong impression about the way you reacted and I'm sure Joel did, too. We thought you were mad at Joel for taking care of Kendricks."

"You're right, I am mad about that. I'm mad not because of who Kendricks is but because of who Joel is. Bram, he's my everything yet he put it all at risk.

How could he dare take the chance of putting me through the loss of having him in my life? Is settling his macho bullshit more important than me?"

"Oh Girlie. Joel believed, rightly or wrongly - but to be honest I do agree with him - that your life would always have been in danger so long as Kendricks was alive.

That incident when your friend got caught in the bear-trap? We're sure Kendricks was behind it. And then, when he sent you on your own to our place? well... that was the icing on the cake, so to speak.

Kendricks probably thought you were dead otherwise there would have been other so-called communication errors and mix-ups resulting in him sending in a team to attack."

"And I get that Bram, I do, but Kendricks never needed to know I was still alive. I have no trouble staying out of his way. I expect my government paycheques are just piling up in my deposit account – darn, I meant to visit the bank when we were in town—-"

"See? That's exactly the kind of action that could have alerted Kendricks and brought him hunting for you.

Yet you're not wrong, you have a right to your money, to your identity, to your life, and it is bullshit that you've been forced into hiding even though you've done nothing wrong.

That's why Joel felt it was imperative that he find a resolution to the Kendricks situation."

"A final solution."

"Yeah well, that's the kind that work."

"Oh Bram, you're college-educated, you've been in the Armed Forces, you're not a stupid man. You know there are alternatives, legal alternatives."

"Think so? Really? C'mon, Girlie. Work it out. You didn't break any laws but Kendricks did. He broke the moral code of the agency, he actively and with malicious intent put your life at risk and then he put you directly in the line of fire. At his command. Yet the law is on his side. You would have to prove his wrongdoing and you'd probably be killed in the process.

The law, unfortunately, has gray areas that let us down sometimes. This is one of those times. And you know it."

"But I devoted my life to upholding and enforcing the law..." I trail off considering what he's saying.

It's a heavy blow to my psyche and my principles, learning that everything I know to be right can be turned upside down in an instant. It makes my sacrifices feel worthless and yet... I couldn't have lived my life any other way.

"Oh Bram, I've made a real mess of things, haven't I? On my last sight of Joel he'd brought the shutters down and his face had no expression whatsoever. He looked like he hated me. He looked at me the way he did when we first met, he was a stranger to me.

I need to use your phone to call him. Oh, that was another thing I wanted to get in town. Oh well, after Christmas we can go back."

He finds Joel in his contacts and calls. I can hear voicemail kicking in. Bram explains that he's calling for me and I want to speak to Joel, that it was all a bad misunderstanding, so call back.

We wait and wait but Bram's phone doesn't ring.

At some point Maggie comes in to ask Bram if she should stay the night but he tells her to go home to her own family, we'll be okay. She pats me on the shoulder but doesn't say anything.

Eventually, I fall asleep on the couch and Bram takes me upstairs. I protest, wanting to wait up for Joel, but he just shushes me and puts me to bed. I get a tender kiss on my forehead and his assurance that everything will be all right.

I wake up in darkness and Joel's place beside me is empty. The house feels cold so I grab his terrycloth robe that I can wrap around myself twice and go back downstairs. Bram is sound asleep in the family room which has grown cold now that the fire's gone out.

I build it up again and sit there staring at the flames and thinking my thoughts. Light starts seeping through the curtains signalling that morning has come and Joel has stayed out all night.

What was he doing? Where was he? Is he okay?

I find Bram's phone on the coffee-table and hit re-dial on Joel's number. He answers *What?* in a thick voice and I'm so happy to hear him, I gasp out something like *You're okay!* and there is a long silence before he replies:

"You. Fucking. Bitch," and disconnects the call.

My tears flow freely as I drop the phone. Bram's voice startles me because I didn't realize he's woken up.

"That's his drunk voice. You've never heard it before and I haven't heard it in a long, long time. I think our boy's on a bender, Girlie. You might as well go back to bed, I don't think we'll see him today."

"Shouldn't we go looking for him? Or maybe just you should go since he hates me."

"I wouldn't know where to start. He grew up here and he'll have all kinds of haunts in this area. Old hang-outs, old friends, old..," he stops there but I'm pretty sure he was going to say *old girlfriends*.

A man with Joel's good looks and his bad boy attitude? He'll have old girlfriends by the dozen.

It's my fault, I have no one to blame but myself. I didn't think I had any tears left in me but I'm wrong.

Chapter 16

Bram

Joel stays away another day-and-a-half, but he never answers his phone again. I'm starting to get worried enough to try to track him down, for Girlie's sake if nothing else.

She's a wreck, not eating and only sleeping when she drops down from sheer exhaustion. She's phoned all the hospitals in the area and even called the morgue. I wouldn't let her contact the police – it's too soon for them to bother searching for an adult, but I wouldn't have called them anyway.

He stumbles in, a stinking mess, and still drunk. His eyes are flaming red and his runny nose tells a story of a bad old habit: snorting coke in order to keep on with his drinking binge. I reach him first, but Girlie is coming in one direction and Maggie from another.

Joel takes one look at Girlie and begins a tirade that I quickly shut up, dragging him up the stairs. He's bigger and stronger than me now but his condition makes him weak. Maggie follows and that set line of her mouth does not bode well for Joel.

I shoo Girlie away and tell her we'd deal with it and she can see Joel in a few hours. Of course she protests but I'm firm. As usual she gives in to me meekly.

I suggest she bundle up and go for a run, the paths are still clear from the last snowfall, and she nods her agreement with the plan.

"I'm just so glad he's come back," she says.

Maggie and I strip Joel down to haul him into the shower. First, though, I shove a couple of fingers down his throat to see if there's anything left to bring up but he just gags.

I have to stand in the shower with him to keep his head up. His knuckles are raw indicating he'd been in at least one fight and he has some bruises on his torso that show someone fought back.

At least it wasn't the police who brought him home. Whoever it was didn't stay, they just dropped him at the door and drove on. Maybe he took a cab.

Maggie leaves to put together one of her hangover concoctions which do work but taste almost as bad as the hangover itself. When she returns with it I see a look of grim satisfaction on her face as Joel obediently chokes it down.

We put him to bed and close the drapes, leaving him in darkness. Now that I know there's no more booze in his stomach I have no worries about him vomiting in his sleep. We leave him, hoping he won't waken until he's sober.

About four hours later Joel wakes up and Maggie gives him another glass of her cure. He drinks it down without a word but does groan when he sits up too fast so his head must still be pounding.

Girlie comes back from her run and finally eats a meal. She's only picked at her food for the last two days. Afterwards she showers and lies down for a nap in my room. I know she wants to go to Joel but I tell her not yet.

Truth is I had no idea what he might say to her but I'm pretty sure it will be hurtful, maybe even something impossible to come back from, so I figure it's best to keep them apart until Joel is back in his right mind.

Girlie spends some time in the kitchen with Maggie and then, when the older woman goes home, she curls up on the couch and watches some TV. After a couple more hours she announces she's going for another run.

By now it's late and it's dark but I know our property is safe and, well with Kendricks taken care of, there's no one to worry about anymore.

There's nothing for me to do but wait. I hear her come in after awhile but we don't speak. At first light Girlie is up again for another run.

Joel wakes up and this time he stays up. He drinks a bit of the soup Maggie left but he's restless. Or maybe he's feeling a bit ashamed at the way he let himself go.

He doesn't tell me where he's been, or what he's been doing, but I can see he's anxious. I tell him to dress warm and go chop some wood. That's always a good way to blow off steam.

He scowls at me but doesn't argue. He probably knows he needs some fresh air in his lungs. I stand at the window on the top landing looking down at the woodshed. Joel works like a machine, smoothly swinging the axe, splitting the wood, tossing the pieces to the side, laying up another chunk.

While I'm watching I see Girlie come running into view. Even from here I can admire her even stride. She slows to a jog and then a walk when she catches sight of Joel. As she comes closer I see him smack the axe into the tree stump and turn around to confront her.

I can't hear what they say but I can see them facing off against each other and I can tell they're yelling. Joel throws his hands up in the air and Girlie violently shakes her head saying *no* to something. I can tell by their body language that they're each trying to make their case. That's good, that means they both still care what the other one thinks.

Girlie turns and hurries back to the front of the house but Joel doesn't follow, he just stands there staring after her.

Chapter 17

Girlie

Bram is waiting for me at the top of the stairs. I can tell from the admiration in his eyes that my color is high and my eyes are probably flashing.

"What did you two say to each other?" Bram asks.

I give a deep sigh. He's always right there, especially when I don't want him to be!

I don't want to have this discussion, but I can't refuse him. I've been replaying my argument with Joel in my head anyhow, might as well say the words out loud to see if they make any more sense that way.

"I told him I was really upset by the risk he took and he said there was no risk he knows what he's doing. He says I'm a killer, Girlie, and I know you've already figured that out so I say wartime action is different and he says dead is dead. Can't argue with that. And now that Kendricks is dead I'm an accessory.

Then I ask him why on earth he would risk his liberty, his life, OUR life together, for a crappy piece of shit like Kendricks and you know what he says? he says he did it for ME. I tell him I don't need to be avenged.

Sure, I wanted revenge in the beginning, in fact it's what kept me going thinking about someday confronting Kendricks and killing him myself! But once I fell in love with Joel none of that was important any more. It just seems so petty and negligible beside the very real thing that I have in my life now which is Joel and me and our feelings for each other.

So I realize it's just Bastard Cousin Kenny all over again. Joel kills the men who harm me so I share the guilt for that. I don't mean that I feel guilty about their deaths, I mean guilt as in being complicit because I'm his motive and I'm his accomplice and, I have to admit it, willingly.

Joel is right when he says that Kendricks was a threat and I could never live freely with him hunting me down. But I told him that living here in this home is perfect. That if this is my prison it's exactly where I want to be because this is where he is, and he is my everything."

Bram looks at me with such loving concern that I start to cry again so he holds me gently, patting my back and telling me he's sure Joel must see and understand how much I love him.

"He's not a stupid man, Girlie."

"I know he's not, but he's still mad at me right now. He says if I don't care about myself what about him? How can we move forward in our lives if he always has to be looking over his shoulder and watching out for me?

What kind of a life is that? I hadn't thought of things from that point of view and I told him so. I've come inside to think over what he said."

Then Bram surprises me by telling me to put on the white negligee he bought me.

"Put it on, add a bit of perfume or make-up, brush your hair and go sit by the fire in the family room."

I protest saying Joel and I need to talk seriously and now isn't the time to play at dress-up, but Bram insists that it's exactly the right time and to do as I'm told.

I don't actually have any make-up or perfume, that's more of the stuff I meant to buy when we were in town, but one look in the mirror shows that I picked up rosy cheeks from my exercise outdoors so my color is good.

I put on the white costume and I have to say, it really is a beautiful garment. All lace, sweeping to the floor, and very low-cut with a bodice tight enough to give my breasts some lift. It's white and my skin shows through it in a sheen of pale pink. I feel very feminine and graceful. Virginal, even.

I walk down to the family room and just get settled in, curled up in front of the fire, when the door opens behind me and Joel comes in carrying an armload of firewood. He glances at me then stops and does a double-take. It's like something out of the cartoons and that makes me smile.

He carefully puts the firewood in the box then comes over and kneels down beside me.

Chapter 18

Joel

Girlie is a vision in white. So pretty, so womanly, so breathtakingly beautiful. She looks angelic and yet her body holds such a promise of earthly, wanton delights.

Funny how seeing her completely naked isn't as sexy as seeing her in this lacy nightgown. Maybe dressing up changes how she feels and moves? All I know is I'm utterly entranced. I want to devour her and I want to worship her – both at the same time.

Of course I can't even give a hint of how I feel. First she came flying down the stairs to welcome me home by jumping in my arms then she really hurt me.

The fact that it was so unexpected made it ten times worse. Despite all the booze I drank I couldn't heal that hurt, I really felt betrayed by her words and thoughts.

Now that she's explained it wasn't anger on Kendricks' behalf but for me, I can see things from her viewpoint and, maybe, understand. But I always knew I was never in danger... still, I guess it's just as well that she has no idea just how deadly I can be... and have been. And, let's face it, probably will be again.

But because she doesn't know she allows herself to worry and imagine the worst.

After I told my story and she screamed at me I felt like she'd driven an icicle through my heart. Everything inside of me went cold. Cold and angry. That anger carried me through my drinking binge. I haven't been on a tear like that in years.

But just now, when she said she was happy to be a prisoner so long as she was imprisoned with me I felt such a flood of warm emotion. The coldness just melted away. Along with my resolve to keep Girlie at arm's-length, at least emotionally.

I knew this little chickie was going to be my downfall, I just knew it. And now she has me in the palm of her hand. God, I hope she never figures that out!

Chapter 19

Girlie

Bram was so right about this get-up. Joel just keeps staring at me. Looking from my eyes to my breasts then back up to my face again. I kind of feel like he's a ravenous wolf and I'm a sacrificial lamb.

To break the spell I lean forward and gently press my lips to his in a close-mouthed kiss. He enfolds me in his arms and I know that everything between us will be right again.

Joel reclines on the rug and pulls me down with him, stretching the length of me against his body, covering me. He rests his chin on my head and we both gaze into the fire but I can feel his eyes traveling over me and lingering on my decolletage. It's amazing how a bit of white lace can transform a very familiar body into something alluring!

"Sing me a lullaby," I request, remembering him singing one to me once before.

"No, but I'll croon to you."

"Croon?"

"Yeah, haven't you heard about those old-time singers who were called crooners? They sang romantic stuff. Singers like Nat King Cole."

"Never heard of him."

"Little chickie, you're so young! But that's good because you won't be able to compare me to him, believe me there's no comparison, his voice is velvet! The song is called *Unforgettable*. Look at the fire, don't watch me when I sing, but I want to watch you. It will inspire me."

His deep voice, the gentle melody, the heart-achingly romantic words... like a little girl I ask him to sing it again and again.

Next day when I told Bram that the white negligee was a great success he said he heard Joel singing and when that happened he was so happy for the both of us because he knew what it meant.

When Joel finally says he's sung enough I turn and push him flat down on his back. Propping myself up to hover over him sets off my breasts to their best advantage and I know that. He stares at me, mesmerized, while I explain that what he did for me was overwhelming.

"Now that I truly understand why you did what you did, I have to tell you that I have never in my whole life felt so cherished, so protected, so profoundly loved, and so deeply honored, Joel O'Shea."

Finally he pulls the negligee off of me and we make sweet, sweet love.

Afterwards I tell him:

"I really hope you like your Christmas present. It didn't cost me any money but in a sense it's costing me everything I have. I've had my birth control device removed because I want to have your baby." He grips me tightly, but lets me continue.

"I want to have a new life with you but... just you. I want us to be exclusive. At least until I fall pregnant and then, if you still want me to have sex with your brothers well..."

"No," he interrupts. "It was never a case of wanting that, that's just the way things turned out."

"When you were gone all night, drinking, were you... did you, uh—"

"No, Girlie. I wasn't with anyone else. You are the only one I want and I've been hoping that's how you feel about me, too."

"Well Bram is a super-hot father-figure..."

"Naughty girl!"

Then I tell him about my trip to Maggie's doctor and he laughs at my description of Bram taking credit for the well-used state of my vagina.

"It's a cunt, Girlie."

"Fuck off, Joel."

"Ohhh I'm going to get you for that. You're going to be begging for it!"

Chapter 20

Joel

I prop myself up on one elbow so I could look down the length of Girlie's body while gently caressing her soft skin.

"Hey, a mama can't be called Girlie and you're no longer Joanne so what's your middle name?"

"Joanne."

"No, I meant your oh... I get it. Okay, what's your first name?"

"You remember I told you my mother was a bit soft in the head?"

"Yeah, so what?"

"Well, she chose my name."

I can see she's avoiding answering so I tease her asking if her name is Raindrop or Moonglow or Precious and she stops me saying:

"Unfortunately, you're getting warmer... my name is Angel."

"Angel? But that's perfect!"

"Oh right, tell that to nine-year-old me who had to listen to all the stupid, cruel comments kids make. That's when I switched to Joanne and I wouldn't answer anyone who called me Angel."

"Angel is pretty."

"Pretty stupid for law enforcement. Can't you just picture it? *Stop! I'm Agent Angel and you have to obey me or I'll get out my handcuffs.* Jesus, Angel is a porn star name."

"Ohhh, wait a moment, don't say anything while I picture you saying that while wearing a tight uniform with your shirt half unbuttoned and a super-short mini-skirt..."

She punches me then suggests that maybe we can act out that fantasy some time... then I bend down for a kiss and say:

"Angel O'Shea, that's a good name."

"O'Shea? Oh! Does that mean...?"

"Of course. I don't want my son born a bastard."

"Joel, that wouldn't matter to me, And besides what makes you think it will be a boy? Maybe we'll have a little girl."

"I would love to have a little girl! Fuck, that will be so great. A mini-Angel that I can spoil rotten from day one."

"You know we don't have to get married—"

"I want to."

"Well, if that's your idea of a proposal... at least you can give me another kiss."

She pulls my head down and kisses me deeply and lovingly but I break it off to say:

"Talking about spoiling someone rotten... hold on a minute."

I reach over to find my jeans and bring a jeweller's box out of the pocket. How many times had I thought about throwing it away in my anger during the last couple of days? Thank God I didn't when I see Angel's eyes go huge in delighted surprise. I open it to display a stunning sapphire surrounded by diamonds.

"Blue, to match your eyes," I tell her, adding:

"Angel Joanne Dwyer will you do me the honor?"

We fuck like teenagers all night long.

Chapter 21

Angel

Finally, a Christmas of happy memories to help cover over the bad, scary feelings from when I was a very young child.

Joel explains to Bram that from now on I'm to be called by my first name, Angel. He's delighted to congratulate us on our engagement. I show him my ring and spend the rest of the day admiring it over and over again. It's gorgeous.

A few times I look up to see Joel watching me and he smiles while I blush at being caught.

Bram points out that before he goes off to cook our Christmas dinner I still have one more gift from him to present to Joel and he wants to see me in it.

"Oh right," I reply, "the Christmas morning costume."

When I come back modeling the last of the three outfits that Bram bought both men's eyes go wide. They applaud as I twirl around showing off for their approval – and no wonder!

The negligee is a baby-doll nightie of pink chiffon with a red satin bolero top held in place by a skinny satin bow. This shoestring of fabric is stretching across about ten inches of breasts and barely holding them in place.

After I tied the bow as tightly as I could I looked in the mirror and marveled at the sheer sexiness of the lingerie. It immediately excited me when I thought of its effect on Joel.

Bram insists I kneel down by the Christmas tree and assume a pin-up pose. I comply, tilting my head and biting my bottom lip and Joel tells me to hold still while he snaps my picture on his phone.

"Send me that, will you?" asks Bram but Joel says no, he isn't sharing any more of me today. Ever since we discussed pregnancy and marriage Joel has become very possessive.

"Aww, but you've at least got to let me watch you pull the ribbon to untie that bow."

"No Bram, she's my Christmas present and I'll unwrap her when we're both good and ready - and in private. Sorry bro, but we're exclusive now."

Bram complains that Joel is a spoilsport but he smiles as he says it.

"Besides, I get to ogle her at dinner when she puts on her new see-through dress."

Joel suddenly asks me:

"Angel, what will happen to your tits when you're pregnant?"

I give him a huge, happy grin answering:

"Oh, they'll get much, much bigger!"

His answering smile is brilliant!

Part Four

"Connubial"

Chapter 1

Joel

Bram did us proud with his extravagant and generous wedding present. When he offers to pay for our honeymoon I'm sure he's thinking two weeks in the tropics sunning on a beach or sipping Mai Tais decorated with little umbrellas while lounging around the pool. He'd hate something like that and, turns out, so would we. Angel says she isn't keen and it's such a relief to hear that.

Not that I have any objection to ogling her in a thong bikini, smoothing sunscreen over every inch of her body, and enjoying the romance of tropical sunsets... but only for a couple of days and not in an all-inclusive package.

Instead, we opt for concierge service in Vegas. So Bram charters a private jet to be met by a limo that will ferry us to the Wedding Chapel. Then on to the Honeymoon Suite of a 5-star hotel after the ceremony. And back to the airstrip when we're ready to come home. He's made the booking and paid for it all.

Wilcox, our driver, is waiting on the tarmac for us as we deplane. The limo is a luxurious stretch with champagne chilling on ice and a bouquet made up of a dozen red and a dozen white roses.

I'm in a suit, but I begged off wearing a tie, and Angel is in a white dress that doesn't hide the red underwear she's got on. For the first time since I've known her she's wearing high-heels, also sexy red, that add another four inches to her height. It makes it easier to reach her for a kiss.

We decide our trip will start with the wedding service so that once we reach the hotel we don't have to leave it again. I confirm the itinerary to Wilcox who says Bram has sent him a text saying *carte blanche*.

"Oh, you know Bram personally?"

He grins and says he first met Bram more than twenty-five years ago when he, Wilcox, was a trainer with the Corps and one of several who instructed Bram in the basic training to become a Marine.

"And you remained friends after that?" I say with a laugh, knowing Bram wouldn't have been the easiest or the best pupil.

"Yeah, after we cracked his head a few times!" Wilcox chuckles back. "Of course it took a few of us to take that big boy down."

"So tell us Wilcox, have you ever driven Bram around Vegas?" asks Angel.

"I sure have, ma'am but that's all I'm gonna say on that subject."

"Aw, c'mon Wilcox. Give us something we can tease Bram about when we get home because we all know he's going to have plenty to say about what we've been up to!"

Angel at her most wheedling is hard to resist and I can see Wilcox thinking about what he might get away with telling us. Finally his grizzled face breaks into a wide grin and he answers:

"All I can tell you is for a man his age I was impressed, mighty impressed, by the company he kept. How's that?"

"Ohhh, it's not nearly enough! but it's better than nothing so thank you."

Wilcox chuckles again and shakes his head. I wonder how Angel will embellish that remark and hope Bram has enough sense to ask Wilcox his side of things before making any accusations.

The wedding chapel is just as awful as we imagined since Bram does have a peculiar sense of humor. It's tacky and shiny with lots of chrome and mirrors reflecting the garish lighting of a spinning disco ball. It's also open at 10:00 pm which suits us just fine.

"Perfect!" declares Angel, looking through the open doors and grabbing her big bouquet of two dozen roses.

Wilcox follows us in with a receipt for payment of the service including a witness and a couple of photos. Wilcox serves as our second witness.

We're back in the limo in half-an-hour, the whole ceremony taking less time than was spent by the photographer's posing of us.

I think he fell in love with Angel because he kept wanting one more shot. When he asks for her number I tell him to send the photos to my phone and I'll bet he thinks I'm jealous, but the truth is Angel still doesn't have a phone of her own yet. And yes of course I'm jealous, this beautiful girl is my wife!

Besides, who figures on getting lucky the bride on her wedding day? Other than her husband, that is.

We step out of the venue into the warm Las Vegas night and Wilcox asks:

"See the sights? or straight back to the hotel, Mr. and Mrs. O'Shea?" which makes me grin and Angel giggle.

We compromise by settling for a ride down the famous Strip so we can see the lights of the fancy hotels and casinos before heading to our honeymoon suite. Driving along we toast each other with a glass of champagne. Well, half-a-glass because we have other things on our mind.

Angel exclaims favorably about how roomy the back seat is, adding:

"No wonder Bram likes doing it in cars, this is great! We're enclosed in a private and dark little space. It's so cozy!"

"Yeah well, Bram's legs aren't as long as mine."

"Well if I hike up my dress and lift my body up while you pull me over you thigh I think we can... ahhh, yes... just like that. No need to complain, husband..."

"Oh! I like hearing that, darling. I really like hearing you call me that. Just shift your leg like this and—"

"Don't lose my panties! I'll never be able to walk into the hotel because this dress is pretty much see-through!"

"Okay, I'll put them in my pocket. Do you want to take your bra off or should I just push it up and over?"

I've forgotten all about Wilcox until I hear the privacy glass that separates us from the driver roll to a closed position. Fortunately not a moment too soon!

Chapter 2

Wilcox

I'm always happy to do my old buddy Bram a favor and driving for his brother and new bride is an easy job. Since I know Vegas well he asked me to recommend a really kitschy chapel, but a top-notch hotel for them.

Years of living in this city has been an eye-opener with things just getting stranger all the time. I've seen way more than I ever wanted to in the backseat of my limo! Sex shows never did appeal to me but boy, this couple are both so good-looking and well-built I am really tempted to watch them. They make such a nice change from the plastic-bodied girls and wealthy wrinklies who normally occupy that space.

Bram now, he's had some fine-looking women in the car and usually more than one at a time, too. If they were working girls they were high-class, and if they were school-teachers or nurses having a blow-out weekend well he sure treated them nicely. Happy memories!

But this is a married couple so I – admittedly somewhat reluctantly – close the window between us once they start getting it on.

But I've left the speaker open and my excuse for that is because I don't want to interrupt them at a crucial moment. Listening in means I'll know if I need to circle the hotel a few times.

Besides, my good friend Bram wouldn't begrudge an old happily married man like myself a bit of a thrill.

Especially when I can hear that luscious girl say:

"Husband, I'm almost naked and you're wearing far too many clothes. I can't wait to get you stripped down and into our honeymoon bed."

Lucky guy!

Chapter 3

Angel

I've never been to Las Vegas before and considering I only got to see a private airstrip, a limo, a wedding chapel, and a hotel I have to say I still don't feel like I've ever been to Vegas!

Wilcox had already checked us in so he just escorts us across the hotel lobby to an elevator that is private to the building's top three floors. He pushes the right button, hands Joel a key, neatly accepts his tip while saying Bram has already taken care of him, and wishes us a pleasant evening with a grin that stretches from ear to ear.

He's put his number into Joel's phone saying just text me with about twenty or thirty minutes notice when you're ready to leave. Tomorrow, the next day, or the day after that. Bram left an open tab for the transportation costs.

It's very nice to have all the details taken care of, leaving us free to concentrate on each other.

The elevator is pretty impressive, the penthouse lobby is awesome, and our suite is exquisite. Joel scoops me up to carry me over the threshold, even though it's a hotel room and not our home, and the first thing we do is kiss long and hard. Then we tour the place.

The decor features artistic photography of lovers with the nudity tastefully done. It's erotic, rather than explicit. Same with the sculptures scattered on various surfaces. The materials are velvet and marble and there are lots of mirrors. One wall is all glass looking out on a balcony with a dizzying view.

The bed is massive and round! It's also got wooden panels that close it into a box and these are all mirrored on the inside. There's a mirror on the ceiling as well. This is going to be quite a thrilling experience! There are a dozen pillows that match the black satin sheets. They're slippery. It's wonderful.

We only brought the clothes we're wearing because we don't plan on leaving the room until it's time to go home so once we undress I'll have to be sure to hang everything up. Hopefully I won't get too distracted to do that!

Joel did ask if I would want to go to a show and I answered *not this time* because I'm sure we'll come here again some day. Gambling doesn't interest me and I don't want to spend my honeymoon bargain-hunting at the outlet malls. I'll go shopping next time we visit.

"Well husband, our married life has begun!"

"So, what are you going to do to entertain me? I hope you're not going to be one of those women who get headaches once they get a ring on their finger."

He's taken off his suit jacket and is sitting comfortably in an armchair. The seating area has two chairs and a couch that look onto a small bathing pool fed by a waterfall.

I slowly strip, dancing to a song in my head, until I'm naked except for my sexy shoes. Of course my performance includes me posing and shimmying just out of his reach.

Meanwhile he's teasing me back by taking his time unbuttoning his shirt. He tosses it aside and I lose the rhythm of the music I've been imagining while I pause to stare at his well-muscled torso that's got exactly the right amount of dark hair. So yummy.

Having forgotten the tune I give up on the dancing and kick off my shoes to walk right into the pool, twirling under the waterfall with my arms stretched up high above my head. I know droplets of water are flying off my body as I spin. I don't hear Joel approach until he says:

"This brings back memories," and pulls me tight against his naked body.

He's right, this is just like our time at the compound when every day we showered outside with cold water. There's a flat ledge just the right height for me to lie back on while a warm spray mists over us as we play, splashing each other like water babies.

He licks the drops from my throat, chest, breasts, and sucks on my nipples. The room is air-conditioned but the waterfall is bathtub warm so I alternate between hot and cold sensations as I pose like a sacrificial well... not a virgin, that's for sure!

I think *maybe I'm a bit of an exhibitionist* as I spread my legs. The O'Shea brothers never made me feel shy about my body and being on display turns me on. Seems to make Joel happy as well.

Standing, he pulls my legs around his waist and we have wet, exciting sex. It's a great sensation. I love touching and looking at his body and I know he feels the same about mine. Being married appeals to his possessive instincts, I can see it in the hungry way he's staring at me. It reassures me as well that this incredibly handsome, hunky man is mine all mine.

After our first round of sex he gives my bottom a slap and sends me to the bathroom for towels. I walk with an outrageous wiggle and hear him chuckling in appreciation.

When I return offering towels and towelling robes he insists on drying me off. Again I relive a memory of him vigorously rubbing me down after the first show I put on for him in the outdoor shower. Back then I really hated Joel yet afterwards I simply melted into his kiss. It was so humiliating yet arousing all at the same time.

"I'm starving," he announces and looked around for a room service menu. I join him to check what's available and am happy to see the prices aren't listed. I'm sure the cost is so high it will kill my appetite and in truth I'm hungry, too.

We decide on dinner and luckily the kitchen is full service 24/7 for these upper floors. No wonder the prices are hidden! So Joel orders a t-bone steak and I choose lamb chops. Since both of us like our meat cooked rare our feast will arrive quite soon.

He pops open another bottle of champagne and we toast each other again, this time while standing naked admiring the view outdoors and our reflections in the glass. We really are a handsome couple.

More intense kissing is interrupted by a knock on the door. I dash into the bathroom while Joel slips a towel around his waist. He comes to get me once we're alone again.

I gather up our robes but he tells me he'd rather we dine in the nude. I've dined topless at home with him and Bram but this is something new. In fact, this whole night is such a fun adventure - and we haven't even tested the bed yet! We'll make that our dessert.

After eating a delicious meal and enjoying a languorous, sensual bout of lovemaking we both fall into deep, restful sleeps. It's pre-dawn when we awaken and make love again while the desert sunrise lights up the room.

I guess the excitement of yesterday caught up with us because we both fall asleep again, for several hours more this time.

It's probably late morning or even noon when I wake to the delicious smell of fresh, strong coffee. Joel got up first and ordered us room service.

I'm not very hungry but I nibble on some fresh strawberries and blueberries. There's bacon and toast and home fries on warming plates which I figure I'll want later. I smile to myself thinking *have to keep my strength up because this man will wear me out.*

Even though I haven't quite finished my coffee Joel takes the cup from my hand and orders me onto the bed saying he wants to take me doggie-style.

It sounds like his need is urgent so I immediately obey, getting on my hands and knees. Joel starts by pushing my hair up off my neck and kissing me there and behind my ears, licking then blowing softly to send shivers down my spine.

"This is my favorite position," he announces. "I'm plugged in looking down at your peach of an ass with one hand full of tits and other playing with your horny button—"

"Oh please," I interrupt in a dry tone, "all this romantic talk will make me swoon."

"Ha-ha. I was going to add that the only thing missing is that I can't see your beautiful face showing me your passion and pleasure. Except..."

He releases my breasts in order to tilt my chin upwards until I'm looking straight at myself in a mirror. I can see my face with Joel poised above me smiling down at my kneeling body.

I've forgotten about the mirrors! And now I can't stop staring. Looking up I meet his eyes and I can see he's enjoying my astonishment and pleasure at this discovery.

"I love being able to see your face," he tells me.

Joel suddenly flings his head back and orgasms powerfully then immediately flips me to mount him. He reaches over and closes the remaining open panels before lying back, instructing me to look around. I see our reflection everywhere and again I can't tear my eyes away.

I see his hands reaching up to gently pinch my nipples at the same time that I enjoy the tingling I feel from his touch. I'm not sure what causes the disconnect between what we're doing and what I'm seeing but I feel like I'm watching a movie of someone else - and being felt-up in the back row of the theater.

I tell him so and he laughs saying I am starring in our very own x-rated porno.

"What?"

"Chickie, can't you see the cameras? We're being shot from," he looks around and counts, "five different angles."

"But I don't want someone filming me, us, like this!"

"It's all automated, nobody's actually watching and no one will see this except us. We get the video on a memory stick or something when we leave. Have you not read the welcome package? Oh of course not, that explains why the chocolates are still there."

"Chocolates? Where?"

"Never mind that now. I want your full attention and concentration on me."

He can be so demanding... and in bed it really turns me on. Outside of the bedroom not so much. But it's our honeymoon and I'm thrilled to submit to my husband's care.

Later, lying beside each other, he kisses me gently but thoroughly. Both of us love to kiss a lot.

With one hand he takes hold of me by my wrists and lifts my arms above my head. Then he uses his long arm to caress me with light strokes from head to toe. Each stroke up and down the length of my body involves a bit of teasing my clit. Or my horny button, as Joel now calls it.

I start to squirm but he tightens his grip on my wrists. I no longer panic at being restrained, he's cured me of that or helped me cure myself by bringing my memories to light. Now I'm fighting and struggling against my arousal, but I'm going to lose this battle.

My breathing quickens and my chest is heaving. I'm writhing on the bed, so hot from his skilled fingers, when I suddenly remember the cameras are on. That sure notches up the excitement meter.

"You want me to perform, don't you?" I whisper in a voice turned husky. He smiles and leans down to kiss my forehead but pulls back again. I guess he doesn't want to obstruct the view, and I discover that yes, I really am an exhibitionist.

I'm so conscious of my pink body wantonly posed on the black satin sheets, legs splayed, breasts straining upwards, pinned in place by my strong, handsome husband. Joel quickly brings me to orgasm and I wonder what kind of spectacle I make as I arch my body in response to the waves of pleasure.

Joel enters me and I immediately cum again. His hands lose their tenderness as they now roughly massage my breasts and grab my ass and he fucks me so well I forget that the cameras are there.

Chapter 4

Joel

I don't know how I'll ever thank Bram enough for this. Something about this room, whether it's the mirrors, the cameras, the luxury... I don't know, but it's turned Angel into a little spitfire. She's wearing me out.

After fuck number whatever – I lost count – I'm lying back trying to catch my breath. She's delicately cupping my balls, her little hands are so gentle. She remembers everything I've taught her, but she's careful knowing my cock is super-sensitive right now.

After a few minutes I pull her up so her head is nestled against my neck and I've got her smooth back to caress. I look down the length of her and comment:

"I'm glad you don't have any tattoos. I like to see your clean, unmarked skin. And if you did have a tattoo I'd probably be jealous of whoever it was you got it done with and for."

She giggles over that saying: "Nobody puts a bumper sticker on a Ferrari..."

"Oh you're a racy sports-car are you?"

"Well, I'm hoping that sometime this year I'll turn into a passenger vehicle."

That confuses me for a moment until I realize what she means. I hug her tight, I love to think of us becoming parents. I don't know where that thought came from but I realize it's 100% true.

"Actually the real surprise is that you don't have tattoos. I mean, macho man and military... isn't it like a prerequisite in Special Ops?"

"You're right that lots of guys there were inked, and most of them pretty heavily too, but no, none of the O'Sheas have tattoos because Papa always said he'd kick our ass if we got one. I told you he was a bit of a criminal in his day, right? Well, he'd tell us *the last thing you want is identifying marks* so we went along with it."

We lay there cuddled together, catching our breath and thinking our thoughts.

"You know, though, maybe I wouldn't mind you and me getting something done together. What do you think?"

"I'm not a big fan of needles, and I'm pretty sure getting a tattoo is damn painful, but husband your wish is my command."

I can't stop myself from making that sound she always loves to hear: a rumbling groan that tells her she's said something that reaches down to my core. I don't know if it's the word *husband* or the word *command* that turns me on more, but the two words in the same sentence? Jeez!

I have to clear my throat before I reply:

"I'll give it some thought, and I'll let you know. But Chickie, if you don't want to do it I certainly won't force you. Although I suspect there might be other things that will turn you on when I force you to do them."

"As if!"

I disengage from her embrace and roll onto my stomach, resting my head on my forearms.

"I need a little nap," I explain. She lies down quietly beside me and I'm just drifting off when suddenly she delivers a stinging slap to my rump.

"What the fuck, Angel?"

"I can't resist, your butt is so tempting. It still is!" she says with a laugh and swats me again.

"Oh baby, you don't want to go war with me," I warn her but she pays no attention and smacks me again, hard.

"That's it, now it's your turn," I declare, sitting up and holding her down.

"No, you can't! You said you'd never punch, or spank, or slap, or hit me and..."

"This isn't hitting, it's retaliating. Different thing altogether. It's not anger, I'm simply giving tit-for-tat. Cold, measured revenge, baby. Believe me when I tell you Angel, that anything you do to me I will do right back to you and probably harder because well, I'm bigger and stronger so hey! sucks to be you, little girl."

I then hold her firmly and give her four good swats – one more than she gave me. I leave my handprint on her bottom as she squeals and yelps. That should make interesting viewing when we eventually get around to watching this video.

"Joel, I really didn't like that," she complains, rubbing her behind.

"Do you think I do?"

"Well I guess not, but your ass is... wow, so inviting!"

"From what I've heard there are plenty of books and now some movies about men spanking women, actually spanking and a lot more, so I figure it's a thing nowadays. I guess. Do women like to give up control? is that appealing to you?"

"I have to admit that the thought of being dominated by you turns me on. I mean, I get so mad when you boss me around in real life but I always seem to do what you want. For me, personally, the idea of being disciplined is a sexy fantasy but I don't like the reality at all. It hurts!

I've heard some women say that their sexual fantasy is to be raped but, again, nobody really wants that in real life. I met a woman who said she likes to imagine having her clothes cut off with a knife. It's just a scenario to fantasize about in the safety of your own bed. Do you ever fantasize about raping?"

"Me? I don't really fantasize. I just have to flip through the pictures in my memory. Like recalling you riding me with your breasts swaying and your eyes half closed and your mouth half open... I can bring up that image as clear as a hi-res photo and reliving that memory gets me hard. See? Just talking about it is having an effect."

"That's not really a story-line though. I mean I'm flattered but—-"

"Oh wait, there is a fantasy I have that isn't a memory because it's never happened but it could and, you know what? it definitely should! And it's sort of a rape fantasy, too I guess."

"Uh, *sort of* a rape?"

"Well, like all good pornos it's a case of the girl saying *No! No!* but her body is saying *Yes! Yes!* Oh, you've probably never seen a porn film."

"Seen no, but I have heard a few. Kendricks used to watch them on his laptop with the volume turned up. He'd always pester Anita and me saying he'd email us the file and maybe we'd learn something."

I feel an instant rush of anger but decide I won't waste a minute of my honeymoon thinking about Kendricks. Instead I continue explaining my fantasy that I hope we will act out some day.

"Okay, so I've been thinking about this ever since you mentioned *Agent Angel of the DEA with her handcuffs*. I imagine you wearing a skin-tight cop uniform with a super-short skirt and a shirt half-unbuttoned.

I easily take your handcuffs away and put them on you with your hands cuffed around a bed post or something. Then I rip open your shirt – you're not wearing a bra - and push up your mini-skirt – you're not wearing panties - and you're struggling and saying stupid cop stuff like *stop it, you're under arrest*.

Meanwhile, I'm fucking you and squeezing and manhandling your body and you're loving it and I tell you I won't let you go until you promise to drop the charges. Yeah, I really enjoy thinking about that and we should definitely act it out some day."

"Forget someday, husband, and deal with this horny slut you've got in your bed right now!" she insists.

Chapter 5

Wilcox

My clients don't come up for air for two days so it's a very tired but happy couple that I pick up from the hotel. And they still can't keep their hands off of each other!

Looking at them in the rear-view mirror I see she's got her head on his chest, he has his arm around her shoulders and they're holding hands, too. At least, I can see one hand from each of them... God knows what the other is doing. They aren't saying much and only murmuring when they do speak so I can't hear their conversation.

"Did you folks try your luck at the tables at all?"

"No, Wilcox. We just got lucky in the bedroom. Oww! Why'd you pinch me, Joel?" She looks quite indignant adding: "He's Bram's friend, he knows the score. Jeez, nobody's gonna be surprised that we fucked on our honeymoon."

For some reason the bad language doesn't sound like swearing coming out of her mouth, it actually sounds cute.

I don't know what he whispers in her ear but she lets out a low, throaty laugh that makes me look at her with renewed interest. We men are such pigs.

"Wilcox, I didn't even get to pull the handle on a slot machine!"

Joel says something else I don't catch but based on a repeat of her husky chuckle I'm guessing it has something to do with pulling his handle.

"Oh, you would have been disappointed, Mrs. O'Shea. The slots are all push button now, no more *one-armed bandits.*"

"Mrs. O'Shea. You're so sweet, Wilcox. We're so glad we have you taking care of us. We're having a very memorable honeymoon and you're helping to make it special."

She's so sincere that even me, veteran of years of schmoozing and fake smiles, am touched. Such a sweet girl.

There's no luggage for me to fetch out of the trunk so after opening the door I just stand and watch them walk to their plane. Well, I watch her and she's definitely worth looking at.

Their clothes are slightly rumpled, but her red panties and bra – with matching high-heels – look damn enticing through that sheer white dress.

When they're almost at the stairs she turns to wave and blow me a kiss. Pure delight! I'm in such a good mood I think I'll take my missus out for a nice meal with the wad of folding money that Joel just slipped me.

Those two are a class act, and even with my jaundiced seen-it-all-before attitude I figure that marriage will last.

Chapter 6

Angel

Bram is happy to see us when we get back home. He says he's had a text and an email from Wilcox so he knows everything has gone according to plan.

I give him a big sloppy *thank-you* kiss and get a hard hug in return.

Marriage doesn't change my day-to-day life until I suspect I might be pregnant. My periods have never been regular but even so I think I missed one and that, combined with morning nausea, makes it seem likely. Although from what Dr. Moro said it's too soon to happen.

Anyhow I ask Maggie to get me another appointment and to drive me there since I don't want to ask either of the men for a ride and I still don't have a licence of my own.

She comes in with me and is so excited when Dr. Moro gives me the good news. I just want to race home. I barely hear the doctor explain about different vitamins and supplements and what kinds of exercise I should take. All I can think of is telling Joel.

I don't know how we get home safely because Maggie becomes a lead-footed driver speeding back to the house. I don't even consider taking Joel aside for a private chat because I'm bursting with my announcement and don't want her beating me to it.

We have an incredible night celebrating! I don't mind my toasts having to be alcohol-free because I've never been much of a drinker.

Neither Joel nor Bram knew I was seeing the doctor so they are both shocked, surprised, and delighted. We didn't expect me to fall pregnant so soon but we're all thrilled.

What's strange is that not long afterwards Bram turns grumpy and he's been in a bad mood for days. I don't remember ever seeing him like this before. He's never been an optimist but was always even-tempered and ready to share a laugh. Now he's snapping at everything Joel says.

We're lingering over breakfast and I'm thankful that I don't feel the least bit nauseous today. That's put me in a good mood and Joel isn't scowling over anything so it's just Bram.

I might as well just ask and find out: "Is something the matter, Bram?"

He frowns at me but I just smile back. After making a hmmph kind of noise that rumbles deep in his chest he says: "It's not you... it's him." He turns his frown on Joel who takes a drink from his coffee mug before asking:

"What did I do?"

"It's not what you did, it's what you have that's pissing me off."

"What do you mean what I have—" Joel begins with a puzzled look but Bram cuts him off saying:

"You don't even realize what you've got and how lucky you are." He counts off on his big fingers: "You've got a wife, Angel, you've got a baby on the way, you're young – well, youngish, and everything in your life is great."

Now I'm the one who's puzzled as I ask: "But isn't all that exactly what you want for your brother, Bram?"

He throws himself back in his chair which creaks ominously and folds his arms over his chest.

"Of course it is but I'm, well I guess I might as well just admit it, I'm jealous. Envious, at the very least."

"Ah, you're feeling lonely." I say. "Maybe there's something I could do to fix you up? Put a smile back on your face?" Now I look right at him with a big grin.

He smiles back but only briefly before saying, "You can't. You two are exclusive now."

"She's already knocked up Bram, so there's no disputing who the Daddy is. If Angel wants to fuck you you two should go ahead."

I give Joel a look of disdain explaining:

"Bram and I don't fuck, Joel. Fucking is for you, with Bram I make love. Other than the very first time – when you rushed him - it's always been that way with us. Bram seduces me with a heavy petting session and then we just... well... segue into lovemaking. It's very, very, very nice!"

From the look on Joel's face I think I've just put my foot in my mouth.

Bram must think so too because he jumps into the conversation saying:

"No, I don't want to have sex with Angel. Well, I do because I'm not insane, but no, it wouldn't feel right to me. She's your wife now, Joel. And besides you're the one I'm pissed off at."

"Yeah I get that, but why?"

"Because you're such a mean prick!"

"Well that's hardly news! I haven't changed."

"And that's the problem! You shouldn't have come out of all the recent shit smelling like roses."

"But you're the one with all the businesses and the big house – lord of the manor! - Papa always said he'd leave you everything and he did." Joel turns to me adding: "Bram can kick us out anytime, we have no right to be here except by his invitation."

"Maybe I should kick you out and keep Angel, whaddya say to that, huh?"

"You can kick me out but don't forget I've got a trust fund so I can certainly afford to take Angel with me – no matter where I go. So c'mon, what's really going on?"

"Aww, fuck it. I'm just grouchy and pissed off because despite being such a mean prick you got the girl."

"Oh, so you're saying I don't deserve her, is that right?"

"Well, you don't," I answer. Now both of them are looking at me with funny expressions so I hasten to explain:

"The way you got me isn't right or fair or normal, even. Basically I was kidnapped, assaulted, raped, confine—-"

"Wait a minute," interrupts Joel. "I don't remember you saying *no* so how did we rape you?"

"Well first of all it was a gang bang, and secondly no one asked for my consent."

"To be fair, Angel, we really didn't need to. I mean you were offering blow jobs and were all wet and ready—" puts in Bram.

"But I'd just been shot at, beaten, terrorized, and traumatized. I didn't have any choice in the matter or, at least, I didn't believe I had a choice. I thought it was spread my legs or die."

Both men frown heavily thinking over what I've said so I hurry to add:

"But I came out of all that deeply attached to both of you," I turn to Joel adding: "and madly in love with you. That's all so crazy none of us deserve to be happy but we are so... why not enjoy the *happily ever after* if we can?"

"Angel just blow him."

I sigh deeply saying:

"Joel, again, pay attention: you get your dick sucked but with Bram I perform fellatio." I sneak a sideways look at Bram and yes! I make him smile with that comment.

"That sounds good, Angel but I don't want Joel to be okay with it. I know, I know that's crazy shit but... I want him to suffer somehow. Don't ask me why 'cause I don't know why. Okay, how about Angel will blo—I mean *fellate* me but Joel you have to watch."

"I was planning to, but now that you're saying I have to, well now it feels... I don't know, kinda weird..."

"Oh, forget it. You're just trying to make me feel better and it's having the opposite effect. You're so confident of Angel's love for you that you don't even care what she does with her body."

"Oh, I care," cuts in Joel sharply, speaking in a very serious tone. Suddenly the whole atmosphere has become tense and somewhat uncomfortable.

I get up and walk over to Bram's chair to sit on his lap. He holds me comfortably while I make my suggestion:

"Papa Bear, why don't we go sit in the family room with the drapes drawn and no lights on so it's nice and dark and we'll act like horny teenagers in the backseat of a car. As a matter of fact, I thought of you when we were in the back of Wilcox's limo, didn't I, Joel?

I tried to get Wilcox to dish the dirt on you but he wouldn't. Even though I pouted. But you could tell me what shenanigans you got up to in Vegas. I'd like to hear about it and I think it will make you feel better, too."

He gives me a squeeze and a smile saying: "Maybe I can talk you into giving me a hand-job?"

"Well, no promises, but if you get me really, really worked up maybe I'll act like a naughty, slutty teenager again. Just like last time."

"Oh, sweetheart," he chuckles: "I feel better already."

He stands up smoothly with me in his arms and turning to Joel adds: "As for you, well you'll just have to wonder about what we're doing so enjoy imagining it."

Joel replies:

"Damn you for talking about my imagination! It's already busy at work and you've got my outlet for release."

Oh I guess that's me – Joel's outlet for release... Charming!

Bram just laughs since Joel's comment cheers him up. He's carrying me to the family-room but I can't resist a peek back at Joel still sitting at the table.

He returns my look with an intense gaze that makes me gulp, knowing I'll be relating every single move that Bram and I make – and probably re-enacting them all – in our own bed tonight.

That thought makes me shiver with pleasure: double the fun!

Chapter 7

Joel

I'm in the bedroom working on a surprise for Angel. I hope to have everything in place before she finishes with Bram and joins me.

Why is it that I don't feel any jealousy about her being with Bram? Because I truly don't. I know that Bram is a good kindhearted man who won't hurt Angel. I love and trust them both so I guess that's my answer.

I know he'll never try to have intercourse with her, not now that she's my wife. But they'll fool around and get naked and spend a lot of time lip-locked. And no matter what one of our President's once said, *oral sex is definitely sex!*

I also believe Bram is playing a big part in Angel's healing process.

He knows all about the psyche warfare training I'd received in the military and how I found the subject fascinating. Even now I still look for new books by the psychologists whose words resonate with me and enjoy educating myself further.

In my mind I've been going over Angel's experiences in relation to what I've learned about psychological trauma and post-traumatic stress disorder.

Angel missed out on essential nurturing. The subsequent abandonment caused by her mother's death when Angel was only three meant she never got the chance to make up for it. Angel was never able to confront her mother over issues of anger and fear - issues that can never be resolved now.

The bottom line is Angel wasn't loved, she wasn't even properly cared-for, and she has an underlying sense of worthlessness that she probably isn't aware of. She doesn't realize what she missed out on, and can't acknowledge the loss.

Deep down, on a subconscious level, she can't believe we think she's a wonderful, valuable, and necessary part of our lives but I hope over time she'll come to accept the truth of it just by living with our love every day.

So I'm grateful that Bram is giving my wife plenty of loving attention while I take care of fucking her endlessly and well.

Chapter 8

Angel

A session with Bram is always so relaxing, and I'm happy to see him acting like his usual self again.

Being with him is always more about the intimacy of cuddles rather than electrifying sex. The sex is always great, but I feel he craves closeness just as much, if not more, than ejaculation.

We're together for about two hours and I spend that time wrapped in his arms while we kiss, caress, and compliment each other with sweet nonsense talk:

"My big daddy is so strong and muscular, I feel completely safe when you hold me."

"Baby girl's kisses are so sweet with her soft warm lips and her little hands stroking my face."

I give him a back massage while topless so I can rub my breasts against him. He turns over and fondles me gently but without any urgency, just in lazy contentment. I drift off to sleep for a bit and I think he naps as well.

After saying goodnight to Bram I continue on to our bedroom without bothering to cover up. Joel raises an eyebrow at the sight of my bare breasts but doesn't say anything.

He's lying on top of the duvet watching TV without sound. It's a huge, wall-mounted flat-screen and other than the morning news I don't remember him ever switching it on before.

"So now you're watching sports? Are you bored with me already, husband?"

"No, and I'm not watching a game. I don't really follow any teams."

I tilt my head in thought and realize that I've never actually seen Joel watch sports on TV. I don't even know what sports he played in school. He gets all his exercise in the weight room these days.

"So since you're handsome and a wonderful lover; and a skilled guitarist and a sensitive singer-songwriter; I suppose you're a brilliant athlete too, hmm Mr. Perfect?"

He smiles at my list of his accomplishments but shakes his head answering:

"Nope, never played any sports."

"Seriously? With your physique you could play basketball, football, baseball – everything!"

"My school didn't have sports so—"

"No sports? You weren't in a seminary were you?"

That makes him laugh out loud before saying:

"A military academy. Lots of physical endurance training: rope climbing, swimming, long hikes with heavy packs, that sort of thing. Boarding school, for me, was a very regimented and unpleasant experience where I was average at everything.

I like watching hockey during the play-offs but I don't play although I can skate. I probably could have done okay as an athlete because of my build but I'm pretty sure I'd have made a lousy jockey."

I laugh at that and comment that he at least he's *hung like a horse.*

"Well, why don't you be my lady jockey and take me for a ride?"

"You know the word for a lady jockey is just jockey. Male or female doesn't matter."

"Oh Chickie, it always matters."

"You're a Neanderthal."

He agrees, grabbing hold of me and insisting he needs to keep me barefoot and pregnant.

I see that he has the iPad on the bed beside him and he's set up screen mirroring. I watch him plug in a thumb drive and then the big screen comes to life. I'm blown away by what we're seeing.

It's the video taken in our honeymoon suite. Several different clips from different angles and we're both nude in every one of them. My mouth falls open as we watch.

The images are so clear, I can see the sheen of sweat on Joel's chest and, as usual, the flush of desire on mine. Now I can see my body and my facial expressions just the way Joel does.

I'm absolutely dazzled by our performance. We're both shameless and oblivious and obviously having a wonderful time! Joel is so energetic and I'm so pliable.

"Just look at that tramp," I say and he answers:

"She's a sex goddess."

"And who is the hunky guy with her?"

"Just some stud they found in the studio, I guess. But look at her. She's loving every minute of it. She's so sensuous and sexy and beautiful! And look at his face, it's like he's in awe wondering how he ever got his hands on such a prize."

"That's not me."

"Yes Angel, it really is you."

"No, that's Girlie behaving like that."

"Ahhh yes, you're right. I recognize that luscious sexual abandon."

"I could be luscious too if I wanted... but I'm a proper married lady now."

"Soon to be a mama."

"That particular fuck there where you're pounding so hard you've got my whole body shaking, that's probably when you knocked me up."

"Yeah, makes sense. It sure looks like I'm in deep."

We turn towards each other and begin kissing. He massages my breasts and soon has me stripped completely bare and is lifting me on top of him.

"Ride 'em, cowgirl," he says in a teasing voice.

I fondle my breasts, rubbing my nipples with the palms of my hands, and reply:

"Giddy-up, Horsie."

He reaches up to claim my breasts for himself and his movement shifts me so I'm looking at the TV of us naked, reflected in all the mirrors, and I get to watch us fucking while actually fucking. I remember feeling the exact same mind-blowing experience at the time when I watched us in the mirrors.

We cycle through the clips, some showing better angles then others, with Joel saying he likes the ones where he could see my face the best. A couple of times we replicate in person what we're seeing on the big screen.

Finally both of us are exhausted and he asks:

"How did it go with Bram, is he feeling better now?"

"Yeah, I think so. He seemed happy and relaxed when I left him. His dick stayed in his pants in case you were wondering."

"I was, but I wasn't going to ask."

"Then I guess you're glad I told you."

"You know, if this is Girlie on the video do you want to share it with him?"

I think about that for a bit but answer:

"No, not yet. I'd like to keep this just for us for now."

He replies with a long, penetrating kiss that leaves me dizzy then in a quiet, contented voice says: "Mine."

Chapter 9

Joel

I'm sitting talking to Bram about clearing some of the woods, thinning out the old and dying trees crowded in there. They catch fire so easily if lightning strikes. There's no urgency right now, though, we're months away from thunderstorm weather. We're both just sitting here relaxed and comfortable.

Angel comes in to Bram's office with a letter she's written to her friends Anita and Matthew Landisman.

"I've explained what happened to me back then and the situation now. I want to get in touch with them but, well it's odd but I feel I need your permission to do so."

I don't like to think of Angel's life before I met her so I wipe my face of any expression and say nothing.

Bram reaches out for the letter and thanks Angel for her consideration. He puts it down on the desk and we both read.

The gist of it tells how she was set up by Kendricks and under fire ran for her life finding shelter with us. She'd been told we were drug dealers but what she discovered was a couple of ex-military men, honorably discharged, with a brother at University majoring in Psychology. She never saw any drugs being manufactured or used.

"I'm not a gardener but I think I would have noticed fields of pot or poppies!"

She goes on to apologize to Matthew saying it's hard for her to admit but she was actually at the compound when he came looking for her. She couldn't let on because she was frightened for her life and for his and Anita's too.

"When I heard that Kendricks was killed in a robbery or mugging or whatever it was, it felt like a ton weight was lifted from my shoulders. I hadn't realized how much fear I was living under.

I know both of you were on my side but I couldn't risk you being harmed. Because it was a field team shooting at me I didn't know who I – or you – could trust.

I've also been thinking of that so-called ambush you and I walked into, Anita. The heavy price you paid is made even worse if it was caused by one of our own. I'm sorry to say I think that's possible... in fact, likely.

If you're willing to forgive me for my deception I'd love to have you come and visit here to meet Joel O'Shea, my husband. Bram you already sort of met Matthew, he's Joel's older brother and my brother-in-law. Danny isn't living here right now because he's away at school."

Angel then wrote out our phone and email details for contact, she still doesn't have her own phone, and signed it adding:

"I'm using my real first name now which is Angel, not Joanne, which is my middle name. But maybe I'll always be Joanne to you? so you can still call me that if you like."

It's a good letter with nothing to compromise us. I think about how isolated Angel must have been feeling for all these months and realize it will probably do her a world of good to re-connect with her friends.

Of course I'm jealous of that friendship but I do want her to be happy. I'm about to say *yes, I hope they can come and visit soon* but the words that actually came out of my mouth are:

"We'll discuss this and let you know our decision."

"What do you mean? What's to discuss? I am allowed to have friends, right?"

"Angel, I just told you that Bram and I will talk about it and let you know."

"You can't just dismiss me like that, Joel." She's angry and I can see her visibly struggling to maintain control. She tries to be lighthearted:

"C'mon, please-please-please-pretty-please Joel, sweetie, husband. I'll do anything you want and I already know the kind of things you want, don't I?"

She's wheedling prettily but I remain impassive and she says: "You know what they say: *Happy Wife, Happy Life.*"

"Who says that?"

"People, I guess... I don't know, it's a line from something: a movie, a TV commercial, whatever, it's become a meme and people repeat it."

"Hmm, well I don't know anything about memes and what people say but I do remember you swearing an oath before God to obey me."

"I promised to love, honor, and cherish. That's it. There was nothing in our wedding vows about obeying," she counters hotly.

"Obey me, Angel."

Bram is watching the struggle of our wills but he doesn't say anything or intervene. The three of us wait in silence until Angel crumbles. Head down, tears barely kept at bay, she nods in agreement and quickly leaves the room.

"How the fuck can you be such a prick and resist that delectable girl?" demands Bram.

"I'm not resisting, I can't fucking move right now I'm so hard. I've got to just sit here and try to think about anything but Angel."

Bram shakes his head in disbelief at my stubbornness so I try to make him understand.

"Listen, I'm inclined to say okay because I want Angel to be happy and I can't see any reason to say no, but that's why I need to talk it over with you. Bram, you're always clear-headed and you'll be able to spot any pitfalls that I might overlook by trying to please her."

"Okay, I get that. Well, let's see... you didn't leave a trail to and from the location where you killed Kendricks, and there's no connection between the two of you. You married Angel, not Agent Joanne Dwyer, so there's no obvious motive, means or opportunity."

"Yeah, and I didn't rob him, but in that neighborhood I'll bet his corpse was stripped of valuables in minutes and since his car keys were in his hand his vehicle was probably stolen too. I'm sure the cops put it down to robbery with violence.

Angel, or rather Joanne Dwyer, might have had reason to go after him - although nothing's been claimed or proven - but she doesn't have the skills to travel undetected. No one can prove she didn't leave here but neither can they prove that she did."

"I got the impression that her friends really do care about her and I can believe that, it didn't take us long to fall for her even though we knew it was probably a dumb thing to let happen. So, I think this is a good letter and she should send it.

Now we just have to hope they've forgiven her for going silent and having them worry all these months. It will be bad if they don't answer at all."

In my mind I'm not convinced that would be a bad thing. Sure, Angel will be disappointed, sad even, but she'll get over it. However I answer him saying:

"Yeah, good. Thanks Bram. Oh by the way, I'm giving you a heads-up, when I go in the bedroom I'm going to really slam the door."

"You're such a mean bastard, Joel."

"I know, I just have to keep convincing Angel of that."

"Why?"

"Fucked if I know, I just know it's something I have to do."

Chapter 10

Angel

I feel so beaten down, it's like I'm worthless. My thoughts, my feelings, my brain – they don't count - nothing matters except my body. He'll talk to me and listen to me but only when he wants sex. Otherwise he just issues orders and makes demands. It's like I'm a child and he's the parent. This is bullshit.

Well, when he comes in the bedroom to reveal the big decision I'll just be passive, no matter what the answer is. I plan to be about as animated as a blow-up sex doll. Because that's all he deserves.

I know he'll seduce me with caresses and teasing but I've got to keep my head clear. The brain is supposed to be the most powerful of the erogenous zones so I need to concentrate on not getting aroused. I'll use all of my power to tempt him without succumbing myself. That's what I'm going to do.

I don't hear him coming down the hall so when the door suddenly swingd wide, bashing into the wall and bouncing back, it startles me. However I hold my pose.

I'd considered something tempting: nude and curvy curled up on the bed; or even lying with my naked back to the door and giving him that over-the-shoulder look that's so popular on glam posters.

Instead I choose a very submissive pose with me lying in the center of the bed, naked, my legs together and crossed at the ankles and my arms stretched above my head and crossed at the wrists. Almost as if I'm tied up.

The swinging door hasn't closed properly so Joel flings it shut with all his might. I've never heard a door slammed so loudly in my life! Now he's looking at me with narrowed eyes. He looks furious and I'm frightened, but I can't let it show. I'm keeping my face expressionless although I feel my breathing has quickened.

Joel approaches the bed with his eyes travelling the length of my body. He looks from my feet all the way up to my hands.

The only thing he utters is: "Very clever."

He then flips me over and drags my body sideways on the bed to position me for sex. He lifts up my hips and tucks in my legs at the knee so that I'm bent almost in half with my arms and torso stretched out flat, my bum in the air and my pussy prominently displayed.

I'm limp and lifeless, allowing myself to be positioned without assisting or resisting.

"Don't speak, don't move, and definitely don't squeeze. Just listen and learn your lesson." His voice is menacing and cold. I feel goosebumps forming on my skin and I'm trembling but from lust just as much as fear.

So much for punishing him by being passive - apparently that's exactly what he wants! And as for me not giving in? I'm suddenly so horny it hurts.

Without warning he enters me in one long forceful thrust. He's never been this deep and I'm uncomfortable but it isn't a bad feeling physically, it's more of a mental discomfort. He's turned things around so it's me being punished.

He fills me up and then just as quickly withdraws and thrusts in again. He's definitely hitting something deep inside, probably my cervix? Joel continues applying these measured strokes as he tells me:

"This is what you are to me: a hole, a cunt, that I can take whenever I want. You belong to me. This hole is my hole, this cunt is my property. I will use you whenever and wherever. You don't ever get to tell me *no* or *not now*. I said DON'T move."

I don't realize I flinched. It's reaction to his hateful words that I want to fight but can't. I'm utterly in thrall to him.

"This is what it means to be my wife. Your body is your dowry to me. You offered, I've accepted, the deal is done."

I feel tears filling my eyes but I struggle not to cry. For some reason I know that showing any kind of weakness will be my downfall, he'll crush me. I have to stay firm.

Yet all the while he continues attacking my body with hard painful thrusts.

My clitoris is swollen and so aroused it throbs. I'm completely subdued, and it seems like this torment will last forever.

After exploding into orgasm he lifts me up against his chest while remaining inside me. With one hand he massages both my breasts and with the other he toys with my clit. I cum instantly but he doesn't stop, he brings me to ecstasy two more times.

Before I made my limbs hang loose but now I have no control over them. I'm shattered. I'm weak and helpless, just a mess of desire.

He's skilled and I can't resist, no matter what I think about him, no matter how this makes me feel about myself.

I'm sticky with his semen, mixed with my own wetness, running down my thighs. I feel like I'm nothing more than a dirty slut who deserves to be used and discarded. Now I do burst into tears.

He's grown hard again so he lays me down on my back and enters me looking into my teary wet eyes all the while. His face holds as little expression as I had hoped to show him. My tears don't move him, he's a master at this game.

When we're both sated I find myself cradled in his arms while he sits with his back against the headboard. He brushes away my tears, gently caresses my face, and bends to kiss me.

It's a glorious deep long-lasting kiss and I totally lose myself in it. I reach up to wrap my arms around his neck, pulling him closer. His hand is cupping my face, his lips are gently exploring mine, his tongue teases me. We kiss and kiss and kiss, and I've melted into a puddle of devotion.

"Chickie, I may not love you the way you want," he says, "but I do love you the best I can and with everything I have.

I force you to obey me – and I will always do so, Angel – because I'm fighting the power you hold over me. If I don't take charge I'll ending up drowning in my love for you."

"Sure, now that you've gotten laid you speak of love but what you said before... when you were, were punishing me... those were terrible words, Joel. I'm not just a cunt!"

He gives me one of his heartbreakingly handsome smiles and replies:

"Well, during the times when I'm thinking with my *little head* then sweetie, that really is all you are. The very best cunt in the whole world, though..."

"You know, people talk about someone *having another side to them* but in your case I think I've met about six different *sides* already!"

Joel squeezes me tight saying:

"And we have the rest of our lives to explore each of those and all the rest we encounter, too."

"Fucking psycho," I mutter, but he just laughs and cuddles me.

Chapter 11

Joel

I find Angel in the nursery. This was home to Bram and me and Danny as we grew up and it shows the wear-and-tear of boys. Scuff marks where shoes were kicked off, strips of wallpaper hanging down where a corner had come loose and been picked at till it peeled, a window slammed open and shut so many times it no longer stays in position.

Taking her in my arms I say: "You can change anything and everything in here, make it however you like, you know that right?"

"I just love the idea of our baby growing up here. It's a wonderful room – although yes, it could do with some fixing up – and this is a lovely home in a beautiful location. Everything is perfect, Joel. It's almost scary. "

"Yeah, that's a funny thing about human nature. It's almost like we're afraid to celebrate in case we jinx something."

"It's just superstitious nonsense but—"

"But," I interrupt her, "I have good news for you and it's something you can celebrate. Anita Landisman sent an email and everything is okay, you're all still friends."

Her eyes light up with pleasure as she exclaims:

"Really? That's so good to hear, what else does she say?"

"Come back downstairs and read it yourself. It's a long email and you'll probably want to read it a few times so you might as well be comfy."

"Oh Joel that is good news!" she hugs me tight but I can tell her mind is on the email, not me, and I'm feeling left out already.

We go down to Bram's office and I give her the passwords to the computer and the email account so she can log-in on her own.

Her eyes are already scanning the message when I say: "I'll leave you to it."

Angel stops reading to smile up at me and suggest I get us both a drink, like hot chocolate, and bring it back to the office so we can discuss the email together.

The fact that she's not shutting me out, and instead is sharing the friendship, chases away the jealous feelings and I'm happy to fetch the hot drinks.

Of course the moment I go into the kitchen Maggie's there asking what I want and insisting she will take care of it so I head back to the office. Bram arrives at the same time and is telling Angel he's happy things worked out with her friends.

"Yes, me too. Anita says they'd love to come visit but they can't get away right now because of big changes in their lives. Turns out they're not happy or comfortable in that unit any more, especially after what happened to me, and now they don't feel they can trust their fellow agents. That's terrible, you have to be able to trust your crew, it could be your life on the line.

Then, what I said in my letter just reinforced a niggling doubt Anita had had about the bear trap and the ambush. Poor woman, she was in such terrible, terrible pain that day, and had a long recuperation and physio after, too.

And they don't like the new CO so Matthew put in for a transfer and got it, but there's no job for Anita at his new posting so she, oh wow, it says she's applied to the FBI and been conditionally accepted!

She can't work in the field, obviously, but still has to go for training, training that's tailored to her disability she's written, so it will be some months before they get leave. Oh, that's too bad."

"But on the bright side if it is months before they visit they'll be able to meet Baby O'Shea too."

"That's right! Oh yes, Joel, that will be something." Angel's hand automatically goes to her belly, although nothing is showing yet, and she smiles.

"Do you know this new CO she talks about?"

"Hmm, let me see what Anita writes about him... oh! Oh I do know him and he's awful. Chris Snyder was Kendricks right-hand man. I never had much to do with him, he's another one of those *all men together* types who ignored the female agents.

I always got the feeling he really hated me, but that was probably just on Kendricks' behalf. Snyder certainly never made a pass and it was very, very clear that he never would. Thank God!

Actually, I don't think he likes women period. There were rumours about him beating up prostitutes, quite badly too, but nothing came of it. I remember that one of the girls was very young, possibly even underage, and her injuries were severe. We thought he'd be booted out and maybe charged, too, but Kendricks must have covered it up for him.

The brass would never have promoted Snyder if there was even a hint of scandal so his bad behavior was kept under wraps. No wonder Matthew and Anita want to get away."

"Does this Snyder have anything specific against you personally, Angel?" Bram interjects.

"No, as I say I don't remember him ever speaking to me. I was never involved in any operations with him. Frankly, I was always glad to stay out of his way, he was obviously such an angry destructive person. I had nothing to do with the accusations made against him so he shouldn't have any kind of a grudge against me."

"Do you think he's a threat?"

She smiles and reaches over to take my hand to reassure me, explaining that while they're still breathing men like Snyder will always be a threat to women, but it's nothing personal, and nothing for me to worry about.

The unspoken thought in the minds of all three of us is *Joel doesn't need to kill him.*

Just as I was wondering what happened to our hot chocolate Maggie appears with a tray that includes three mugs and a platter piled high with homemade cookies. "

I saw Bram come in so I brought an extra cup, and here are some sweets unless you'd like sandwiches? Although dinner time's not far off so you can probably wait."

"Yes, Maggie, we can wait. Besides, I can eat Angel's share of the cookies while she's on the phone to her girlfriend."

I turn to my wife saying: "We're going to have to get you your own phone, and the sooner the better."

Chapter 12

Angel

We enjoy a leisurely dinner, especially me since I'm in such high spirits. Getting Anita's email is a delight and a relief. I'm so glad my friends have forgiven me for what I put them through. It wasn't by choice, but that doesn't make it any better. I'm lucky they're so understanding.

My good mood must be infectious because Bram is kidding around and even Joel is smiling at his jokes. Actually, Joel is looking at me quite intensely. He's got that possessive look he gets. I think he might be a teensy bit jealous of my friends. And... oh yes, he's turned on!

"Angel, I've had enough to eat. Let's go," he announces.

"Oh not yet, Joel. I want to have dessert."

He gives me a penetrating stare but I do my best to keep a straight face.

"It's chocolate mousse and you know how much I love chocolate."

"It will keep. Come with me."

"I will, but not yet. It won't take me long to eat, I'm only going to have one serving of dessert—"

"Angel, my love" interrupts Bram, "I think Joel's planning on you being his dessert!"

He's laughing at Joel and I make the mistake of joining in. Joel sighs heavily then says, in a very stern, cold voice:

"I would have thought you learned your lesson the other day but I guess I wasn't hard enough on you. Otherwise the lesson would have lasted longer."

He pauses and stares into my eyes. I've got that deer-caught-in-the-headlights feeling and, dammit, my body betrays me by starting to tingle. I say nothing.

"Go to the bedroom immediately or I will punish you right now, right here, and in front of Bram."

I don't move, I can't, but I've forgotten how fast he can. Suddenly he's right here and even though I'm no longer frozen in place I've missed my chance to get away.

He lifts me up and turns me around so that I'm kneeling on the seat of my chair and he pulls my arms over the back and holds me pressed into place. I'm wearing cut-off fleece pants and he just rips them down.

So there I am, on display, bared from waist to knees. Is he going to spank me after all? I'm helpless to prevent Joel from doing whatever he wants.

Joel slips his hand down the front of me to cup my vagina and then he starts rubbing his fingers against my clit. He quickly develops a rhythm that I can't help but respond to.

He's putting on a show for Bram with me as the reluctant performer. It's shaming and degrading and my arousal only makes those feelings of humiliation worse.

I know my bare ass is fully exposed and quivering, my thighs are trembling, and my hips will soon be gyrating although I'm doing my damnedest to keep myself in check, to try to hold on to some shred of dignity.

When his fingers start eliciting a wet, sucking sound I start to cry.

"Joel, please. Please stop. I'm begging you. I'm so sorry, I really am. Please, please stop doing this to me."

But Joel won't let me keep my pride intact.

I hate him, hate him, hate him. Normally, I enjoy getting turned on when playing the part of his helpless submissive but this time it's more than a game. Joel is determined to subdue and dominate me but not in a horny tingly way. Usually I find scenes like this so sexually exciting... but this time is different. There's no shared pleasure or joy.

Just as I'm about to explode in orgasm he stops and my devastation is complete when I start to whine.

"Do you want more my little cum-slut?" Joel asks.

I don't respond but my panting breaths sound loudly in the silent room. He slips two fingers inside me and presses lightly against my g-spot. I need him to press hard.

"Yes, I want more," I finally cry out.

"Do you want me to rub harder and faster, cum-slut?"

"Yes! Yes!"

"Tell me who you are."

I'm sobbing as I answer: "I'm, uh, your... your cum-slut."

I hear Bram clear his throat and my shame deepens but a moment later Joel's fingers drive me into a frenzy of sexual pleasure. Shaking and vibrating in a blinding lustful response.

Joel wipes his wet fingers across my ass before releasing me. My whole body sags and I'm wailing out my hurt.

But my ordeal isn't over yet.

Holding me by the nape of my neck Joel starts again but this time he slicks up his thumb along my wet slit before pushing it against my butt-hole then manipulating my clit once again. His hands are so big and his fingers so long it's an easy fit for him.

"Are you sorry for your defiance, Girlie?"

I quickly answer, "Yes, I'm so sorry, Joel."

"Will you be my obedient cum-slut now?"

He pinches hard on my clit making me scream:

"I am your obedient cum-slut, I am, yes!" and then words fail me as my vision goes black and I hear a roaring in my ears.

All of my senses have overloaded. Awareness seems to take a long time to return although I'm sure it's only a moment. My utter debasement makes me wish I could remain detached from the reality of this dining-room, these men, my wet pussy, my shame.

"Leave us, Angel, but apologize before you go."

I turn around to face Bram with my cheeks scarlet from embarrassment and wet with tears. Having him witness my humiliation is what's made this episode different.

Several times the three of us have played Joel's game of statues where I have to remain motionless while the two of them objectify me then, when I'm hot and horny, take me bed together and we have fun. This hasn't been fun.

I can't meet his eyes and there's a hitch to my voice but I do manage to say:

"I'm sorry you had to witness that, Bram. Joel, I promise I'll do better."

"Go take a cold shower, we can smell you. I don't want to see you or be around you right now."

This is worse than I thought if Joel doesn't even want to fuck me. He must be really mad to be so disgusted with me. I mean what kind of person reacts the way I did?

It's like the very first time I laid eyes on him. There I was, bent across Danny's knee having my ass beaten, when I looked up and saw Joel's smiling face and something inside me went ZING.

Is that the necessary combination? Physical pain plus shame that my predicament is amusing a handsome man equals me falling in love? That's... despicable. No wonder Joel doesn't want to take me to bed. He knows how flawed I am. I bet he regrets putting a baby inside me.

With my head hanging down I pull up my shorts and leave the room dragging my feet and sniffling. As I go through the door I hear Bram give a long drawn-out *fuuuuuuuuuuck.*

Chapter 13

Bram

"I know what you're going to say so just don't," JoeI says to me. "I'm an asshole, prick, bastard, and a cruel motherfucker who doesn't deserve her."

"Okay I won't say it, I don't need to since you're saying it yourself. But seriously Joel, what the fuck is wrong with you? You know that what you just did was all kinds of wrong, right?"

He drops his head into his hands and just mutters,

"I don't know, I don't know."

When he finally sits up his hair is mussed and his eyes look lost. That makes me angry.

"Well if you don't know what you're doing why are you doing it? If you don't have a plan why are you muddling around hurting both Angel and yourself?

When that girl – any girl – has an orgasm it should be a moment of joy, not punishment, and certainly not humiliation. These games you play with her just aren't right, Joel. It's pretty sick, actually."

"I can't help having this overwhelming need to keep her under my thumb, under control, because I'm afraid that if I don't well... I'll be... I'll, fuck I don't know!"

"Well then why not just threaten to put her across your knee? I do, and it works great."

"With Angel? You spank Angel? You know that's a sex thing that really doesn't do anything for me and besides, she told me she'd hate it."

"Well of course she'd hate it if I actually did it. Jeez, have you seen the size of my hands? No, you don't get it, the idea is simply to threaten and be menacing about it. She then gets to shiver and quiver and beg for a second chance to be a good girl while promising to do anything you ask.

It's lots of fun, actually. She gets to fulfill her fantasies of submission and I like making her happy.

You'll like it because you get to play the stern, dominant male. Next time you order her to do something you tell her you've come up with a new consequence if she's disobedient. I swear to God she will immediately perk up at those words and you will never need to actually spank her.

I don't know why corporal punishment is a turn-on for her, maybe something from her childhood? Maybe she thinks she deserves it? or sees it as the ultimate power play? I don't know, and I'm not about to guess.

I stick to the things I do know and both you and I know that Angel loves you. She loves you deeply. She will never willingly hurt you and she will always be there for you, accepting you exactly as you are.

You're so fucking lucky to have her. It's up to you to make sure that she feels she's equally lucky to have you."

I see something harden in Joel's face. I don't know if it's resolve or pigheadedness but his expression goes blank while he masters his feelings. In a stiff tone of voice he says:

"I also owe you an apology. I am sorry about what went on here, it won't happen again."

"Joel, listen. First off, what happens here with us is always gonna end up being okay. We're brothers and I love you and I know you love me back.

This thing with Angel, well you've never felt like this before for any woman. I've never had the luck – good and bad, I'm not sure which it is – to feel like that myself. I can't say I understand, but I can say that the two of you belong together. It's obvious to anyone who sees you with each other. I know, this... this whatever-it-is will work out, I'm sure of it."

A fleeting expression of hope crosses his face but he suppresses it. I can tell he's struggling to come to terms with his emotions but I don't know if he'll manage it. I don't know if he can.

He's an intelligent man and a caring man and, deep down, I'm sure he realizes just how much he needs her. Unfortunately he's the type of man who believes that kind of need makes him weak. He's wrong, but that's something he's got to figure out for himself.

"Look, I'll just say two more things. First of all: you're being a real asshole and this so-called fear of falling too hard is bullshit and we both know it.

Secondly, you owe Angel an apology, too," I conclude.

Chapter 14

Joel

I silently open the bedroom door and creep in with a dish of chocolate mousse that I leave on her nightstand. The light from the hallway shows her tear-stained face and I feel awful. I should gather her in my arms but I can't, not yet, I'm not ready. I need to figure out my feelings and thoughts first.

Then I stay up late leafing through my psychology texts but I can't concentrate on reading. I'm pretty sure they aren't going to give me any insights into my own pathology but reading gives me a few hours' distraction.

I hope Angel is still sound asleep by time I go to bed. I've never felt this way before. Going to bed has always been a pleasurable anticipation.

We have sex every night and every day as well. Just watching her bend over to pick something up is enough to whet my appetite. And she knows it – I swear sometimes when she's reaching for something she deliberately contorts her body into some lascivious display to turn me on. It works, too! I can't keep my hands off her.

And she herself has always been responsive, right from day one, even when she hated me. Sometimes she still does hate me but I always win her affections back. Have I gone too far this time? Fuck, I don't want to break her.

I can't believe I didn't run after her and bed her, that I actually told her to take a cold shower! I can't believe I told her she smelled. God knows I love the smell and the taste of her.

I realize I'd fucked up when she started crying and it wasn't a game but I just kept going. Bram's right, an orgasm should always be a wonderful, beautiful experience yet I acted like she was dirty.

Shit, I do need to apologize to her. I need to let her know that she is a blessing in my life and I think I behave badly because I'm afraid I'll lose her if I don't hold on tight.

I tried to explain some of this last time but she called me on it, and she was right. I can't call her nasty names then afterwards talk of love. But I realize now that through jealousy or fear my grip is too tight. I have to learn not to crush her, not to destroy her spirit.

I don't know if I love her so much that I'm afraid of losing myself or am I terrified of losing her? Is this how Papa felt about Mama? Is this why he treated her so badly? If I keep acting like this I'll lose Angel's love for sure. I have to find a way to express what I really feel.

I hate to admit it, but I think all of this come about because of her friends. I'm jealous and that made me need to push myself front-and-center in her thoughts. Damn.

I don't think I can deal with any more emotion tonight but when I eventually go to bed Angel turns towards me – still asleep – and pulls me close. I'm so moved by the gesture I wonder if I'll cry. I'm glad it's dark so she can't see my face all screwed up fighting back tears if she wakens.

I get my ridiculous feelings under control and clasp her to my chest whispering *I love you, I love you, I love you* over and over again to my sleeping wife.

Chapter 15

Angel

I wake up very early, not sure what time it is, except it's barely light out. I'd gone to bed, alone, very early last night.

I 'm glad to see Joel in our bed but he's turned his back and rolled away from me. It doesn't feel right reaching out to touch him. I've never hesitated before, this feeling is awful.

I decide to go out for some fresh air to clear my head. Just for a walk because Dr Moro said no to jogging and running while I'm pregnant. I don't think it's really a problem, he's probably just one of those people who don't understand the endorphin rush, but I've been following his advice.

So instead I've been taking long walks because I still need to stretch my legs and exercise my core muscles.

As I slip out of bed to get into my track suit I see the chocolate mousse dessert. Is this a peace offering? or is it a test? I'm tempted to eat it but decide I'd better leave it untouched. I hate feeling like this, but I'm going to wait and see what Joel says when I come back.

I feel everything is fragile right now. It's like I'm walking on a tightrope and I can so easily say or do the wrong thing and then – disaster!

Last night I cried myself to sleep. It was horrible. Our bed felt so big and empty, and I was so cold and lonely without Joel beside me. I felt like a horrible person who deserved to be abandoned.

I'm so ashamed of myself for being such a dirty cum-slut showing her true colors in front of the men. The same two men who took my virginity. Did they suspect the depravity that lay within that untried flesh?

How can I fix things between us? I have to, somehow! He's my whole world and I can't live like this.

I need Joel, my husband, father of my child, to love me so I can redeem myself. He tells me he does, but then I act up and push him away.

It's never been this bad before, though. We've always resolved our issues through sex. That allows me to tell him with my body the things I can't manage to say with words. But if he thinks I'm tainted, and can resist my body well... what do I have left to offer?

Chapter 16

Bram

I didn't sleep well last night, too much worrying about these two people, my family, who I love so much. When I wake up I figure I might as well stay up, if I'm tired later on I'll have a nap.

So I'm in the hallway looking out the window when I spot Angel leaving. She goes for a walk every day but usually not this early.

I realize I want to talk to her. I really, really don't want to interfere between the two of them but if I don't mention Joel, if I just talk to her about what *she's* going through and what *she's* thinking and wanting well... I won't be coming between them, I'll just be showing my concern for her.

I've got to convince her how much we all love her. Even Maggie remarks about Angel being so good for Joel. When he came home after he got his discharge there were times when it seemed he'd never find a way to be happy again. But we've all seen how he's come alive now that he's got her by his side.

Just as I make up my mind to get dressed and go I hear the door close and looking out I see Joel hurrying to catch up to her. He must have called out – or Angel heard his footsteps - because she's turned and is waiting for him.

My conscience isn't the least bit disturbed about spying on them. I'd eavesdrop if I could!

Her stance is very submissive, cowed even, almost as if she's expecting a blow. But her head is tilted up, to look at Joel, and that's a good sign. He gets close and stops. The two of them are just standing there staring at one another.

I'm waiting for them to dash into each other's arms, but that doesn't happen. Instead, and I can't believe what my eyes are seeing, Joel suddenly drops to his knees on the gravel path, holding out his hands. Kneeling he stays absolutely still while looking up at her. I wish I could see the expression on his face but maybe not, the emotion might be too raw, too uncomfortable to witness.

Angel tentatively steps forward, reaching her hands to Joel to lift him up but he pulls her down into his embrace. They hug for a long time, rocking each other, then they kiss for even longer.

I laugh lightly to myself when I realize I've been holding my breath.

I am shameless in my enjoyment of their reunion, certain that they're apologizing to each other and promising to never do that again.

At least that's what I hope because I can't take much more of their nonsense, I'm a busy man and getting on, too, so I need to get a good sleep at night.

I yawn and decide I'll head back to bed after all.

Chapter 17

Angel

I'm absolutely flabbergasted. Maggie has dropped a bombshell on us and I don't dare look anyone in the eye.

After we met up and made up this morning Joel and I walked on a little ways, hand in hand, but both of us were irresistibly drawn back to our bedroom.

We enjoyed lovely sex and an emotional reunion where we agreed that I am his cum-slut but only when he's being my Fuck-Master.

We're happy again, but we've acknowledged we have problems. First we need to identify our issues and then work together to solve them. We've drawn closer after this latest conflict so I'm hopeful.

The three of us finish a late lunch when Maggie brings in the coffee and pours herself a cup. Sitting down at the table she announces she has something to say. I immediately feel apprehensive because she isn't behaving like her usual self.

Well, no wonder. She says she's embarrassed by the conversation, but I'm mortified!

"I have two things to say. First off, we're going to have to get someone in, like a nanny, to help when the baby comes and I'll look after the hiring because well, obviously we need someone understanding and discreet."

"Discreet?" I'm puzzled by her word choice but she continues quickly, explaining:

"Because of the sex games that the three of you get up to. Don't think you've been fooling me, I know what goes on here."

My face feels frozen and I definitely can't look at either of the men. It's Joel who breaks the spell asking:

"What exactly are you saying, Maggie?" at his most forbidding.

"Don't you take that tone with me, Joel. You're too big to be spanked now but I'll wager you still remember when I took a strap to your backside for being cheeky."

Her unintended pun makes me sputter with laughter and Bram immediately joins in. Joel simply looks discomfited, obviously he does remember Maggie punishing him as a boy!

"Listen, I'm not criticizing. If somebody else told me this story sure I'd be thinking *hmm, fine goings-on there* but I know you three. You're all good people, and you're healthy, fine-looking adults who are living closely together and very happy with each other.

And I'm so glad to see you all like this. In fact, Joel, I've never seen you this happy before. It warms my heart. Angel, you truly have been a godsend."

"Um, I'm so embarrassed Maggie, but thank you for saying that. And, uh, what was the other thing?"

"Oh right. Well, none of you knows a damn thing about pregnancy so I've booked an appointment for the three of you with Dr. Moro. You're seeing him after today's surgery."

Bram says: "I don't have to go."

Just as I say: "I better go get bathed and dressed. I started some laundry but..."

"I'll finish your laundry," Maggie offers. "This is an important appointment because I told the doctor that he needs to explain everything about sex during pregnancy. You're all too old and think you're too smart to just let nature take its course, you'll be worrying and questioning everything so it's best that you get all the facts."

"Sure, but I don't need to be there…" Bram begins, but Maggie just glares at him saying:

"I don't care if it does confound the doctor about who's doing what to who - you all need to hear this stuff so yes, the three of you have to be there."

With that she drains her cup, puts it back on the tray, and leaves us alone.

"I don't know whether to laugh or cry!" I exclaim.

Joel starts to chuckle saying:

"Do you think that maybe one time when we thought she'd already gone she came back in the room and saw… well, something… and just left quietly?"

Bram laughs as he reminds Joel:

"I wouldn't have expected her to just leave quietly but hey, don't you remember when we were kids Maggie always knew what we were up to? We couldn't hide anything from her."

"Oh I remember alright, just like I remember her with that belt that she used to hang on the kitchen door handle *where it's nice and handy.*"

The two men laugh again recalling how their younger selves used to run and dodge Maggie's swinging arm.

"But she knows about me getting naked with you two, and all of us having sex!" I wail in embarrassment.

"I bet she doesn't know anything about Danny, though," puts in Joel.

"No, you're right there. I don't think she'd approve of that at all," agrees Bram.

Chapter 18

Joel

We're all quiet for a moment, thinking about Danny and that situation. I know Angel feels badly, she thinks she's caused the rift in the family, but it's not her, it's Danny himself who is the problem. It's his nature.

Since the incident with him at the cabin back in December he's pretty much stayed clear of us. When we were together, just before Christmas, we pretended nothing had happened but it was obviously on everyone's mind. I was relieved when he got that phone call to say his Christmas week ski-trip was starting early.

Bram and l talked about it. Danny is the baby brother and we both spoiled him but mostly it was Bram.

I have to go along with whatever Bram decides, this is his house so his rules, but I make sure he knows how I feel. I don't want any of us to be tiptoeing around shit.

Angel and Bram talked things over as well. Afterwards she told me she was honest about her feelings because she can never lie to Bram.

So she explained to him that Danny had frightened, disgusted, and finally angered her by his actions and words.

She goes on to promise that she can forget what happened in order to keep the family peace but she never wants Danny to ever touch, or even try to touch her, again. She adds:

"Of course this is Danny's home and he will always be welcome but it's my home now, too. He might have the history but I have the greater need. I married into the O'Shea family and have a baby on the way.

Joel and I will leave if you tell us to, but I don't believe any of us want that."

Bram reassures her that this is her home for as long as she wants it to be. He tells me afterwards that she then looks at him with her lovely open face and says:

"Thank you so, so much! I want to live here with Joel and baby and you and Maggie forever. I've never had a happy home until now. It will kill me if I have to leave."

And he says that makes him feel quite emotional. But then he asks her:

"What happens if Danny asks me if I have to be 'hands-off' with you as well?"

And Angel answers:

"What you say is up to you. Say whatever you like. But I don't feel the need to justify the choices I make. If he asks me I'll tell him the truth. Or if you prefer, I could just say that's none of his business?"

So the situation isn't resolved but we're all hoping that at least it can be buried and, with luck, forgotten. I'm sure things will change for the better once the baby arrives and Danny realizes that Angel isn't Girlie any more.

Chapter 19

Angel

If Dr. Moro is surprised to be meeting with the three of us he doesn't let on. Today is my third doctor's appointment and I really like this man. He's always so calm, unhurried, and receptive.

I begin by telling him I plan on having a home birth and he recommends a midwife. Her Hungarian name starts with a Z and is completely unpronounceable so she's called Mrs Zee-Zee.

After doing his usual tasks of measurements, weighing, blood-pressure, stethoscope, etc.. he returns to the chair behind his desk. Smiling at the three of us he says:

"Mrs. Clarke has asked me, well actually she *told* me, to talk to you about sex during pregnancy. I'm not even going to ask why I'm having this conversation with the three of you because that's not my business.

Basically, you just want to do what comes naturally." He pauses and smiled a little adding, "Whatever that might be. So, go ahead and have as much sex as you want. And, now that you're in the second trimester Mrs. O'Shea, you're probably going to want it a lot.

The hormonal changes your body is going through include an increased blood flow to your genital/erogenous zones meaning you'll be more easily aroused," The doctor pauses again, this time at Bram's strangled snort of laughter, but ignores it adding: "and your orgasms will be stronger, as much as 50% stronger."

Joel swears under his breath saying: "Jesus fucking Christ, it isn't possible!"

Just as Bram adds: "She's gonna kill you, bro."

Despite a rosy blush that shames me but heightens the doctor's interest I asked: "Okay, um, thanks. What do we.. uh, I mean I, need to avoid?"

"The most harmful thing is worry so, for example, if you have an... er, active night and next morning you discover a few spots of blood you don't need to be concerned. Make sure what you do feels good and stop if there's any discomfort. That would be unusual though, so if you are experiencing pain during intercourse then you should come back to see me.

Performing, and having oral sex performed on you, is fine but be gentle with anal—"

"Oh, that's probably not going to be an issue."

"Okay, the only other thing to avoid is tight bondage restraints..."

Bram suddenly stands and flees the room barely able to hold his laughter long enough to excuse himself. His behavior makes Joel smile but I glare at him before telling Dr. Moro:

"Again, doctor, that won't be an issue."

"Not that you can't engage in—-"

"Right. Got it. My last question is about my breasts, if Joel overstimulates me," I turn and give him an *as if* look, "will I leak milk and, if so, is that a bad thing?"

"Your breasts won't make milk until after you deliver. Right near the end of your pregnancy your breasts will produce a high-nutrient fluid called colostrum. It's what will nourish baby until your milk starts to flow. Colostrum is yellowish in color and you might leak a few drops during sex but it's not very likely and it's not a problem if you do.

I can see since your last visit that your breasts have grown and you'll probably gain another cup size before too long. Most husbands enjoy that aspect of pregnancy," he adds with a twinkle, "of course we only have one here to ask right now—-"

Joel interrupts to say: "There is only one husband and that's me. Only one husband and only one father."

"Oh! So, you're sure both are yours?"

"Yes, of course I'm...WHAT?" shouts Joel at the same time as I exclaim:

"BOTH??"

Dr. Moro is tickled pink to deliver the unexpected news.

"Yes, Mrs. O'Shea, you're carrying twins. I can very clearly hear two heartbeats."

Joel jumps up and shakes the doctor's hand which doesn't make sense to me, but I'm too stunned to make much sense of anything. Next thing I know the doctor is putting his stethoscope in my ears and positioning the instrument in the right place so I can listen.

"You might not be able to hear the beats or be able to distinguish between them since you're not a medico, but I'm absolutely certain."

I listen and can hear faint pitter pitter sounds but he's right, I can't tell them apart. I can't even identify my own heartbeat although my heart sure is pounding right now.

Then Dr. Moro has Joel bend down to get the device into his ears to listen. Joel's face fills with wonder and he pulls me close and covers my face with kisses.

Bram returns, looking slightly shamefaced as he should. And when Joel tells him the news he grins and shakes the doctor's hand too! What's up with that?

Then he gives me a full and lingering on-the-mouth kiss that no doubt validates all of Dr. Moro's suspicions regarding the three of us.

"I'm going to have to redecorate the nursery!" I cry.

"That's right! We'll need two of everything. I'll take you shopping," Joel answers.

I look at him and just shake my head saying: "Twins! My God, you O'Shea's are going to destroy my body altogether!"

Chapter 20

Joel

Everybody's been telling me that Angel is having a great pregnancy and she's doing everything exactly right. Weight control, gentle exercise, vitamins, and prenatal classes to learn breathing techniques.

I'm the one who's a mess. Only recently, but that's because she suddenly ballooned after months of just looking, well, stout. Like she wasn't even pregnant, just chubby. Then bang her stomach's out to here and it looks so heavy.

They're all making fun of me for the way I keep fussing over her. I know Angel is healthy and I'm being nothing but a nuisance but I can't help myself.

I want to help her to sit and when she has to move I want to help her to stand. I want to carry her coffee mug for her but I also want to take the coffee with its caffeine away from her.

I don't dare, though. Her coffee intake is rationed and she guards every drop. In fact, she sits with the mug balanced on her belly like she's afraid to let it out of reach.

Since she's stopped drinking I've stopped as well but that's not a hardship. None of us smoke or do drugs so nobody's had to make any big changes except for Angel.

My poor baby is suffering because of our babies. She's grown huge, although she doesn't like it when I say so, and it's become difficult for her to find a comfortable position. She has a lot of trouble sleeping through the night.

I think she's the most beautiful woman in the world and I'm overwhelmed by this sacrifice she's making for me.

And I can't stop touching her stomach. Actually I only stop so I can touch her breasts. They're enormous and look full to bursting. Creamy white with the blue veins showing through and her nipples have grown too. I'm in awe, she's so womanly.

I can't believe I've ever been mean or bossy or cold towards Angel. She's my beautiful, wonderful wife and soon she'll give birth to my children and I'm just so fucking lucky.

Being a father was never a hope or a desire for me. Not the way it is with other guys I've met. Men who want a son to carry on their family name. Some to have them follow in Dad's footsteps, while others want to give their children a better life. Either way they're devoted to the idea of fatherhood.

I guess it was something I always thought would *probably* happen, but it wouldn't be a big deal if it didn't. I would never, ever in a million years have thought I'd react this way.

Bram and Maggie are both laughing at me. Once the babies are delivered and Angel is safe and well I'm sure I'll be able to laugh too but meanwhile... I'm fucked.

Chapter 21

Angel

The nicest, most incredible thing happened with Joel today. He knows that I've been feeling blue about the way my body looks with me being so heavy and my boobs being at least two cup sizes bigger... I'm nothing but tits and tummy.

He tells me he's discussed my depressed state with Maggie and she's come up with a suggestion. What surprises me is that Joel agreed to it. He's booked me into a session of what he explains is called *Boudoir Photography*.

I don't know how Maggie even knows about this stuff but somehow she convinced Joel and he's taking me whether I want to go or not. I mean, do I really want to memorialize this ugliness?

Of course he says my body is beautiful like this but seriously? he's only talking like that because if he doesn't I'll burst into tears. There's no need to drag anyone else into the delusion just because I'm unbearably sensitive and emotional.

But we end up having a wonderful afternoon with Bobbi the photographer. From the moment we arrive she does her best to put me at ease, offering water or herbal tea, asking when I'm due and have we picked out baby's name yet? Basic small talk for preggers.

She shows me a selection of filmy, frothy negligees. I'm a bit ungracious and tell Joel to pick whatever he wants since it's his idea, after all.

He makes a good choice: a floor-length sleeveless robe with a mandarin collar. It's a lovely gown in royal blue velvet which is perfect for my coloring. And not a frill to be seen!

Bobbi also recommends that she shoot some film of me in a sheer white wraparound.

"Two very different looks and you'll be stunning in both."

I take that comment with a grain of salt but decide since I'm here anyhow I might as well behave myself and go along with the photo shoot.

Bobbie is really skilled at what she does. She soon has me relaxed and smiling naturally, despite my misgivings about the whole venture.

Starting off in the white wrapper she has me standing in a little girl pose with my hands clasped behind my back and my chin tucked down to my chest. That makes the whole front of me really stick out and she makes me laugh about it.

Then she has me kneeling on a sort of couch, it's round and quite large. Then she orders me to assume different poses and show a variety of facial expressions calling out:

'Winsome. Shy. Happy. Sassy. Teasing. Pouting."

I look over at Joel and he is mesmerized. He keeps looking from my face to my body.

Of course as I move into the selected positions the wrapper falls open but Bobbi stops me from fixing it. She says to just let it fall about naturally. Before long it has slipped down my shoulders to my elbows and is now wide open. She takes quite a few shots of me like that.

Then it's time for the gown and Bobbi insists that Joel be in this series of photos, too. He is amazingly co-operative and follows her directions to pull his shirt loose from his jeans and unbutton it. She has him recline on the divan and then I'm told to lie in his arms.

He smooths my hair back from my face and kisses me. All the while I can hear the clicking and whirring sounds of the camera. Bobbi tells Joel to caress me, strip me, and worship each inch of skin as he exposes it.

I quickly forget about both the camera and the photographer while Joel lies me down flat and fondles, nuzzles, and gazes with adoration – not disgust - at my distended stomach and swollen breasts. Soon we can't take our eyes off each other and share such an amazing feeling of intimacy.

At some point Joel took off his shirt and now he starts to pull off his jeans before remembering where we are, but Bobbi encourages him to continue saying:

"I don't mind and you'll love these photos for all of your lives."

As usual he's gone commando so now he's naked alongside me. We make love awkwardly, slowly, and gently in this room full of boudoir props, while a stranger snaps pictures, and I am grossly, heavily pregnant. Joel whispers loving endearments crying *oh, Chickie* when he climaxes.

Next week, when we come back to pick up the photo album I'm going to give Bobbi our honeymoon video to see if she can edit all the different feeds into a short film as a surprise for Joel... and maybe we'll share it with Bram, too.

Chapter 22

Joel

Holding Angel in bed tonight I'm overwhelmed by the emotional day we experienced.

I explain that I have always enjoyed every minute of sex with her whether it's hot and heavy fucking or slow and gentle love-making but today, for the first time ever, I feel even more. I've connected with her in a way that adds real meaning to my life.

I need to think of something special I can buy for her. She really doesn't want much... in fact, she doesn't even nag me about the things she does want like her drivers licence and a phone. Maybe there's something I can do for her that she'll really like?

"I've known for a long time now that I love you right down to my soul but today, making love, I just felt so heartbreakingly close to you. I felt like I couldn't be tender enough and I was almost afraid to move inside, it felt crowded. That was probably my imagination, don't you think?"

"Maybe not. I mean, everything's in the same vicinity but Dr. Moro did tell us the babies are well-protected in my uterus so it's all okay."

"Yeah, I guess. I do know that I've never had such a slow orgasm. It just lasted and lasted and felt really great."

"I noticed that, your body shuddered and you groaned but you stayed gentle the whole time."

"Well it was a new sensation and I'd like us to try to achieve that again but we can wait until after the babies are born.

Meanwhile, I'm going to get all sentimental with you my sweetheart, my darling, my adorable Angel and tell you that my love is eternal. Forever, infinite, undying, endless, neverending—"

She interrupts me to say: "Joel, I do know what the word eternal means."

Chapter 23

Angel

I feel more than ready for this pregnancy to be over even though I'm still ahead of my due date. And I keep hearing that first timers usually go late. But my arms are aching to hold my babies, and God knows my breasts are aching, too.

I have to admit I'm pretty frightened about the actual birthing process. Especially for two of them! When I asked Maggie if there really is a lot of pain or if the movies exaggerate it she tells me:

"There is pain, but you forget all about it once your babe is in your arms."

"That kind of sounds like sentimental you-know-what," I reply doubtfully.

"That's as may be, but think about it: no one would ever have more than one child if the pain was so bad they couldn't forget it afterwards."

"Yeah, that makes sense. And it's not like I can back out of the deal now," I laugh.

But Maggie senses that I still feel scared so she gives me a hug and a reminder that I'm healthy and fit and Dr. Moro has had no concerns throughout my pregnancy.

"And that Mrs ZeeZee the midwife? she's confident she'll get you through a home birth of twins with no difficulty whatsoever. I have faith in you, Angel. You'll come through this with flying colors."

Maggie's words are prophetic because not long afterwards I go into labor and... it was far better than I thought it would be. While dozing in the bed afterwards I hear Maggie and Mrs ZeeZee bragging about me to each other:

"Quickest and easiest birth I've ever witnessed. One of each, too! Absolutely perfect children. Just wonderful."

"Strongest vaginal muscles I've ever worked with," agrees the midwife. "She held when I told her to hold but when I said *push* that girl just popped those babies out. Everyone healthy and doing well. A good job all round!"

After hovering around me to the point of distraction these last couple of weeks Joel isn't even here when my water breaks. The delivery is half over before he arrives back home. I shouldn't blame him because no one expected the babies to come today, but I do feel a bit put out. Okay, actually a lot put out.

He comes in just as Mrs ZeeZee cuts our son's umbilical cord, and the look on his face is priceless. He's in time to witness our daughter's birth and actually cries tears of happiness.

He's squeezing my hand and kissing my forehead while murmuring:

"You're marvellous, marvellous, you've created a miracle, two miracles. So beautiful, Angel you are so beautiful and I love you so much, so very, very much."

He pulls back so he can look into my eyes and despite the incredible weariness I feel I'm surprised – and delighted – to look back at his clean-shaven face.

"You shaved! Joel, you're so handsome!" I exclaim. He grins at me explaining:

"That's where I've been today, I went to a barber to have my beard taken off. I wanted to get you something special, but I couldn't think of a good gift to buy. Besides, I'm sure these two have tender skin and I don't want rough hairs to rub against them. But shit I really wanted to be here for their births and for you, to hold your hand and let you yell at me." "I would have yelled too but now your face is so perfect, so handsome, I can't even think straight." "Well, I remembered all the hints you've been dropping and I thought okay, this will make Angel happy."

"It does, Joel, it really does. Thank you sweetheart. Come closer and let me feel."

I reach up my hand to his face but he brings it to his lips instead and kissing my fingers says I need to get my sleep now.

"I'm so happy... and so sleepy," I comment drowsily.

He leans on the bed to hold me and whisper endearments and compliments and praise as I thankfully drift off to sleep.

I remember thinking: *when the babies have been fed and diapered and cuddled but still scream and squall remember you played a part in all of this, too.*

Chapter 24

Bram

The O'Shea twins are born just in time for the holidays, and we're able to have them home for Christmas. Keeping up the family tradition of biblical names the children are called Adam and Eve.

Watching these tiny creatures being tenderly held in the massive arms of Daddy while watched lovingly by Mommy makes me feel so emotional. Every cliche now makes sense. My heart is full.

Danny, with his pretty girlfriend Stacey keeping close by his side, insists on family photos around the Christmas tree. They all pose in various groupings finishing with Angel and Joel and their babies.

Joel passes over his phone to me and I think he wants a picture taken too but instead I find myself looking at the photo taken last Christmas of Angel in her pink lingerie.

I finally get to look at it. Her breasts are straining to break free from the skinny red bow and the expression on her face is both knowing and innocent. This might just be the sexiest and most erotic thing I've ever seen.

I smile at Joel and pass the phone back saying:

"Girlie was great and one-of-a-kind, but Angel is better. Angel has given us all the best present. Merry Christmas, bro!"

Chapter 25

Joel

I love feeding time when it happens during the day and we're all wide awake. In a couple of weeks the twins will be introduced to a bottle of breast milk for night feedings. Mrs ZeeZee explained the benefit of combining breast and bottle feeding so now Angel is willing to give it a try.

Meanwhile, my favorite thing is to sit on the bed watching Angel with a baby suckling each breast propped into place with pillows. This afternoon Bram has *just happened* to wander by so he's come to sit in the bedroom as well.

Angel is sleepy but happy. She welcomes Bram with a smile as he brings the armchair closer to the bed to watch. It certainly is a memorable sight.

Maggie comes in right him after saying:

"Oh good, you're all here," She pauses to give an approving look at our happily thriving family. "I spoke to Dr. Moro about having sex again now that the babies are born. I asked because Angel can't be wasting her energy running back and forth to doctor appointments but I know you're all wondering."

I'm careful not to catch Bram's eye because we'll both burst out laughing. Maggie has been trying to run our lives for us since we were kids. I can look at Angel, though and her expression says she's mildly interested in the subject.

"So, the usual recommendation is to wait four to six weeks after the birth but there are no hard-and-fast rules—"

Angel interrupts to say: "I don't want Irish twins, Joel."

Bram leans forward and with a frown says: "Hate to break it to you, honey but you've already got them. The O'Shea family came from Ireland way back when."

Maggie just shakes her head at him before explaining: "*Irish twins* is an expression used when talking about babies born within twelve months of each other. It's quite common back home, but Angel's right: it's too hard on the woman's body."

"Oh shit Angel, I don't want to wear a condom and you can't take birth control since you're breastfeeding," I complain.

Well, breastfeeding is supposed to act like a natural birth control method," answers Angel.

"And it works just about as well as the rhythm method does," puts in Maggie. "I specifically asked Dr. Moro about this and he said you can have another IUD put in."

"Really? That would be best because I don't want to fall pregnant again."

"You don't want more children?" I ask, but just out of curiosity. I'm perfectly satisfied with the lovely family we have.

"I don't want to think that far in the future. I want to enjoy these two first."

I lean over Adam to reach Angel's lips and give her a lingering kiss, adding:

"Me, too."

"Yeah, yeah enough of that until we can get Angel fixed up with that device. Also, if you do decide on more kids you should wait a year or two anyhow."

"Or seven years, like our parents did," Bram puts in, with a chuckle.

"Abraham O'Shea you know perfectly well, oh! maybe you don't... but your poor mother suffered miscarriage after miscarriage between your births. That's why there's such a gap."

"Oh poor woman!" says Angel. "That must have been heartbreaking for both of them."

"Hmmph," snorts Maggie. "If Matthew O'Shea had shown a little restraint his wife wouldn't have had such a hard time of it. But that's all water under the bridge now.

So, back to the facts straight from the doctor's mouth. Right now you're low on estrogen which means vaginal dryness and low libido. Chances are you won't be that keen. However, considering how Joel has had the luck of the devil with you so far Angel, you'll probably turn out to be one of those women who enjoy sex even more after giving birth."

"Oooh, another kiss please," Angel says. Of course I comply.

"Yes, apparently some women, hang on I wrote it down here, okay some *women become more sensitive to stimulation* according to the doctor who, for some reason, found that very funny."

As do Bram and I giving in to our urge to laugh. Maggie just purses her lips and walks away in disgust with Angel calling out *thank you for finding out all this for us* after her.

Bram leaves as well and I can hear his guffaws all the way down the hall.

"Well Mrs. O'Shea, prepare yourself for a good time. I will wait the full six weeks but I'll sure be ready for you then."

"I can take care of you now, Joel. Just not with my pussy—"

I interrupt her to point out: "Chickie, you can't even keep your eyes open. But when you're ready you better believe I'll be issuing plenty of orders and demanding instant obedience... or else."

Her eyes open at that and now she's definitely looking interested. "Yup, I've been considering some new methods of disciplining you when you're defiant."

"Oh, I'm never defiant any more. I'm so bland and boring now. But I used to have a real smart mouth on me, remember? I miss being that way."

"Oh I remember all right. You thought you were so tough and I enjoyed subduing your sassiness. Hmmm, good memories."

"I'm older and wiser and not so easy to control now, mister. Although you're welcome to try."

I give her a wicked smile:

"Keep it up, Chickie. I'm memorizing every word. By the way, I had another look at our honeymoon video that you had that photographer put together for me, us, and I found myself lingering over the part where I give you four good hard smacks on your luscious ass."

She's quick to remind me: "Spanking doesn't interest you, you said so."

"Welllllll, I might have been a bit hasty. As I say, that video clip of you squirming while your pretty bum turns pink is very, very enticing. Maybe that is something we should explore..."

I hear her breathing quicken and give silent thanks to Bram for his timely suggestion.

"No, I don't think we need to think about that. In fact I'm sure of it, Joel. I promise I'll be your good and obedient wife."

I lean in close to whisper in her ear: "Maybe a naughty wife is what I really want."

She's closes her eyes again, not from sleepiness but to avoid my gaze, as she whispers back:

"Promises, promises."

Part Five

"Consensual"

Chapter 1

Bram

Our lives have settled into happy, comfortable routines – especially now that we have day and night nannies for the twins.

Angel only breastfeeds in the morning and she's out running every day, working to regain her figure. Personally, I think she looks fantastic but she's aiming for a pre-babies something-or-other.

Both Joel and I use the weight-room but he's working out way more than I am. His longer routines started out as a distraction from not having sex – hard for a couple who indulged at least twice a day - but the doctor has since given the all-clear. They just haven't done it yet, I can tell because they're both so edgy.

So, I'm in a shit-disturbing mood at lunch and decide to get the kids, that's how I think of Joel and Angel, worked up.

"Last night I was up late working on the taxes and I had the TV on but wasn't watching it, you know how you put it on just for noise, or company, or something. Anyhow, there's this old Western playing and what catches my attention is John Wayne has got the leading lady across his knee and he's spanking her! It's set in the time of the Wild West and she's wearing a white camisole and bloomers. I've heard about that Fifty Shades movie—-"

"It's a book actually, a trilogy I think," puts in Angel.

"Oh, I thought it was just a movie. Anyhow, even I've heard about it so I thought this spanking thing was a new kink but the Western I saw was from the sixties. Tell me Angel, why do you think women are turned on by this?"

"What makes you think I'd know?"

"Well you've been squirming in your seat ever since I said the word *spanking*."

"No I haven't! Besides, maybe it's the men who are turned on."

"Well, yeah I think you're right. I mean, I managed to ignore the whole movie until that scene came on and it sure grabbed my attention."

"Older movies are very sexy," declares Angel. "They don't have swearing or nudity or explicit scenes but you know all the characters are adults and they're having sex and they get the point across in such a seductive way instead of shoving it in your face."

"They had to be creative to get around the censors."

"Like the British crime dramas having to deal with criminals and solve mysteries without guns. Those detectives need a completely different skill set then the cops in North American shows."

"That's true. Remember when we disarmed you on that first day so you couldn't rely on your gun for protection—-"

"And I developed new skills rather quickly? Of course I remember!"

The two of them are ogling each other so I figure I've given them enough of a push and say,

"Well, back to working on my taxes. Poor me!"

"Bram, I've taken a lot of accounting courses, mostly forensic stuff but I could give you a hand."

"Thanks, honey. I'll keep it in mind if I run into any snags but, I have to admit, it's all pretty straightforward right now."

"Bram, before you go I just want to let you know that Angel and I are going to go use the big bathroom, we need to have a long talk."

That makes me smile, sure that there won't be a lot of talking going on.

Chapter 2

Joel

The big bathroom is a luxurious extravagance my grandfather installed in the house. It's like a Roman Bath or something and has a soaker tub that's big enough for me to stretch out. There's also a tiled surround of beautiful mosaics and the room is only lit by candles.

In my father's day the tub was converted to a jacuzzi and those streaming jets are so relaxing.

The rule is no sex in the water but there are piles of soft blankets and pillows piled along one side of the room. Nice and handy when you're feeling romantic or just downright horny.

Angel and I haven't been in the big bathroom since the twins were born although she did find some relief from floating in the water during her pregnancy.

Mrs. ZeeZee told us it was okay so long as the water wasn't too hot and Angel didn't stay in too long. Since I was happy to supervise and wash her back – among other body parts - we both enjoyed bath time. I look forward to bringing the babies in here with us when they're older.

After Bram leaves I turn to Angel and explain:

"I do have something to tell you about and I think we should be comfortable and without distractions. It's a highly personal story that I'm going to confide in you."

She directs a quizzical, slightly worried, look at me so I give her a soft kiss as reassurance.

We go straight to the big bathroom and undress each other along with more kisses and caresses as well. I'd noticed her squirming too and sure enough when I give her a quick stroke she's already moist.

Taking a good look at her body I'm thinking maybe we could delay our talk but Angel has already turned away and stepped into the water. She's still a bit shy about her post-baby figure but I see nothing to complain about.

I know she'll submit to me if I make a move, but I'd prefer to have her initiate sex. Just because Dr. Moro says we can fuck doesn't mean Angel herself is ready. So although I want her very badly I have to wait, it has to be her decision.

There are other types of intimacy besides fucking, and I think what I tell her will have a profound impact, I've never shared this story with anyone.

The whirlpool jets are turned down low so we feel the movement but aren't distracted by any noise. I lie back and stretch out with Angel nestling against me. I'm stroking and caressing her, but staying away from erogenous zones. Other than an embrace she isn't touching me at all.

"So, this isn't a pretty story but I think it will explain some things about me: about the way I am, and the way I think.

One day when I was fourteen I heard strange noises from my parent's bedroom so I went to investigate. I knew it wasn't sexual – it sounded like fighting - and it was sort of both things.

Papa was spanking Mama but not with his hand – he was using his belt. He was standing at the far side of the bed and she was lying across it. He was facing towards me so I could see everything. Mama still had her dress on, but he'd pulled it up which showed her naked behind. I looked away from that but seeing her face was even worse because she was really crying. I mean really crying, sobbing hard, but he was smiling! and it was a mean smile.

There must have been a few dozen red stripes all over her behind and her thighs that looked really painful. What I had heard was the slapping sound of his leather belt hitting her flesh and he was putting everything into it. He meant to hurt her.

When she sees me she calls out: *Go! Go away!*, and he says he'll come see me later. I'm not happy about what's going on but I have to leave because Papa's word was always final. He definitely ruled our household.

I was wishing Bram was there for me to talk to but he'd already joined the Marines, and Danny would only have been about seven at the time.

It wasn't something I could ask Maggie about because I sensed this was some dark family secret I had to protect. I don't know why, a mixture of embarrassment and shame, I guess.

It was quite awhile later when Papa came to my room and gave me the most ridiculous explanation - which even then I thought was totally unbelievable – about what I'd just witnessed.

He said that sometimes, in order to do his Christian duty, the man of the house has to punish his wife to maintain peace and harmony in the home. He called it *domestic discipline* and claimed it came down from the Old Country.

"Luckily your mother is a good and obedient wife, mostly, but I can't control my house if I can't control my woman and there are times when she needs correction. Wives will provoke their husbands into punishing them because they enjoy the release they get from the pain, the mastery, and their tears.

It's something you will face someday, son, and I hope you're man enough to shoulder the responsibility."

"But if you don't want to do it.." I started to say but he stopped me and replied:

"It's not a question of want, but of need. Listen, I love all three of my sons in different ways but equally, and I would gladly give my life to save any one of you, however, and I hope this doesn't shock you, I love your mother more.

The love I have for your mother is both a blessing and a curse. I'm lucky to have her but I'm terrified of losing her. It falls to me, as head of the family, to keep her in line. Knowing that I'm there to guide and instruct - in any way necessary - is what makes her happy. It makes her feel secure in her place within our marriage.

After three boys and over twenty years of married life my love for her has only grown stronger. She is my life."

Well, how could I argue against a statement like that? I didn't have the experience or the knowledge to challenge him. I hated to know that he physically hurt her but I do believe he was deeply in love with her. To me the two things are impossible to reconcile but we never truly know what goes on in other people's hearts and minds."

I stop speaking to give Angel time to absorb what I've said. I discover such a feeling of relief at having told that secret after so many years.

"Did your mother ever mention it?" she asks.

"Only once. The next day, after we'd eaten breakfast, and Papa went out. Mama took me into the living room so we could see the driveway and when we saw him pull away in the car she spoke quickly, all the time keeping watch in case he returned.

"Joel, I'm sorry for what you saw," she said to me, "but just know that your father has certain needs and I have a wifely duty to fulfill them. We have been married a long time.

You've never known my family, they disowned me because of the choice I made, but there's always been a lot of money waiting for me if I needed it. I could have left your father at any time. I'm here because I love him, and I love my children, and this is the life I chose."

I interrupted her then to say I couldn't stand seeing her in pain like that and she smiled briefly then hardened her voice to tell me that wasn't my business although she thanked me for my concern.

So it was an unsatisfactory conversation and I never, not with her or Papa, spoke of it again. And I never did get around to telling Bram. He always idolized Papa but he truly adored Mama and I didn't want to ruin his memories."

"So that's why the idea of spanking turns you off."

"The violence of it turned me off. Angel, I'm no stranger to inflicting pain and even death against an enemy, but to a loved one? Seeing any man ever hit a woman or a child – for any reason - is just sickening to me.

So that's mostly why, but I looked into this *domestic discipline* idea further and what I learned was disturbing. Remember I'm an adolescent at the time, looking at Internet Chat Rooms and, well...

there was no censorship of any kind. What I saw and read was pretty bad.

As Bram mentioned there are a bunch of movies and stuff out now about spanking and domination so this sort of thing is still going strong. You could look it up right now and get tons of hits for articles, websites, blogs... everything. Including photos and even video clips.

I'm telling you now Angel, I know I will never be able to spank our children and I hope you won't either. I don't blame Maggie for hitting me, hitting all of us actually, with the belt when we were kids because boys can be difficult.

Plus although she's always been devoted to the family we're not her children. When it comes to my children I know corporal punishment isn't something I'll ever be able to inflict on them."

"No, and I agree completely. I mean, I could see that if your kid is hanging over a window ledge on a high floor and you have to be all calm until you get them safely back inside then I could understand reacting by walloping them out of sheer relief that they're okay, and anger that they terrified you."

"Yeah, I can see that. Oh fuck, kids do stuff like that, don't they?"

"Well I'm sure some people's children do, but ours will be perfect, of course!" she laughs.

"But... now, after what I've told you does the idea of being spanked still turn you on?"

"Wait, these blog posts you read, is it supposed to be a turn-on or a punishment?"

"Ah, you're right. The domestic discipline practitioners make a clear distinction between spanking for pleasure and spanking for punishment.

They recommend differentiating by using the hand for pleasure spanking and an implement for punishment."

"Implement?"

"Like a paddle, belt, switch, whip, cane - each item sounds even worse than the other, doesn't it? - and to refrain from sexual behavior when punishing.

Some of those blogs described the *alpha male*, the *dominant man*, the *head of the household*, and I swear they could be talking about me! but I never meant to become this mean macho type. I evolved into it through necessity because of my military experiences.

However, I do meet the criteria of being intimidating when angry, gentle with my children, tender with my wife, but no matter how disappointed my Papa would be I will never be *man enough* to cause you physical pain. I could never in a million years become a practitioner of that lifestyle."

She turns her head and kisses me deeply and I kiss her back with pleasure. This intimacy, this closeness, is what our marriage means to me.

"Wow. I really can't wrap my head around the sort of things you've been telling me. None of that arouses me. I didn't realize stuff like that happened among regular married couples.

I mean, I know there is the whole BDSM community and that's what? BD is Bondage and Discipline, DS is Doms and Submissives, SM is Sadists and Masochists. I think that's right. Anyhow, that scene has no appeal for me. I'm a real suck when it comes to pain. I can't take it and I can't inflict it.

What you've described sounds more like some kind of marriage contract, some so-called Christian thing, where the husband must punish and the wife must accept her punishment. How can you have a normal marriage with a man who treats you like a child? I mean, even you sometimes act like a father instead of a husband and I resent it every single time."

"I know. I love seeing you trying to hold back your feelings because you know anything you say is just going to make you sound even more childish - you get yourself into quite a dilemma!

But here sit back," I pull her off my chest and lean her against the wall, "because I want to see your face when you explain why spanking arouses you."

"It doesn't, it's the thought of being spanked and the threat of being spanked that turns me on."

"Explain it. I know you have scenarios in your head so look at me and describe everything."

"I don't know about looking at you, I always fantasize and touch myself with my eyes closed."

"Not this time. I want you to look at me and I want to hear you say all the words that trigger your response. For example, I know that the words *bare bottom* get your attention but bum, butt or ass doesn't. So, give me the whole screenplay."

She tilts her head and looks at me in a speculative way before saying:

"And if I don't want to?"

"Then I'm going to think we've landed right in the middle of your fantasy since you're being a brat, and you know what will happen then, don't you?"

She laughs and admits: "You got me. Okay, here goes."

Chapter 3

Angel

"First of all, to the best of my knowledge I was never spanked as a child, and I never saw anyone else get spanked. So it's nothing to do with my repressed memories. Not this time, that is.

No, the fantasy of you giving me a spanking is a sexy, playful thing that I've brought on myself by acting saucy and deliberately pushing your buttons. You warn me that if I don't behave you'll put me over your knee for a good old-fashioned spanking on my bare bottom. It's verbal foreplay between us and it's hot.

I stick out my tongue and you're like *that's it brat, you asked for it* and you grab me but then I start to struggle and apologise and promise to be good, in fact I suggest you'd enjoy me licking your balls way more than punishing me. But you just shake your head and say *No, you had your chance and you chose disobedience.*

So of course now I'm begging you not to discipline me but you're so hardhearted you tell me you've been looking forward to spanking my lovely ass until it's rosy red. Well of course that makes me struggle even more, but I'm no match for you.

You easily overpower me and moments later I'm across your lap, facing the floor, and you're pulling my panties down.

You make sure I hear your mmm-mmm sounds of appreciation. Then you comment on how enticing my plump bottom looks quivering in anticipation. I immediately feel ashamed that here I am, a grown woman, being punished like a naughty little girl.

There are a few variations such as me begging you to leave my panties on and you insisting I need to be spanked *on the bare* in order to learn my lesson, or you chuckle saying you've been looking forward to this and warn me to *prepare for a lengthy session.*

Usually I've orgasmed by now so that's where it ends, but sometimes you actually give me a few smacks and it stings so I'm squealing and squirming right on top of your hard-on. You tell me how much you're enjoying the spectacle and that my humiliation is exquisite.

My fantasy is 100% pain-free and yeah, I have to admit I find it sexy. In fact..."

I reach for him and Joel gives me a deep, powerful kiss. He can't hide his erection while we embrace, so obviously the scenario I described has aroused us both.

We step up out of the water at the same time and head for the blankets, not even bothering to dry off.

"You're such a bad girl," he growls at me. "I think a blow job might let you off the hook but I don't know, you've got a bum like a ripe peach and it's so inviting..."

"Oh no husband, there's no need to spank me. I'll be good and I'll make it up to you. I know how to make you happy."

"Okay I'll let it go this time so long as you make me really, really happy."

I enjoy the sex talk but am a little anxious. This will be our first time since the twins were born and my body has changed, I'm sure it's changed down there too.

But Joel's kisses and caresses on top of the arousal I already feel from sharing my fantasy are enough to make me crave sex. I tell him so.

"I need to feel you inside me, I want you so much."

He enters me quickly but gently, insisting I tell him to stop if I feel any discomfort.

"The only pain I feel is the ache of my neglected clitoris," I admonish him.

He promises to make me pay for my wanton naughtiness and turns me over so he can enter from behind while rubbing my clit till I'm crying out with delight.

He is relentless.

The feel of his strong hands stroking and fondling me, his warm breath in my ear as he whispers - oooh! - delicious threats, the promise of what he'll do to my body and what he's already doing... I have missed this closeness so much.

He smells good, he feels good, and he knows exactly how to make love to me with just the right amount of strength. I've orgasmed in the doggie-style position – one of our favorites – and now he's slid me over and on top so I can ride him cowboy style.

Another fun position. He likes this because he can look into my eyes, I like it because - finally - I can see his handsome, clean-shaven face, and we both like it because he can squeeze my breasts and tease my nipples.

Omigod we can't take our eyes off each other as we climax together. Powerful orgasms and overwhelming emotion. Life has been very full since the arrival of the twins but now I'm ready to give my attention and my body back to my husband.

I'm glad we didn't rush this and I'm so happy to know how much Joel loves me. He has shown me his love by his restraint, and now he's showing me with his abandon.

And he's not complaining about my pussy being too big or loose, or my breasts and butt not being firm. He seems to be enjoying my body just as much as I'm enjoying his. I'm so lucky!

I'll make some time later to replay the story of his parents in my mind and give some serious thought about how that might have shaped his outlook. But for now I'm happy to just lie here in his arms and.. aha! now he's sliding into me for leisurely missionary-position lovemaking.

He's definitely making up for lost time and I love feeling him inside me so much. I'll have to hold on tight and make this moment last forever... at least until bedtime.

Chapter 4

Joel

I left out part of the story when I told Angel about the kink in my parents marriage. I didn't tell her that Danny became aware of what was going on and believed it was the natural order of male/female relationships.

After what Maggie said about the many miscarriages Mama suffered between our births I have to wonder if Papa caused them.

I suspect as the years passed my father's arousal might have become wholly dependent on my mother's pain. Frankly it's not something I like to think about so maybe I didn't give Danny a fair hearing when he told me what was going on. I just dismissed him by saying I already knew.

But where I was appalled he was intrigued. I think that's always biased me against him.

In retrospect, I was wrong not to talk it out and teach him another viewpoint. And I was wrong to keep Bram out of the picture. If I'd been more open then maybe these future events, what we're dealing with now, wouldn't be quite such a shock. Maybe none of this would have happened.

Danny brought his girlfriend Stacey to stay for a few days the Christmas the twins were born. She barely opened her mouth but there's nothing wrong with the quiet type. I remember Angel smacking me when I said it makes a nice change...

We all thought Stacey was a very pretty girl, slender and petite, and she clung to Danny. We all liked Stacey, even Maggie, and we thought she was good for Danny. Little did we know.

Now that they're visiting us again during the University's Spring Break we've all noticed a huge change in the girl.

Angel found out that Danny first got involved with Stacey during that ski trip the previous Christmas, the year Angel and I got engaged.

Danny was actually pursuing a young woman called Sonya who had money, brains, and beauty but no heart, no kindness, and no compassion. It was a long time afterwards that we heard the story and even from that distance we were horrified.

Apparently Sonya, Stacey, and Danny were the only ones still up late one night in the chalet. They huddled by the fire drinking red wine and telling stories.

Then Sonya suggested they play the game of *Truth or Dare* but just the *Truth* portion. Each had to tell a true story about themselves behaving badly.

Danny's true story was him spanking Girlie. He didn't mention the ins and outs of the situation at the compound, just that he'd beaten a girl's ass till she was red hot and then he and his two older brothers all gangbanged her for a few days.

Sonya's *Truth* was setting up her stepfather for a dirty weekend and then sending her mother to the hotel, pretending it was a birthday surprise. She laughed imagining the look on her stepfather's face when he opened the door expecting seduction and instead discovered *same old, same old*. She hoped her mother realized she wasn't the intended guest.

Stacey's story fell short. She talked about a very handsome piano teacher who came to her house once a week for her lesson. The female staff would all make excuses to be in the vicinity of the front door or the music room in order to see and be seen by this dreamy young man.

Stacey had such a huge crush on him she was nervous and couldn't concentrate when he sat beside her on the piano bench. One day he got fed up with her mistakes and threatened to break her little finger but he was overheard and fired for that remark.

Both Sonya and Danny look at Stacey, waiting for the punchline.

"That's it. I just felt really guilty about him losing the job because I was such a bad student."

Apparently Sonya then thought about this story and decided that Stacey craved punishment for her part in the teacher's dismissal. Sonya declared that the *Dare* portion of the game will be for Danny to break Stacey's little finger and then Sonya will have sex with him.

"Stacey gets the punishment she was promised all those years ago, I'll get turned on watching Danny hurt her, and Danny gets to do me."

Of course Stacey had no intention of letting Danny break her finger but somehow she found herself compelled to do so. She hunched her shoulders and screwed up her face in defence against the pain and held out her hand. Danny caressed it for a few strokes then broke her baby finger. Stacey's scream of pain was drowned out by Sonya's shout of excitement.

Stacey was left to awkwardly try to wrap her finger by herself while Danny and Sonya started fucking right there in front of her. Stacey's heart was broken along with her finger.

For the rest of that semester Sonya and Danny were a couple but their affair was one long battle with Sonya refusing to be submissive to Danny's self-proclaimed superiority over her. She left for the summer vacation and refused to have any further contact with him.

Danny then took up with Stacey who had been patiently waiting her turn, and soon had the girl completely under his thumb. She'd been very quiet at Christmas but on this, their second visit, she never speaks.

We also see that Stacey has become very thin which isn't surprising as she hardly eats a bite at any of our meals. She's very pale, probably the lack of nourishment, and has shadows under her eyes. Stacey is still a pretty girl because she has lovely features but there's no life or sparkle to her.

At Christmas she was painfully shy but always quick to smile, especially when looking at the babies. Now she doesn't seem interested in anything and just keeps darting nervous glances at Danny whose watchful eye never leaves her.

The blow-up happens late this afternoon. We're all gathered in the family room getting ready for dinner when Danny orders Stacey to go mix him a drink.

As she walks across the room towards the liquor cabinet Angel notices something caught on the hem of Stacey's dress and points it out to the girl. Giving a loud laugh Danny grins at Angel and explains that that's Stacey's *tail*.

Turns out this is a butt-plug with a long furry piece attached that he's making her wear a tail to prove she's his *submissive*. A tail worn with clothing that deliberately shows it off, in this case a mini-dress.

I saw some sights during my military tours – as I'm sure Bram did as well – particularly when I was embedded in the poorest places where life is cheap, but this is sickening.

I make sure my expression is neutral but I can see the confusion playing across Angel's face.

Danny, showing off, orders Stacey to strip so she can properly model her tail for us. The girl bows her head with embarrassment but quickly pulls the dress over her head and holding it in one hand displays her thin, naked body with the bushy tail protruding from between her tiny butt cheeks.

I have to grab hold of Angel to stop her from intervening because I've been watching Bram and know he's about to act.

We cam all see how Stacey's bones protrude and how she bears the marks of a strap or belt on her back, bum, and thighs. Her breasts are small and show signs of bruising. She's been roughly shaven and there are red marks all over her pubis.

Danny claims I'm too wrapped up in Angel to enjoy another woman so he orders Stacey to crawl over to Bram and suck his dick. The girl immediately drops to all fours and starts crawling.

I can feel Angel's eyes on me and when I meet her gaze I see blazing anger but I just tilt my head towards Bram and then Angel understands.

Stacey reaches Bram's chair and putting her hands on his knees tries to pull his legs open so she can obey Danny's command. But if Bram doesn't want to move nothing and no one is going to move him.

He looks down at Stacey and in a friendly, interested voice asks her if she is able to remove the *tail* by herself. She explains that yes, she *can* do it, but only with Danny's permission.

Bram just nods. He tells her to stand up and take the plug out. She looks to Danny who, churlishly, agrees.

Bram then lifts Stacey onto his knee and cuddles her in his lap. He tells her to put her dress back on, she's still carrying it, and says that from this moment forward she is finished with Danny.

"What the fuck, Bram, she's mine you can't—-"

Danny's protest goes no further. Bram – who is suddenly incandescent with rage – roars at him to leave the house saying no sexual sadist will ever stay under his roof. That he is ashamed and disgusted to have a brother who tortures the weak and innocent. He says he will beat Danny to a pulp if he ever lays a finger on Stacey again.

None of us have ever seen Bram this angry and we all fall silent. Maggie has come running into the room but she stops cold once she feels the tension in the air.

Bram tells Danny it's time to come to grips with his own secret self and admit that he's gay. Danny screams back that he's *not a fucking faggot* who likes men, but Bram replies:

"Well you sure as hell don't like women. You leave, now, and Stacey stays here, with me."

"No, I'm taking her back with me," argues Danny.

Bram stands up and, with a sigh because my presence is totally unnecessary yet necessary in a way that only makes sense to us brothers, I stand up as well.

Danny's glance darts between us and he curses. His choice of words shows little creativity which is disappointing for a University student. He stomps out of the room and loudly slams the front door when he leaves the house.

Stacey hasn't moved a muscle since she stood to put on her dress and now she looks frightened and lost, fighting back tears.

Bram explains she can stay with us until she has to go back to school in September.

"You'll feel much stronger in body and in mind by then," he says and Maggie chimes in to add:

"I'll see to it that Stacey here is eating and sleeping properly. We'll all take care of her."

The girl bursts into wracking sobs and Bram calmly gathers her in his arms and sits back down in the chair wrapping her securely in his embrace. She buries her face against his chest.

"Dinner will be ready in about fifteen minutes," is Maggie's only comment.

Angel and I just look at one another and shrug.

Chapter 5

Bram

Danny has broken my heart. I've always been guilty of spoiling him a little. There's fourteen years between us and I'd get a kick out of the way he'd cling to me once he started walking. As a toddler he was forever following me around.

So yeah, I've always had a soft spot but right now I'm disgusted and still so, so angry. His behavior has been depraved and despicable.

I'm really having a hard time believing any of this is true but I've seen the marks on that poor girl's starved body and... I have to accept that my baby brother is responsible. Something about him is warped.

For most of his growing up I was away with the Marines but that's no excuse. I always thought I was a pretty astute judge of character so how did I miss all the red flags with him?

I mean, I did witness his roughness when he beat Angel, and then when we found her after Bastard Cousin Kenny's attack Danny just froze. I thought he was in shock, and maybe that was part of it, but now I'm thinking – although it makes me sick – that the sight of her bloodied face and bruised body excited him.

I remember next day he called her ugly and told Joel and me to leave her alone. Ugh, I don't even want to guess at the dark thoughts he was harboring.

When I made the homosexual comment he really flew off the handle, screaming at me. I only said it to point out he doesn't like women but now I'm wondering... if he is denying his true nature that might explain why he's such an angry and dissolute man.

I couldn't care less if he is gay and I know Joel will feel the same: he'll always be our brother who we love. But I find it hard to love him right now, knowing what he's done to Stacey.

Maggie got the girl tucked up in one of the spare bedrooms and took her a hot water bottle for comfort more than warmth. This house has always been comfortable, and it's important to me to keep it well-maintained.

I sat up for awhile talking to Joel and Angel, then, after she yawned her way to bed it was just Joel and me. Although it's absolutely none of my business that didn't stop me from asking if they'd re-consummated their marriage. His satisfied smile gave me the answer I'd already sensed.

I'm glad for them. It's good to know one brother is normal, well normal-ish. I accepted the fact that Joel is a killer - although a justified killer by his standards - long ago. He follows his own set of rules. Maybe my moral compass has gotten skewed by the shit I've seen and gone through in my life but to me Joel is, and always has been, a good man.

Danny, now. That's another matter altogether. I want to get some sleep though so it's time to put thoughts of him out of my mind. I've just stripped off when I hear a timid knock on my door. It can only be Stacey.

I step back into my jeans, not bothering with my boxers, and open the door to see her tiny frame standing in the dark hallway.

In the light spilling out from my room I can see that she's wrapped in a quilt and clutching the hot water bottle to her chest. Her face has a scared expression and her body language screams *beaten down and cowed* but she politely asks for permission to come in.

I usher her into the room and she just stands there shivering, still hunched over, talking to me in a voice that's barely above a whisper. This is silly. I pick her up and carry her to my bed. I pull the duvet over top of her and I sit down on top of the cover.

"Now, repeat what you just said because I didn't hear a word of it."

"I'm afraid to be alone, can I stay here with you?"

"Aww baby, there's no need to be afraid. You're perfectly safe here in my home. You know I don't expect anything from you, right? so why would you want to stay in my room with me? "

"Because I'm not scared when I'm with you."

That touches me. This girl hardly knows me but it feels good to hear she trusts me. So I tell her of course she can stay and if I snore too loudly she's free to go back to the spare room.

That makes her shake her head saying nothing will make her leave.

So we lie there with the duvet separating us and I stroke her hair and kiss the top of her head. Eventually I can sense that she's fallen asleep. I get up and she stirs, opening her eyes but not really seeing, and I reassure her that I'm still here.

I take off my jeans again and put my boxers back on then I slide under the covers with her. She's stark naked and I didn't expect that. I'm sure Maggie would have put the girl to bed in a borrowed nightgown.

By now I'm too tired, and I've had too many conflicting thoughts today, to stay awake over any other mysteries. Mindful to keep my arm outside the duvet I place it over Stacey, holding her safely.

Just as I'm drifting off I feel her small, warm body pressing against me as she snuggles deeper into sleep.

Chapter 6

Angel

Stacey has turned out to be such a great help to our family. She's always willing to lend a hand and has appointed herself head of baby laundry which means we keep her very busy.

I did notice that she never holds either of the twins and part of me feels glad about that because I have to admit I'm not 100% convinced that everything is okay in the girl's head.

I mean, she was not only totally submissive to Danny sexually but she allowed him to control how much food went in her mouth, and how much sleep she got, and, because of that damn tail, how often she could use the toilet!

Now that her first month with us has passed she's already put on about four or five pounds and her long hair has a nice shine to it. The bruising under her eyes has disappeared and, after I got her to come outside for walks, she's developing a healthy glow in her complexion.

"Joel, are Bram and Stacey having sex?" I ask one night when we're cuddling together after just finishing a round of lovemaking ourselves.

"I would guess yes, because I know she sleeps in his bed every night, but I'm not sure. Why do you ask?" he answers.

"Because I'm nosy, and I want to know."

"Oh well then ask Maggie, she's the one who always knows what's going on around here."

"I'm not that nosy!" I say indignantly. But my lofty ideals come crashing down when Maggie takes me aside to ask what I think about Bram and *that girl*.

"Well, I don't know exactly how close they are," I hedge but Maggie soon sets me straight.

"She's sleeping in his bed but if he's spilling any seed she's swallowing it up."

"Maggie! TMI or what?!" I exclaim in a whisper-shriek.

"Well I change the bedding and I do the laundry so I can't help but know these things."

"Oh! but then that means you know how often... oh, oh from now on I'll take care of our own linens," I say, my cheeks flaming with embarrassment.

Maggie just pats my arm and tells me:

"There's no shame in a husband and wife loving each other as often as they can. You make Joel real happy, Angel, so you just keep doing that."

"He makes me very happy, too."

"Hmmph, I can tell that just by looking at you. The kind of happy glow you've got doesn't come out of a bottle of make-up.

Anyhow, Bram's got a soft spot for you, Angel. He'll tell you if you ask him what's going on with the two of them."

So I do. I find him in the family room where he's just poured himself a scotch and I take him by the arm saying:

"Walk with me Bram, I want to have a chat."

I lead him to the back door, planning on a stroll around the garden, but Joel steps out of the office to intercept us.

"What's going on?" he asks, eyeing me with suspicion.

"Bram and I are going to stretch our legs outside."

"Maybe I should join you?" Joel says, narrowing his eyes.

"Nah, bro. Angel wants to dig into my relationship with Stacey, probably at Maggie's instigation, so I'm going to satisfy her curiosity. You can come if you want but I think Angel will speak more freely if you don't."

Joel has to smile at his brother's frank reply and bows us out the door.

"So I've been outed, eh?"

"Oh Angel, you've always been transparent to me. Even when you were Girlie."

"Girlie's gone, Bram."

"Oh, I'm not so sure about that. Are you?"

I figure I know what he means and I think about it for a moment before nodding and saying,

"Yes. Girlie is gone."

"Well then, I guess it's my sister-in-law I'm talking to now, mother of my niece and nephew - the two most perfect children in the world."

"Ahhh, we're on the same side again."

"Were we ever not?"

"Possibly, I felt a bit of antagonism when you were just speaking to Joel."

"Oh honey, never worry when people speak their minds. It's when they're trying to hide something that you've got to watch your back. I can't imagine you and me ever being on opposing sides in anything."

"I'm not so sure, if we discover that Stacey plays cards then Joel and I might give you two a run for your money in a friendly game some evening."

By not pushing the subject that's on both our minds he blurts out his thoughts without prompting:

"Stacey wants to have intercourse with me and I would very much like to make love to her but I can't stop thinking about the fact that when she was ten years old I was thirty. That feels really wrong. So, what do you say to that?" He sounds defiant and sad.

"I point out the fact that when I was ten years old you were thirty-*two* and Bram, you busted my cherry, remember?"

"Oh for fuck's sakes, you're younger than Stacey?"

"Uh-huh."

"Well, you and me we've... well, it's been... many's the time we've..."

"Go find Stacey and take her to bed. You're not forcing her into doing anything, and she's lived here long enough to know there's no obligation. Go ahead and make love to her since that's what you both want.

You're a big guy Bram, and she's a slightly-built woman but don't worry, she won't break. When you're under the covers these things sort themselves out."

Bram leans over and gives me a loud, smacking kiss. Then he turns it into a lingering kiss with one hand cupping my breast to toy with my nipple.

"Thanks, honey," he says with a sweet smile. "You've given me back my confidence."

I wait until he'd gone back in the house before wandering in myself. I'm thinking pleasant thoughts when both Maggie and Joel pounce on me, eager for news. I'm happy to repeat the conversation I've just had.

"And what was with the kiss and grope?" queries Joel with one eyebrow raised. God, that man notices everything!

"Oh, I think Bram just needed a little stimulation to set him on the right track," I brag.

"Well it worked for me," he replies and, giving me a gentle swat on the ass, shepherds me down the hall and up the stairs to our bedroom.

I hope Bram and Stacey's afternoon delight will be as soul-shaking an experience as ours is sure to be!

Chapter 7

Joel

Strangely, I found myself surprised to see Bram stroking Angel's breast. I have to share her lovely tits with the twins but I never thought I'd be sharing them with anyone else ever again. My reaction makes me wonder.

Am I jealous? No, but I feel possessive and that makes me hard. I love getting an erection when Angel is within reach. Too bad we have to walk all the way upstairs. I swat her bum to make her hustle but, being contrary as usual, my wife slows down.

I told Angel on our honeymoon that anything she does to me I will do back to her but longer and harder so I will definitely draw out the foreplay and make her wait. She's been forewarned.

In fact, I feel like something different today and I wonder if she'll accommodate me? What am I thinking, of course she will – I can always bully her into letting me have my own way.

That's not something I feel proud about, I just accept it as the way it is for me and for her. She's willful and I have an overwhelming need to dominate, that's our dynamic.

Finally, we're in our bedroom. Angel is peeling off her clothes as she heads for the bed and I stand back to watch, enjoying the view. She flops down and rolls around in different positions asking me if I want her like this, on hands and knees; or like this, on her back spreadeagled; or like this and she raises herself up on her knees indicating her being on top. She's such a sexy tease!

"First I want you to undress me slowly, kissing every inch of my body, and when I'm naked I want you to jerk me off."

"What?" she exclaims in surprise.

"Yup, I want you to give me a hand-job and when you're finished that I want you to start sucking my balls and cleaning up my cock until I'm hard again. Then I'll decide what position to take you in."

She frowns and pouts saying:

"But I'm ready now. If I have to do all that I'll have to wait forever to get fucked. Please, let's have sex now and then I'll do the other stuff."

"No."

"No? Just *no* that's it? You're not even going to consider how I feel? We'll see about that!"

She climbs down from the bed and hurries over to make me change my mind by putting her arms around my neck and pressing her naked body against me.

She coos and squirms and I enjoy feeling her tits warm against my chest. My hands fall naturally to her ass which I squeeze and pinch. She's kissing my throat and neck and whispering in a little girl voice about how much she needs me inside her right now.

"Please love me, Joel. I'm so turned on. Here I am totally naked rubbing against you and you're still fully dressed. It's not fair. Come on, come to bed with me. Fuck me, husband."

I *almost* capitulate.

But I know she enjoys the games as much as I do. She's well aware that her current discomfort will be soothed again and again.

I've already told her to undress me and I'm not about to repeat myself. I lean back against the door and lace my hands behind my head, waiting. I can see her struggle but finally she's figured out that the longer I wait the longer she's going to wait.

Quickly she undoes a couple of buttons but I remind her that I want it done slowly. Then I give her a hard stare advising I won't say it again.

"Do as you're told... or else."

At my commanding tone she gives a shiver of pleasure that sets her tits bobbing and I give them an admiring glance.

Angel plants a kiss - sometimes a lick - on my skin as she slowly unbuttons my shirt. She has to tug to pull it out of my jeans which are tight with my hard-on. Her hands hesitate over my belt buckle but she's already gotten into the game so she doesn't go there yet.

Instead she pulls my shirt wide open and I lower my arms long enough to let the sleeves fall down and the shirt to fall off. She puts my arms back in the same position.

Now she strokes my shoulders, lingering over my biceps, and caresses my arms. She leans in and licks the hair in my armpit. It's a few hours since my morning shower so I'm sure I'm salty with sweat and the idea of her tasting me is a real turn-on.

Her mouth travels from one nipple to the other, sucking hard on each, and then she licks and kisses my other armpit. She repeats the process with my left shoulder, bicep, and arm. Now she's rubbing my torso with both hands, kneading and massaging.

She's really getting into it, the little vixen, and I have to struggle to maintain my self-control.

My daily workouts keep my abs firm and defined. She traces their shape with her tongue. I think I'm going to explode, but of course she's not done yet. She replaces her hands with her breasts and rubs up and down and all over my skin.

Now she's murmuring, her lips vibrating against my body, and giving contented little sighs that have me biting down hard on my bottom lip in order to hold on.

"You are the most annoying and adorable creature in creation," I gasp while she looks up at me with a delighted smile. My arousal fuels hers and she's reveling in her power.

Finally she's unbuckling my belt, unbuttoning and unzipping my jeans, and pulling them down over my thighs. Oh. So. Slowly.

Now, of course, is when I want her to hurry up and she knows it, too the little brat.

I usually don't wear shorts so I've sprung to life once the denim's out of the way and, at last! she's wrapping her hands and fingers around me. She barely has time to pump before I explode and I hear her throaty chuckle.

"On your knees," I order, trying to regain control.

"It's my pleasure to obey, Fuck-Master, the saucy wench eagerly replies," she says with a self-satisfied giggle.

Licking the length of my shaft, sucking on the tip, probing the hole with her tongue, kissing my balls then taking them in her mouth soon has me stirring again. She teases my pubic hair and reaches her other hand round to caress my ass and squeeze and pinch it, too.

When I'm ready again I bend down to lift and throw her on the bed. She lands on her back laughing gleefully, and arches her back in anticipation.

"I can't decide which position so we're just going to have to fuck in all three, wife. And now that I've already cum you can count on being twisted and turned and bent out of shape before I'm through with you.

And, I can promise I'll have you calling me Fuck-Master without the sass!"

Chapter 8

Stacey

I'm a little nervous about Bram, I mean he's a huge man so I figure he's going to be huge all over. Danny is well-endowed but we never had a lot of intercourse, he usually just ordered me to perform oral sex. When he went down on me he did a wonderful job but, sadly, it didn't happen very often.

Bram never has to order me to do anything. He's just naturally in charge. He's big and strong with a deep voice that always speaks kindly to me. He wears his beard short and it tickles when he nuzzles me. We kiss a lot and I really like it.

I get so hot imagining his big hands fondling my naked body, his thick fingers probing my pussy and pinching my clit, and when he cums I'll bet it's with a roar.

I've made it clear to him that I hope things between us will go further. Now I just have to wait for him to make the next move but I've learned to be patient. In fact, my whole life feels like it's been one long lesson.

I'm the typical poor-little-rich-girl. Growing up I had every luxury but there was no one around to give me love or affection, and every person in my vicinity was paid to be there. Some of them resented me and were mean, but most just ignored me.

Both of my parents came from wealth and Father grew their fortunes through hard work in the family business. When he died at a young age my mother stepped into his place and ran it all herself. I was effectively orphaned by the company and grew up in boarding schools.

I've never been a scholar and Mother made it clear the family business will go to her chosen successor, who won't be me, but that I'm a wealthy young woman who will always enjoy a rich income.

I feel badly about how I've disappointed her, and guilt because I enjoy the distance that disappointment has created between us.

I am smart enough to realize that being starved for love made me an easy target for an aggressive man like Danny. That, and my past experience in European BDSM clubs. Desperation made me the perfect submissive.

All of my life I'd been warned to stay away from poor men, who'd only be after my fortune, but Danny's family is rich so I figured he'd be a safe bet. Another one of my poor life choices...

I also realize that Bram is the ideal father-figure and he is, truly, the perfect Daddy. He is warm and protective and affectionate. I'm happy to obey and not fearful of punishment, knowing that if he does discipline me it will be fair. But that will never happen because I plan on being his perfect good girl.

We won't have a Daddy Dom and Little Girl relationship because I don't get any Dom vibes from him at all. Yes, he's a strong, confident man but I get the feeling games of challenge wouldn't appeal. Joel on the other hand... phew! I bet Angel has her hands full with him.

First, though, we've got to have sex. After I made my feelings clear he said he was going to have a drink and think things over. I prepared myself, brushing my teeth again and combing some perfume through my hair.

Now I have to wait. I wander over to the window and looking out see Bram talking earnestly with Angel. They both share a laugh and... he kisses her! Then he really kisses her and it looks like he's fondling her breast. She just smiles at him.

Where is Joel???

Chapter 9

Bram

Stacey is standing by the window when I come in and I realize she's probably seen me kissing and touching Angel. Good, we need to have this discussion anyhow.

"I was just outside with Angel, did you see us?" She nods so I continue saying: "Stacey, honey, don't be shy with me. Always answer, I like to hear your voice."

She bows her head but gives me a sweet smile answering:

"Yes, Bram. I did see you two together."

"Angel is a wonderful friend to me and I'm sure she will be to you as well as you get to know each other. What do you think?"

"I'd like that a lot because I was pretty isolated growing up so I don't have many friends. Bram, doesn't Joel mind when you tou.. I mean, kiss his wife?"

"I want to talk to you about that."

"Is this a serious-serious talk?"

"Yes, but we can be comfortable. Would you rather go sit in the family room? It's not too warm to light a fire."

"Could we lie on the bed and talk?"

That makes me smile. It brings back memories of being a young guy persuading a girl to lie back and we'll *just talk*.

Now that I've decided we can let nature take its course my libido is very interested in Stacey's suggestion so I reply:

"That's a great idea."

Stacey props the pillows up against the headboard and pulls back the comforter. She then pulls her dress over her head and slips into the bed in her underwear. She never wore any when she first came to us but I took her shopping for bras and panties.

At the time my motive was consideration for her modesty but now I'm wondering if I was planning to indulge my predilection for unhooking bras and peeling down panties even back then?

I'm not getting under the covers in my jeans and flannel shirt so I strip down to my usual bed-wear when we're together which is my boxers, and join her. She immediately snuggles against my chest and I wrap both arms around her.

Stacey looks very frail but I know there's a wiry strength under that waif-like exterior. She definitely has a strong will although I'm sure she thinks she keeps it well-hidden.

"Well, let me begin by explaining that I'm skipping the beginning of the story because it's not mine to tell, it's Angel's. And I say that because both Joel and I were shocked – and disturbed, actually - by something she told us not that long ago that showed how differently she viewed how things were when we first met than we did.

Now, I still don't believe we committed rape but she's absolutely right that nobody actually asked for her consent. We made assumptions and looking back, yeah that was wrong.

But all I can say is at the time Girlie, as we called her then, was the hottest thing I'd ever seen.

Have you ever heard the word *gobsmacked*? One of our Irish cousins uses it and it fits perfectly when describing how Girlie made us feel.

So, I'll start this story a couple of days after that meeting.

Danny, Joel, and I were living together in this ramshackle compound – we were practically camping – and Girlie was with us, shared between us, for sex.

Danny found her and thought that gave him rights but it was obvious that Joel was taking more than his fair share of turns and Girlie was smitten with him. Despite the age difference and the constant bickering between them.

Girlie had a sassy mouth on her and she just kept pushing Joel's buttons, trying to provoke him and it worked, too.

He tormented that poor girl but looking back now it was obvious she enjoyed him immensely – even while yelling at him *I fucking hate your guts!*

I laugh for a moment recalling some of their encounters. I'll have to remind them, they'll enjoy reminiscing.

"It was Girlie that Danny spanked so hard!" exclaims Stacey and I'm curious how she heard about that.

"Danny must have told you that story but why would he?"

"It was at the ski lodge with Sonya and..." she stops and folds her lips tight together, holding back the words.

"Honey, tell me."

She just looks away and shakes her head.

"Stacey, you started to say something and I've asked you to finish so I expect you to do so."

I settle back to wait, figuring there'll be some tears but determined to make her tell me. Sure enough she eventually turns back so I can see her eyes are brimming and she's chewing on her lower lip.

I calmly return her gaze, my expression open and expectant. Finally she huffs a big sigh and says:

"I did tell Angel, but I don't want to tell you because you're gonna get mad."

"Stacey, your past is not my business. I have no right to judge about anything that happened before. Aww honey, do you really believe I would ever get angry with you?"

"Not with me well, just maybe... because I let it happen but..."

I study her for a moment realizing she really is upset. Upset by a memory but also about something that will anger... oh, of course. Danny.

"Stacey, I know Danny has hurt you, we all know because we saw the marks on your body, and yes, I'm really angry with him about that but I'm not going to take it out on you!"

I pull her tight against me and stroke her hair, commenting on how pretty it smells. I feel her loosen up a bit and she starts to speak saying the words quickly:

"Sonya wanted to play a *Truth* game so Danny told us a story about giving some girl a really severe spanking and then him and his brothers gangbanging her."

I start to interrupt but then stop myself and indicate she should continue.

"Sonya's story was about agreeing to meet her stepfather in a hotel but sending her mother there instead, pretending it was a birthday surprise or something. She was mean when she speculated on whether or not her mother figured things out and hoped she did."

She stops there, but I know there's more to tell.

"C'mon, honey, what was your *Truth?*"

Stacey lets out an even bigger sigh and in a hesitant voice explains it isn't her story that will make me mad but the aftermath:

"The housekeeper overheard my piano tutor threatening to break my finger if I made another mistake. I had a major crush on him and that made me clumsy and shaky when he was around. Anyhow, he got fired and I felt guilty.

The really bad part was... well, Sonya. She said I should have my finger broken and if Danny would do it right now she'd have sex with him."

I close my eyes for a moment, not wanting to hear the rest of this story but knowing I have to.

"I wish you were going to tell me that Danny flat out refused but you're not, are you?"

She just shakes her head and lets the tears spill over. I pick up her hands and start kissing each finger from nail to knuckle.

She giggles, saying: "It was just this one," and wiggles the bent pinkie finger on her left hand.

"They all need to be kissed," I answer and proceed to do so. Then I answer her original comment:

"Yes, Danny spanked Girlie and although we thought it was a joke, to shame this law enforcement officer, it soon turned into a brutal beating. It was Joel who told him to stop, and I commented that Danny had better do an equally enthusiastic job licking her clit to make up for it."

"So did she taunt Joel to get him to spank her too?"

"No. Girlie doesn't want to be spanked, but she does like to be dominated as foreplay. Once she gets in bed she gives back as good as she gets!"

"You've been to bed with her a lot, huh?"

I look into her eyes, noticing they're a pretty hazel color. They go with the bit of red in her hair that shows up when the light catches it. I suspect Stacey has some Irish blood in her, too.

"Sorry, I was distracted by noticing what beautiful eyes you have."

She smiles at my compliment but says: "Now it's you who has to answer my question."

"Oh, I wasn't avoiding it, not really. It's just that that time has passed, long passed. But yes, I spent many hours enjoying Girlie's body and giving her as much pleasure as I could. She's a wonderful woman.

But I always knew I was only second in her affections. Joel is her man."

"How did he feel about you two getting in on?"

"Well, quite a few times the three of us had sex together."

"Lucky her!"

I laugh at that remark, remembering how at the time each of us felt we were the luckiest one in the bed.

"Girlie slept in Joel's bed every night. They always had sex before sleep and as soon as they woke up. She never said *no* to any of us. It was easy to see that Danny was in a snit so she avoided him and he didn't pursue her. Especially after she got beat up—"

"Who did that?"

"I'll save that story for another day, hon. The point is, Danny believed Girlie's injuries made her ugly but to me and Joel she remained beautiful and always will. He no longer showed her any interest, but that didn't stop him resenting us for loving her."

"I see. I guess that explains why he got so mad at everybody and set the fire."

That remark makes me sit up in a hurry and my sudden movement startles her. I frighten her when I shout out:

"WHAT? It was Danny who started the fire?"

She scuttles to the edge of the bed and cowers, hunched up against my anger. I immediately feel sorry and reach for her speaking in a soft voice:

"Sorry I scared you Stacey, I was just so shocked at what you said. I'm not mad at you, I'm mad at Danny, but you're only repeating what you heard. Come back here, baby, let me cuddle you."

She stares into my face for several long moments before trusting me enough to get close again. I've got to keep in mind that this girl has been traumatized and tortured and her ordeal will only have been made worse by knowing she allowed it to happen.

Once I have her snug in my embrace again I kiss the top of her head repeatedly.

"I know other men have hurt you but I can promise here and now that I never will. I will never harm you or let anyone else do so. You are perfectly safe with me.

Now, relax and let me finish this story. I'm almost done and then we don't have to talk about it ever again.

So, Joel and Girlie were having a hot-and-heavy affair and sometimes I joined in, sometimes I just watched, sometimes he made her perform for both of us. She does a wicked lap-dance and that girl has no inhibitions about her body. If Joel told her to masturbate she'd reply:

I'm going to have to... God knows you're not doing your job.

"So he'd grab hold of her and stroke her till she screamed with pleasure and then he'd do it again and then again and then once more. By time he'd be done with her she'd be wrung-out, limp, and whimpering but that wouldn't stop her from saying:

Okay, you're getting a bit better.

That makes Stacey laugh. She asks if Joel would then stroke Girlie again and I explain:

"No, he'd usually toss her onto my lap and tell me to fuck her till she shut up because if I didn't he might just kill her. She'd immediately climb on my cock and omigod she would be soaking wet and so hot inside.

Naturally I'd enjoy being fucked by her but I never kidded myself, it was Joel who got her in that state and it would always be Joel who really aroused her."

"So what changed between the three of you?"

"At some point those two stopped fighting long enough to realize they were deeply in love with each other. It was almost Christmas and Joel had gone away on a business trip when Girlie asked me to take her to an appointment Maggie had set up with her doctor, Dr. Moro.

Turns out Girlie used a uterus device, I can't remember the whole name, for birth control and she wanted it removed. Her Christmas present to Joel was that she would be exclusively his for intercourse so they could try for a baby and everyone would know that the child was definitely his."

"Ohhh, that's really touching. He was happy, right?"

"I guess, because he'd already bought her an engagement ring."

"That's so romantic!"

"You know it really is but if anyone would ever have used the words *Joel* and *romantic* in the same sentence I would have laughed myself silly – and so would he!

Anyhow, he decided then and there that Girlie wasn't the right name for a Mommy and asked if she wanted to go back to using Joanne. Her real name is Joanne Dwyer, except that's when we found out Joanne is actually her middle name, it's just the name she always used.

She said no, she didn't feel like Joanne anymore, and told him her Christian name is Angel. Joel loved it. He thought it suited her perfectly. I guess she'd been teased about it as a kid but it is her real name so ever since that moment she's always been Angel."

"It really does suit her," Stacey says. "I've only known her since she had the babies but seeing her with them she really does look angelic and heavenly and just beautiful with her big blue eyes and blonde hair."

"Angel is a beautiful woman, inside and out. She was always very generous with her body and in bestowing favors. One time, after they'd already gotten married, I got cranky over something and Joel suggested I take her to bed which surprised me but he pointed out she was already pregnant.

And Angel was willing, but it didn't feel right to me, not now that she was his wife. I'm pretty sure they were both relieved when I declined the offer.

However, even now I could ask Angel to sit in my lap so I could fondle her breasts and she'd be unbuttoning her top as she walked over to me. Joel wouldn't allow Danny to make a request like that but with me and them it's always been loving and respectful."

Stacey pulls herself out of my arms and turning towards me she slips her right leg over my thigh, well not quite over since she's too little for that. She holds my face in her small hands and with determination in her voice says:

"From now on when you want to fondle breasts you fondle mine, even though they aren't as big as Angel's."

I look down at her chest. She's wearing a lacy bra in pale pink and it matches her panties. Her breasts are on the slightly small side although they're filling out more now that she's eating properly, but the skin looks so soft and smooth.

I feel her tremble under my scrutiny and I tell her: "They look perfect to me."

I brush my hand across the front of her bra and feel that her nipples are hard. I continue to admire the view but when she reaches up to unhook the bra from its front closure I stop her saying:

"That's my job."

But of course I don't expose her yet, I start kissing the swell of cleavage her push-up bra causes. Placing my hands on her sides I stretch my thumbs inwards to rub her nipples through the lace.

Stacey squirms in my lap which has the desired effect on me and I transfer my lips to hers and we kiss deeply. Poor girl doesn't understand yet that with me foreplay lasts a long, long time.

Chapter 10

Stacey

Bram is big but I accommodate him without difficulty. Well, with a bit of squirming from discomfort to begin with, but it all works out well. Very, very well as a matter of fact!

He teases me for the longest time ever and I love every moment. When I try to rush him he stops me and I have to obey his authority. Such an erotic experience.

My body is like a musical instrument that first he fine-tunes and then he plays. By time he pulls my panties off I'm delirious with desire.

We're pretty much limited to me being on top since he thinks his weight will crush me. I'm not so sure but I'm willing to go along with whatever he wants. I do think that if we find a piece of furniture that's just the right height he'll be able to take me from behind while standing. I look forward to exploring our options!

After ages of over-the-bra caresses he finally unsnaps the clasp and pulls my bra open to expose my breasts. My nipples are throbbing. He compliments me, saying:

"You're beautiful, Stacey. Your breasts are so round and I love your brown nipples. Look, you nestle nicely in my hand. You look and feel just lovely my delicate little sweetheart."

He then strokes, kisses, licks, nuzzles, and fondles until I can't stay still a moment longer. I rub hard against him and enjoy feeling him respond in kind.

"Let me touch you," I beg and he smiles but said *later*.

When he finally finishes adoring my breasts he lays me flat on the bed and gently strokes me from shoulders to groin with his fingers walking up and down my flesh. I'm all over goosebumps.

His fingers keep edging closer to my slit and I feel myself pushing my bum up trying to nudge my clit against his hand. I can't stop writhing and when I try to shove my panties down he takes hold of my wrists and lifts my arms over my head. I love having him pin me down. Danny often restrained me but only for punishment, not pleasure. Bram can tie me in knots and it will make me cum.

He gently flips me over and continues stroking the back of my body. Again, as his fingers get close to the elastic of my panties, I wiggle in anticipation. Finally he bares me and kisses my bottom before turning me over once more and taking a good long look at my vagina.

Danny insisted on shaving me down there but Bram told me he prefers a natural look so I've let my pubic hair grow and now have a reddish fuzz. It must please Bram because he keeps running his fingers over it and tells me again that I'm incredibly beautiful.

His touch is so light and loving. I can't keep my legs together, it's embarrassing but I just want to spread as wide as I possibly can.

He can't help but see what I'm doing but he only smiles down at me. I'm desperate to feel him inside me, preferably his cock, but his fingers and his tongue will certainly be welcome.

He leaves me to plead with my body and just when I'm near tears he finishes drawing my panties down my legs and tosses them aside.

Finally he lifts me on top of him and I discover he's already removed his shorts. Indignantly I tell him *that's my job!* and he delights me with a rumbling chuckle.

I need two hands to guide him inside. My wetness allows me to slide down his shaft easily until I'm absolutely engorged with him. I hardly begin moving before I orgasm.

He whispers: "Good girl. Now, again."

We spend the next few hours playing with each other: fucking, kissing, and finally collapsing in joyous exhaustion. I am utterly worn out but so, so satisfied.

Chapter 11

Angel

Joel and I both enjoy a well-deserved nap after our *active*, as Dr. Moro calls it, afternoon.

When we wake I'm lying on my stomach and Joel rolls on top of me. His dick probes me like a heat-seeking missile so I pull up my knees and he lifts up to give me room. Once my pussy is fully exposed he enters and we have a slow session, me with my face turned sideways so he can kiss my cheek and mouth.

He catches hold of my hands and squeezes. There was a time when I would have pulled free but now I know I'm completely safe with him. If he holds me tight it's for our mutual pleasure and needn't cause me any grief.

Of course with both of his hands occupied and his dick in me from behind my clitoris is being sadly neglected. I point this out to him so he frees one hand but then tells me to take care of it myself.

"Lazy bastard," I comment but my hand slips into position and has just gotten busy when he pulls it away and quietly questions:

"What did you just call me?"

"Um, I wasn't.. oh I meant.. damn let me have my hand back!"

"Apologise for calling me names."

"Okay, I'm sorry I shouldn't have said that. I didn't mean it. Can I have my hand now, I'm getting desperate."

"Good. And no, you'll just have to suffer an over-stimulated clit until I'm finished."

"But it's so nice when we finish together, don't you think?"

He pauses to consider for a bit and then he releases my hand telling me he'll let me off the hook this time.

I immediately start stroking and in moments I'm out of my mind in orgiastic ecstasy. Joel quickly joins me and when we finish he turns me over and claims my mouth for a soul-stirring kiss that goes on and on.

I think we doze again because next time I open my eyes I'm lying with my head on Joel's chest.

"Joel, do you think Bram and Stacey finally got it on?"

"Probably, I guess. What exactly did you say to him?"

"It was so simple and so stupid really. He was holding back because of the age difference. He told me he's twenty years older than her so I explained that he's twenty-two years older than me so then he realized age wasn't an issue.

That's when he grabbed my tit and stroked my nipple. Then he thanked me for giving him back his confidence and went upstairs."

"Oh okay, then they're definitely fucking now."

"Jo-el, I told you before, Bram makes love."

"An-ge-el, I saw him fuck you the first time you had sex. There was nothing loving about that, it was all about his pleasure."

"Yeah, and as I recall he'd barely finished when you yanked me off him and had me bent over the arm of the chair. That definitely was a fucking."

"I love fucking you, and I always have. Every single time has been a real pleasure. I really love you, Angel."

"Yeah? What was the best time?"

"Next time."

"Wait, wha- oh! I get it. Good answer, Joel"

Of course I just melt when he talks like that and I know it's not just talk, I can see it in his eyes and in the way he holds me. Some devilish impulse in me pipes up to say:

"Are you interested in Stacey? Do you want to fuck her?"

Joel gives a loud, hearty laugh. I didn't mean it to be funny so I smack him on the chest. He looks at me shaking his head. Then he gets off the bed and pulling me to my feet marches me over to the cheval mirror that gives us a full-length view of our naked selves.

"Look at yourself, Angel. Why the fuck would I want Stacey? Sure, she's pretty but she's got the body of a child with tits - and small tits at that.

You have a magnificent rack, a slim waist, an adorable baby fat pot-belly that I hope you don't exercise away, a fantastic ass, and shapely long legs.

You are a gorgeous woman who puts up with a lot from me, who has given me the world's most beautiful babies, and who is always generous and responsive in her loving. Why the fuck would I want anyone else? Ever?"

With a speech like that what can I say? Nothing! so I drop to my knees and blow him.

Chapter 12

Joel

Inside I'm still laughing at Angel's question. Can she possibly be jealous? It's so ridiculous I can't even contemplate such an idea. I got a great blow job, though. Maybe I should try to make her jealous?

Chuckling, I walk into the dining room where Stacey and Bram are already seated.

"Since we're all late Maggie just served up and left so I guess if you want your food hot you'll have to fix a plate and take it into the kitchen to nuke."

"I will because I'm starving."

"Worked up an appetite, did you?" asks Bram slyly.

I look from him to Stacey, her face still flushed from sleep, and answer:

"I did, we both did, and it looks to me like you two did as well."

I hear Angel come in behind me and I don't have to look to know she's rolling her eyes. She immediately starts filling two plates with ham and scalloped potatoes which she takes into the kitchen.

A minute later she returns with one and puts it in front of Stacey then goes back into the kitchen just as the microwave dings again and gets the other heated plate for herself.

Bram and I just look at each other while the women add bean salad and begin to eat. I stare Angel down.

"What? Stacey's a guest and I'm a new mother who needs her strength," says Angel when she sees my face.

"Stacey's no longer a guest if she's screwed the host, and you should be serving me before yourself because that's what a good wife would do."

"Oh, sorry for your luck, Joel but you didn't get a good wife, you got me." She takes a big mouthful of scalloped potatoes and makes mmm-mmm noises smiling at me all the while.

I reach over and spear a slice of ham off her plate. She almost gets me with her fork but I am very quick. I don't bother to cut it because I don't dare put it down, and just eat it in a couple of big bites from my hand.

Meanwhile Stacey has slipped onto Bram's lap and is hand-feeding him off her plate.

"See?" I tell Angel, adding: "And they're not even married."

"That's *why* she's doing that, because he's not being a demanding husband."

I lunge towards her but she leaps from her chair so I promptly sit down and eat her food.

"You're nothing but a spoiled baby, Joel O'Shea."

"You're right, and I'll wake you up tonight with loud cries and demand some breastfeeding."

I hear her snort of laughter and pull her down onto my lap for a kiss. Obviously none of us got quite enough of each other this afternoon.

I'm surprised when Stacey giggles and tells me Bram's been entertaining her with stories of how we used bicker and taunt each other way back when.

"Nope, Bram got it wrong. It was always Angel, or rather Girlie, taunting me, I was the victim."

That makes the three of them laugh but I keep a straight face and continue:

"I'm serious. They'd gang up on me, Bram encouraging her bad behavior. One time is burned into my brain, into my heart, actually," I add dramatically. "It happened when Angel was playing with my cock. All of a sudden she tosses it down and tells me she can't look at it because it's too ugly. She says:

Joel just look at all these knobby veins, and the dark color, I mean it might feel smooth as silk along the shaft and velvety at the head but it's so ugly.

And I'm devastated! How can she not love my cock? It always makes her feel great. But then she really twists the knife in my heart when she tells me that Bram has a pretty dick and his balls are the softest skin she's ever touched."

I stop and blurt out: "Oh shit! am I saying stuff I shouldn't?"

"No bro, I already talked to Stacey about the three of us," Bram says, reassuring me.

"Oh thank Christ. Anyhow, after totally dissing my cock Angel turns her back to me and starts playing with Bram's cock and talking to it – saying it's so pretty and she just loves kissing it.

I'm so upset I go straight to the weight-room to work out my feelings on the punching bag. I beat on that body-bag until my knuckles are aching and bruised. I'm exhausted and dripping with sweat so I shower till the water runs cold before dragging myself upstairs to bed.

I look up when I reach the landing and see Angel leaning against the wall looking out the window with her back to me. Her head is resting against her upraised arm and her body is all shapely curves. When she hears me and turns around the moonlight catches her face and makes it shine. She gives me the biggest, happiest smile and right there and then I realize I'm crazy in love with her.

"Joel, that's so romantic! Aww, lucky you, Angel."

My wife practically spits saying:

"I remember that night very well and you can wipe that self-satisfied smirk off your face right now, Joel O'Shea!"

Turning to Stacey she explains: "He didn't finish the story. He literally threw me over his shoulder and carried me into our bedroom like some caveman then he pushed me down to my knees and ordered me to worship his cock."

Stacey gasps out a laugh and Angel says:

"I'm serious! He'd come upstairs wearing an old pair of sweatpants which he kicked off so he could shove his dick in my face.

Well I'd only been teasing him before but he's determined to make me say that I like his cock way better than Bram's, that I love it actually, and I just want to fawn all over it to prove that I think his is the very best."

By now the two women are laughing heartily and Bram gives me a look that says *they're nuts* and I know he totally understands me.

"Hey this might be a bit forward or pushy or something, I don't know, but I think it matters so I'm going to give you two a suggestion. And since it's unsolicited advice you certainly don't have to pay any attention to it but..."

Stacey looks from me to Angel to make sure we're listening. When I nod she continues.

"You guys need to have one night of D/s role-playing and I know the perfect scenario for you."

"What's D/s?" I ask.

"Dominant and submissive. You'd be the dominant one, Joel."

"Well duh..."

"I'm not submissive!" declares Angel.

"That's why it's called role-playing. You try it and see how it makes both of you feel. Unless you already do explore?"

"Everything I know about sex I learned from these O'Shea brothers. I've never had any other experience although I've heard stories from girlfriends and I read romance novels that are pretty explicit," answers Angel.

Not only is that news to me, it's very interesting news.

"How come you haven't shared any of those stories, wife?"

"Ooh, I will when we retire for the night, okay?"

I smile at her commenting: "There's always something to look forward to with you, Angel."

"And when you're ready to play let me know and I'll suggest a scene," adds Stacey with a knowing smile.

We finish eating, heating some of the food and having the rest cold, then carry the plates through to the kitchen. We're not allowed to tidy a thing under Maggie's strict instructions but the girls put the perishables in the fridge while Bram and I scrape and stack the dirty dishes.

"Does anyone want coffee?" asks Bram.

Angel surprises me by saying:

"I want wine. I have a craving for red wine and lots of it."

I just look at her but Bram says that's a good idea and heads down to the wine cellar. He comes back with three bottles reassuring us that there's more if we need it.

We carry the bottles into the family room where the glasses are kept behind the bar. Bram opens the bottles and pours out four glasses. He and Stacey toast each other but when I turn to Angel she's already finished her first glass.

"I'm thirsty," she explains, pouring herself another and giving me a defiant look.

"Hey, it's your hangover. Go for it."

Angel told me this afternoon that she challenged Bram and Stacey to a card game some time so I ask if anyone is interested in playing a four-handed game of gin rummy or euchre or whist. I get a second surprise, from Stacey this time, who says the only card game she knows is poker.

"That sounds like fun!" says Angel, just as Bram asks:

"What are we playing for?"

Stacey smiles and says: "Why not strip poker?"

Angel, now on her third glass of wine, nods with enthusiasm. Bram and I exchange smiles and he fetches the cards while I clear the floral centerpiece off the table and we all sit down.

"First rule is everyone has to start with an equal amount of clothing," announces Stacey, continuing: "I have three pieces on: my dress, my bra, and my panties."

"I have a shirt, jeans, boxers, and socks," replies Bram.

"No socks allowed, take them off and then you'll be down to three pieces, too."

"I only have two pieces," I tell them. They all glance at my shirt and my jeans and then at my face and start grinning.

"Well, you better not lose then, Captain Commando," is Bram's response.

"I have four," says Angel, "my top and shorts and bra and panties."

"You should take off your top then."

"No, I'm the youngest so I should get a handicap."

"Well, I'm the oldest so I should, too," replies Bram.

"But I've never played poker and you probably have."

"Then you'll probably have beginner's luck but okay, I say we let Angel have four chances to lose,"

She sticks her tongue out at him.

"First, let me run upstairs and check with the nanny that everything is okay because I don't want her coming down looking for me if we're... you know."

Angel leaves and the three of us get comfortably settled.

"Any other rules? And what game are we playing?" I ask.

Stacey starts shuffling the deck answering:

"Texas Hold 'Em."

Bram produces a rack of chips and gives us each a stack.

"At the end of each hand we count chips and determine who lost that round."

Angel comes running back saying everything is absolutely fine upstairs and the children are sleeping like babies. Then she hiccups and giggles.

"I've never actually played poker but I think I know all the hands except, does a Full House beat a Flush?"

We all answer *yes* and the game begins.

Angel loses the first round, her top comes off and she says: "Oh well, someone has to be first".

The second round her shorts come off and this time she complains that "Somebody must be cheating".

The third round she chooses to remove her panties saying: "You can't see under the table so..."

"It would have been smarter to take off you bra, Angel. Then you would have distracted the men and had a much better chance," admonishes Stacey.

Bram loses the next round and loses his shirt. He always wears a t-shirt in the weight room so it's been awhile since I had a good look at his physique. Damn, he's in terrific shape. Both Stacey and Angel are enjoying an eyeful as well.

Angel loses the round after that and now she is fully naked. She's allowed to play until she loses another hand. She looks at her cards, takes a drink of her wine, and folds – for the first time.

"There's an old Italian saying that I can't remember, *fortuna carta malfortuna amore* something or other but it means *lucky in cards, unlucky in love* or the other way around but same thing. I always get lucky," she adds with another giggle.

Bram drops out after the flop and Stacey and I bet big against each other at the turn. I win the hand and she gives me hell:

"You rivered me! You should never have called my raise, you didn't have the cards."

"And yet, I won!"

Counting up the chips means Stacey loses her dress.

Angel keeps folding and I'm not sure if this is a clever strategy or if she's tipsy and has lost interest in playing.

Bram loses his jeans and then Stacey loses her bra. I make a point of having a good look at her bare chest knowing Angel will be watching me. I very slightly tilt my head towards Angel and wink at Bram.

He sees her scowl and hides a smile.

Bram ends up naked, and I finally lose a round and, following Angel's idea, take off my jeans. I'm naked except for my shirt but it's long enough to provide cover so long as I don't stand up.

Angel's folding strategy finally fails her and she's now out of the game. She casts a doubtful glance at her glass and pushes it away. Standing she declares:

"No orgies allowed!"

We all just look at her and snicker. She's buck naked, slightly swaying, and drop-dead gorgeous.

I lose my shirt next round, the hand after that puts Bram out of the game, and after the next hand I declare that Stacey is the winner.

"Where'd you learn to play poker like that?" I ask her.

She confesses that she played poker for years while in boarding school adding:

"Girls are so mean! Believe me, you don't want to get naked with a bunch of tweens and teens. Talk about body shaming!"

"Well, I raise my glass to you, you're one hell of a poker player, Stacey."

"That's my girl!" grins Bram.

"I am, aren't I?" she grins back at him.

Three of us are naked, one only has a pair of panties on, and we've all been drinking. Angel's ban on orgies has suddenly made the idea very appealing. I really don't have any interest in banging Stacey but the idea of screwing my wife in front of the other two does make my cock perk up.

"Come here, Angel. We won't have an orgy but we will fuck right here, right now. Those two can watch, or they can distract themselves, or they can leave the room, I don't care, I just know I want you immediately."

Angel totters a bit as she walks over and I grab hold of her arm and pull her onto my lap before she can fall.

"Oh Joel, I'm a terrible poker player, aren't I?"

"Yes Chickie, you are, but you're the best lay in the whole world."

"Really?"

"Uh-huh."

"We haven't had sex in a chair for a long time."

She kneels to spread her legs over my thighs and holding onto my shoulders lowers herself onto my cock. God it feels so good. There's something about being naked around other people that's such a turn-on.

Actually, I've heard there's this whole *nude in public* thing. I guess it's something like the *mile-high club*. Maybe it's the idea of being naughty in a crowd or getting aroused at the possibility of discovery.

Angel is definitely tipsy so I hold her ass and lift her up and down. She starts grinding and next thing I know she's thrown her head back and her hard nipples are in my face. I have to nibble! Her hips spasm signifying she's cum seconds before her hot wetness gushes down my shaft. A few more thrusts and I join her.

Holding her tight against my chest I look over her shoulder to see Bram and Stacey watching us with undisguised interest. Stacey's on Bram's lap now and her panties are gone.

"Your turn," I tell them.

They exchange a glance and then he smoothly lifts her into position. I turn Angel around so she can watch them, too. She settles with her head tucked under my chin and my arms wrapped around her.

In the past whenever I saw Angel astride Bram I marveled at how little she looked compared to him but Stacey is really tiny. She wiggles her narrow hips way down the shaft of his cock and her tiny ass shimmies as he holds her in place with one hand on her back. With the other hand he plays with her tits, bending his head to take one brown nipple into his mouth. After awhile he holds her by the waist and swivels her in a corkscrew kind of motion until she cries out with pleasure.

Bram doesn't even break a sweat, he just keeps rocking her and in just a minute or two more she cries out again but this time he pulls her close and buries his head over hers so we don't see his face as he orgasms. We do hear his rumbling groan, though.

I forget about them after that as I turn Angel towards me for a kiss. We both get lost in our long kisses. She closes her eyes and I kiss her eyelids while she makes contented sounds. I close my eyes too and when I open them the two of us are still snuggled in the chair but covered by an afghan.

One light has been left on so I can see well enough to carry my wife upstairs to our bedroom. I find my robe and slip it on before going into the nursery to visit the babies before I go back to sleep.

Chapter 13

Angel

I'm breastfeeding Eve and Adam and I can't stop crying. I feel so badly about having to skip a day. When Maggie saw four wineglasses she really gave me shit. And she was right. She said I can't feed them until all the wine is out of my system. That was yesterday and Maggie says it will be safe enough today.

Looking down at my two little loves I feel so guilty. Joel is lying down with us and he says:

"Don't cry, honey, they'll never find out that their Mama's a drunk who—"

"Joel DON'T!" I wail with fresh tears pouring down my face.

"Hey, I'm only teasing, Angel. And look, the babies don't like the noise so you have to stop crying. You're a wonderful mother and having one day of just bottles didn't do these two any harm. I know you've had some nipple pain from nursing but you've persevered for their sake so you've always done your part."

"But I think they do know, Joel. They've really sucking extra hard today to punish me. You shouldn't have let me drink that wine."

"Let you? Angel, you're a big girl and you have to deal with the consequences of your actions."

"You forgot, too!" I exclaim.

"I forgot, too," he admits.

"Thank God these poor children have Maggie to look out for them," I say. Maggie, who is putting linens in the hall closet, comes in then and tells me to dry my eyes.

"Don't be crying and turning your milk sour. You've already drunk the wine and now it's over. Don't forget about it, but move on and give your handsome husband a big smile."

"He is handsome, isn't he?" I answer wiping the tears from my face.

"Now that he's shaved off that horrible beard, yes he's passable."

"Oooh, *passable*! High praise indeed. Don't let it go to your head, Joel," I laugh.

He looks up and gives Maggie a lazy smile and a wink. He knows he's her favorite. She shakes her head at him saying:

"I know what that look means. You've taken Dr. Moro's advice. Other than Angel's mistake with the wine and sweetie, truly no harm done we had plenty of your milk bottled, everybody is all relaxed and happy again. And I mean everybody... we've got a happy household, indeed."

"And a lot of laundry to do, I'll bet," adds Joel slyly.

"You're right there! and feel free to lend a hand," Maggie retorts.

Joel immediately gets up, his face showing concern as he asks her seriously:

"Maggie, are we giving you too much work? You must hire help if you need it, you know you can just go ahead and make that decision yourself. We don't want to overwork you."

"No, no we're fine now that we have our two nannies. That girl, Stacey, she's been a big help too. She does all the babies' laundry, you know. She's a good girl."

"Bram's really happy with her," I say, adding: "It's lucky they found each other."

"Well... she is awfully young."

Laughing, Joel tells: "Don't go there, Maggie she's two – almost three – years old than Angel."

"Never! She's just a slip of a girl."

"Right, whereas I'm still a whale with all my baby fat..."

"Don't be silly," Maggie dismisses my complaints as nonsense. "That reminds me that photographer, that Bobbi, she called saying she wants to do a photo shoot with you two and the twins. You know, this here makes a lovely picture with the four of you. I'll call her and say to come by at this time tomorrow."

"Joel? What do you think," I ask doubtfully.

"Oh Angel, Maggie's suggestion is absolutely right on. It's a great idea, thanks! This will be our most beautiful picture. And Angel, you and I have got some terrific photos," he adds with a leer.

"Okay, if you guys are sure... then yes, let's save this for posterity. If you don't mind calling Bobbi for us Maggie, that would be great."

"Consider it done."

Chapter 14

Bram

When I hear the Boudoir photographer is coming to the house I insist that Stacey and I get to watch her in action.

We all got to see Angel's pregnancy photo album but they also shared with me the album of the shots including Joel. Great stuff. This Bobbi produces fantastic results.

I want to hire her to photograph Stacey. Not yet, the girl still needs to put on a few more pounds, but when her body is back to 100% health I think sexy and beautiful photos will do wonders for her morale.

Maggie is stubbornly trying to figure out a way to cover most of Angel's breasts with a shawl while still showing the babies nursing. We all realized some time ago that it can't be done but Maggie is insisting.

The photographer is certainly a patient woman. Finally Maggie throws the shawl across the room and exclaims only dirty-minded folk would see anything but beauty in this natural act.

We all quickly agree so we can move on.

Bobbie tells Joel to strip off and slip under the covers beside Angel. She then takes shots with the babies held in their parent's arms, lying on their parent's chests, cuddled by their mother who in turn is being held by their father. It's really beautiful. Especially when he starts singing love songs to the three of them.

Both Angel and Stacey are too young to know the music but Maggie nods along to familiar tunes and we both enjoy the sound of Joel's voice.

With all the shifting to pose in different positions the sheet gradually slips away. Joel stretches out on his stomach, and Angel sits curled up beside him with her arm across his back, and both of them are looking at the babies on their pillows. Everyone is naked and everyone has great-looking asses. Maggie says this wasn't quite what she had in mind but admits it is artistic.

Now Joel starts singing a lullaby to the babies and Angel shifts position so that she's looking up at him with a face full of love. There are many more poses of those two adoring their children and each other. It's really a moving experience and I'm glad they let us be a part of it.

"I've taken so many pictures of people wearing pasted-on smiles that it's an absolute pleasure to photograph a truly happy, loving family," replies Bobbi to our thanks.

I realize then that I've never seen Stacey hold either of the babies so I ask her why not? She admits she's afraid of dropping them, telling me that their skulls are very fragile, and that makes her nervous.

"As an only child whose parents were both only children themselves I've never been around babies or even small children."

I get her seated in the rocking chair and Joel passes Adam to me to take over to her. I stand close beside her so she knows the baby is secure and can't fall.

Adam immediately starts searching for a nipple and Stacey gives a gentle laugh saying:

"Sorry Adam, but I have no milk for you. My breasts are too small anyhow."

"They will be exactly right for feeding when your time comes," I tell her.

"Do you think I'll ever be a mother, Bram?"

"Of course! But first I'll come and dance at your wedding."

Her face falls and I realize it's time for us to have a talk about where this relationship is, or rather isn't, going.

We return Adam to his Daddy and I take her back to our bedroom. I want to strip and fondle her while we talk since I've gotten turned on after watching Angel and Joel naked and kissing.

Gently stroking and caressing as I speak I explain to Stacey that what we have going on is really wonderful but it's only temporary.

"Don't you want me?" she asks in a small, hurt voice.

"You know I do... very, very much, and I'm going to enjoy every minute of our time together until you go back to school in the fall. Where you'll find a guy your own age."

"Huh! like Danny, you mean?"

"Hush now, you know that's not what I mean. You'll find a nice man who will love you, take care of you, and raise a family with you."

"You take care of me."

"I do, and I consider it a privilege. I'm well-rewarded with this sexy sinuous body," I pause to nuzzle and kiss her skin.

"Sinuous! Oooh, I like that!"

"Sinuous, slender, slim, and sinewy."

"What if I don't want to go back to school? What if I want to stay here with you?"

"I'm flattered, but you need your education, honey."

"Pfftt, it's just a piece of paper."

"Stacey, you know it's much more than that and all three of us here have had our schooling, I don't want you to miss out on your turn. You've invested so much time and money already. My mind's made up, honey. You're going back to University to finish your post-graduate degree."

"If I don't meet anyone, and I won't because my heart belongs to you, can I come back when I graduate? That will be next Spring."

"If you promise to try and meet someone, to attend parties and other stuff, and to keep an open mind, then... if you still feel the same way about me well... I'll be honored to welcome you back."

I surprise myself with what I've told Stacey. I had planned on making it clear that we're just having a fling so she will go back to her life – without Danny, this time – and have all the wonderful experiences a young woman should enjoy.

Instead, well... but she is sinuous and sexy and smooth and soft... and I can't resist her tender, young body. I'm a greedy and selfish dirty old man and she truly is a gift.

Chapter 15

Angel

I'm so excited! today's the day that I will finally get to see Matthew and Anita. It's been so long - too long. They're going to come early so we've got plenty of time to visit. They couldn't be sure when they'll get here so I've brought the babies downstairs for their morning feed instead of doing it in the bedroom.

Both Eve and Adam have suckled and had their little backs rubbed till they burped, but I think they might want to nurse some more so the three of us are just dozing a bit. I make everyone in the family call them Eve and Adam because Adam and Eve sounds too biblical – especially since their mother is called Angel.

Joel has had to run out to the liquor store because at the last minute I remembered Matthew and Anita are Southern Comfort drinkers. When I hear the door open again I wonder why he's come back so soon and call out:

"What did you forget, hon?"

The body of a big man, though not quite Joel's size, fills the doorway and a voice harshly snaps at me:

"I forgot to kill you when I had the chance at that meth cabin, you fucking bitch."

I sit up gasping. It's Snyder! Chris Snyder from my old unit at the DEA. What the hell is he doing here? and Danny is with him! How do they know each other?

As soon as I see Danny I slide the babies off my body and behind me, pulling up the afghan to hide them from view.

Luckily Danny doesn't even look in our direction, he hustles straight across the room and grabbing Stacey by her hair he delivers a painful slap to her face and then another, and another.

Maggie comes in then and Snyder knocks her down. As he pulls back his leg to give her a kicking I jump up and rush over, yanking on his arm to pull him away.

Meanwhile Danny is dragging Stacey towards the door snarling at her: "You're coming with me, you bitch-cunt."

"Yes of course, Danny. I want to come with you."

I feel betrayed by Stacey but then realize what she's doing is getting Danny out of the room and away from me and the babies. One less angry male to deal with. From the hallway I can hear the sound of Danny hitting her and Stacey's squeals of pain.

Snyder shakes my hands off his arm as he turns to me. I'm only wearing a dressing gown that has gaped open showing I'm nude underneath. He stares for a moment then reaches out to squeeze my breasts and painfully twist my nipples.

He grabs me roughly and it hurts but when milk leaks out his face shows disgust and he jumps back. It would be comical if I wasn't so terrified. He slaps the side of my face open-handed then wipes the milk off his fingers and onto my skin.

Since my milk has disconcerted him for a moment I'm tempted to attack but I can't. I can't risk trying anything with the babies in the room. Oh, if only Joel was here! And where the hell is Bram?

Danny yells from the front door that they've got to go, they can finish us off at the cabin, but they have to leave the house NOW.

I can see that Snyder is nerving himself to grab me so I hold my breasts up towards him feeling the milk leak out and knowing the pearly shine will distract, fascinate, and appall him.

"Snyder, listen to me, I can't go anywhere. My babies need me, they need this. This milk right here, it's nature and I need to nourish them."

I see him screw up his face, sickened, and realize the moment is lost. He couldn't care less about my babies or what they might need. He has one goal and that's to hurt me before he kills me. I have no idea why, and I don't know how I know this, but I do know it with certainty. I'm so frightened.

Danny calls out again, more urgently this time, and Snyder jumps into action. He grabs my upper arms and I try to fight him off but I'm not even wearing shoes so kicking is having no effect.

I try twisting my upper body away from him but he rabbit punches me and I feel myself falling. As I'm being dragged out of the room and out of the front door I'm dazed and struggling to stay conscious.

I feel my body being lifted up high, into a truck, but my mind can no longer hold on. I black out, slumped against the door.

Chapter 16

Matthew

"We're almost there, hon. I'm really looking forward to seeing Joanne again."

"Remember we're supposed to call her Angel now."

"Oh, right. Angel is an okay name, I think I can get used to that."

"Angel O'Shea is a pretty name. I wonder what her husband is like? Ever since we got her letter and looked up the O'Shea brothers, well, that was a lot of information to absorb."

"They're not the first military men to get involved in drug operations."

"Which we don't know for sure is true and hey, maybe they were running an op for our Government? Sorry to say it wouldn't be the first time!"

"I can't imagine Jo... I mean, Angel with twins! Last time we saw her she was vowing to stay single the rest of her life and now she's got a husband and children. You know it doesn't feel like it's been all that long since the three of us met up in training."

"I know. I wonder if Angel knows about Snyder being such good friends with Danny O'Shea? I bet she doesn't, she never mentioned it."

"She probably doesn't know then. I'm pretty sure she wouldn't like it. Every time those two come to one of our social club evenings they're always so obnoxiously loud and arrogant and abrasive. It's like they bring a wheelbarrow full of testosterone with them. Why can't Snyder be normal and bring a date? Instead of one of his whoring companions."

"Maybe Danny is his date?"

That makes me laugh out loud but then I get thinking:

"I know you're joking but... what if? That might explain their meanness towards women. Remember that quote or Shakespeare line about *the lady doth protest too much*? Maybe it's a case of that with them."

"Well, both Snyder and Danny O'Shea are big, tough guys so I suggest we keep our speculation to ourselves, right?"

I give her a nod and I'm just about to comment on the pretty countryside when Anita yells:

"HEY! Look! That's Snyder's truck racing towards us."

"No, it can't be. All those souped-up, jacked-up pick-ups look alike. You've got Snyder on the brain."

"It *is* him, I'm sure that's his truck. He didn't get the custom package, just the cheapie version, and you can see how the truck doesn't balance right on those ridiculous tires."

"That truck's going so fast we're not gonna get a good look inside but see what you can do 'cause since he and Danny O'Shea are pals it is possible he's here. We're almost at the O'Shea residence now."

The black pick-up is moving erratically and I have to give all my concentration to keeping us safe because a sudden swerve from that truck will knock us off the road. If it's not Snyder behind the wheel it's some other idiot who drives like a maniac.

The pick-up has to be doing 100 mph as it blows past us but Anita is watching closely and snapping pictures with her phone set to auto. She now yells out:

"It is him, it is. And I swear I saw Joanne sleeping, or unconscious more likely, against the window. Let me check if anything shows up on my phone…"

I don't care if Anita's right or wrong, I'm not taking any chances on Joanne's safety so I squeal into a u-turn and start pursuing.

"Who can we call for back-up!" I ask my wife and she says:

"I'm phoning Joel O'Shea."

"Good, you're armed, right?"

"Always."

Chapter 17

Bram

"What the fuck is going on here?"

The front door is open when I get home and I'm walking into a hell of a mess. The hallway mirror is swinging on one hinge, the coat-rack is tipped over, and the floor runner is all twisted up.

As I hurry into the family room I hear Joel come running in behind me, echoing my words.

The first thing I see is Maggie crumpled up on the floor and bleeding from her forehead. I kneel down beside her and hearing her ragged breathing I gently turn her into the recovery position.

Joel has found the twins on the couch, tucked under a blanket, and their little faces are soaked with tears and red with bawling.

"Where the fuck is Angel?" Joel hollers just as I'm looking around for Stacey.

His phone rings and he quickly yanks it from his pocket saying:

"It's a private number, kidnappers? WHAT?" he demands. I can hear a female voice yelling on the other end but not angry, just trying to be heard over the noise of car engines revving high and tires squealing.

"Joel? It's Anita Landisman, Matthew's wife—"

"Were you here?" he interrupts.

"No, on our way but not now, LISTEN, don't talk just listen. It's hard to hear. We're chasing after a vehicle being driven by our unit's

CO, Chris Snyder, and I think he's got Joanne, I mean Angel, with him. He's really speeding and, well, it doesn't look good."

Because she's shouting out the words I can hear her too. Joel notices me listening and hits the button to put the call on speaker. Suddenly he's dead calm as he asks her exactly where they are, what direction they're headed, what vehicle they're driving, and what this Snyder is driving.

Anita Landisman answers his questions competently and says the last sign they saw was for a secondary road if that's any help. It is, we both know exactly where they are. That secondary road is the usual route to our family's hunting cabin since it shortcuts through the woods away from the highway.

She tells Joel that she'll call for back-up but he tells her no need, we're on our way.

"You go, I'll follow as soon as I tend to Maggie. Just holler upstairs for the babies' nanny. I'll be right behind you, bro."

His face is full of anguish and anxiety but he just nods and heads out of the room stopping sharply at the door when he hears Maggie cry out:

"Where's Danny? He was here, I heard his voice..."

Fuck! Now I've got to keep one brother from killing the other one.

Chapter 18

Stacey

I'm determined to fight back and not to waste all the time and effort Bram and Maggie spent getting me well. Not for a piece of shit like Danny O'Shea. I know why he's grabbed me, he hates to lose any of his *possessions*, but I can't understand why they brought Angel, too?

He's got to know that Joel is going to be gunning for him. Maybe Bram, too. Actually yes, for sure Bram will be because he loves Angel, too. And... maybe he'll come for me as well.

At the house I was trying my best not to make Danny angry but now that we're in the truck it doesn't matter. If I can deflect him from hurting Angel then anything he does to me is worth it. She's shown me such kindness, they all have, and I'll do what I have to to repay that debt. God knows I'm used to feeling pain at Danny's hands.

"Danny, there's no point taking me with you because I don't want you anymore. I'm in love with Bram now. He's a real man and he takes care of me so well, and in every way. So, very very well..."

Smack! He's slapped my face again and oomph, he's almost winded me with a punch to my stomach. Now he's hitting the top of my head, swearing at me and calling me names. I don't care what he does to me, I can take it, but I'm not going to take it quietly.

"You're such a fucking loser, O'Shea. A real man doesn't beat up on women."

I rake my nails across his face and he yelps as blood beads in a trail of claw marks. I can't punch but I can jab at his Adam's apple holding my fingers rigid, just like I learned in that self-defence class the school put on. It makes him choke.

Then I bite down hard on his arm.

Chapter 19

Danny

What the fuck is going on? I think as Stacey, little door-mat Stacey, starts fighting me. She's scratched my face and it stings! Stupid little bitch, I'll teach her a lesson she...

"OW, STOP! JESUS FUCKING CHRIST SHE'S BITING ME! LET GO! LET GO!"

I beat her down with repeated punches to her head and the back of her neck. I'll break her fucking neck if I have to. Finally, Jesus, I can shake my arm free. Fucking cunt bitch, my arm hurts badly and I'm bleeding heavily.

She's half-fallen off the seat and I see her eyes roll up. She's out cold. Good, she'll keep until later. Now I notice that we're really speeding and we're coming up to our turn soon.

"Fuck, Chris what's going on?"

"Well if you're done with your little playmate look out the window and tell me who the fuck is chasing us."

"What? It can't be Joel already, let me see." I twist round to look out the small window at the back but I don't recognize the vehicle.

"It's a brown SUV, looks like two people inside, and I don't know them or their ride. Actually, the driver kind of looks familiar but he's wearing sunglasses and a ballcap and I can't see him clearly."

"Okay, you watch out the windshield and be ready to grab the steering-wheel while I turn and have a look."

Chris Snyder looks out his side mirrors and then leans as far over the back seat as he can before saying:

"I know that car. I've seen it in the lot at work. Who, who, who... oh, I know, it's the fucking Landisman's. What are they doing here? They transferred out of the unit.

You'll know them, you've seen them at barbeques, she's the gimp. She shoulda been dead but we can thank this bitch Joanne Dwyer for keeping her alive."

"Listen we're almost at our turn-off and it goes straight to the cabin. It's actually quicker to use from our house but it's not a good road, so we don't take it much anymore. It's really twisty and it goes deep into the bush so maybe we can lose them on it? We gotta try. The turn-off is coming up pretty soon so you'll have to slow down."

I don't know what Chris would have answered because suddenly he's standing on the brakes to avoid smashing into a car that's come blasting out from the side-road I was just talking about.

It's covered in mud with a bunch of leaves stuck all over but I'd recognize Joel's old Challenger anywhere.

He leaves it blocking the exit to the side-road, and slews sideways across the oncoming lane, our lane. He jumps out and lifts a rifle to his shoulder, taking aim.

Chris starts swinging the steering wheel round but Joel has always been an excellent shot. With any type of firearm. Firing through a windshield is no problem for him. Chris dies instantly from a bullet to the brain.

We've slowed right down since Chris had braked hard when Joel's car came out of nowhere in front of us.

The SUV behind us screeches to a halt and a man and a woman jump out of each side with their weapons drawn. They come up alongside us at a run yelling: *Law Enforcement, put your weapon down.*

I reach for the wheel to steer us to safety and when I look up I meet Joel's eyes. Now he's aiming the gun at me.

The SUV behind us screeches to a halt and a man and a woman jump out of each side with their weapons drawn. They come up alongside us at a run yelling: *Law Enforcement, put your weapon down.*

Just then a midnight-blue Lincoln Continental – Bram's choice of car for his entire driving life – comes racing down the side-road. He squeals to a stop since Joel's car is in the way and just leaves it there before bellowing:

"Put the gun down, Joel. Joel, weapon down. He's not worth it. There are two babies to raise and your wife needs your help to do that. The law can deal with..."

He doesn't need to finish because Joel carefully lays his weapon down and with the look of a man nerving himself to face the worst walks stiffly to the pick-up. He doesn't even glance my way, his eyes are only searching for one person and when he finds her he comes running.

He's on the opposite of the truck from Angel but he doesn't waste time running around the vehicle. He opens the door, pauses only a moment to lift up Stacey and gently lay her on the ground before jumping inside to grab his wife.

Angel doesn't open her eyes but she gives a little moan and I see Joel's lips move in a *thank you, God* prayer. He meets my gaze and I feel the chill of his look go right through me.

Without a word he carries Angel out of the truck and takes her over to the cops. Both the woman and the man cluster round the two of them, checking on Angel.

Bram hurries over and kneels by Stacey. He strokes the hair back from her face but pauses, studying the angle of her neck, and stops himself from gathering her in his arms. He seeks me out and shoots me a look of pure red-hot hatred. My oldest brother, the hero I always looked up to, my favorite, my family.

I don't carry a gun having never gone that whole military route like my brothers did, but I know Chris is always armed. I feel around his corpse until I find his side-arm.

I flip the safety and then I give Chris a long look. The bullet that killed him has only left a small hole, his face is still intact and he's as handsome as ever. I'm looking at him when I put the gun in my mouth and I'll keep my eyes on him as I pull the trigger.

Chapter 20

Joel

I don't even flinch when I hear the report of a handgun. Danny can't shoot so we're safe from him, and I have no interest in what he might have done to himself.

It's probably best if he took the coward's way out... neither Bram nor I should be committing fratricide. But I know I would have killed him too if Bram hadn't shown up when he did. Thank God he did.

The words he said bring me back to Angel and I experience deep, gut-wrenching fear thinking that something has happened to her. Well, something has, but I'm terrified I'll find her dead, so this is a blessing even if she is unconscious.

I'm trying to hold her gently but it's a struggle not to squeeze tight. I can't make myself let go so her friends have to administer first aid by working around me. Anita pats my shoulder while Matthew is lifting Angel's eyelid and feeling the pulse at her neck.

"She's coming round, she'll be with us real soon," he says with relief evident in his voice.

He waits until Angel opens her eyes and then the two of them go check on Stacey. I heard her coughing so I know she's alive but the Landisman's are making concerned noises about her neck.

I hear Bram's deep voice rumbling words of compassion and passion: *oh my poor baby, such a beautiful girl,* and *I love my brave little girl.* I hear him, but my brain isn't registering anything except Angel's blue eyes gaining focus and finding me.

I see her joy and relief and I'm overwhelmed. I can't even kiss her yet because I can't take my eyes off her. I noticed when I picked her up that her breasts dripped milk and now she's whispering:

"Take me home, Joel. Please. I need to hold my babies right now, I have to make sure they're okay. I know we have to deal with all this shit but I can't do that yet. What I need to do most is finish feeding Eve and Adam. Please take me home."

She's clutching my arm in her urgency and I don't even bother speaking to anyone else. I carry her to my car and once she's safely buckled in I race down the highway because I can't get around Bram's car for the shorter route. Just as well, Angel doesn't need to be bounced around on a bad road.

I'll settle her with Maggie and the twins and the nanny, and then I'll come back to help Bram clean up this mess.

I'm already thinking about the best solution and decide we should run the pick-up into a tree then set the truck on fire. But I have to remember to dig out the bullets first...

The Landisman's might take a bit of convincing but Bram can be very persuasive.

Chapter 21

Stacey

Three long weeks later and the one bright spot in all this is that there's been no more talk about me going back to school.

I know my attitude is selfish but I've had plenty of real-life education in the last couple of years and now I just want to stay here. Safe at home with Bram.

Focusing on my recovery delayed his reaction to Danny's suicide.

The official story was one of those unexplained single-vehicle crashes. Me being thrown from the pick-up was a miracle because the other two occupants died on impact with the tree. And if they managed to survive the crash they were burned to death in the subsequent fire.

There were no bullets in the bodies, and no shell casings or other evidence of shots fired at the scene. The statements from the witnesses, both employed in law enforcement, confirmed the jacked-up truck was speeding out of control when it passed them on the road.

Once my safety was assured Bram went into a badly depressed state but he's been mourning the boy Danny used to be, not the man he became. And I think Bram feels guilty that he doesn't care more.

For at least a week Maggie sported a black eye and a goose-egg bump on her forehead from the blow that Chris Snyder gave her. The whole nasty episode aged her, but she has recovered and the twins bring her joy every day.

No one talks much about what happened and it's almost like Danny is simply away at school. Nobody mentions him.

The back of my neck was damaged from the punches he delivered but Dr. Moro is taking good care of me. I wear a neck pillow to sleep but that's an improvement because at first I had to wear one of those immobilizing collars all the time.

I claimed that I was lucky not to get the *cone of shame* they put on dogs after an operation but everyone feels so badly for me they had trouble even smiling at my joke.

I have no memory of the state I was in when we were found. I've been told I was very lucky, it seems I was scarily close to paralysis from a broken neck.

Fortunately Joel was strong enough to lift me straight up and out of the vehicle so I didn't flop around or move at all. And Bram and the Landisman's recognized the danger and kept me still until the paramedics arrived.

I heard there was quite a scene at the hospital. No one had ID - or none they were willing to show - so Bram, claiming he was my father! said he'd pay cash.

Authoritative and angry... I can only imagine how intimidating he was.

A phone call home resulted in the day nanny driving Maggie to the hospital carrying crisp bundles of money, and loud with complaint and criticism. Even the ER doctor, trying to check her injuries, backed off from her tirade about money-grubbing, cold-blooded so-called health professionals. I was sorry I missed the excitement but by then I'd been sedated.

I was pretty battered and bruised but no broken bones, and no damage to my spinal cord. It's lucky for me that everyone worked hard to get me eating and sleeping and healthy again before this incident meaning I've been able to heal quite quickly.

I'm proud of myself for fighting back, and the headaches are mostly gone now.

Angel and Joel are working something out between them. I don't know the details but Angel and I have become quite close so I'm sure she'll share when she's ready.

Meanwhile the two of them are wrapped up in their babies and each other and that's exactly how it should be, so it's my job to provide Bram's ease and comfort.

The weather has turned glorious, warm and sunny and the woods are full of new growth. I persuade him to come for a walk. He doesn't want to go out but arguing takes too much effort so he does come with me.

The fresh air, a gentle breeze, and my hand swallowed up in his big paw helps to lift his spirits. We walk slowly for about forty minutes then head back to the house.

He's napping a lot, a symptom of feeling low I'm sure, so as soon as we arrive back we go upstairs and I tuck him into bed. Then I strip down and slip under the covers as well.

He lets me snuggle into spooning position and gives a contented sigh but I know a better way to cheer him up. I reach inside his boxers and let my little fingers find the tip of his penis then I gently tap and tease and stroke until I feel him harden and respond with some pre-cum.

I'm so happy to feel him pull me close and start kissing my shoulder. I wiggle my ass till I'm pressed tight against him then I maneuver myself into a position that let's us screw while lying on our sides.

It's a slow lovemaking that is healing for both of us. As usual Bram murmurs that he loves me before drifting off to sleep. I know it's just words, just a phrase, but it feels so good to hear.

I'll work on making him fall in love with me for real, but in the meantime we're both enjoying the girlfriend experience.

I'm so lucky to have found such a good and loving man in the oldest and kindest of the O'Shea Brothers.

Part Six

"Catharsis"

Chapter 1

Angel

Both Joel and I are so thankful that Bram has Stacey in his life. She suffered the most physically, and he is still suffering emotionally, but she's been there for him 24/7.

He's come to rely on her and she's happy to accept that role. She's a much stronger woman that we knew.

Because of this, Joel and I have been able to take the time to discuss our issues and, hopefully, we'll be able to resolve them. Although we've been at an impasse for some time.

Lots of great sex but... Joel has been different since the kidnapping and crash.

One night after dinner Stacey and I were in the kitchen folding baby laundry and I burst out with a revealing confidence. I told her how I've always fought against Joel's dominance despite getting so aroused when forced to submit to his authority but... he hasn't been pushing me lately. She just looked at me and shook her head saying:

"Poor Joel, you're going to drive him crazy. You need to reconcile your two warring selves, Angel. Bram's told me about the days when you were Girlie so maybe she needs to come back? Girlie can be the bad girl who craves discipline though she fights against it, while Angel remains the loving mother and wife."

Her idea blows me away. I think it might be the perfect plan and tell her so.

"Oh, I have lots of good ideas," Stacey brags with a smile. She's finished folding one pile of baby clothes and now she's starting on the twins towels and bedding. There's always so much laundry!

"Well, I'm all ears because I've got to do something. Lately I've been cranky and irritable and I keep snapping at Joel."

"You're trying to push him into punishing you."

"Oh God, no, I'm not into that."

"How do you know?"

"He told me about Christian Domestic Discipline and I told him it sounds awful. And he agrees, well he would considering how he felt about his parents but... oh shit, Bram doesn't know about this. Stacey, please don't say anything."

"Umm, don't worry because you haven't told me anything. *Yet*, that is..."

"Shit, shit, shit. Okay listen, the O'Shea parents were C.D.D practitioners and Joel discovered them in the act but it was was more than just a spanking. It was a real beating. Joel was disgusted and ashamed for them so he never said anything to Bram or Danny.

Quite a few years later Danny mentioned it to Joel but he, Danny, thought it was a good thing – as in *the natural order of things*.

Joel regrets keeping quiet about it but he can't say anything now because he doesn't want to shatter Bram's thoughts and feelings about their parents with this ugly truth."

"Oh, that is messy. Angel, I think you're suffering a mild depression."

Although my mouth's dropped open in shock I can't think of a thing to say. How does Stacey know? I haven't told anyone about it because this is my problem to deal with privately. She doesn't show any surprise at my reaction and just goes on to say:

"I'm fairly knowledgeable in the D/s world and, if you think this is something that might work for the two of you then I can help you and Joel identify your wants and needs. We'll determine where the deficits are, and then we can develop a good working plan to move forward.

Personally, I *don't* think it is the right solution for you, I think your problem is self-loathing, not being good enough, that sort of thing... but, structured discipline is one option to help you overcome low self-esteem, it's all based on the motivation."

I've given up folding and am just staring at her. Because she's so petite and young-looking I forget that Stacey is a well-educated woman with an undergraduate degree and a variety of experience and knowledge that I haven't given her enough credit for.

"You did mention creating, no crafting, a scene for Joel and I?"

"Yes, of course. I already have something in mind. I either tell both of you, or just you and you have to share it with Joel. Think about how each of you might react to such a conversation and let me know what you think works best."

"Um, I guess it might be best to tell me and I can tell Joel."

"You won't be shy about it?"

"Well if I am I can just wait until we're in bed with the lights out and whisper it in his ear. I'm guessing we don't do it immediately, we both think about it and prepare ourselves, right?"

"The anticipation is half the fun."

We share wicked grins.

"Okay so I'll just set the scene without any commentary, what you guys experience sexually and emotionally is entirely your own private thing. Of course you can share if you feel the need to discuss it afterwards.

So, you'll be in a private room and Joel will command you to get in position. That means you strip off and kneel before him with your back straight, your eyes cast down, and the palms of your hands laying flat on your thighs. You do not move, not even a finger, without his permission.

Joel will then feed you his dick, slowly or roughly, however he pleases and you will lick and suck and swallow – all according to his directions – without using your hands at all.

Performing naked and carefully following his instructions will turn you on but you cannot move, you can't squirm or press your thighs together. He'll no doubt comment on your hard nipples and bare breasts and his praise will arouse you even more.

Once he completes – to whatever degree that means for him – he'll order you to get ready on the bed. That means you again kneel but this time with your arms stretched out and your cheek flat to the mattress. You ass in the air and your pussy spread wide for him.

I think the next step should be anal play."

"What? No!"

"Angel, just listen for now. Joel will rim you with his fingers and then he'll lube up the small plug I'll order for you insert it in and out while strumming on your clit.

The anus can't lubricate itself so you need to use lots and lots of lube. Also you need specially designed anal toys otherwise you could lose something up there and have to go to the hospital."

"Omigod! That would be so embarrassing!"

"No doubt, eh? And apparently it happens a lot, believe it or not. Anyhow, I'll get you everything you need including the special solution to wash your toy with afterwards.

I think you will get really turned on with Joel handling your ass so much and I'm positive he will. Eventually the two of you will want to progress to his dick in your back-door and with his fingers bringing you to orgasm I know both of you will enjoy the experience."

"That sounds, well... hot."

"I know! Joel's gonna love having you naked and pliable, and you'll get turned on by him forcing his will on you. The anal play is something new and extremely personal for the two of you. Afterwards you'll get one hell of a fucking! Oh and I'll order the special candles, too."

"Oh doing this by candlelight sounds nice but we've got plenty of—"

"No, no. First of all your D/s night isn't about romance and you need the lights turned up, no hiding your blushes or your arousal. No, the candles are for hot wax play, you know dripping it on bare skin can be very erotic."

"Oh I'm a real suck when it comes to pain, Stacey. I don't want to do that."

Stacey laughs and clarifies that the wax isn't for Angel it's for Joel.

"What? But I thought he was the Dominant?"

"In the next scene you two act out you get to be in charge. You tie him naked, spreadeagled and face up on the bed while you strut around in a sexy costume. You're not allergic to latex are you? And you'll be the one wielding the candle. I think Joel will love it.

There are two tricks to make sure it's pleasurable. The first is to buy candles specifically made for this, they don't burn as hot as regular household candles. And the second is to hold the candle high. The wax will cool as it falls through the air so the further the journey it has to make the less likely it is to burn his skin although it will still be hot.

You'll drip wax on his chest, slowly working your way down his body and giving him something to worry about until you veer over to his thighs. Leave the entire groin area alone and I guarantee when you're ready to ride him he'll be a bucking bronco for you."

"Oh that sounds so good but I don't think he'll go for the hot wax."

"That's why you're not going to tell him in advance. You'll have some nice body oil to give him a massage and then you'll bring out the candle that *oh, Stacey must have added this too.* He'll be tied up so what's he gonna do about it?"

Angel gasps and says she isn't sure she could trick him like that but Stacey just smirks.

"Okay, you order everything and I'll no, wait. I'll talk to Joel first and make sure he's on-board before you order the stuff but I think he will be. And you're right, he'll love the idea of me worshipping his body with massage oil."

"Meanwhile, we all need to sit down and talk openly with each other. You need to tell Joel that you told me about his parents and that he needs to tell Bram. I get what he said about destroying the sentimental memory Bram holds, but it explains so much about Joel and especially about Danny.

I truly do think that Bram needs to hear that because I believe it will help him."

I consider for a moment and agree that what she's said makes sense. We finish our work – although folding the cute baby clothes is hardly a chore! and I tell her:

"Let me talk to Joel about it tonight. I'd like to see the four of us sit down and get everything out in the open. Maybe we can do that tomorrow."

"For sure, the sooner the better and good luck with it. I want to do whatever I can to help Bram, I.. I care for him very much."

"I do too, but in a different way. You're in love with Bram, aren't you?"

Stacey only hesitates briefly before beaming a beautiful smile and happily agreeing.

I say goodnight and head up to our bedroom, stopping in the nursery to drop off my basket of tiny outfits. I hear Joel singing softly and see that Eve is awake and staring at her daddy with rapt attention.

The night nanny is hovering in the doorway that joins the nursery to her room. She's also staring at Joel with starry eyes and I realize this young girl's got a major crush. I'd better warn him to be kind but distant so she doesn't get the wrong idea.

Will he get the wrong idea? Will he think I'm just jealous? I give the girl a detailed inspection and concede that she is very pretty, very gentle, and very feminine. Traits Joel finds attractive.

Maybe I won't say anything to him, maybe I'll have a word with Maggie instead. Oh yeah, I am jealous.

I kiss Eve goodnight and Joel gets up and kisses me as we turn to go to our own bedroom. His hands drop to my waist and propels me forward while he nuzzles my neck. I soon forget all about our nanny.

"Hey, before we get carried away I want to tell you about a conversation I had with Stacey."

"Can it wait?" he asks impatiently.

"No, and it's about sex so... Ah, now you're interested."

I tell him everything Stacey said to me. Well, not the hot candle wax part. I still haven't decided about doing that.

I can tell Joel is getting aroused thinking and talking about the role-playing idea but then he says:

"I don't think I want Stacey ordering us sex toys like a butt dildo, Angel. Can't we scrounge a carrot or something out of the kitchen?"

"No, she explained that it's got to be stuff specially designed for anal play. Apparently there's an inner ring inside the anus with a muscle that involuntarily pulls. I think I've got that right.

Anyhow, she said while body parts like fingers and dicks and... ugh... tongues are okay foreign objects can get sucked in somehow and people have to go to the emergency room."

"Oh I have heard about that," he laughs. "Not this inner ring thing but about people, mostly guys of course, getting weird things stuck up their asses and having to go lie about it at the hospital."

"Yeah, so I guess these sex toys all have a wide base at the end to prevent them slipping in too far. But I understand what you're saying. Because of all the time I spent getting naked with you and Bram I sometimes forget that this is a pretty private thing after all. Soooo, if we do that part I guess it will have to be your finger."

After mulling it over Joel declares: "It's a good idea. Because of the attack I never did get around to punishing you for your irresponsible drinking while breastfeeding. But it's never too late to be taught a lesson in obedience."

I give a little gasp of shock but... he's not wrong. Drinking all that wine wasn't something naughty it was hazardous, and I took a foolish risk. He takes hold of my chin and looks deep into my eyes saying:

"Tomorrow after lunch, at 2:00 pm sharp, you will meet me in our sitting-room."

I'm overwhelmingly turned on, so much so that I can't speak so I only nod *yes*.

He warns: "Don't be tardy, Angel." In such a menacing voice I feel a gush of wetness slicking my folds. I start nodding again before correcting myself to shake my head *no*.

The anticipation both of us are feeling about tomorrow leads us into a passionate and very satisfying encounter. Sometimes minimal foreplay so we can hurry into straight sex is exactly what we both want.

Afterwards Joel rolls me onto my stomach and straddling me says:

"I'm going to give you a back-rub and tell you a story."

"Oooh! sounds lovely! Is it a true story?"

"Well... it could be. I've actually told you this one before – the basics, anyhow – when we talked about my sexual fantasies. Ever since then I've been making up little scenes – stories – in my head and I'm going to share one with you every night."

"Just like Scheherazade."

"What's that?"

"Who, not what. A woman who told the King a story every night so he wouldn't get bored and kill her, I think she had a year's worth of stories. Or maybe it was 1,001."

"Uh-oh, I only have a week's worth so am I in danger of boring you? and signing my own death warrant, Angel?"

"Not yet..."

"Wench! Okay, you relax while I tell you a bedtime story..."

A Joel O'Shea Fantasy Story:

featuring Agent Angel of the DEA

pursuing Criminal Kingpin Nasty Nick

"You're Under Arrest!"

Agent Angel of the DEA pursues criminal kingpin Nasty Nick to the back room of the betting shop on Garden Street.

"Aha! Caught you at last, Nasty Nick! You're under arrest," she triumphantly cries. Pulling her handcuffs loose from her belt she announces:

"Put your hands behind your back, you're coming with me, mister."

Nasty Nick, who is much, much bigger than Agent Angel looks down with an amused expression on his dark, handsome, beardless face. She has to tilt her head way back to show him the earnest look in her big blue eyes. That also gives him a great view of the buxom blonde's impressive amount of cleavage.

He easily pries the handcuffs from her hands and snaps them around her own wrists.

He slips the chain over a coat-hook on the back door and, in a cruel twist of fate, the young policewoman is swiftly rendered helpless. Stepping back Nasty Nick takes a good long look at his captive.

Agent Angel is a luscious little package from the top of her police hat, precariously balanced on a mane of golden hair, to her ridiculous stilettos with impossibly high heels. She isn't wearing stockings under her extremely tight and extremely short black mini-skirt.

Her bare legs are shown off to advantage as she stretches to hold on to the coat-hook and keep her balance.

The shirt of her black uniform is equally tight, in fact the top three buttons won't close because she's filled it out so fully. Nasty Nick enjoys a nasty thought and decides to act on it.

Powerless to prevent the assault Agent Angel suffers Nasty Nick's groping. He's popped open the remaining snaps of her uniform shirt and is delighted to discover she's braless. He begins squeezing and kneading and fondling her bare breasts while softly grunting in appreciation.

Agent Angel bites her lip to keep from moaning because his rough hands feel surprisingly, incredibly good when rubbing and pinching her hard nipples.

After enjoying some more play time on top Nasty Nick then focuses on her plump derriere tightly encased in black serge. He can't find the zipper so he grabs hold of the skirt's hem and yanks hard to drag it up and over her enticing round bottom.

She isn't wearing panties!

Reaching to the front of her body he finishes pulling the skirt up over her mound, pausing to tease the blonde curls and press a finger against her wet clit, and rolls it up to her slender waist. Now he's got naked tits in one hand and a juicy bottom in his other hand. He massages and caresses the fistfuls of soft, smooth skin.

Nasty Nick can't resist her inviting body a moment longer. Spreading Agent Angel's legs he quickly enters her and starts pumping. She's warm and soaked and oh so delightfully, shockingly tight!

He growls in her ear: "Lose the arrest warrant, Agent Angel."

She squirms and struggles but she's utterly exposed, defenceless, and completely at his mercy. She can't fight back when her wrists are handcuffed and her arms are raised high above her head. She can't even protect her breasts which sway and bob with every thrust he makes.

She can't pretend he isn't a handsome, skilled lover driving her mad with lusty excitement.

He knows he can't hold off for much longer and is relieved when he hears her cry of delight and agreement:

"Ohhhhh, yes! yes! Okay, I won't arrest you!"

Then Nasty Nick joins Agent Angel in orgasmic release and pleasure.

Afterwards he leaves her hanging for a bit while with both hands he strokes from her belly up over her tits and along her arms then back again. She rests against him, and he enjoys the sweet scent of her.

Then he finally lifts her up to unhook the chain and hunts around for the handcuff key. He finds it and is about to unlock the cuffs but he's distracted by the sight of her beautiful naked breasts.

Her flesh is milky white, and her hard little nipples are rosy red. He's already filled his hands, now he can feast his eyes. Lost in admiration until a sniff and a hiccup catch his attention and he sees that Agent Angel is crying! Her tears make him feel an unaccustomed tenderness.

"Why are you crying?" he asks, bewildered, "Are you ashamed about having sex with me? Didn't you enjoy it?"

"No, no I did enjoy it. It was my first time and it was great. Now I know what all the fuss is about!"

He pulls opened his shorts and notices some blood mixed in with the stain of his semen.

"Oh! Did I hurt you? Is that why you're crying?"

"It hurt a little but no, that's not why I'm crying."

"Then why?"

"Because I'm such a lousy cop that I can't even manage to make an arrest!"

Joel announces: "The end."

He had stopped the back-rub quite some time ago in order to concentrate on doing to me what Nasty Nick was doing to Agent Angel. He fucked me gloriously and like her, I too enjoyed it immensely.

Although afterwards I smacked his chest exclaiming:

"Hey! I was good at my job!"

Chapter 2

Stacey

I can't stop thinking about what Angel told me regarding the O'Shea parents. Philip Larkin sure got it right in his poem. It makes me wonder about Bram, about whether or not it's an explanation...

First off, I hope she can convince Joel to talk about this. I think it's really important that Bram knows the history so he can put the whole Danny episode in perspective. I know Bram blames himself and that's just wrong.

Danny observed sexually violent behavior while growing up and it had an effect. As an adult he kept bad company and made bad choices but they definitely were choices – his and nobody else's.

Secondly, it makes me think Bram might have witnessed something too, while very young, and then buried the memory. Because I soon realized that Bram's kink – and I believe we all have *at least* one - is that he's a voyeur.

He doesn't go creeping around in the dark spying on women undressing in their bedrooms, but he does like to watch. I expect his history with women would often involve threesomes where he would enjoy seeing two women together.

Also, there were all those times he was invited to watch Angel, or I should say Girlie, and Joel.

I discovered this quite quickly so I'm sure Angel's figured it out as well, but it's something we'll never discuss. We both love Bram enough to keep his secret.

Not because I think it's shameful, but because I think that for him the secrecy is at least half the thrill. Once or twice I caught sight of him in the mirror looking at me. That's what made me start thinking about voyeurism.

Bram never married and, so far as I know, has never been in a long-term intimate relationship. He went from military boarding-school right into training to become a Marine so I don't know how much sexual experience he could have had apart from the visits he and his fellow soldiers would have made to hookers when on leave.

I'm guessing the backseat-of-the-car fantasy stems from real make-out sessions that ended well before he wanted. As a boarding-school grad myself, I know there wouldn't have been many opportunities. Mixed dances once, maybe twice, a year, then trying to hang out with the local kids when home for holidays.

He's already in bed, but I tell him that even though I'm really tired I still need to shower and wash my hair adding:

"If you hear a thump that'll be me falling down. I have to close my eyes to keep the shampoo out, but I might get sleepy and disoriented."

"Leave the door open, hon. If I hear a crash I'll come and rescue you."

Of course that whole bit of by-play was simply a way to let him spy on me. So, now I'm in the shower with my hair full of shampoo and my eyes closed. I tilt my body so he can see the water splash off my breasts like a waterfall over the boulders. Well, in my case those boulders are very small.

I keep turning and twisting this way and that so he gets a good eyeful of my body shiny and wet with suds. I'm having such fun posing and teasing.

I run the bar of soap down my throat and across my chest, soaping up each breast and playing with my nipples. I think my big nipples help make up for my breasts being small.

I keep moving down with the soap until I've reached my pussy. I spread my legs and start rubbing the bar back and forth then round and round my clit.

My eyes are closed and my head is tilted back. I keep rubbing the soap-bar and soon my hips are bucking to the rhythm of my strokes. I don't let myself finish, but I pretend it's because I can't.

Again, I caress my breasts and my ass and then I try more stroking, with just my fingers this time, but I still can't get myself off. Apparently. Finally, I give a frustrated sigh and standing under the spray rinse all the shampoo out of my hair.

After I give my body a quick rubdown I use the towel to dry my hair.

When I come back into the bedroom Bram is still sitting up in bed with his newspaper, but I'm certain he hasn't been there the whole time.

I'm sure he witnessed my sexual frustration and now he beckons me over. I'm eager to snuggle into his warm embrace and when I squirm around I can feel that his cock is ready for me.

We kiss and he caresses me. Then I fling myself onto his lap complaining that I'm so horny and I need him so badly. Since he's already aroused we make love quickly and with deep satisfaction for both of us.

Chapter 3

Bram

I'm not sure what I think about this stuff Joel's told me. He and Angel and Stacey all came into my office this morning saying there was something we should discuss.

"From the looks on your faces you're not about to suggest something fun like a game of naked Twister, are you?" I quip but it doesn't lighten the mood. I can see the girls are puzzled and don't understand what I'm talking about. Damn, they're young!

Once Joel starts talking about Mama and Papa I get agitated, verging on angry. It's good Angel and Stacey leave us to discuss this on our own.

I tell Joel I can't believe what he's saying but he assures me that, regrettably, it's all true and it did happen.

"Then how come I'm only hearing about this now?"

I can see Joel is uncomfortable having this conversation. He's walking around the room - which really isn't big enough for pacing - and he's picking things up and putting them down again without paying any attention. He's trying not to make eye contact. Finally he admits:

"Because I didn't have the balls to tell you back then when I should have. You know I was always scared of Papa."

"He was hard on you but that's because he loved you."

"Yeah, easy for you to say Bram, you were the favorite. He was a real prick to me. From the minute I entered my teens nothing I did was ever good enough. He rode me all the time."

"Well, you gave him a lot of attitude."

Joel pauses for a moment and I can see him processing an idea, then he says:

"I wonder if it was connected – me witnessing Papa beating Mama and then him always being angry with me and picking on me. Maybe he realized I never bought his explanation about the *rightness* of what was happening between the two of them."

"Well, what exactly was it? Are you sure it wasn't some... God I hate to think, never mind say, this but... was it some kind of sex play?"

"I think it was sexual but there was nothing playful about it. This Domestic Discipline stuff is supposed to hurt, that's the whole point. They claim that wives need to be beaten painfully and humiliated—"

"Like how?" I interrupt. It's so hard to believe because Mama was always a very dignified, classy lady.

"Being made to stand in a corner to reflect on their punishment, shit like that. All to make them feel happy and fulfilled. I mean, what motherfucker came up with that?"

"Listen, I do believe you, Joel, but I just can't imagine it happening. If you saw it then of course it did, but as I say it's just too fucked up to get my head around."

"Which explains a bit about Danny, right? I mean, you never knew it happened, and you're the nice, stable, good son. I saw it happen, once, and as we know I have some anger and power-tripping issues.

But Danny lived with it while it was happening a lot. Maybe it was common for him to see or hear it happening. And, maybe that's how Danny picked up his twisted ideas about women and hurting women."

"Do you think so?"

"It kind of explains things, doesn't it? and that's why I'm telling you now after all these years. Actually I'm telling you now because the girls told me to. See, I told Angel oh... two-three months ago? and that was the first time I ever told anybody.

I've got to admit it was a real relief to share that secret.

Anyhow yesterday she was talking to Stacey and part of the story slipped out. Angel swore Stacey to secrecy saying it would hurt you to find out – because that's what I believed, and that's what I told her - but Stacey said *no, that's not Joel's decision to make* and she convinced Angel to persuade me to tell you."

"That little girl has a good brain to go with her good heart and she's right. I guess that, without realizing it, I was trying to figure out what went wrong – what I did wrong – to shape Danny into being the person he became. I've been feeling guilty and now, from what you've told me, well... maybe it isn't all on me."

"Oh, Bram," he said. "None of the blame is on you."

Maggie comes in to tell us to get a move on 'cause we're holding up lunch.

"Wait a minute, Maggie, I've got a question. Do you know if my father ever beat my mother?"

"Oh," she shuffles her feet looking uncomfortable, but then squares her shoulders with determination.

"Well, I always wondered if this would come out and what I'd say if it did. The answer is *yes*. Your father called it *home correction* or some damn-fool thing but that was just a fancy way to excuse him beating up his wife. What they call *spousal abuse* nowadays, and your poor mother just had to take it.

Well, I told her she didn't *have* to take it, and she admitted that she knew that, but your Papa had convinced her it was her wifely duty.

It got worse and happened more and more as the years went on. He turned mean and jealous even though he certainly had no cause!

But why are you asking about this now?"

"Joel was wondering how much Danny would have known about it. Do you think he knew?"

"Oh I know he did. Your Papa never hit your Mama in front of us, but it seemed hardly a week went by when he wasn't ordering her to leave the table, or the family room, or the kitchen, and go up to their bedroom to wait for him to come and punish her. He'd acquired a taste for it. I guess Danny got it, too. Yes, looking back I'd say that explains a lot."

"Yeah, I think it does. Thank you, Maggie."

"You know that expression *let the dead bury the dead*? well... it makes sense when applied to your parents, so come along and eat now."

She leaves, and turning to Joel I give him a light shoulder punch. He understands what I mean by it and just nods at me. We head into the dining-room where our ladies are already seated.

I smile at both of them so they know everything is okay with all of us, and give Stacey a kiss as well.

"By the way Joel, I need you to help me after lunch with some calculations I'm trying to work out. I'll get everything ready so join me about ten minutes after we finish, okay?"

"Actually I'm planning to take my wife to bed after we eat."

"Oh, well make it fifteen minutes then."

"Ha-ha, Bram," says Angel, then she turns to Joel saying: "I'll head up now since it's almost 2:00."

He doesn't answer her but I swear the look in his eyes is positively hungry. Stacey notices and whispers under her breath *Sir Dom!*

Chapter 4

Angel

I've actually got about ten minutes before my deadline but I want a little time to myself to get into the right mind-set.

Today's little adventure is all about me catering to Joel's need to dominate. I fully expect him to act completely over the top with macho *MINE* vibes. It should be fun.

I'm in our sitting-room stripped naked and kneeling in the proper submissive position trying to blank my mind. I really do want to make this special for him which means he doesn't need to see me making faces or huffing complaints.

My meditations have lulled me into a calm, relaxed state and I'm not bothered that Joel is late. I look down at my nude body and am pleased to see that motherhood hasn't ruined my breasts and the stretch marks on my stomach aren't too noticeable.

I sense Joel's presence and looking up see he's entered the room silently. He meets my gaze before barking out an order to keep my eyes down. I comply, resisting the urge to roll them because all of a sudden *it's showtime!*

He doesn't speak as he prowls around me, pausing to get a good look from every angle. I find I really have to concentrate to remain motionless.

This silent scrutiny is disconcerting. I'm used to hearing Joel compliment me, often very crudely, whenever I'm naked. I find myself wishing the lightbulb in the overhead fixture was a lower wattage.

Completing his slow circling Joel ends up standing way too close to me, his crotch practically butting my nose. Oh yeah, he's already hard. He unbuckles and unzips and his dick springs free, right in my face.

When I reach for him he snaps at me to stay still. I obey while he strokes himself and when the tip is glistening he tells me to open very wide.

"I'm going to rest my cock on your tongue and you're not going to do anything except let it sit there. You won't close your mouth or your lips. You won't move your tongue or any other part of your body. I don't want my cock to touch anything but your tongue so keep that mouth open wide."

I follow his instructions but it's hard. My jaw is aching from being held motionless and stretched wide. I can't swallow the saliva that builds up and it pools in my mouth before spilling over my lips. It's shaming and I'm fighting the urge to cry.

Joel simply stares at me, his eyes feasting on the sight of his dick sitting in my mouth with my chin dripping wet. Tears fill my eyes and I can't blink fast enough to stop them streaking down my cheeks. Joel's eyes hold me captive.

He starts rocking his dick back and forth along my tongue and pushing in further and further. When his tip nudges the back on my throat I start to gag but force myself to breathe through it. We continue this way for what feels like an eternity before his rhythm suddenly picks up tempo and he orders me to get my mouth working to suck him like an industrial vacuum-cleaner.

It's such a relief to release my jaw and draw my cheeks in tight. I start swallowing spit and my tongue gets busy swirling and stroking. He's managed to get right inside my throat. Pulling back he instructs me to breathe in at the sides of my mouth so I inhale deeply. He plunges in again and now he's thrusting hard, his balls banging against my chin.

When he cums he holds my head tightly as he unloads. His breath is a drawn-out hiss of release as his hips spasm a few times. We're both panting and he doesn't move away.

I can't see his face because he's still holding my head down. He pats my head and tells me I'm his good pet. I know I should rebel against the contempt that comment shows but instead I feel proud of myself. Maybe my voice will be hoarse from him pounding my throat but his is already ragged since I've taken him apart.

Chapter 5

Joel

Angel is fucking perfect. She's such a good girl doing everything I want, exactly as I tell her. Looking at her beautiful face flushed red, her eyes sparkling with tears, her lips thinning as her mouth stretches makes me rock-hard.

I drive deeper into her throat then I ever have before and she's taking every inch like a fucking rockstar. My gorgeous wife, so eager to please me because she's mine.

My cock explodes like I'm a teenager and I have to hold her head down so she doesn't see my face because God knows what I look like. Utterly fucking destroyed.

I almost tell her what a good girl she is before catching myself and switching to *pet*. I know she craves my praise but she has more work to do to earn it.

I leave her kneeling on the floor while I go into our bathroom to clean myself up. I do up my jeans but take my shirt off. Coming back into the room I study her bowed head and submissive pose and something feral rises up inside me. Once again I savor how fucking perfect she is.

Spying her tee-shirt on a chair I hand it to her saying *Wipe your face dry then bend over the arm of the sofa*. She does as she's told, presenting her smooth, round ass and pretty pink pussy to me.

I swiped a jar of petroleum jelly from the nursery and now I grease my fingers before running them around the rim of her asshole. She clenches but then forces herself to relax.

I don't think I've ever looked closely at anyone's anus. I've definitely heard about guys getting a finger poked in their ass during sex and hating or loving it. I don't think I'd like it... but I want to do this to her, now.

I'm massaging Angel's plump cheeks with my left hand, enjoying the softness of her skin, while delicately probing with my sticky lubed finger. As I edge into her passage I'm aware of a powerful muscle, real tightness, and heat. I'm in as far as my first finger joint and she grunts gently. I withdraw and add more lube before sliding back in. I enter more easily this time so I slowly push in deeper.

Stacey's told her there's something called a P-spot in here and pressing on it can bring pleasure. I slip my finger in and out and her hips are rolling along with the motion.

Once we've established a rocking rhythm using my right hand my free hand reaches for her cunt and she spreads wide for me. I trap her clit between my thumb and knuckle, kneading and pinching, while she moans encouragement.

It only takes a minute more before Angel shatters and her whole body spasms with her ass muscles clenching tight and her legs shaking. I pound the fingers from each of my hands into both her holes and she feels so fucking good.

"You're so wet and ready for me, wife. This is exactly what you want, exactly what you need, isn't it?"

"Yes, yes sir. Yes, husband. Give me whatever you want, I'm yours to use however you please."

Her words drive me to the brink but I hold back, needing her orgasms to feed my possessive desire. With every stroke in: mine, mine, mine. Her limbs are flailing beneath me as she's maddened with ecstasy until the final orgasm that sends her rigid giving me the tightest grip and draining every drop.

I wanted to fuck her ass as well but I flop back down on the bed, wiped out. I'm done. This was the best ever. My mind's eye immediately begins replaying the scene going back to the very beginning.

Click - coming into the room and finding Angel in the proper submissive position. Slowly stalking her and admiring everything I see. Instant lust.

Click - my cock is in her mouth and her eyes are filled with longing while she patiently awaits my command. My good girl. Seeing that reminds me of dog owners who place a treat on their animal's snout but don't let it eat until they give permission.

Click – her cheeks red and tear-stained as I choke her throat but her tongue and lips are working overtime to keep me going.

Click – a sparkling glimpse of mischief before she casts her eyes down once again. She's owning me and can't resist letting me know.

Perfect obedience, perfect trust, perfect devotion.

This is what Angel has given me this afternoon. She's acted on my whims with nothing but a desire to please and satiate me. She's let me indulge my dominant nature and the sex was explosive.

We'll definitely play these roles again plus we'll try that other thing she spoke of, um... *tying me up for massage and tantalizing torment.* Oh yeah, I like the sound of that!

In our daily lives she definitely doesn't give me perfect obedience and I'm sure she doesn't always trust me, but I always know that

I have her full devotion and love. Angel is my wife. She is mine – utterly, totally, completely, undeniably – mine.

And I am hers.

Chapter 6

Angel

What an experience. I can't call it *afternoon delight* because *titillated to exquisite joy* is a far more accurate description. Joel can't take his eyes off of me, and I need to keep touching him.

Leaning into him is always comforting, but brushing my hand against his arm and feeling the heat of his skin is electrifying. I'm a bit anxious, a bit emotional, but physically connecting with him reassures me.

Joel eats a big dinner but I find I'm not too hungry. Guess my appetite was fully sated already. I'm toying with the food on my plate when he asks:

"Do you want to go for a drive, maybe grab an ice cream, Angel?"

"Later on I'd love to but I can't right after dinner because Nanny is *finally* going to let me help bathe the babies."

"Really? I want to come too. I want to discuss swim lessons with Nanny."

"I've heard of teaching infants to swim," interjects Stacey eagerly, "I think it's a great idea."

"Yeah, I heard that since they've spent nine months floating in water it's a familiar and comfortable environment which kind of makes sense," Joel replies.

"And if they do learn, we can take them in the big bathroom and not be panicking every second," I add.

"That's a sight we definitely want to see, too!" Bram declares giving Stacey a squeeze. We all smile at each other, enjoying our family life, our wonderful lives together.

Chapter 7

Joel

We had so much fun playing with the babies in their bath that I forgot about taking Angel out afterwards. It felt like Nanny was never going to finish - she does love to lecture!

She explains that you don't really teach infants how to swim, you teach them how to survive in water. It makes sense, and we're all in agreement that Nanny will find an instructor for us.

I'm feeling traditional so we have a nice session in the missionary position. Since I'm on top it's easy to pin Angel's wrists down by her head and then watch her wriggle. I love to watch the way her breasts move, and I love to see the challenge in her eyes.

"I have another Agent Angel and Nasty Nick story to tell you after."

"Ooooh, tell me now while we're screwing, that'll be fun!"

"No, I want to concentrate on enjoying every sensation. I'll tell you once I cum."

She squeezes her vaginal muscles tight then releases and squeezes again, rhythmically. I don't stand a chance and finish quicker than I'd planned. I let my weight drop down on her while I'm still inside.

"No fair, Angel! But I've really got you pinned down now." She squirms and undulates beneath me and I feel it from head to toe.

"Tell me a bedtime story, Daddy."

"Ha! naughty girl. This story is particularly appropriate!"

A Joel O'Shea Fantasy Story:

featuring Agent Angel of the DEA

pursuing Criminal Kingpin Nasty Nick

"Charges Pending"

Nasty Nick is on the landline in his office in the back room of the betting shop. He's doing a deal when, once again, Agent Angel storms in loudly announcing he's *under arrest.*

The crook on the other end of the line hears her talking and immediately disconnects the call.

Nasty Nick is so angry about losing the deal he grabs hold of Agent Angel and pulls her across his knee.

"How dare you come in here hollering about charges and an arrest? This is my place of business, little Miss Buttinsky and I'll teach not to interfere with my work."

He then starts spanking her, hard, and she yells at him to stop so he does but only long enough to push her skirt up over her bum, up to her waist.

As usual, she isn't wearing any panties so he enjoys the spectacle of her bare bottom quivering from his punishment. The sight of her plump derriere already turning pink inspires him to renew the spanking with enthusiasm.

Soon she's kicking her legs and wriggling her hips from side to side trying to escape his punishing hand. He just keeps smacking away despite her begging him to please-please-please stop!

"Will you drop the charges if I do?"

"Yes! I promise, just please stop spanking me."

Nasty Nick was going to finish anyhow because all that squirming in his lap has given him a hard-on.

He quickly unzips and lifts her onto his cock for hot sex. She's as hot inside as her red bum feels in his hands. In no time at all they reach climax together.

"The End," I announce. Then I continue saying:

"I forgot that I promised you ice cream so hop out of bed and get dressed."

"Oh I forgot too and I love ice cream. Let's go."

"So with that little tale to think about I'm guessing when we do go to bed for the night our sex will be extra hot, hmm?"

"Husband... why wait until we're back in bed? If you bribe me with ice cream we can make out in the car."

"Oh, I do love an insatiable wife!"

"And I love a husband who works so hard to satisfy my appetite," she replies.

Later, on the way back home, I detour down a deserted lane I remember from my younger days. After a delightful interlude that leaves us both happy and sated I ask:

"Do I truly satisfy you, Angel? And, I don't just mean the sex although I do want your honest answer about that, but also in our life together."

"Joel, what brought this on?"

"Oh something you mentioned once before about when things are going good it almost feels like it's too good and we're tempting fate.. but first I have to know that everything is good."

"Everything is way more than good, Joel. For awhile there it felt like something was missing but our role-playing games, both the planning and the actual enacting, really lift my spirits.

I am fulfilled in every aspect of my life even though this isn't the life I ever envisioned for myself."

"You mean your career."

"Yeah, but mostly my background. I think I always had a chip on my shoulder to prove myself because look at the career I chose: a challenging job in a male-dominated field.

Stacey said with what I went through when I was young I probably have deep-down feelings of low self-esteem, low self-worth, and I believe that *might* have been true but it's not true any more.

See, I never thought someone like me would ever win over a man like you, Joel. A handsome, healthy man to give me beautiful babies, a beautiful home, and his beautiful wonderful fulfilling love.

I never dreamed about this life, this goal, because I never believed it was attainable. Not for me. Now that I'm living it well... it's real and I'm not dreaming and I'm the luckiest woman ever."

"Girl, sweetheart, you're the luckiest girl. And yes, I know you're a grown-ass woman, a wife and a mother, but you will always be my girl."

Chapter 8

Bram

I'm standing at the door with my arms crossed and a serious expression while waiting for Angel to come downstairs for her run. I'm here to remind her that Dr. Moro said *no running*.

"Oh Bram, he fusses. I checked this out online and I'm doing everything I'm supposed to. I feed the babies then put on this solid contraption of a bra, and I only run for a short distance. I need the endorphins and the fresh air."

"But the doctor said a brisk walk that won't tax your energy is plenty of exercise for a nursing mother and—"

"And he's wrong. I take the twins out for a walk every afternoon, but the morning run is for me to clear my head and get a good start on my day."

She's bouncing on the balls of her feet, eager to get outside, so I give her a stern look and pointedly look at my watch adding:

"Keep it short."

Angel races out the door with her ponytail bouncing and her long legs stretching into a running stride. I watch her follow the path into our woods until she disappears from view.

I decide to wait breakfast until she returns and we can eat together, but I need a caffeine fix now and head to the kitchen. I'll never understand this passion for running and jogging, especially first thing in the morning.

I get what she means about the feel-good chemical reactions exercise provides, that's why I work out in the comfort of our climate-controlled gym.

Carrying my coffee mug back down the hall I'm startled by the front door banging open with Angel bursting in red-faced and panting from exertion.

"Bram!" she gasps, "there's someone out there in the woods, he followed me..."

"Get Joel," I order before running into the woods myself.

I hurry down the path Angel took and once I'm out of sight of the house I stop to study the grass along the edge, moving into the cover of the trees. It's still early enough that the sun hasn't burned off the light morning mist and the ground is damp enough to show telltale signs.

A man, judging from the size of the shoe print, apparently paced back and forth in this spot. Watching the house? or specifically waiting for Angel to appear?

I start walking deeper into the woods and call out *I'm in here* when I hear Joel holler.

"What's going on? Angel said there was some guy out here—"

"Yeah, look. Somebody was here and it looks like he left in a hurry, see the broken ends of the bushes where he raced through. He wanted to get away and didn't care about making noise."

We follow the evidence, but we're only led to the far edge of the woods bordered by the road. Anyone could park a car there and walk to our home, and then just as easily make their getaway.

Our place is pretty isolated and we've always felt perfectly safe here. The cost to surround the place with a fence would be astronomical. I honestly can't think what to do.

"I'll get on to a security team to get us set up with motion sensing cameras and lights feeding into a home surveillance system," announces Joel pulling out his phone. "We still have deer, elk coming through here now and then, right? I'll have to let them know about that so they can calibrate accordingly."

"Had a young moose wandering around last Fall but that was the first one I'd heard of around here in years."

We walk back to the house where Angel has been joined at the front door by Maggie and Stacey. Stacey's the only one who looks worried, the other two are pissed.

"Well? Did you see anyone?"

"No, but there were signs. We saw where he came in and where he got away from too. I can't believe this happened."

"We've never had any trouble like this before," states Maggie.

"We still don't," declares Joel saying it will all be taken care of.

"I'm still going for my runs," insists Angel quickly adding that she'll be armed with her service weapon.

Joel and I both look at her shaking our heads.

"Hon you can't ever fire that gun, the ballistics will be on record. I'll get you another one, one that's safe to use."

"Angel! Joel! You've got babies in the house, you can't have guns around the place," cries Stacey.

I smile as I lead my girl into the kitchen so we can all eat our breakfast while I explain the *other* facts of life to her before Joel and I get to have our meet-up.

He's certainly playing it cool about everything. My so-called project was just a ruse to get him away from the girls. The thing is, I've had disturbing news but he doesn't seem to be in the least bit concerned.

"You realize this is the FBI I'm talking about, right?" He just nods so I continue: "Sheriff Stein said the agent was asking very probing questions about the family, especially you."

"Christine Stein, that name just kills me. At first I thought she married a Jew but then I find out that's what her parents called her because her mother liked the name! It cracks me up every time I hear it."

"Joel, this is serious shit."

"Not really, Bram. I mean, what have they got? Somebody said *hey, since Danny O'Shea was in the truck with Chris Snyder when they crashed we better go investigate the O'Shea family* – how likely is that?

If this agent was asking questions about Danny then naturally our family will come into the conversation, especially since the paramedics took a young unidentified woman to hospital. Do the Feebs think she's another witness? Why would they care? They don't need one, not with two law enforcement personnel making statements."

"But they're digging around, looking for something, otherwise why not come straight to us? In fact, why get involved at all?"

"Yeah, I don't understand that bit. Why would the FBI be interested in a single-vehicle crash even if the driver was a CO with the DEA? Unless.."

"What?"

"What if Snyder's their target? What if he's the one who's been under investigation by the FBI and now they're tying up loose ends? Or pursuing some other line of enquiry that's tied into their original investigation?"

"That's a possibility... hmm, and because Snyder is connected to Danny they're also checking out the O'Shea's. Well, there's stuff they could find out about us online but it's all third-hand shit because none of us are on Facebook or Twitter or any of those social media things."

"Well Danny might have been, I've never looked, have you?"

"I never even thought of it."

"Ask Stacey, she'll know. Meanwhile, don't worry about the FBI. They've got nothing on us."

"Okay, yeah. Actually, I think I'll get in touch with my buddy in Intelligence, he owes me one so I'll ask him to look into this and see what's what."

"Sounds good. Now, who the fuck is watching my wife and why?"

Chapter 9

Angel

I should be feeling antsy from not getting my run this morning but the adventure has stoked my adrenaline and when the rush fades I'll want to crash.

The twins were fed and are in the Nanny's care, Joel's gone to help Bram with whatever it was he wanted, and I'm avoiding the females of the household. Stacey wants to lecture me on gun safety, and Maggie wants to share her speculations and dire predictions so I'm just going to stay in our bedroom.

I know the urge to sleep is going to hit me soon and my whole body will shut down. I'll wake up in about forty-five minutes without having moved a muscle.

How do women without nannies manage? The babies wear me out and I've got lots of help here at home. I honestly can't imagine how working mothers do it, or single moms – especially teenagers – struggling on their own.

I really am fortunate... even if I don't think I deserve to be.

I shake my head to clear those thoughts. I still can't believe Stacey sees so much, it really is disconcerting, but her advice was good.

Before he left the room this morning Joel explained that he's given it a lot of thought and he just can't bring himself to give me a spanking although he will definitely threaten to do so and is happy to deliver the occasional swat to reinforce the *or else*.

I tell him, again, that although talking about it turns me on I really, really don't want to be spanked so that's absolutely fine by me. What I told him is the truth, but does he listen?

Then he fetches my Kindle saying he's bought me some spanking-related short stories to read. I didn't know such things were even available!

So after a refreshing sleep I'm now in the family room reading. And... I have to admit, feeling horny.

Stacey comes in the room commenting: "You're reading!"

She sounds so surprised I'm a bit snarky when I reply: "Well, yes I can read, you know."

Stacey just gives her gurgling laugh explaining that she knows I don't have time to read.

"I've never seen you just sit back and relax. I have no idea what type of novels you like, or what authors?"

"You're right. Now that I think about it it's been ages since I've had the chance to just kick back and enjoy a book. Even now, I wouldn't be reading if Joel hadn't got these stories for me. They're all about, believe it or not, spanking!"

"Really? Who wrote them?"

"What? You mean the author isn't *Anon*? she actually gives her name?"

"Yes, and I'll probably recognize the spanko even though it will be a pen-name. Angel the whole BDSM scene is a really hot commercial property – in every sense of the word! There are many, many people writing about it and quite a few are well-known with good reputations for writing an accurate depiction."

"Are you serious?"

"Absolutely. Can I see?"

I pass her the Kindle and she clicks back to the beginning of the eBook I have open, nodding as she says:

"Oh yes, she's been part of the scene and is basing this on her own experience. I read an interview she gave a few years ago where she said she still gets spanked several times a month even after years of being in the same relationship."

"Oh! is she in a domestic discipline marriage with her husband? or the dom-sub thing?"

"Well, it might not be a male/female relationship. I really don't know. But her stories indicate that the female character always feels calm and relaxed after her punishment, right?"

"Yes, which is crazy because so far the actual spankings are severe. A hard hand-spanking and then he takes a belt to her. Sounds like overkill to me."

Stacey laughs at that saying of course it would since I'm not a natural submissive.

"What do you mean?"

"You like to be dominated but you fight it, you don't give in unless you're playacting a role.

Bram told me, oh the first time we had sex actually, about some of the comebacks you'd say to Joel and there was nothing submissive there!

No, I see you hiding the effects and refusing to cry so as not to give him the satisfaction of seeing your feelings were hurt, but that's a different thing altogether. From what Bram told me you guys had a real fiery relationship."

"You're right, we did. Sometimes I miss being so feisty and sassy."

"Well, you don't have to stop being that way."

"It's hard to keep up all the time. And now, well, how can I taunt him when we're each holding a baby?

Don't get me wrong, Stacey, we both really enjoyed that little scene you scripted for us—" I begin, but she interrupts saying:

"See? All you need to do is set aside time for role-playing. When I say you're not a natural submissive that doesn't mean you wouldn't enjoy being forced to play a part. I think you'd find it extremely arousing. I get what you mean about how the reality of being a wife and mommy makes it difficult to act like a badass rebel, I really do, but like we talked about before: Girlie could return."

"I did think about that, but decided Girlie is gone. Long gone."

"She doesn't have to be, she could come back to visit for special playtimes with Joel. Trust me, it will spice things up. Or..." Stacey pauses for a moment in thought. It looks like she's forcing herself into making a decision when she says:

"Angel, would you like Bram to give you a spanking?"

I'm turned on from what I've been reading, and since I appreciate that Stacey is making an effort to share her man I don't just snap out a *No!,* but I do answer in the negative.

"Um, no... but, thanks?"

"I really didn't think you'd say yes because I don't believe that's your kink. I think all you'd get out of a session across Bram's knee is plenty of embarrassment and a sore bum!"

"Does he.. do you two, uh—"

"No, he's always been gentle with me in every way. He's not into playing games so anything we staged would just make us feel silly."

"So what do you think my *kink* is?"

"My guess is you want to be dominated by Joel but only if you can make him work for it, make him conquer you while you fight against it."

"Okay that feels right to me, but then why did I get so turned on when we played our little game of me being a submissive?"

"I think the answer to that lies in your feelings for Joel. Angel, he's definitely a strong A-type personality and you want to please him so playing that role, knowing how aroused you got him, empowered you.

I really believe this is a battle the two of you will fight over and over again throughout your married life and also that you'll both enjoy it."

Angel hmphs softly. "I would have agreed with you except for the last time we had one of those battles between my defiance and his dominance. Joel ground me down so badly... it was awful."

"When was this?"

"Oh quite a while back, before the babies came—"

"Well I knew that! Because now Joel adores you and worships the ground you walk on, Mommy!"

"Yeah, well I was pregnant but it was early on. And the funny thing is it sorta started like most of our little sex games, I mean between the three of us. We didn't even know you then so it was just Bram and Joel and me.

We'd had dinner and I got into a sassy mood and Bram was egging me on so at first I didn't realize exactly what was going on in Joel's mind. I mean, I still don't know why but he'd gone into his icy-cold mean mode and he really humiliated me and didn't come and fuck me afterwards. In fact, he didn't come to bed until after I'd cried myself to sleep."

"Oh Angel, that must have been so confusing. And it sounds horrible."

"It really was. I felt like dogshit on his shoe, just utterly worthless. The lowest of the low."

"He attacked your self-esteem, oh it's good I wasn't here. I'd have ripped him a new one!" Stacey declares fiercely. "And Bram didn't stop him?"

"No but... I wouldn't have expected him to. I mean, first of all Bram and I thought we were still playing, and secondly when Joel acts that way everyone's on edge desperately trying to keep him from exploding. But we did have make-up sex the next day, and he's never acted domineering since then."

"So you forgave him?"

"Well, he probably won't like me telling you this, but he got down on his knees and begged me to forgive him. Everything inside me just melted."

"Omigod yes! That would have been so powerful. But... you definitely have to do the hot wax thing now. After that humiliating experience Joel put you through? just think of this as evening up the score.

Even if you never put it into words you'll know, in your own mind, that you've had payback and it's a good retribution because he'll get a phenomenal sexual experience out of it."

"Oh you are evil!" I exclaim with a big grin."

Chapter 10

Stacey

Bram gave me a bath before dinner tonight. This was the first time we used the big bathroom and it was delightful. He explained the *no sex in the water* rule but that doesn't mean we can't get all soaped up and steamy. And we did.

Sex is a straightforward fun and natural function to my man, and I love that about him. No hang-ups about pain or fear, and no need for tears in order to perform. A thankful change from Danny!

There is the voyeurism, but so what if men like to look at women's naked bodies? that doesn't bother me.

Actually Bram and I more closely fit the role of a Daddy and his Little. He treats me with tenderness and loving care - like I'm his darling princess – and he enjoys being nostalgic.

There's no question that he's the boss, and I find that reassuring and comforting. Just hearing the rumble of his deep voice is enough to calm me.

So, he's announced that he's giving me a bath and carries me up to the big bathroom. The jets are already turned on in the jacuzzi and swirling foamy bubbles smelling of honeysuckle. Such a sensuous scent.

Bram undresses me – slowly, as usual – then he strips off and escorts me down the few steps into the warm pool. It's big enough for me to swim and for Bram to stretch out his arms and legs.

Turning me this way and that he makes sure to scrub and rub every inch of me with a soapy washcloth. Of course some spots get more attention than others!

I stand while he rinses me off and I can see in his eyes that the shine of the candlelight on my wet skin makes me alluring and beautiful to him.

I know we kind of fell into our relationship through proximity, and initially I made all the moves, but every now and then I see him looking at me speculatively. I think he's starting to see me as me, Stacey today, not the poor waif he basically had to free from his brother.

He scoops me out of the water and into a big warm towel but carries me back down to our bedroom saying that a couple of blankets on a tiled floor are too uncomfortable for a man of his size and age.

I love our big bed and as soon as we're in it I scoot between his legs and start licking him from his balls to the very tip of his cock. He grows harder with every caress of my tongue. When he reaches for me I clamber on top, legs spread as wide as I can, and he kisses me thoroughly while playing with my clit until I'm wet and welcoming.

Our skin is still damp and fragrant from the bubble-bath and I just want to kiss and lick and love every inch of him. Bram's feeling the same way and our lovemaking is unusually energetic, actually frantic. He's such an attentive lover: always gentle yet able to use sufficient force when I need him to bring me to a finish.

He loves it when I cum and never tires of teasing me to ecstasy again and again.

"It's so hot to see you all flushed with excitement, turned on and horny, and I know you aren't faking orgasms, but if you ever want more, Stacey, if you ever want me to do more just say so."

"If I ever do want more you'll be the first to know, Bram. But I am so happy with you. I know we've put the *back to University* discussion on hold right now and I'm glad because I really do want to be more than just an interlude in your life."

"I've never gone for anything but interludes. Joel called me *the good, stable son* but the truth is I've never even *wanted* a committed long-term relationship. I've certainly had plenty of women, and I do like threesomes, the kind of thing that's fun while it last but never goes anywhere – just short-term - and that's always suited me."

I give myself a mental high-five for guessing right about the threesomes.

"Are you saying I should ask Angel if she'd like to join us?"

"God, no! In fact I'm saying the exact opposite – I'm trying to tell you that I'm really enjoying being with you and only you, Stacey. When you were injured... no, that makes it sound almost accidental and it's time I faced facts:

When Danny beat you within an inch of your life, literally, I realized how deeply attached I am. I held back because I didn't want you to know.

It would be selfish of me to hang on to you when you, a young woman, have so much life ahead of you. So I tried to distance myself and normally that's very easy for me to do but with you...

With you I want to be selfish. I want to have your firm, young body in my bed night after night. I want to keep you close and away from the young men who might tempt you away from me."

"Oh my darling man," I sit up so I can kiss him deeply then look into his eyes to say:

"Please understand that I have had my choice of beautiful young men, men anxious to marry me, men my own age, men your age, and even men much older than you, because I'm a very wealthy girl.

I've been pursued by both handsome fortune hunters who would marry me for my money, and equally wealthy men who wish to form an alliance with my family. But you are my choice. You're the man I want to be with.

Maybe you did feel obligated to take me in, and maybe you think I was only repaying you for that kindness, but no matter what you *thought* this is what I want you to *know*: I've fallen in love with you, Abraham O'Shea. I love you and I'm in love with you."

I don't want to hear an *I love you, too* until he truly means it so I kiss him again then turn away and snuggle down for a little rest before going down to dinner.

Bram doesn't answer but I hear him expel a deep breath slowly. I can tell he's thinking about what I've said and I know my words interest him because he's grown hard again.

He kneels in the bed and lifts me up so I'm splayed over his thighs and he enters me from behind. He holds me easily one-handed and I feel his warm kisses on my neck while his other hand strokes me from my throat to my pussy. He circles around my clit, teasing with very light touches but not stroking. Not until my hips grind and

I hear his breathing quicken before he shudders into a powerful orgasm.

Happy and sated we lie in each other's arms and doze a bit before stretching and getting up. Feeling a bit mischievous I ask if it's okay for me to quiz Angel and Joel about their sex life when she was Girlie.

He chuckles and gives me a squeeze saying I should *go for it*, and that he's sure to be highly entertained by that conversation.

So I consider my approach and decide that once we're all seated with full plates before us I'll start teasing Joel.

Chapter 11

Angel

I didn't like the spanking stories – too brutal, too painful, too humiliating - but of course I read them all, one after the other, and *got sick to my pants* as Anita used to say.

They were basically the same story using different implements for different reasons.

In most cases the man was punishing the young woman for doing something potentially dangerous like walking home alone in the dark instead of calling him for a ride, and of course he'd warned her before not to do that but she's forgotten, or doesn't want to bother him, or she's in a mood...

So the reader has to agree that the man is only acting in the girl's best interest when he teaches her a lesson, and, since she already knew not to do that she is further punished for her disobedience and defiance. And if it's a repeat offence? then she's in for a week's worth of discipline with the whole toolbox!

Of course the girl fights and swears, or cries and pleads – depending on her nature - but no matter how it begins it always ends with her sobbing over a very sore red bottom and sleeping soundly in the knowledge that her man cares enough to correct her - at length - and that proves he truly loves her. What bullshit!

I realize these are just stories but I can't suspend belief long enough to get into that. Yet I am aroused, which confuses me. Personally, I'd prefer being orgasmed into oblivion by Joel's magic fingers and, oh yes that has actually happened. In fact, it happened a lot to Girlie.

I'm delighted to recall those times and am still smiling over one particular memory when I come into the bedroom for our *nap time* before dinner.

He's already lying on the bed, naked, hands folded behind his head and just waiting to be admired. I react accordingly and appreciatively then add:

"Joel, we've been having an awful lot of sex lately."

"Is it too much so soon after the birthing?"

"Oh no, I'm not complaining! It's all pleasure, no pain, and I'm enjoying every minute. No, I just wondered about well, can we maintain this pace? Is it normal?"

He laughs and cuddles me close, kissing the top of my head and breathing in my scent.

"No, it's not normal but I think it's well, two things. One is we're healing. We're taking care of ourselves after your horrible ordeal with Snyder and we're grateful that things didn't turn out worse. That makes being together and safe even sweeter and more precious."

"Aww, you smooth-talkers sure know how to pull women's heartstrings."

"This girl's heartstrings are the only ones I'm interested in."

"Woman."

"Girl – and before you argue, in forty years I'll still be calling you my girl so there!"

"I'm going to start calling you my boy."

"I'd love that! I want to be your boy."

"You always have to have the last word."

"No, but in this case there's still the second reason... remember? I think we're responding to Bram and Stacey's love affair. They're shooting out pheromones and sex vibes at each other and we're getting caught in the crossfire."

That makes me really laugh hard. After I wipe my eyes I tell him:

"I'm pretty sure we're self-starters! Which reminds me, I read those stories you got me—-"

"All of them?!" he interrupts incredulously.

"Well, they are short stories," I explain, on the defensive, "and while they're awful stories they do fulfill their purpose, admirably, which means you're off the hook for extended foreplay."

He rolls me on my back and lazily removes my clothes all the while eyeing me with lusty appreciation. The way he looks at me... God, it never grows old. Slipping a finger inside he quirks an eyebrow and I feel myself blush.

"So let me get this straight: *you* don't want to be spanked but you like to know that *other* girl's are getting their asses tanned, is that right?"

I try to adopt a world-weary tone as I say: "Oh Joel, just fuck me already."

"No, no. I savor extended foreplay," he replies, nuzzling my breast, "And I have another Agent Angel story for you so lie back and enjoy the ride."

A Joel O'Shea Fantasy Story:

featuring Agent Angel of the DEA

pursuing Criminal Kingpin Nasty Nick

"Undercover Assignment"

Things aren't going too well in Agent Angel's career with the DEA so she's been transferred over to the AML, Anti-Money Laundering.

That unit got a lead that funds are being moved through a billionaire gentlemen's club called The Billionaire Gentlemen's Club so they send her in undercover to get intel.

The hotel manager agrees to let her pose as a "quality control clerk from head office" in order to check out the club, the patrons, and the employees.

Agent Angel's idea of going undercover is to remove her police hat, belt, handcuffs, and ID.

She's disappointed to learn there are no good-looking young billionaires but plenty of dirty old men who grope and drool. She does catch the eye of a middle-aged billionaire who tries to grab hold of her but he's smoothly intercepted by the bartender. The bartender who turns out to be none other than Nasty Nick who's there casing the joint!

He apologizes to the angry billionaire, but says they've just found out the woman is actually a reporter for some scandal mag and he's been told to kick her out of the club pronto!

The billionaire recoiled at the word reporter but now, with a lascivious look in his eye, asks if she's going to be interrogated... and can he watch?

Ignoring the question Nasty Nick hustles her to the elevator. He knows it's a fast ride but figures there's time for a quick blow-job.

"Get on your knees, babe, you owe me for rescuing you."

Agent Angel complies then looks up at him blinking her beautiful big blue eyes. She doesn't have a clue what he wants. Even though her mouth is open.

With a sigh Nick quickly unzips and pulling his dick out he grabs her head and directs her mouth close.

She breathes out an *Oh!* then leans in and licks him like he's a popsicle. It feels good, but there's no time for *extended foreplay* so he rattles out instructions and Agent Angel obeys his commands.

For a first-timer he concedes that she'd done a damn good job.

"The end," says Joel with a smile.

"I love the ad-lib about *extended foreplay*." I comment.

"I'd love to interrogate you... I can think of many fun and interesting ways."

"Save that thought lover, we're already late for dinner."

Chapter 12

Bram

Joel's face is an absolute picture and the more he scowls the more he fits right in with what Stacey is saying.

"I'm serious Joel, you could be the poster boy of BDSM Clubs, I mean you are the spitting image of Sir Dom."

"Who the fuck is Sir Dom?"

"Well, he's a myth really. I mean it's like saying *Joe Average*. He's not a real person he's just the ideal for Dominants the world over."

He narrows his eyes at her and she claps her hands with delight, saying:

"That look! Picture this: if I could dress you up in a black motorcycle jacket, no shirt, faded low-rise jeans over cowboy boots and wearing that exact same expression – I could post the photo online and have you booked solid for the next two years."

"What are you talking about?" Now he's really frowning.

"Selling your services as a Dom. You'd make thousands a day or, better yet, you could train a stable of submissives and their masters would pay you big bucks."

"Stacey, how do you know this?" I ask, and my lovely innocent girl proceeds to tell me about a BDSM club she'd belonged to while in a European boarding school. She makes it sound like she'd joined the volleyball team.

I decide to just sit back and listen although I find myself feeling like the parent of the kid in a Spelling Bee who can spell cunnilingus without hesitation.

Both Joel and Angel are wearing amazed expressions, and I guess my face is a match.

"You see a lot of submissives want variety but their Doms aren't about to let them wander off just anywhere, are they? No, of course not, they have to maintain control. But if it's the Dom's idea to bring their sub to you for some extra training well... everyone has fun!"

"Fun."

Only Joel could utter that word like it's poisonous. He's wearing his *I don't have an emotion in my body* expression but I know he's seething just under the surface.

"Yeah, well it is to them. If you're queasy about corporal punishment I can take care of that."

"You? I thought you were a submissive?"

"I was a switch which means exactly what it sounds like. I'm just an average-sized woman, even a bit on the small side, so I don't have enough strength in my arm to be very effective at punishing - especially male subs. However, there's a particular whip called The Flicker which is ideal for someone like me.

As you might have gathered from the name it's administered with a flick of the wrist."

She pauses to demonstrate the wrist movement and I, inappropriately, think she'll do well casting a fly-fishing line.

"The Flicker has a soft end so it never cuts or welts the skin but it really stings! It makes contact like a kiss but after one second the impact is felt and the blood rushes to the afflicted area.

The closest thing I can describe it to is being flicked by a twisted-up wet towel in a shower room, has anyone experienced that?"

Joel and I both nod, both having been subjected to the puerile humor of adolescent boys during our growing years in boarding school. Even after all this time I can still remember how much a flick would sting and how pissed off I'd get.

"So, Stacey... you've been on the giving and receiving end of this Flicker whip?" asks Angel a bit hesitantly.

Well, I can understand that because it is a pretty personal question. However my girl isn't fazed in the slightest answering:

"That's right, and believe me it's *much better to give than to receive*," she chortles. I have to remind myself that this is Stacey, the scared little girl we had to rescue from Danny.

"Each of us schoolgirls were subjected to some sort of discipline. Usually a Dom delivers *six of the best*, I'm sure you've heard that phrase, but for us it was just four. *Just* four, my God I thought I was going to die!"

"How old were you?"

"Let's see it would have been ten years ago, no more than that, twelve years ago so I was seventeen. And I can still recall that stinging pain! See, what people like about The Flicker is the sub's reaction. By time they've received four strokes their flesh is bright red and they're shimmying like a go-go dancer. Oh, I should have mentioned that the sub is always restrained for a whipping.

With The Flicker only the wrists are tied and pinned up on something so that the sub can entertain everyone by twisting and turning frantically. Whippings are usually performed publicly because it adds to the humiliation knowing the frenzy of your pain is entertaining an audience."

Joel intervenes quite forcefully at this point saying:

"Stacey, this truly sounds terrible and abusive and I don't ever want to whip anyone, or see anyone get whipped, for any amount of money. Is that clear?"

"Sure!" she replies cheerfully continuing: "But there are plenty of other things you can do. You can put the boys in cock rings, and give-—

"Boys?" interrupts Angel in shock, just as Joel says:

"Cock rings?"

So Stacey goes on to explain that while BDSM Clubs are very strict about keeping their membership exclusive to adults and any guests must be above the age of consent, subs are always called *boys* and *girls* no matter how old they are. Turning to Joel she explains that:

"A cock ring is a way to restrict the sub's arousal. It's put on him easily enough but grows tight if he gets a hard-on so his discipline is to keep his excitement in check.

Girls are really easy because there are so many different types and sizes of vibrators for both vaginal and clitoral stimulation and orgasm denial is a big thing. The Dom will bring his sub to the brink again and again and then withhold satisfaction. He can even do it remotely with his phone."

"Don't even think about getting an app like that for me, Joel," inserts Angel.

Stacey just laughs and continues: "And of course anal plugs and dildos can be used on either sex."

I catch Joel's eye and we're both stunned by the matter-of-fact way Stacey recites these arcane practices. I'm beginning to have my doubts about my own performance.

"Other things are having a submissive kneel or kowtow, naked of course, and be told to hold the position for hours, or be tied up and held in uncomfortable positions for long periods of time.

See the overall idea is to play on the sub's masochistic tendencies and to painfully abase her – or him - by making them realize how unworthy they are.

Sometimes this is done by spitting on them or peeing or putting them in a dog-collar and leash, or doing anything that shames and humiliates, and a real submissive gets sexually aroused and/or emotionally satisfied by this treatment."

I have to interrupt here to tell her I agree with Joel and it really does sound horrible.

"It does, you're right," says Stacey, "but what you don't realize is that the sub is the one controlling the action.

The sub sets her limits with the Dom before anything ever happens. He – or it could be she but for convenience I'll say he – crafts a scene that the two of them then act out. The Sub never does anything she doesn't want to, no matter how much she might plead and protest and squirm, because if things go too far she'll stop the action with her safe word."

"Oh I've heard about that, well I've read about it in novels, usually the word is *red*, right?"

"Yes, just like a stoplight. A good Dom will know when to check in and if the sub is good she'll say *green,* but if she's getting a bit anxious and maybe wants him to ease up she'll say *yellow*. If she says *red* her Dom must stop immediately because the safe word is spoken.

Now, the activities from the original contract between them will develop and become more intense, more sophisticated, as time goes by so that the sub is never quite sure what comes next and that's a huge part of their excitement: a thrill of fear and anticipation.

By the way Joel, with a stable of trainees you would get tens of thousands a week," she concludes.

I'd stopped eating awhile back and have completely forgotten about my food which is now cold. I'm glad I wasn't trying to swallow a bite because I'd have choked for sure.

"That's insane money for sex!"

"I know but remember it's not sex, even if it is sexually-based. Besides, most of the people running these places and owning slaves and subs are part of the filthy rich jet-set. They're bored to bits with their lives and looking for any kind of a thrill and they'll pay any price."

"More money than brains," Angel comments.

"Well I showed a distinct lack of brains when I got involved in it but at least it didn't cost me any money.

A group of older girls from our school invited some of us to come along and, well teenagers are stupid and none of us wanted to back down and look like little kids. That experience sure was an eye-opener.

One of the really surprising things was how gorgeous most of these submissives are. You'd think they'd only have to snap their fingers and men would come running. And that's probably the case but these women want something different.

I went a few times before deciding that scene wasn't for me, in either role. So I moved on but when I met Danny, years later, he sensed a weakness in me and exploited it."

None of us speak of Danny any more and while that's probably sad it works best for us this way. I reach over to take her left hand and kiss the slightly crooked baby finger saying:

"You weren't weak, sweetheart, just achingly lonely and that made you vulnerable to predators like him and that Sonya."

She comes over to me and climbs into my lap telling me she's not lonely any more.

Chapter 13

Joel

Stacey's talk about the BDSM scene, me being the perfect Dom type, and earning big money to deliberately physically hurt people – willing though they may be - has got me unsettled. I truly love sex and I don't think I'm a prude, but this stuff?

I try to catch Angel's eye but she's deep in thought looking down at her plate, not eating, just pushing the food around.

Usually she can feel my stare and will look up to meet my gaze but not this time. I guess she's thinking about all the things that Stacey has said and I don't like that, I don't like not knowing what's going on in her head. I make sure my voice is soft when I call to her:

"Angel? What are you thinking, hon?" She gives me a startled look, obviously her mind was a million miles away, and says:

"Oh! Uh, just about some of this stuff Stacey's been telling us."

"Why?" I can hear my voice growing harsh and add: "Look, I know I sound rough and I don't mean to, I want us to be able to discuss this freely and openly."

She gives me a helpless look and shrugs her shoulders. I gesture for her to come sit in my lap like Stacey and Bram are doing. I think physical contact will help us verbally communicate. Angel seems strangely reluctant but she pushes her chair back and lets me pull her close.

"Okay then, I'll go first. These things we've heard disturb me. I hate the thought of being the prototype for *Sir Dom*. You know I love to fuck but Jesus this is something else altogether.

515

I can't imagine getting turned on over the sight of someone being beaten bloody or pissed on."

Stacey is earnest about explaining when she says:

"But Joel, don't you agree that if other people DO get turned on by that sort of thing then, so long as both parties are consenting adults, it's okay?"

"Yes, of course," I answer quickly. "But that doesn't change the fact that I think they're suffering a mental aberration – I'm not going to say a mental sickness because I don't know enough to speak to that – but definitely something out of the norm. Thank Christ it's not the norm!"

Stacey gives her high, clear laugh. It's a sound I usually enjoy but right now it grates on me. Maybe there is some truth in what she said about me because suddenly I'm feeling mean. Angel must sense it because I feel her body grow still, waiting, and listening closely.

"Bram, you've been awfully quiet. Normally you talk more than I do. So what do you think about all this stuff we've heard?"

"I feel like I'm having one of those dreams where everyone else knows what's going on but I'm just standing there saying *huh?* because this shit blows me away.

But you know, Stacey, I'm not sure that I believe in this consenting adults bit. I mean, you could argue that you consented to Danny's treatment of you but it really wasn't what you wanted, was it?"

"Bram's got a point, Stacey," puts in Angel with a concerned look on her face.

Stacey exhales slowly, thinking about her reply. "You're right that I've *since* discovered that wasn't what I truly wanted, but I thought I did at the time. I'd been carrying a torch for Danny for awhile, he sure was a handsome guy, and I wanted to make him happy."

We're all quiet while we think about Danny then Angel says, gently, "But he didn't feel the same about you, did he?"

"No, my feelings for him were always way stronger. I thought that was normal, that there was always one person who loved much more than the other but... I don't think that way any more."

She squeezes Bram's hand and he gives her a hug. I can tell that he isn't jealous or resentful of the feelings she had for Danny because that's all behind her.

"Getting back to what Stacey's been telling us about this lifestyle," he says: "Well, hell, I'm not sure if I want to know even that much."

"Yeah, it's like looking at something that you know is going to be nasty but you can't help yourself, you look anyhow, and then afterwards think *why did I look?* Damn."

Stacey is still merrily chuckling. "I guess you guys aren't big on horror movies either!"

"You got that right!" declares Bram.

I get an idea that's come out of nowhere but it seems worth pursuing so I tell Stacey:

"I like to look at beautiful things, like beautiful women. Especially beautiful naked women because I'm well, normal. Anyhow, I haven't seen you stripped down for months now Stacey, and I'd like to observe how much you've improved since then.

Before, I could see your rib-cage, and your hips looked painfully sharp, but now I'm guessing everything's covered with a nice soft layer. So how about you show me... show us."

I hear Angel inhale with a hiss and she sits ramrod straight and unyielding. I try stroking her arms but she tenses up and leans forward, moving her body away, though she's still in the confines of my lap.

When Stacey turns to look at Bram's face I sharply order: "No! It's not Bram's choice, it's yours. You don't need his permission."

She tilts her head at me and smiles saying: "But maybe I enjoy asking his permission for this and... other things, too."

I smile back with my eyes boring into her. Like I'm trying to mesmerize or command her with my gaze. Angel stands up suddenly freeing herself and she moves a few steps away before turning to face me:

"I know what kind of look you've got in your eyes and it's worked on me before, Joel, but it's not going to work on Stacey."

"I'm really proud of Stacey for all her hard work to get healthy again. She's got a fantastic body and if she chooses to strip for you bro, I'm sure you'll agree that she looks terrific."

"NO!" shouts Angel. She's now standing beside Bram with one hand on his shoulder and the other on Stacey's. "Joel can NOT make demands like that. It's just wrong."

Is Angel jealous? We already discussed the foolishness of that kind of thinking – didn't she believe me? All three of them appear aligned against me and I can't read anybody but it sure seems like I've pissed off everyone.

I don't know what to do next, that's a new and unpleasant feeling.

Stacey breaks up the tensions saying: "I won't get naked, Joel, but I will show off this pretty lingerie Bram bought for me that really flatters my body."

Stacey slides off Bram's lap and quickly pulls her dress over her head. The same gesture she'd made all those months ago on Danny's orders but with a much different result this time.

She's smiling with confidence as she spins slowly giving us all a good look at her slender proportionate figure clad in chocolate brown lace.

If you like girls with a completely different body type than Angel has then yes, she does look terrific, and I tell her so saying:

"Wow Stacey, you really have been working at sculpting your body. I can see well-defined muscle development and good tone, and you look strong."

"Strong, beautiful, and sexy!" declares Bram.

"Well she certainly owned that moment. Stacey you have poise and courage and my admiration."

She gives me a sweeping bow then happily climbs back on to Bram's lap and snuggles close, leaving her dress on the floor.

I look at Angel and I can't read her expression. Normally she's an open book. She returns my gaze with a hard stare and looks angry or maybe... challenging?

I sit up, intrigued. She registers my interest right away.

"Stacey," Angel asks, "I wonder if you know anything about Shibari? I read something in a magazine about it..."

Stacey cuts in with enthusiasm saying: "Oh, Shibari is fantastic! It's the art of Japanese rope tying.

"It's an artistic form of bondage. The knots can be quite exquisite and worn publicly – on the arms or legs – or privately underneath clothing.

Very often the bondage involves suspension from hooks. I don't think it's origins were sexual but it's certainly been adopted big-time by the BDSM crowd. Look it up online, it's worth checking out."

"Ah, yes well, thank you. I'll say goodnight now," replies Angel quickly before leaving the room without a glance at me.

I don't realize I've narrowed my eyes speculatively until I hear Bram mutter *that poor girl is in for it* while Stacey stage-whispers: *Sir Dom!*

I glance over at them with a lazy look but they aren't deceived by my supposed casualness and just grin back at me. Walking over to the bar I pour myself a shot of Southern Comfort. I bought this liquor for Angel's friends who never did get a chance to drink it. I like it.

I hold the bottle towards Bram and Stacey but they both shake their heads. I down my drink and pour two more which I carry out of the room with a nod goodnight to my brother and his girl.

Angel is still up. She's pulled back the duvet and is sitting on the bed with the iPad open. She's changed into the kimono thing that she calls her silk wrap. It's midnight blue and that color does wonderful things to her eyes.

I hand her one of the glasses and she takes a good sip, giving me an enigmatic look over the rim of the glass.

I'm definitely intrigued by tonight's rapid mood changes. Then I realize I've been on a bit of a rollercoaster ride myself.

She shifts the iPad to share the screen with me and together we start looking at the many photos depicting Shibari. I see that yes, the intricate designs of the knots are truly artistic. I don't know if the strained looks we see on some of the faces are real or the invention of the models.

There are lots of images, some drawings but mostly photos, showing a huge variety of bondage. In a few of the pictures it's just a mannequin with the rope tied enticingly around the breasts and between the legs. A woman could wear that underneath her outer clothes and be stimulated all day.

I find myself lingering over those pictures and considering the idea.

"What do you think?" I ask my wife.

"It's kind of hot but it's also way too much," she replies.

"Yeah. You would never go for that, eh?"

"Joel, I trust you. You got me over my phobia of being restrained and although it still feels a bit dodgy when you pin me down I would be wiling to indulge you if you wanted a very scaled-down version of this. Although it might make me say the word *yellow*."

"Well tonight's story just happens to include a little bit of bondage play so let's see what you think after you hear it."

A Joel O'Shea Fantasy Story:

Police Officer Angel still trying

to nab Criminal Kingpin Nasty Nick

"In the Holding Cell"

Agent Angel is no more, she's been kicked out of her department and demoted back to basic police work. After an official reaming Police Officer Angel is thankful she's kept her job and is hurrying away from her angry boss.

Nasty Nick is at headquarters paying off a superior officer when he gets on the elevator and discovers Angel there by herself. He looks at her the way a pirate looks at the buried treasure he's just unearthed.

Without a word he sends the elevator to the sub-basement and then sets it to stay stopped. Slipping off the necktie he wore to look respectable while in the police station, he effortlessly secures her to the rail.

Now she's standing with her hands behind her back, completely helpless, while he pops open the snaps on her uniform and her naked breasts spring free. He ogles her wolfishly asking:

"Don't you ever wear underwear?"

"I can't. I'm only allowed to wear my regulation-issue uniform and it didn't include a bra or panties or tights."

He just shakes his head at her naivety before filling his hands with her tits and rubbing his face over them. His five-o'clock shadow is abrasive on her tender flesh but since her hands are bound she's unable to stop him so he spends a few minutes enjoying himself.

Pulling back he sees her skin has reddened and brags that he's so manly the only time his chin is smooth is for a short while in the morning after his daily shave.

He steps away admiring the sight of Angel with her chest bared and forced forward by her restrained arms. He grabs the hem of her tight mini-skirt and pushes it up to her waist enjoying the discovery that she is, indeed, panty-less.

He's never had a good look at her and drops to his knees to enjoy letting his eyes explore her cunt with its pink clitoris showing through her blonde curls.

He strokes and pokes, cupping her mound, manipulating her clit with his thumb. She tries to squeeze her milky-white thighs together but he easily pulls them apart.

Now that she's fully exposed he leans in and begins to lick and kiss and tongue her until her legs splay of their own accord and she slumps against the wall as waves of pleasure course through her.

She's got her head thrown back and is chewing on her bottom lip. Looking up he can see her smooth belly, swaying breasts, hard nipples, and her pretty face.

When Angel opens her big blue eyes they make contact with Nick's gaze and the two experience a moment.

Then he screws her, retrieves his tie, and whistling walks away while she quickly pulls her clothes together before anyone can see her like this.

"The end. I know I rushed through the last bit but I need sex right this instant."

"Yes! Yes! We can talk later."

Now my Angel has turned warm and responsive, now she's her usual self. Her skin is soft and smooth and she smells wonderful.

I run my fingers through her hair which she's never cut since we've been together and it's grown out to a gorgeous wavy blonde mane. My beautiful, beautiful girl.

I grab her ass and pull her tight against me, my balls throbbing as they slam into her with every thrust. She is so hot, so wet, so perfect. She's pressing her tits tight against my chest and every inch of her that I can feel against me feels so fucking good.

"I was imagining that I had you cuffed and helpless while I knelt before you."

"Well, maybe we could try some kind of restraint some time."

After we both finish I repeat what she said and ask if it was a heat-of-the-moment comment? or if she meant it.

"Both!"

That's her usual kind of reply and it always elicits a grin. She sits up, cross-legged, and offering me wonderfully distracting views but her words soon draw my attention to her face.

"How come you don't get mean and bully me or try to dominate me against my will any more?"

"Because... you hated that?"

"Yes... and no."

"That's a typical Angel answer."

She smiles at that and says:

"I hate when you humiliate me and make me crumble to your will, but I love the arousal I feel as I fight against you. I've missed that, but I have to admit that it seems like our relationship has reached a new level of closeness and intimacy lately."

"I stopped trying to exert my authority when Snyder kidnapped you and I showed my true colors. I let you - and everyone else - see how deeply I love you and how I'd be nothing without you.

I fell apart, Angel. How can I pretend to be a tough guy when I prayed my thanks to God with tears running down my face once I realized you were safe and okay?"

"Oh Joel, oh darling. You're such a guy... any woman would tell you that that kind of display is as macho and heart-stirring as she could ever want. It's all I ever want. I love you so much."

"Oh sweetheart... is it time for us to have boring married sex now?"

"Absolutely, husband!"

Chapter 14

Angel

Lots of sex usually results in a sound sleep for me but I ended up waking early. I spend some time in our gym but it's really not my thing. Still, I manage to lose some of my anxiousness. Now I'm sitting in the kitchen nerving myself to question Stacey about our previous conversation.

When she gives me an enquiring look I finally blurt out: "Stacey, when you said you thought I was depressed what did you mean?"

"Oh, I hope I didn't offend you, Angel?"

"No, not at all, I just wondered what makes you think that?"

"You mean you're not feeling depressed at all?"

"Well, sometimes, maybe, but that's normal. I mean at times... oh hell."

Stacey has switched off the iron and pulled out a kitchen chair to sit down beside me. Taking hold of my hand she looks right into my eyes.

"Despite the fact that I told you you're not a natural submissive I do get a very strong vibe from you, a vibe that says you feel unworthy. If you are experiencing that kind of self-doubt then your interest in the whole D/s scene, or rather in being spanked – punished - makes sense.

Angel, it's not uncommon for women – and men – to suddenly feel they don't deserve their good fortune and become anxious and worried. You have a beautiful home and a wealthy family, a handsome husband who adores you, two utterly perfect babies, good health, good looks—-"

"I keep waiting for someone to discover I'm really a fraud and I shouldn't have any of these things," I interrupt, feeling tears spill down my face.

Stacey tightens her grip on my hand but just nods, waiting for me to continue.

"I'm a nobody, in fact I don't even know who I am. No idea who my father was, and my mother was a crazy drunk. I might have grandparents and aunts and uncles and cousins but I have no idea if I do. And if I do they could be anybody: violent criminals, drug addicts, lunatics... What kind of mother can I be when I don't even know my own history? Not even my medical history?

You said that the family is wealthy and that's true, but what person from some other wealthy family would ever want their child to marry one of mine? How can my babies ever overcome my sordid past?"

"Oh sweetie, your past isn't sordid. The circumstances aren't ideal, but the fact that you rose out of that is a testament to your strength and resiliency. You trained in law enforcement, a demanding profession, and graduated into an elite division.

You achieved something to be proud of, and you are only responsible for *your* actions not those of your parents, no matter who they were."

"It's comforting to hear you say that but—"

"Hey, never mind *comforting*, it's the truth and I majored in psychology, my career choice was clinical psychologist, so I can back my words. Angel, I know what I'm talking about.

Some people worry when things are going *too well*, and they're afraid to even acknowledge their good fortune in case they somehow jinx it. Some people even subconsciously sabotage themselves. But you know what they say: *it's bad luck to be superstitious.*"

That makes me smile, and her words do bring me some comfort.

"You know there really was someone out there, I didn't imagine being watched and then chased."

"Omigod I didn't realize he chased you, that must have been so scary!"

"Well I'm fast and once I overcame my initial fear - because he did startle me – well, then I got angry."

"Anger can be empowering but also enervating."

"Yeah, I had to go back to bed for a nap, such a wuss!"

"Angel you are a strong woman and I think the world of you."

"Oh Stacey, that's so nice. I realize one chat over the laundry isn't going to solve my problems but talking about my thoughts to someone who understands, and doesn't judge or tell me not to be silly well, it helps a lot, so thank you."

"I don't think Joel would tell you you're being silly. I think there's a depth and a feeling to that man that he tries very hard to hide although he does reveal quite a bit of himself in his music."

"That's very true and I am lucky to have him. Which reminds me. I'd like your help in preparing a little surprise for him."

Chapter 15

Bram

I finally finished working on my taxes and I've reached out to my Military Intelligence contact, as I told Joel I would, but I won't hear back before tomorrow.

So, I decided to find Stacey and suggest we go out for a drive. The weather is nice and we can stop for a drink somewhere and just relax and enjoy each other's company.

Maybe I'll find an abandoned lane on the way home where we can park and neck like teenagers!

Both Joel and I figure we're probably being surveilled by the FBI, but what if we're wrong? What if it's another sicko like that Snyder guy and he's after Angel?

Joel's going with her on her run tomorrow morning and hopefully before the day is out I'll have some answers. It's crazy but I hope it is the FBI. We can deal with them.

Meanwhile, I need to get my head clear.

I go looking for Stacey but find more than I expected. She and Angel are sitting in the kitchen having a very serious talk. I probably shouldn't listen but of course I do. I like to know what's going on in my home, and I like to know what's going on with my ladies.

I'm surprised at the direction their conversation takes. Joel and I once discussed the likelihood that Angel might have some underlying issues way back when but I never suspected she might be depressed or feel unworthy.

She's a beautiful woman with everything she could want! How did Stacey figure that out? She says it's a vibe so maybe she is empathetic. If so, I guess she will make a great clinical psychologist some day.

It sounds like she's managed to help Angel, for the time being at least. Angel's tears have stopped and she's smiling.

Now the two of them have lowered their voices and are giggling. I can't hear what they're saying but damn, I'll give myself away if I come any closer. I guess I'll just have to wait for their conspiracy to be revealed.

I back up a few steps and taking care to make noise head into the kitchen. The two women are looking at the doorway and smile as I approach. I give Stacey a kiss and present my offer, she's delighted.

"Give me ten minutes, hon, and I'll meet you at the car. I want to run a comb through my hair and grab my purse," she says.

I watch her and Angel hurry upstairs, knowing they're plotting something, then I go out to the garage to fetch my Lincoln.

Chapter 16

Angel

Stacey follows me into our bedroom and after a quick look round comments *perfect, I hoped so...* before hurrying out of the room. She's back a moment later with a rope arrangement.

"This is such a handy prop," she explains showing me what looks like a half-completed macrame project: artistically intricate knots loosely tied together forming a tube about eight inches long.

"Slide your hands in here, hold them in front so you can see," she instructs, and when I do she shows me how to give my wrists one twist that locks the binding in place. I try pulling my wrists apart but can't, and twisting again had no effect. I'm restrained good and proper!

"You can slide your hands, once you've secured them behind your back, over this door handle on the wardrobe. We have exactly the same one and I noticed that it would work with this piece. The long handle will fit alongside your forearms and securely hold you in place.

Then, this end bit of rope that hangs down here," she lifts the piece to show me, "unlocks everything with one tug." She demonstrates and the ropes immediately loosen and I'm free.

"That's amazing!" I exclaim, studying how it's made.

"It really is, and it's my gift to you and Joel. It's made to be used again and again."

At those words I feel a delicious thrill go right through me.

"That is so kind of you! But are you sure you want to give it to us? Just loan it for now." I say, sure that something like this must be very expensive. I realize Joel has a lot of money but I don't have any, or at least I don't have access to my bank accounts yet, so I can't pay for this device.

"You know I'm like 99.9% sure that Bram and I will never want to use something like this. I mean, if I tell him I really want to he'll probably go along with it but only for my sake. He's very vanilla in his lovemaking and I'm happy with that, he satisfies me fully.

Other than pretending we're making out in the back-seat parked in lover's lane or something, I don't think he'll ever choose any form of role-playing. So, please accept this with my blessing."

"Well thank you very much, Stacey. I don't know for sure that Joel will be interested but after you told us about Shibari we looked it up online and while going through the photos, a lot of them, I could tell it intrigued him.

Also, he tells me these stories, little fantasy scenarios created from a couple of characters he's made up, and in the latest one the girl - who is a very inept cop, by the way - gets tied to the hand-rail in an elevator by the criminal who ravishes her and performs oral sex."

"I'm getting turned on just listening to the story line. Get Joel to write down his stories and share!"

"Oh, I don't think he'll do that, he's not a writer."

"C'mon, those lyrics he writes? Fantastic stuff. Like that line *this love comes from my heart, but the lust is in my soul* I can totally relate to that feeling."

"Okay, you tell him to do it, maybe he'll listen to you. I've been saying he should record Tik Toks or YouTube clips of his singing and playing but he just brushes me off."

A beeping horn sounds impatiently and Stacey gasps:

"I forgot Bram's waiting in the car! Gotta run," and dashes away.

I go to find Maggie to let her know not to bother with our meal. I tell her Bram and Stacey have already gone out, and Joel and I will either go out too, or fix something later. She agrees that it's a good idea to get out and enjoy some private time away from home from time to time.

Returning to the bedroom I have a quick shower, not washing my hair but not caring that it get wet at the ends, then I pat myself damp-dry. I don't know how long I'll have to wait for Joel but I want to look freshly scrubbed.

I'm wearing my wraparound shortie robe, artfully loosened to show plenty of cleavage and leg, because it has a big bow in the sash that Joel will be tempted to untie. But then I realize because of the ropes he'll eventually have to rip if off me and satin is hard to tear. Plus, I like this robe.

So, I settle on wearing just a towel. I don't bother with make-up but dab on some scent. Then I put both hands through the rope tube and snug it into place behind me. The towel shifts down a bit but holds and now looks even sexier.

I hook my bound wrists over the wardrobe door-knob and sure enough I am very effectively pinned. It all feels so erotic!

That was all accomplished a few moments ago. Now I settle in to waiting for Joel. Replaying his fantasy story in my mind, and squirming around a bit to test being incapacitated, has excited me and I'm enjoying the pleasant tingle my thoughts have aroused...

Chapter 17

Joel

Nobody's around. I check the family room, Bram's office, dining room, kitchen – there's no sign of cooking – and finally I head upstairs. Maybe everyone's in the nursery? But the babies should be sleeping now. I want to wash up first anyhow so I go to our bedroom.

Angel is just standing by the wardrobe planning what she's going to wear since she's obviously just come out of the shower. Then I realize she's leaned up against the wardrobe door and she's looking really hot. Her eyes have a dreamy look and her lips appear soft and inviting. She's posing for me.

That towel doesn't cover much but even so I feel an overwhelming urge to rip it off. I should go slow and draw out the pleasure for both of us but I can't, suddenly I want to be rough, I want to grab hold and manhandle her.

She tilts her body slightly and I can see there's something behind... oh it's rope! There's rope around her arms! tying her up.. there's a rushing sound in my head as my blood surges and I'm thinking fuckfuckfuckfuckfuck so hot, so fucking hot. I hear her voice, breathless and whispery say:

"I'm utterly helpless, I can't move, I can't escape from you, Nasty Nick. I'm your captive."

Nasty Nick! The words inflame me. I fling the towel open but it catches behind at the back so I reach around her bum and yank it away. My fingers brush against both soft skin and rope and the fire rips through me.

I grab handfuls of her ass while staring down at her naked tits. The flesh is goose-bumping under my gaze and I see the aureoles pucker while her nipples grow rock hard. I say nothing but I'm squeezing and kneading her ass and her breathing turns shallow.

Now she says: "You're looking at me the way a pirate looks at buried treasure..."

And chuckling, I give her my best imitation of Nasty Nick's hungry, wolfish smile.

"I AM Nasty Nick and I'm going to do all kind of nasty things to this luscious, helpless body. It's all mine to use however I want! And I want nasty. Nasty, dirty, slutty sex.

You're going to obey my every command, you have no choice slave, and I'm going to make you beg for mercy."

She's writhing out of lust but also partly in performance since she knows how it excites me to see her squirm seductively.

"You're going to ravish my poor naked body and there's nothing I can do to stop you. I'm just your sex toy to play with, a living doll to amuse you, I'm bound and exposed..."

I bury my face in her tits, rubbing it up and down and from side to side and my five-o'clock shadow does make her skin flush pink. Just like my fantasy.

Her skin is so incredibly soft and smells so sweet. I start kissing her tits but I don't want to be tender and loving so instead I grab and squeeze her boobs just like I was doing to her ass.

I drop down to my knees and though her legs have fallen open that's not nearly enough for me. I roughly pull them apart as wide as I can. I feel her sliding down a bit but the rope holds firm. I throw her right leg over my shoulder to give her some stability.

And to open up her most delicate, tender spot to my eager lips. She tastes so sweet and her smell drives me wild. I suck and nibble and torment her with my tongue.

Chapter 18

Angel

I struggle against my ties to reinforce the thoughts running through my head: I am helpless, utterly totally completely at his mercy, his captive and he is my ravisher, I am his toy, his sex doll, his slave, nothing but a body to use as he pleases. I offer, but he only wants to take.

I feel his teeth on my most sensitive parts and hold my breath while he nibbles gently then licks like he's catching a froth of whipped cream as it spills over the rim of a steaming hot chocolate... and tastes just as sweet.

I'm held in place with one foot anchored on the floor and my other leg over his shoulder. With my hands tied and my legs spread wide I can't cover myself. I'm utterly exposed. It's so erotic I'm melting with passionate longing.

My pussy flames red-hot while he brings me closer and closer to the edge.

He cups my ass in both hands and pulls me in tight bringing my pussy – my cunt – towards his mouth. But that doesn't cool me down. His tongue gets to work and he owns me. I have no will, I'm simply a quivering pleading wet-wet-wet mess of desire with my legs forced wide, wide apart and held firmly in place.

Our eyes meet – me looking down over my heaving chest, and him looking up over the underside of my flushed breasts – and I see the dark hairs on his chin are glistening.

He quickly stands and pulls, unsuccessfully, then lifts me up and off the door handle. Turning me belly down on the ottoman he studies the knots that bind my wrists together. I can feel him running his fingers over the rope, stroking it and my forearms. Then he smacks my ass once but hard so I sure feel it.

"That's just a reminder," he growls in my ear.

Then he's entering me from behind, grabbing my knees and lifting me up. He's watching his cock plunge in and out and I know he's looking at those knots, too. After he cums he stays inside me but drops my legs back down.

Now he's kneading and massaging my ass. It's still stinging from when he gave me a spank and I wonder if he'll smack me again. There's nothing I can do to stop him if that's what he desires.

Instead, he reaches his arms under my chest and lifts me, pulling my body tight against his. Now he's kissing and murmuring endearments. He's fondling my breasts, kissing my face, loving me. This feels much, much better than a spanking.

"Do your wrists or arms hurt being tied up like this?" he asks.

I wriggle my shoulders and I feel okay. I say so, asking *why?*

"Because I'd like to keep you like this for a while, so long as you're not uncomfortable. In fact, I'd like to take a picture of you on my phone. Then I want to fuck you again."

I look him right in the eye and respond: "Anything you want... Fuck-Master."

Chapter 19

Joel

"Stacey I'd like to thank you for helping Angel prepare for our little game yesterday."

"Ah, it was a success was it?"

"Mmmm, but they say practice makes perfect so we'll probably give it another go sometime soon."

"What's this? Secrets?" asks Bram, inquisitive and interested.

"Only from me, I think. Angel enlisted Stacey help so we could enjoy experimenting with a bit of bondage."

"A bit of bondage? I see... Stacey, why didn't you tell me?"

The four of us were having our breakfast outside, enjoying the fresh morning air. Stacey now looks at Bram with her head tilted saying:

"I never thought twice about it. In fact realizing I'd kept you waiting in the car put all other thoughts out of my head. It wasn't until I was falling asleep last night that I even remembered and wondered if things worked out. I guess they did."

She gives us a cheeky smile that makes me laugh. I tell her that if she ever wants to know real secrets to ask Maggie, because she knows everything that goes on here.

"Maggie can be trusted, Joel. Just not to keep sex secrets."

"Oh right yeah, you told me about our sheets," I reply.

Angel laughs saying: "Omigod, yes!"

Bram chuckles as well until Angel tells him he wouldn't laugh if he knew what Maggie said about his bed linen.

We both ask *what?* but Angel shakes her head.

"Oh no, it's too embarrassing to repeat."

Just then Maggie comes out with fresh coffee saying:

"Hmmph, no need to be shy on my account, Angel. I stand by what I say and unless I ask for your discretion you're free to repeat word for word anything I ever tell you.

Besides, the time for embarrassment was when I walked onto this very patio and Angel you were sitting on Bram's lap in that chair, without a stitch of clothing on, him with his hands full of your breasts and you, she points to me, were on your knees doing... well, something Angel was obviously enjoying.

To be honest my first thought was to find the old belt and just lay into all of you but then I realized you men weren't degrading her, and she wasn't corrupting you. The three of you were engaged in something joyous and loving and I'm glad I witnessed that, it gave me a new understanding. Now I know why you all got on so well together.

But things are even better now that Bram has a girl of his own," she adds, smiling at Stacey.

None of us utter a word while she pours our coffees then goes back inside. I can't even make eye contact with anyone or I'll burst out laughing.

"I still haven't heard what she said about my sheets," complains Bram in a much more subdued voice.

"Ask her yourself!" replies Angel in an equally hushed tone. Turning to me she says: "I'm too embarrassed too breathe right now, but I'll tell you later."

"Hold up!" cried Stacey, "I want to hear about you three out here on the patio."

Bram looks at me and we both start laughing. Angel pulls a face but that just makes us howl.

"You go ahead and tell it Joel since you obviously want to," she huffs, but I know she's only pretending to be mad.

"There's really nothing more to add to the story, Stacey. I'm sure Maggie described it exactly as it was. We didn't know she saw us but... well what she saw happened a lot so—" but I'm laughing to hard to continue.

"Stacey these guys had this rule about me having to get naked as soon as all the employees left for the day. Now only Joel and I were having intercourse because we were trying to get pregnant but that didn't stop these two passing me from lap to lap and honestly it was mostly just cuddling."

"There were a few times when we ganged up on you though, Angel. I'd hold you down while Joel licked your pussy till you screamed with joy. You'd be squirming and struggling and I'd get to feel you up. We were out here one night in the winter with the heaters going and we were too busy playing to notice how cold it was."

"Oh I remember that night... half my body was on fire and the other half was freezing cold to the touch! We're all lucky we didn't get pneumonia."

Now that Angel's laughing too I'm happy. I've got another Fantasy Story to tell her at bedtime.

A Joel O'Shea Fantasy Story:

Now a Police Officer Angel

and Criminal Kingpin Nasty Nick

"Collared!"

Agent – now officer - Angel has been demoted to a beat cop. Nasty Nick has pulled strings with the higher-ups on his payroll to get her assigned to his area. He wants to keep tabs on what she's getting up to.

An old lady in the neighborhood discovers her cat has gotten itself caught in a tree and can't – or won't – come down. Officer Angel to the rescue except that, no surprise, she gets stuck as well.

"I'll have to call those firemen again," complains the old woman.

The ladder truck arrives with a couple of men who make quick work of the rescue job. The lead guy says:

"Here's your pussy, ma'am", then turning to his partner adds *sotto voce* "and here's ours," keeping hold of Angel and bundling her into the fire-truck.

"Lucky girl," the cat-owner thinks to herself.

Back at the fire station the veterans tell the young crew that they've brought back a new mascot to replace the late Spotty, their Dalmatian.

"Don't wreck her," they warn, adding that: "It's end of shift for us and we've got to go home but we'll want piece of her when we get back."

The four young firefighters decide the older guys are playing a prank. They figure Officer Angel is really a hooker or a porn star: *remember that photographer from the calendar shoot talked about doing a video?* And immediately get into the game.

They strip her, a quick job since she's naked under her uniform as usual, and put the dog's collar on her.

Officer Angel is thinking the call of duty for policewomen is really expecting quite a bit more than she ever imagined...

The men get her up on the bed, positioned doggie-style, attach the leash to her collar and toss the hand-loop over a hook on the wall. One of them grabs a deck of cards from the table to draw for who takes the first turn when the fire alarm bells go off and they have to hurry away.

Officer Angel is alone and struggling to unbuckle the collar because she can't reach the end of the leash when she hears footsteps. It's Nasty Nick! and he's seeing her completely naked for the first time.

Since she's on all fours with her privates exposed he figures the four young guys have fucked her and gets angry. Sliding off his belt he tells her she's getting punished for her bad behavior and he wants her to count off the strokes.

The first lash makes her yelp but she calls out *one, Nick* and he tells her to address him as *Fuck-Master Nick.*

Once four hard swats have striped her wiggling bare bottom Nasty Nick discovers he's turned on by the sight. He feels her up and she's moist from the spanking but there's no semen inside her.

He asks: "Did they screw you?" and she replies through her tears,

"No, Fuck-Master Nick."

Happy to learn he called in that false fire alarm in time Nick screws her doggie-style, then helps her get away before the firefighters return.

"The end."

"Aww, no fair! I want to hear about Officer Angel enjoying sex with four buff young firefighters..." complains my wife.

I remind her that I also own a belt and she quickly suggests a blow job.

"I'm changing the name of your horny button to a submit button."

Chapter 20

Stacey

Bram is so sweet. Obviously my experiences at the BDSM Club intrigue and concern him so much he's wondering if he really does satisfy me. We're getting ready for bed and he says:

"Stacey, love, you know you can tell me if there are any uh... games, or anything um... that you'd like us to play, right?"

He's so uncomfortable and obviously hating every word he's saying, but he's making the offer and that's so sweet. I know he'll feel better if I can suggest something, something that gives him back the power but also enjoyment.

I pause to give it some thought because I don't want to give in too quickly or he'll know I've been planning for just this situation.

"Welllll, as a matter of fact, there is something I would love for you to use on me. It's something I was given by one of my schoolmates but we never got the chance to try it out. I mean, if you don't mind, if it's okay with you?"

He's trying not to frown as he nods for me to continue.

I get my suitcase from the closet and pull out a flat box that's tennis racket size. Bram is watching intently as I open it up and remove an ivory-handled wand holding a spray of ostrich feathers. His eyes light up as I shyly offer it to him saying:

"I would love to have you torment me with tickles from these feathers. They're so soft, they're sure to make me crazy with desire."

I knew this type of toy would be right up his alley. Although our foreplay usually involves lots of semi-clothed caresses now he immediately strips me in his eagerness to test it out.

"Oh," I say as if a thought has just occurred to me:

"Maybe you should take my silk scarf that's on the dresser and secure my wrists to the headboard so I can't scoot away trying to escape the feathers."

Bram laughs off the idea, I was pretty sure he would! and quickly lays me down with one of his hands easily encircling both my wrists to keep me securely in place. Propped up on his elbow he looks down at me and begins to slowly tease and tickle my body.

This was supposed to be a treat for him but I'm sure enjoying being held tight while the tingling sensation plays up and down me from head to toe as he turns me front and back and doesn't let up no matter how much I swivel and wriggle and writhe.

I didn't expect much sensation from the feathers because they really are extremely soft but the continued tickling strokes have stimulated all my nerve endings. I'm not play-acting when I arch my back and spread my legs, those movements are involuntary reactions to being super turned-on.

I'm mewling like a kitten and tossing my head, my fingers flex and clench, my breath is a panting rasp. I can't fake this arousal, Bram knows it's all real, yet he's relentless in administering each delicious stroke.

I cry out as heat floods through my body, radiating from my clitoris to all my erogenous zones. I hear his sensuous groan and I match it with a gasp of pleasure.

Much later that night, actually it's the wee hours of the next morning, I wake from an erotic dream with my fingers cupping my pussy. I begin playing with myself: rubbing my nipples, stroking my clit. I feel Bram stir and waken.

Before he can speak I tell him to go back to sleep, or to watch quietly, because I can't stop. I explain that I dreamt of all the things he'd done to me earlier and how utterly deliciously wickedly wonderful every touch, kiss, and lick had been and now I'm reliving it all.

He can see my face, my hard nipples, and my rapidly moving fingers in the glow from the under-lighting in the bathroom. I put on a performance for my voyeur that is 100% real emotion and physical sensation. God, how I love feeling his eyes moving up and down along my body.

I roll over and lift myself up on my knees, showing him my back view and giving him a good look at my fingers sliding across the wet folds of skin. He can see, hear, and smell my arousal. I'm so close, so close...

"Please! May I finish?" I beg.

I don't hear words, just a rumbling growl that sends me right over the edge into that white light exploding in my mind and in my pussy. My gyrating hips have shot my body upright and bowed back in an arch.

Suddenly his big hands are everywhere, nipples, clit, ass, and his mouth is kissing my face all over.

Hungrily I search for his dick and yes, it's hard, and in my mouth it grows harder still. I fuck him with my mouth and swallow his hot messy mass of cum. He pulls me against his chest and into a bear hug that makes me fear for my ribs!

I don't know if I fall asleep or pass out. Seriously, I'm so completely shattered and overwhelmed by this night's experiences.

He's so strong, so mighty, yet it's a quiet strength. I mean I'm always aware of the manliness of Bram but he's not in the least like those testosterone-fuelled boys constantly flexing and bragging and vibing – he's just simply, immovably, safely there.

At some point I remember circling my arms around his neck and calling him my big oak tree.

Chapter 21

Joel

By choice I prefer working out in my gym, but this morning I'm escorting my wife on her run through the woods. I don't think the watcher will return but there's no way I'm taking chances on her safety.

Over the past few years Bram has gradually eased us out of the illegal businesses and dodgy partnerships we inherited from our father. Many of which were established in my grandfather's time. We ended on good relations so I'm confident there are no enemies and no threats.

That means it's the so-called *good guys* we have to worry about. Ironic when you consider the three of us all had exemplary careers in the military and law enforcement.

I don't believe Angel is in any true physical danger, but I know our life together could be irreparably damaged. There are certain facts and truths that are better left hidden and buried. Angel knows most of it... but not all.

I'm hoping Bram's contact in Intelligence can shed some light on what the FBI's up to, but I'm going to add the video home surveillance anyhow. We should have done this a year ago, at least. It will be expensive but what better way to spend money then in protecting your family? I don't want Angel to ever worry about her and the twins security in our home.

Her voice interrupts my thoughts when she calls back:

"You're awfully quiet back there old man, having trouble keeping up? Do you need me to stop so you can catch your breath?"

"I'm an arms-length behind you babe, which means your ass is well within reach of my hand so just keep that in mind when you're mouthing off."

"Ha! I'm just giving you a heads-up that it's time to put on some speed."

And with that my wife shoots forward setting a much faster pace. I have to admit that I'm having a good time out here in the crisp fresh air. There's always some noise in the woods: birds chirping in the trees, rodents rustling in the grass, the rushing water from the stream that's just out of sight, and the steady tap-tap of our feet on the path.

Angel has done a remarkable job of losing the baby fat and looseness gained during her pregnancy. She was careful throughout and that, combined with her efforts since, has paid off. She looks trim, sleek, and strong.

Every time her foot hits the ground the corresponding ass cheek tightens into a hard round ball, then it happens again on the other side. I'm mesmerized watching the bounce back and forth. It gives me a delicious idea.

This last spurt signifies that our run is nearly at an end. We've completed the circuit and are coming up to the house now. A few stretches to cool down and then into the shower. I'll put my plan into place before breakfast.

Once we get in the house I hoist Angel up and over my shoulder to carry her up the stairs. She protests that it's too far and she's too heavy but I just swat her bum and tell her to keep quiet.

"This is how I react when someone calls me *an old man,* Angel, I have to prove myself. It makes me want to treat you like a little girl. So from now until I tell you different you do not speak or make a sound. You've been a brat and your *old* husband is putting you in a *time out.*"

"I was only—"

Swat.

"Joel don't do—"

Swat.

"Hmmph."

I give her ass a soothing rub since she's finally figured out how to behave.

Silently she heads to the bathroom and turns the shower on. I follow and admire her body as she strips off. The look on her face is hilarious: scowling and pouting. I'm getting a preview of how the twins will look when they're thwarted, and it's so cute.

I quickly join her under the water and removing the soap out of her hand I take charge of washing us. Angel is soon obediently following my directions to bend and turn as necessary as I tell her where I'm cleaning next.

"Now I'm going to get this soap all foamy and clean your neck down to your shoulders and across your upper back. That feels good, doesn't it? Now turn towards me so I can get those tits all sudsy."

I let my hands and my eyes linger over her pretty tits, all wet and shiny, with the nipples a hard red. They lift invitingly when I raise each arm to wash her armpits.

She's keeping her mouth shut by biting down on her bottom lip and my cock has noticed that gesture. But this session is all about Angel so I turn her around again saying:

"Now to massage these bubbles all over that lovely round bum with one finger probing your ass-hole since it needs to be squeaky clean for later."

Her body twitches when I say that but I can't see her face. I do plan to have sex with my wife's ass but I still need more time to prep her first so it won't be happening today. But... I'm happy to leave her wondering.

"Your ass cheeks are so squishy, I love grabbing a handful to squeeze, but right now I want you to tighten up... oh yes, good girl, just like that. Now your cheek is round and hard, just like my balls get before I explode. This shows me you've got strong muscles in your bum which are going to give me so much pleasure when I'm buried deep in your ass. Mmm-hmm. Now turn around.

I need to get a good lather going in order to clean this cunt because just when I think it's washed I feel a sticky slimy spot. Damn, it just happened again. Hmmm, seems the more I scrub the more it gets slippery"

By now Angel is wiggling and panting while I keep bringing her to the brink then easing back. Leaving her unfulfilled I move on, chuckling as she whines.

"Good strong thighs and long, sleek legs, oops got to do the other leg too. And now we're at these ticklish feet."

Other then groans of pleasure my girl is sensibly keeping quiet.

I pull her close and telling her to wrap herself around me I get enough soap off her and on to my body for a quick wash. Then I unhook the handheld shower-head and begin her rinse.

Naturally I spend extra time on her erogenous zones and she responds lustily when I aim the water inside both holes and then directly on her clit. I finish up just as the water is starting to cool.

Hope everyone else has already showered this morning or they'll have to wait for the boilers to heat up again.

I give us both a vigorous rubdown with a big fluffy towel and when I pull it away she puts her arms around my neck and drags me down for a kiss.

"Take me to bed, husband," she commands and I smile at her before looking in the mirror and seeing her naked reflection. There's a faint pink mark on her ass from when I swatted her on the stairs. Watching, I give her a sharp smack and see her flinch.

"I said no talking."

The frown is back. Angel reaches her hand round to rub her behind but I pull it away and tilting her chin turn her head to look at her image saying:

"See how I've marked you?"

She gives a discontented grumble but I notice she's staring at the reflection of her handprinted ass.

I fold up the towel and place it on top of the vanity. That gives some padding when I lift Angel up so she's kneeling on it.

"Both palms flat on the mirror and don't make a sound," I instruct. She complies and I inch her knees wider and wider until her pretty pussy, all pink and clean from the shower, is fully exposed.

"Look at you being such a good girl for me. You want to please me, don't you?" I watch her face in the mirror. She's ducked her head down but lifts up her eyes to meet mine as she shyly nods.

With her hands against the glass her tits hang free and I grasp one in each hand to squeeze and fondle, keeping my eyes on hers.

"My pretty baby, my sweetheart. You make Daddy so happy he's going to make you feel extra good, baby girl."

Since Angel never knew her father and grew up without a male relative it's likely she has a Daddy fixation. She's definitely got a praise kink. Her body was already trembling from the edging in the shower and now she's practically purring.

"Time to play, baby. I just need to..."

Looking around I consider my options. I'm too tall if I stand, too low down if I sit, but there's a stool in our walk-in closet that will work perfectly.

"Don't move," I order as I go fetch it.

Returning I see her face in the mirror looking a little apprehensive. Does she think I've gone to get some spanking implement? She really should know me better than that. I haven't enjoyed giving her these swats, it truly does nothing for me, but it's part of this playtime and I hope Angel is getting something out of it.

I pull up the stool until I'm close enough to massage both cheeks and the backs of her thighs while dragging my tongue from her ass-hole to her clit. All the way down and then back up again.

I dried her thoroughly but she soon begins to slick for me as I continue licking and tasting.

I pause to circle her clit a few times and when I pull back I see she's closed her eyes.

I bark her name and then meet her startled gaze in the mirror and order her to keep her eyes open.

"I want you to watch your own face while I destroy you with pleasure," I explain. "It's about time you see what you look like up close, closer than what you saw in the honeymoon video."

Then, sitting back so I can see both views of her, body and reflection, I start scissoring my fingers to torment her clit. I can see the flush forming across her chest, her nipples hard and her tits swaying. Her eyes are still watching but from under lowered lids, and her mouth has fallen open.

Angel rocks but I pull her back into place. With one hand around her hips I reach down to attack her clit from a new angle while I insert two fingers inside her hole from behind. Stretching in and up her sudden jerk shows me I've reached her g-spot. I massage it rapidly while simultaneously giving her a clitoral orgasm. Her whole body spasms and shudders in a wave of deep pleasure.

"Uh.. ah.. Joel, oh! oh! ohhhhhhh!" she cries out her delight and, of course, that earns her another smack on the bum.

"Ow! Joel, I can't control—"

Smack.

"You'd better learn some control wife, because I've only just gotten started on giving you your orgasms. You need this discipline to keep you obedient and I prefer using the carrot method instead of the stick."

I repeat the process of driving her pleasure to a peak then pushing her over the edge again and again and again, until finally Angel collapses on the counter-top in a boneless mewling heap.

I love seeing her like this, lewd and lusty and satisfied. I'm so thankful that Angel is such a receptive lover and always has been.

Staying on the stool I pull her onto my achingly hard cock, still facing away from me so we can both watch ourselves in the mirror.

I roughly fondle her tits while she squirms her ass against me. Pressing her feet against my shins she gains enough leverage to lift her pelvis up and down my shaft. I grab her by the hips and knowing I can't last long I press two fingers down hard on her swollen clit and she explodes yet again and I join her.

I put Angel back up on the counter, sitting this time, while I run warm water over a washcloth and clean us both. Her folds are so puffy and red. I capture her mouth against mine and kiss hard until both her upper and lower lips match in swollen tenderness.

My lovely wife is rocking that freshly fucked look. I can't wait to show her off downstairs. I don't think I'll be hearing any more *old man* comments for awhile.

"You can speak now, Angel. Anything you'd like to say?" I smirk.

"Just... that was lovely, thank you Fuck-Master."

Chapter 22

Angel

Stacey and I are sitting on a blanket on the lawn, playing with the babies. The sunshine is so warm on our skin and every one of us is greased up with sunscreen. Plus sun hats and sunglasses.

I'm still in a happy haze from this morning's activities with Joel. He's never spent so much time with his mouth on my pussy before. It actually got to the almost-painful point but then I'd shatter all over again.

When Bram brought the food into the dining-room he took one look at me and said:

"No wonder we've run out of hot water."

Joel smirks saying: "I was inspired by our morning run, watching her pussy twitching each time her butt clenched on a down step."

I have no idea what he's talking about but I don't care, I'm just thrilled at what he did in our playtime, and because my post-babies body still excites him.

Everything is fantastic. I have a wonderful home and family, friends and husband. Life is fucking great! There, I said it. I'm not crossing my fingers or touching wood or anything like that - I don't believe in jinxes.

Now that the twins have passed the six-month mark they're awake for longer periods each day and very interested in everything and everyone around them. Interested enough to move. Both enjoy rolling onto their tummies and lifting up their heads. They try to sit but usually end up toppling each other over.

They need to be watched constantly but it's a pleasant task. The smallest thing – like a lady bug – entrances them, although when a butterfly flitted past Adam cried because he couldn't catch it. Eve studied her brother for a moment then burst into tears as well.

I sighed, reaching over to cuddle before I realized it wasn't Adam who made her cry – it was strangers. I could see a long shadow falling over our blanket. Turning I looked up into the shapes of two men but I couldn't see more than that since the sun was bright behind them.

I scramble to my feet and move so that I can get a better look. Maggie brought the men out which means they came to the house, not from the woods. Now she moves past them to fetch the twins, telling Stacey to give her a hand.

"We'll be right back," she says, and her voice is sounding a warning.

The strangers produce ID wallets and introduce themselves as FBI agents wanting to speak to Joel O'Shea. They won't say why so I decide I'm not feeling co-operative and refuse to let them come inside to wait.

"If you don't know where your husband is, or when he'll be back," says the younger man, Agent Dexter Williams, in a tone of blatant disbelief, "Can you at least call him?"

"I don't have a phone," I answer. Now both of them give me a look but actually that's the truth, I still don't have a phone.

"It's on my to-do list," I tell them.

Just then the nanny comes out and stops short seeing the FBI agents. She stares and blushes then quickly bends down to gather up the twins' blanket, toys, and other baby paraphernalia before hurrying back indoors.

Stacey comes back out and stands beside me without saying a word, while Maggie is blocking the doorway with her arms folded. The Feds realize we're not in the mood to be helpful and leave their business cards with me insisting I must have Joel call as soon as I see or hear from him.

I acknowledge that I'll pass on their message.

As soon as they leave Stacey and I run into the house and confer with Maggie over what that could possibly be about.

Bram and Joel are out on some project but we're expecting them home for dinner so we'll just have to wait until then to get some answers.

Chapter 23

Joel

I can tell Angel's unhappy about my attitude but really, what else can I say? I don't know why the FBI is interested in me but I can guess it's about Kendricks's death or Snyder's or Danny's, or all three.

"But aren't you worried?" she asks tearfully. I gather her in my arms and rocking her say:

"What's the point of worrying? I'm going to deny any accusation they make and the onus is on them to prove their case. They can't do that so no, I'm not going to worry about it."

"But they came to our home! They think they have something—"

I interrupt telling her:

"This is what's called a *fishing expedition*, hon. They're going to make some outlandish statements and gauge my reaction. We both know I'm pretty good at keeping my expression wooden when required."

"And even when it isn't required." she admits with a pout. That makes me laugh.

"Angel, the only weak link in any possible chain of evidence is the Landismans and if they were to admit anything now they'd both be criminally liable so they're not going to talk.

I'm sorry your friends have been put in this position but they agreed willingly. They really do think the world of you, Angel."

"But what if they're offered a deal if they speak out against you?"

"Why would such an offer even be made? There's no reason. And as federal agents they'd still be subject to a record and job loss even if they did avoid imprisonment so no deal would ever be good enough.

You know that, you know from your own career that you guys are held to a higher standard and if you fall, you fall faster and harder than civilians do."

"But what about me? Why didn't those two agents question me?"

"Now as to that, I'm not sure." I pause for a minute while I run several ideas through my mind before discarding them all. The only thought left is:

"Maybe they didn't research me as well as they thought because I'm guessing they don't know who you are, or rather were. It looks like they have no reason to connect DEA Agent Joanne Dwyer with Mrs. Angel (Joel) O'Shea, housewife and mother."

"If that's true then this can't have anything to do with Kendricks."

"No, you're right. I don't think it's about him at all. Of course if they are pursuing an enquiry into Snyder and Danny well, your identity could still come out and then they might connect the dots. But even so, all they've got is guesswork and supposition.

They don't have anything arrest-worthy so we don't have anything to worry about."

I can see she's still not convinced but she is inclined to be a worrier. Which is why I don't tell her that this Agent Williams has been nosing around for awhile, asking questions about all of us.

I debate sharing the thought that her morning stalker is one of these agents, but because I don't know if she'll think that's good news or bad I decide to keep quiet.

Bram has passed on to me the gist of Angel's conversation with Stacey when she confessed to feelings of unworthiness. We decided not to discuss this with her, but to increase our compliments and praise. We thank her for creating a very comfortable home, for keeping the staff working together happily, for being a devoted mother, and working hard to keep us all healthy with walks and jogs and good healthy meals.

It will take time to see results but I believe Angel has grown more confident this last while. I hate to see that weakened by an unfounded threat.

Now she looks up at me in wonder asking: "Joel aren't you afraid of anything? or anyone?"

"Angel, sweetheart, of course I am. I'm terrified about anything happening to the twins or to you so that's three people I'm afraid of because of the power you three have to destroy me. What's that expression... hostages to fortune?

And of course there's Bram, Stacey, Maggie – if any of you were in trouble or in danger I would do everything in my power to bring you home safely. But that's the only kind of thing I'm afraid of. Not threats.

Although of course there's always Silvana D'Allessandro."

"Oh? And who might she be?"

"She's the colonel who tried to have me killed when we were stationed in the Middle East. I'm sure I mentioned her..."

"Not by name. I have to admit I completely forgot about her. I mean, I thought her betrayal was enough revenge – shouldn't it have been?"

"You'd think so but... woman scorned, etc.."

"She couldn't still hold a grudge just because you never returned her affections. Joel you're drop-dead gorgeous but come on, that happened several years ago so she must be over you by now. Especially now that you're a happily married Daddy who's no longer in the military."

"Well you've bruised my ego deeply, wife... but I'm afraid with a possessive nature like Silvana's my current good fortune might just make her even more vengeful."

"Oh, it's *Silvana*, is it?" And I hear how her tone of voice hardens.

"You can't possibly be jealous, you don't even know what she looks like."

"Of course I'm not jealous but how come she's not D'Allessandro? You call all of the other soldiers from your unit by just their surnames."

That makes me think, and she's right. I do think of Silvana as a woman first and a soldier second. I guess that's because of the way she came on to me by stripping off to show me what she had to offer. Before that happened I'd never thought of her that way.

It was her behavior that made me view her differently - and not favorably. And that was before she set me up to be captured and likely killed. Bitch.

"I don't really think Colonel D'Allessandro is a threat to me - to us - Angel. She's just the only enemy I could think of when you asked.

And yes, you are jealous and, once again, let me reassure you that I will never have eyes for another woman now that I've met you."

"Pfftt, I'm not jealous!"

"Ha! You're such a liar, naughty girl."

"Never mind that. Getting back to the FBI, what are we going to do now?"

"*We're* not doing anything, but *I* will call back one of these agents and see what they're after. Which one was in charge?"

"One guy was definitely older and I think he was the superior, but the younger guy was the most talkative and really the way he spoke was like he was trying to provoke me."

"That would be this Agent Dexter Williams?"

"Yes, Williams is right. He's going to want to see you, to talk to you in person, maybe to take you in for questioning."

"I'll tell them to come here and Bram and I will meet them in his office. I won't go anywhere unless they produce an arrest warrant - which they won't be able to do - and even if they did I wouldn't say a word without my attorney.

They have to play by the rules, Angel. And you and I both know how those rules can tie their hands."

"Oh Joel, I'm going to fret until all this is over."

I wish I could allay her fears but I'm helpless against her nature, formed by her own life experiences. She's been taught some hard lessons. All I can do is hold her and give reassurance and hope that my calmness and lack of concern will somehow ease her anxiety.

"Who - or what - are you afraid of, Angel?"

"Me personally? Nothing. It's losing everyone and everything in this life we've built that scares me. But as for me I'm tough. I'm so tough I could have been a superstar champion of the WWE."

"Maybe if they added mud-wrestling to their competitions..."

"Oh, you'd LOVE to see me mud-wrestle, wouldn't you?"

"Yes, I would. In fact, I'd love to see you in a wet t-shirt."

"I might be able to arrange that, husband."

"Good! Meanwhile, I have another bedtime story for you."

A Joel O'Shea Fantasy Story:

featuring Police Officer Angel

and Criminal Kingpin Nasty Nick

"On Probation"

Officer Angel comes by the betting shop early the next morning. She tells Nasty Nick she's following his instructions on how to see him clean-shaven.

He lets her feel his smooth face and then pulls her into a long kiss. And a lengthy grope. Then he sits her in his lap and they neck and fool around a bit.

He asks why she chose to join the police force saying:

"After all, you're not much of a detective, are you?"

She confesses that she's on her last warning at work.

"Do you like being a cop?"

"Well, I never really thought about it. Daddy was a policeman but he died when I was very young so I never really knew him. But Mama always told me I should be proud of him and so I figured if I became a policewoman then when he looks down on me from heaven he can be proud of me."

"Oh Angel, the people in heaven have way more important stuff to do then to be watching us. Maybe when you were a little girl he would have watched over you but not now that you're a grown woman and doing private, grown woman things."

He then opens up her uniform top and, as usual, enjoys the sight of her bare breasts. He plays with her nipples and massages her tits till her squirming in his lap makes him hard.

"And you're associating with known criminals and well... that doesn't look too good for a cop on her final warning does it? I guess I could keep it a secret... for a price!"

"Well, but... you're the known criminal so you have to keep it a secret, don't you?" she asks with a puzzled frown.

"I may be the criminal, but I'm not the one who's being fondled like this, am I?" and with that Nasty Nick slides his hand under her skirt and starts teasing her naked pussy.

"Oh Nick, please don't tell on me."

"Well, maybe you could persuade me to keep your secret if you agree to owe me a favor AND give me a blow-job as a sign of good faith."

"Oh! I can do that. I did it before, and you said I did a good job sucking your dick."

Nasty Nick smiles and sets her down on her knees. Officer Angel performs with satisfactory enthusiasm.

"The end." I say.

"He really enjoys taking advantage of her innocence, doesn't he?" complains Angel.

"Oh, I think he's just showing her who is in charge of that relationship."

"Well, he certainly *thinks* he's in charge..."

Chapter 24

Angel

Joel phoned that Agent Williams first thing this morning and the agent wasted no time in coming back again to see both Joel and Bram at home.

They all go into Bram's office and Joel shuts the door in my face. I'm tempted to take in a tray of coffee but I know Joel is keeping me away because of what he calls my *transparent looks*.

And I don't feel like offering any hospitality to these FBI people invading my home.

The trouble is I don't know how forthcoming Joel will be with me once they leave. Will he tell me everything? or leave out crucial bits to *protect me*. I don't want to be protected, I want the truth so I can face it head on.

Sure that I'll find Stacey in the laundry room off the kitchen I head that way but first I encounter Maggie preparing lunch so I complain to her.

She hears me out then comments that so far as she can see there's nothing I can do.

"But I need to know what's going on, what's being said, and I can't be sure Joel will tell me the truth."

"Joel doesn't lie—-"

"He might to protect me."

"No, I'm serious. Joel does not lie. He might refuse to answer but he won't tell you an outright lie. You can at least count on that much."

"I'm worried, Maggie."

"Well Angel I can see that, but I don't know what to say. You've just got to trust the men to take care of this business. After all, it is their business – not yours."

"But the trouble happened because of me and—"

"No, that trouble was caused by Danny. He didn't have to bring that Snyder person here but he did. He didn't have to tell that lunatic about the hunting cabin but he did. He didn't have to batter Stacey half to death but—"

"He did," finishes Stacey coming in with a basket full of baby washing.

"Angel, you could just as easily blame me for what happened."

"Oh I don't know any more, Stacey. My head's just going round and round. Snyder had it in for me although I don't know why, and Danny had it in for you so I guess we can share the blame."

"Neither of you is to blame," insists Maggie. "It's the crazy men who caused the trouble – and that's nothing new!"

"Maggie what's your husband like? I don't know anything about him except you leave after your shift here to go home and feed your family and that's all I know."

"Well he's an invalid so my family consists of him and my sister who lives with us and whichever of my kids are around. I've got four and they're grown but that doesn't mean they don't land on my doorstep, like as not with their own kids too, every now and then. I bitch and complain but I love it."

And she does look like a happy woman satisfied with her lot in life. How the hell do I achieve that? It's not that I want more... I think I want less because I still can't believe I have all this.

Sometimes I wish Joel and I were still back at the compound having a so-called shower with buckets of cold water and Bram cooking the meals and then me cleaning up naked under Joel's watchful eye.

Back then my head was a mess because I didn't understand what had happened to me, and I had no clue where I was going, but for some reason those anxieties didn't keep me awake at night. Living in the moment with the men, especially Joel, making all my decisions for me was, strangely, enough.

"I'm going to demand Joel repeat this conversation they're having word-for-word and Stacey? I want you to back me up on this."

"Sure thing!" she smiles.

Chapter 25

Bram

Joel's never been good at answering questions so, as usual, it falls to me to do the bulk of the talking. That's okay though, Joel is sufficiently intimidating even when he's silent. Maybe even more so then.

"So our information is that Anastasia Somerton, known as Stacey, has been living here since March. She came with Danny O'Shea, the youngest of you three brothers but stayed after he left, is that correct?

"I didn't know that Stacey was actually called Anastasia but yes, the rest is true."

"Why didn't she go back to the university with your brother?"

"How is that relevant to your enquiry?"

"We're wondering if she is the unidentified female who was thrown from the vehicle Danny O'Shea and Chris Snyder died in. The woman the two witnesses called the paramedics for, the one taken to hospital as an emergency case?"

"No, she isn't," I reply.

The four of us sit quietly for a minute or so.

"Why is Ms. Somerton living here?"

"That's a private matter," I answer.

"Mr. O'Shea I'm conducting an enquiry on behalf of the Government of the United States of America. I demand that you answer my questions."

"Mr, I mean Agent, Williams, I'm a citizen of those same United States and refusing to answer is my constitutional right."

"Why did Danny O'Shea leave his girlfriend behind and why, more than three months later, is she still here?"

"She wasn't his girlfriend," says Joel. Three pairs of eyes swing his way and he returns our gazes blandly.

"Danny and Stacey were friendly at college, but she got sick and Danny didn't want to be with her any more. He had no patience with the patient," he gives a grim smile, then says:

"He knew it wasn't right to leave her behind on her own so he brought her here. Because Stacey was anorexic - or borderline - or something. We have two nannies because of the babies, and our housekeeper is a trained dietitian. Bringing Stacey here to be looked after made sense because she knew us. She spent Christmas here."

"Well, sorry but it really doesn't—" begins Agent Williams but Joel interrupts him to say:

"We have money, we're well-off, but the Somertons have real wealth. They want their daughter to make a well-connected marriage someday and they don't want any medical records showing mental or physical illnesses.

Stacey has never been officially diagnosed and she's well on her way to recovery now. She's eating and she's got all of us watching that none of that food is coming back up. She exercises with my wife and we've just started her lifting weights so she can build muscle and get toned."

"I told you it was a private matter because we don't want any word of Stacey's problem getting out. We think she just let too much pressure build up over her post-graduate studies. The fact that the situation is resolving itself so well shows it was just a temporary illness," I add.

"So who was the female in Christopher Snyder's truck?"

"She could have been a hitchhiker for all we know, but isn't it likely she was Snyder's girlfriend?"

"There's no record or report of Snyder having a girlfriend."

"Well we can't help you there, neither of us ever met the man."

"Your brother knew him."

"Evidently, but we didn't, and he was never a guest in this house."

The second agent, an older man, hasn't uttered a word beyond greeting us first thing. Now he stands thanking us for meeting with them and telling Dexter Williams it's time to go.

Williams isn't happy about it but there are no further questions left for him to ask.

"I'd like to see Ms. Somerton before we leave," he says with a trace of desperation in his voice.

"You already saw her, with my sister-in-law and her babies. Stacey didn't want to speak to you then, and she doesn't want to speak to you now."

Agent Williams has no choice but to give up. As we walk the two men to the front door one of the nannies comes into the hallway, sees Williams and bursts into tears before fleeing back up the stairs. We all just look at one another.

Joel nods a goodbye to the FBI and turning to me says:

"I'll get Maggie to take care of her." Before he goes upstairs as well.

I've left my phone in the office and hear it ringing so I say goodbye to the two men and hurry back. It's the call I've been expecting from my friend in Intelligence.

Chapter 26

Angel

Maggie joins us for lunch to relate the story she's gotten from the night nanny.

Turns out the girl had been complaining about strange goings-on here while at an Easter family gathering. She's overheard by her cousin, FBI Agent Dexter Williams, who decides there's a case for a charge of conspiracy or some such thing. So all on his own initiative he launched an investigation.

"But why?" asks Stacey.

Bram replies:

"Because he's an ambitious climber, that's why. I had a call from the friend I asked to look into Agent Williams and he told me that's what's being said about the man. He's a young agent who wants to make a splash so he jumps feet first into anything likely to propel his career upward."

"And that's all it was? That doesn't make sense," I comment.

Maggie continues saying:

"Oh, the girl got carried away with having an audience hanging on every word so she told about Danny and that Snyder coming here and beating on Stacey in the hallway and you, Angel, screaming your head off.

She said it was a kidnapping because the two of them took you and Stacey in the truck. But then both of you came back home although Stacey ended up in hospital overnight, badly injured.

She told a story of Joel bringing Angel home then going back out swearing about the trouble Danny caused even when he was dead and how did he know Danny was dead?

So this cousin, the FBI Agent, starts looking into Snyder's death and tries to make two plus two equal five. The nanny never imagined things would get this far and she's regretting her big mouth. She panicked when she saw him the first time, and the second time well... as you saw for yourselves, she burst into tears."

"I noticed that she'd developed a crush on Joel—" I start to say but Maggie cuts in telling me:

"Oh, they've all got a crush on him. He's a wonderful Daddy and a heartthrob."

"Sir Dom," whispers Stacey under her breath.

"Maggie, I think you have to let that nanny go," begins Bram and she tells him that's already been done. She leaves us then and we finish lunch soon after.

"Joel, Bram, come into the sitting room please. Bring your coffees, both Stacey and I want to have a chat," I order.

Joel shrugs and come through with Bram and Stacey following.

"How did Stacey and I miraculously get thrown from Snyder's truck just before he crashed into a tree and it burst into flames killing the two men while Anita and Matthew just happened to be driving down that secondary road on the way to nowhere except the hunting cabin?"

Then, before anyone can tell me any more lies I continue:

"And Joel, how did you come to so conveniently be there in time to bring me home? And same with you, Bram, why were you on that road - and thank God you were - but how did that happen?

And finally, why the hell is everyone feeling so guilty about Danny if his death truly was just a tragic accident?"

Joel tries to stare me down but I'm as angry as I've ever been in my life.

"I KNOW I've been lied to and I'm FURIOUS about it. I don't care why you've lied, I don't care if it was deliberate or a sin of omission, I don't care what you thought or why, I just care about being told the truth now."

"Okay, first of all, in case any of this comes up again, Stacey – or should I say Ms. Anastasia Somerton the wealthy heiress to Somerton Industries – I told the FBI that you are here recovering from a bout of anorexia brought on by nerves and pressure from your university course.

You've never been officially diagnosed because your family doesn't want a record of the illness, and you're now recuperating nicely under our care. I could hardly say my brother had been slowly starving you to death hence the anorexia story - sorry.

You were never in Snyder's truck, either of you, and we have no clue as to the identity of the female the paramedics took to hospital. No one could find any ID for her.

Angel, and this is the truth, your friends passed Snyder on their way here. They recognized his souped-up truck and Anita thought she caught a glimpse of you in the vehicle. Matthew turned around and pursued them while Anita phoned me.

Bram and I had just arrived home to find evidence of a fight in the hallway, Maggie bleeding on the floor right there, and the twins bawling their heads off. That's a terrible sound, by the way. There was no sign of you two.

As soon as Anita told me what road they were on Bram and I realized Danny was heading to the hunting cabin, and somehow I just knew they would kill you there.

Bram stayed behind just long enough to get Maggie and the babies safe in the Nanny's care while I came after you.

I used my car to block the road and before the truck had fully stopped I shot and killed Snyder. I turned the gun on Danny but Bram had arrived by then and talked me down. The Landismans were there as well, witnessing everything. I put my gun down and rescued you.

Danny got hold of Snyder's side-arm, put the gun in his mouth, and killed himself. Just then you opened your eyes and told me to bring you home to your babies so I did.

Stacey's neck looked broken so the Landismans called the paramedics. Bram went to the hospital but refused to give out anyone's name. He paid cash for the treatment so there would be no paper trail.

The Landismans called the police and stayed to give their statement. They told how the pick-up was racing wildly before the accident. Luckily the young woman was ejected and not in the truck when it crashed."

I want to cry, I want to scream, but instead I take a deep breath and then very calmly ask:

"Why didn't the bullets in the two bodies raise any red flags at the autopsies?"

"Because I went back to the scene and before staging the crash and setting the fire I cut the bullets out of the corpses and cleaned up the evidence.

We'd asked the Landismans to delay making their emergency call until I finished and they agreed to that and to not mentioning me being there at all. They kept their word for your sake, Angel."

Joel says these horrifying words so matter-of-factly, as if he's not shredding everything inside me to pieces.

I feel utterly numb. What I thought was a kidnapping was actually an attempted killing by an ex-coworker and one of my brothers-in-law. What I believed was an accident was actually an assassination and a suicide, committed and covered up by my husband and my best friends.

Everyone knew the real story except stupid, gullible Angel. Too weak, or maybe too untrustworthy? to be told truth.

I walk out of the room, blinded by tears, unable to speak. I get as far as the staircase before I collapse with deep wracking sobs that stem from my very core.

Why doesn't he believe in me? Why do I keep having to prove myself, my love, over and over and over again? I am sick and tired of constantly being tested and always-always-always failing. Of just being not quite good enough.

I can't go forward, I can't go back, but I sure as hell can't live in this moment of heartbreaking agony. I feel utterly bereft.

Suddenly, I'm gathered up in a strong embrace and I know it's Joel and I don't want him to touch me, or see me, or talk to me. I want to kick and scream and bite and fight against him, but I'm no match for his strength. Not his physical strength, nor his mental, emotional, moral, or amoral strength.

I cannot fight Joel and win. He's right, I am so weak, too weak.

He easily lifts and carries me up the stairs. I expect him to throw me on our bed and try to make everything better again with sex. Instead he climbs another flight of stairs to the nursery.

I can't let the twins see me in this state so I'm gulping and shuddering trying to stop crying and somehow tamp down all these boiling-over feelings.

He sets me down on the carpet and Eve and Adam immediately work at crawling towards me. Joel helps them along and soon I'm covered in excited drooling babies who frown at my tears but giggle when I smile and say *Hello Lovelies!* to them.

"This is why I did what I did, Angel. For these two and for you." I meet his gaze and I know my eyes are filled with pain but I'm struggling to understand because his eyes show just as much hurt as I'm feeling.

"Every time I treat you cruelly I tell myself I have to keep you under my thumb or else I'll lose you. But the truth has always been me being afraid of losing myself to you. It *is* possible to love too much, I know because it hurts so much just thinking about it.

"When I aimed the gun at Danny your friends yelled *put the weapon down* but I didn't listen to them because I didn't care. No, it was Bram's urgent reminder that my wife needed me to help her raise our two babies that finally penetrated through my red-mist rage.

I rescued you because I love you with all my heart and soul, but everything else I did – the cover-up - was for these two.

Angel, I have no conscience but you do and knowing certain things will only hurt you and weigh on you so I tried to take that burden away. Not because I ever thought for one second that you aren't strong enough to handle anything, but because I love you so much I never want to see the slightest shadow darken your life."

I just shake my head *no-no-no*. It's all too bewildering and I can't get past the pain of not being good enough and I tell him so.

"Oh Christ, you couldn't be more wrong! Look, Angel please listen," Joel is sounding desperate and the babies are goggling at him so we're all paying attention when he says:

"Remember when Bram was so upset, after we found out you were pregnant and he was all moody and mad and it was because he felt I didn't deserve you? Well, he was right, I've never deserved you. You came into my life a complete innocent and a good person. I'm not a good guy, I really am a prick and I know I'll never be good enough for you. Do you hear me? I'm not good enough for you, but I don't care, I'm not giving you up, not ever."

I still can't put names to the many feelings running through me but I do know I love this man. I love him more than I hate him. And I need him so much it hurts.

I reach out a hand and he bends down scooping all three of us into his arms.

The twins tumble between us laughing that delightful baby chuckle before one says *Mama,* for the very first time, just as the other one says *Dada.*

A Joel O'Shea Fantasy Story:

ex-Officer Angel and

Criminal Kingpin Nasty Nick

"Verdict and Sentence"

Nasty Nick follows ex-Officer Angel to her home. She lives on the ground floor of a house, which he later learns is her house that she inherited and where she lives all alone.

He comes back later that night and waits for twenty minutes after he sees the lights go out. Then he breaks in.

He finds her sleeping in her bedroom where, through a gap in the curtains, moonlight streams in on her young face.

She is beautiful.

He sits on the bed and wakes her up. She's wearing a baby-doll nightie with matching frilly panties. The baby-blue color matches her eyes. He's never seen her wear anything other than her black uniform. She looks so sweet and rosy and innocent.

After further questioning he discovers she's an orphan who is almost twenty years old.

Nasty Nick came here tonight intending to punish ex-Officer Angel with a *guilty* verdict for stealing his heart. He planned on putting her across his knee for a sexy spanking which he would thoroughly enjoy administering to her luscious bottom, but instead he proposes! sentencing them both to a lifetime of matrimony.

For the first time ever they make love in a bed in the missionary position, then cowgirl, then reverse cowgirl, doggie-style, etc...

He forgets all about spanking her and so they live happily ever after.

I would love to hear what you think of the book in a review, (reviews really help other readers decide if they'll enjoy a book), or email comments to authorlorilaidlaw@gmail.com. Thank you so much for reading **"Girlie"**.

Also by Lori Laidlaw

Alpha + Omega Wolf-Shifters
Dominant + Violent + Hot = An Alpha Male
Her Claiming Bite = True Love

Standalone
Lockdown + 3 Alphas = Heat: An Omega's Thrilling Dark
Romantic Adventure
Girlie: Undeniable Attraction Enemies to Lovers Steamy
Standalone
Cruel Obligation
Jane's Special Adventure
Captive's Deception
Finn and Marbeth
"Princess Weds Killer" = Fake News

Watch for more at https://lorilaidlaw.com.

About the Author

Lori says:

I love the fun and excitement in the Adult Romance genre and all of its sub-categories. It's such fun to write!

I'm half in love with all of my characters... and their moods range from playful to dangerous and everything in between!

The men are unfeeling and cruel until the innocent heroine melts the ice from their hearts and turns them into OTT possessive touch-her-and-die alphas.

My stories are multiple POV expressing mature themes and passionate encounters with enough steam to stimulate your imagination.

It's all about the love.

Email: AuthorLoriLaidlaw@gmail.com

Website: https://lorilaidlaw.com

Bluesky: https://bsky.app/profile/lorilaidlaw.bsky.social

Facebook: https://www.facebook.com/people/Author-Lori-Laidlaw/61555470454210/

Goodreads: https://www.goodreads.com/author/show/29566696.Lori_Laidlaw

Read more at https://lorilaidlaw.com.